HALLOWED BONES

Elemental Dungeon #3

JONATHAN SMIDT

PORTAL BOOKS

Honestly, I'm sure I was a nightmare to put up with as I worked on Hallowed Bones...so I want to thank my amazing wife for being understanding and supportive during this whole process, without her, none of this could have happened.

Also, my heartfelt thanks goes out to the team at Portal Books, for being an awesome and understanding team that put a lot of time and devotion into helping me accomplish this book. Finally, a special thanks to Dimi, he knows who he is, for coming in at the final hour and helping this story cross the finish line. And thank you to the readers, for supporting my journey.

Chapter One

RYAN

"For your sins against the Church—" Ryan could hear the cold words clearly, the moment of his untimely death flowing through his mind.

"—We hereby assign your punishment...Death!" Those words, said with such conviction, had been the end of his normal life. Ryan finished playing through the memory, something he had been doing over and over, ever since the God of Death had unlocked his memories. Initially all he had felt about the memories, the truth, was rage. Now the moment of his unjust death didn't even elicit...anything. What was done was done and there was nothing he could do about it.

At least I know now why the Goddess of Justice sealed them away. Had he remembered his death fully when he first awakened, there was a good chance he would have been less than willing to help her out. While it had been the Zealots of the Light, the smallest portion of the Church of Justice that had killed him—unjustly, might he add—they *were* a part of the Church. An extremely radical and controversial one but a part of the Church, nonetheless. Meaning, in the end, it was the Goddess's fault he was dead.

Sure, she may have brought him back as a dungeon core, giving him a second chance at life. He remembered that bit clearly. His consciousness floating in the darkness, unseeing and unknowing as confusion flitted through his mind over his death. She had claimed she was righting the wrong that had befallen him in her name. If that had truly been the case, why had she locked away his memories? It didn't add up.

Likely, the Goddess had some other motivation she wasn't willing to reveal. Combined with what he had gone through since becoming a dungeon core—the constant manipulations, the half-truths, the lies...Well, what Death had given him had solidified a single truth. Ryan could really only trust himself.

"Ryan." A soft voice pulled him away from his own mind, which had turned to an image of his human self, a longing welling up within. Being confined to a dungeon core in a singular existence was a lot more depressing now that he knew what he used to be and the freedoms he used to have.

"Ryan." The voice, soft, almost childish. Erin whispered once again. Ryan turned his focus away from his longing to see what the fairy wanted. He had been angry, verging on furious, with her after his memories had been unlocked. However, just like with Hel, the magic that linked cores and fairies together dulled that rage. It didn't take long for his anger to be washed away; in part due to his own understanding of the situation, and hastened by ancient magics. While he'd forgiven the fairies in his heart, the awakened human portion of him was still a little bitter when reflecting on his newly restored memories.

"What do you want?" He allowed his tone to hold a tinge of emotion in it. He had gotten a lot better at controlling his feelings and masking them through the bond with the two fairies. In the past few months, he had grown a lot more than he had during his first year as a core. A given, considering he had just had two decades worth of memories as a human returned to him by Death.

Erin flinched at his tone and he could feel the hurt come through the bond from her. She was still having issues fully controlling what she let flow through the bond. That, or she was intentionally doing her best to let him feel all her emotions as a way to try and redeem herself. He may have been a little...harsh to her when his memories had been returned. What should have been a joyous occasion, as they had just reached Platinum along with defeating Marissa and the Cult of Chaos, had turned into one of accusations, bitter words, and strong emotions. Things had been rather tense since then, especially when the memories were on his mind.

"Don't you think it is time we start building your fourth floor?" She spoke softly. Ryan could tell she was picking her words carefully. She was worried about him, and scared. He wouldn't do anything to her, and he wasn't even that mad at her anymore, not truly, but she didn't know that. Honestly, he had no reason to be angry at her. She was, generally, quite poor at keeping secrets. Meaning he was ninety-nine percent sure she'd had no idea his memories had been locked away. Even if she had...her innocence and blind devotion in the Goddess of Justice were enough to lead her astray. In other words, Erin wasn't really deserving of how he'd been treating her. Which was also why he was starting to feel a tad guilty about acting so cold toward her.

Especially considering that he had locked her and Hel away from his core room for a good while when he'd first regained his memories. Ryan had wanted some quiet time to process everything. But, in doing so...he'd lost track of time, and they'd been locked away in solitude much longer than he'd intended. Oops.

Maybe it's time I finally let her know I've forgiven her? The thought passed through his mind while he flicked mentally through the dungeon. As was the norm, he had closed his dungeon off to adventurers in preparation for his ascension to Platinum. Doing so allowed him to completely absorb all of his mobs and work on his dungeon in peace. For his first three floors, Erin had played a large part in his design. Something the two of them had enjoyed doing together. The thought was a fond one, and he couldn't help the rush of emotion flowing through at the nostalgia.

"She has a point darling." Hel, his Chaos fairy, decided to join the conversation. Perhaps she had noticed the ever so slight pang of guilt that had seeped away from Ryan's emotional control through the bond. He thought he had stopped it before either fairy could notice, but it made sense Hel would have picked up on it. She was extremely… skilled… when it came to emotions. Especially manipulating them. Something she had been doing to Erin in an effort to make Ryan more malleable. Something she had been quite successful in until Marissa and the Cult of Chaos had attacked.

Funnily enough, the moment Hel had learned she was a clone and was simply a tool being used by the Cult of Chaos, her entire attitude had changed. The Chaos Fairy had dropped her nice girl act, relinquished her manipulation over Erin's emotions, and completely lost control of her temper as she sought revenge against Marissa. It seemed Ryan's accusations against her and his banning her from the core room during that revelation had been enough to push the Chaos fairy to her own moment of self-realization.

Following that battle Hel had changed ever so slightly. She seemed to consider her words more carefully, and Ryan had noticed she and Erin were getting along a lot better these past few months. Which Ryan felt partially responsible for, as he had given them a common goal. They had been working together to pull him from his solitude and rage. Again, he still felt he was owed those emotions. It was only fair he got to feel the sense of betrayal and anger over what had been done to him. He'd been lied to and manipulated, by the both of them to some degree. Directly or indirectly, intentional or not, it still hurt. But, he should probably be the bigger core, and just move on. There were things that needed to be done.

"The demon attacks have decreased, meaning your growth cannot just be fueled by them anymore. And the adventurers are likely getting antsy about resuming their dives. Plus-" Hel paused, her eyes focusing on his core, her gaze serious. "Being closed for too long may cause suspicions to arise." And there it was, the other thorn in his side.

During the fight against Marissa, Samuel and Xander, they had used an item called a Sphere of Subjugation, which prevented anything, but a given mana type from entering the sphere, or using mana within the sphere. It was an item which Hel had informed Ryan was used specifically to kill dungeons. While Marissa and the others were within the sphere, he had been unable to do anything to them. At least, that was until he had fused his skeletal mobs with blood-stones, at Hel's behest. Doing so had given his normally Dark mobs a demonic nature and they had been able to break into the subjugation zone.

Unfortunately, they weren't strong enough to take on the Platinum-level cultists, and to add insult to injury, Marcus, the Platinum 2 rogue who was in charge of the dungeon town, had taken notice of Ryan's new demonic mobs. The rogue's final words to Ryan after Marissa was defeated were short, sweet, and ominous. Ryan needed to prove he hadn't been corrupted. Otherwise, Marcus's parting words implied Ryan's life might be at stake. Even though Ryan was now a Platinum 5 dungeon, he knew all too well that the Adventurers' Guild had the power to bring him down if they wanted to.

So, on top of dealing with his renewed memories, Ryan had been doing all he could around the Bone Zone to try and prove he hadn't been corrupted. He figured one of the easiest ways to prove his continued existence should be allowed, and even encouraged, would be by continuing to protect the town. Part of his focus therefore had been on ensuring no demonic force, no matter how large or small, made it past his Bone Zone and the walls he had established as markers for his influence. He was also still continually spreading his influence further out, giving him an even earlier alert to whenever an attack may occur. This allowed him on a few occasions the opportunity to kill the cultists before they could create a demonic portal. It was the cultists, after all, who were using the portals to summon the demons from the countless dungeon's they'd corrupted.

Even still, Ryan hadn't seen Marcus since that day, and he wasn't sure if his actions were enough to prove his importance. The only humans that made their way towards his dungeon entrance were the occasional adventuring party, checking to see if he was opened yet, or a contingent of Church members. The latter of which had initially angered him to no end, thanks to his returned memories. It had taken all of his self-control not to kill the five-man party of Church members, easily recognizable because of their all-white outfits, emblazoned with the Goddess of Justice's golden scales. He knew killing them would seal his fate. And Ryan quite liked living, even if his existence as a dungeon core was not his ideal existence. Being a dungeon core was still preferable when compared to being dead.

"We will open soon." Ryan muttered aloud. He could just as easily send the words mentally to Hel and Erin. Afterall, he was connected to the fairies through a magical bond, allowing them to communicate mentally if needed. He'd just stopped doing that, as he was done with secrets, and doing so felt secretive. Instead, he had decided every form of communication from here on out would be out loud. They may all be bonded by magic, but he wanted to now make sure the trust they put in each other was legitimate and earned, not artificially formed.

"How soon, Darling?" Hel sat atop his core, tracing her finger over its top. "Don't we have to completely build an entire floor still?" Her finger stopped as a small smile crossed her face. "Or have you been keeping secrets from us?"

"How about I show you." Ryan sent them both an amused feeling through the bond. Sure, he wanted them to be completely truthful with each other. He wanted to ensure he could trust them. However, that didn't mean he couldn't keep *some* secrets from them. He hadn't betrayed them, and his secrets weren't dangerous. At least, that was how he was justifying his actions. Besides, he doubted they really believed he had been simply mulling in a dark, angry mood for the past few months. Ryan had gotten bored with that after the first week. Since then, he had been hard at work on many other things, including the creation of his fourth, and greatest, floor.

Chapter Two

For Ryan's fourth floor he had decided to go with something a little…different. As a result, his fairies' reactions when they first saw it were rather amusing. When he'd first begun creating his dungeon, he had been instructed on how to craft his floors according to 'dungeon etiquette'. Something Erin insisted was the proper and right way to build a dungeon based on teachings she had received from older fairies under the guidance of the Goddess of Justice. Though Hel was far older and more experienced in dungeon making than Erin, she hadn't mentioned anything about improving the layout of his floors. All Hel ever spoke about was increasing the lethality of his floors. In her opinion, the more quickly he could kill adventurers and gain experience, the better.

"I love what you've done with the place Darling," Hel purred as she hovered over the floor. She held a skull shaped crystal pendant in her hand as she spoke. The pendant was based on the ones Ryan had absorbed from all the adventurers he'd slain. They were special pendants that had a multitude of purposes, one of which was communication between party members. Ryan had made one for Blake, long ago, and now for both of his fairies in order to speak with them, audibly, when they weren't in his core room. He was also testing out the efficiency of these new and improved pendants, which he'd inlaid with silver and gold, to enhance their aesthetics, because he intended to make a few for select persons of interest outside of his dungeon.

Mainly Marcus, the rest of Blake's party, and few other adventurers that had caught his eye. Additionally, Ryan had implemented larger versions of the crystals, also shaped like skulls, throughout his dungeon. Theses crystal skulls would serve as a way for him to interact on a more personal level with any adventurers who entered his dungeon. Hel had once mentioned that in the past Dungeons had been revered as Demi Gods. So, Ryan felt it was about time he started connecting with his people. This was all a part of his plan to ensure the dungeon town, and through them the Adventurers Guild, realized he was a much more valuable asset than a threat.

The way he saw it, he needed to mitigate any and every chance or threat for there to be a misunderstanding about his loyalties. He needed to make sure they understood that while yes, he killed adventurers for experience, he was not evil. Ryan was set on making sure the Adventurers' Guild left him alive so he could reach a point at which they would no longer be able to bring him down. Ryan's dream was to grow strong enough that he wouldn't have to fear anything ever again. And, even more than that, Ryan wanted to make sure he could have complete control over his own fate. Which, in the long run, meant reaching God Tier. In the short term though, it meant, Ryan had done his best to make this fourth floor completely unique.

"I-" Erin was hovering beside Hel, her eyes wide as she took in all that lay below her. The two were slightly larger than children, perhaps adolescents in size. He was currently

Platinum 5, though he was nearing Platinum 4. Killing off demonic mobs en masse was doing quite a good job of gaining him experience, even if it was decreased because he was of a higher rank than the mobs he was slaughtering. Experience was still experience, and he wasn't one to question the laws of being a dungeon.

"It's definitely unique." Erin's voice quivered slightly, and he could tell her emotions were a mess. Hel shot the Celestial fairy a warning look, but Erin didn't seem to notice. "Is this, your village?"

"Well, it was…until the Church killed me." Ryan responded dryly.

"I-" Erin started, but Ryan cut her off.

"Don't. You don't have to apologize for them. I don't blame you for what happened to me." It had been long enough. Ryan sent his reassuring emotions through his bond with Erin. At his words the fairy's eyes lit up, even as tears began to stream down her face.

"The past is the past." Ryan continued. "This new floor, the moment we open the dungeon back up, will start a new phase in our existence. There are to be no more secrets, no more ulterior motives." Ryan ensured his voice was firm at that last part. "Hel."

"You've nothing to worry about, Darling. Believe me." The Chaos fairy let her rage flare in the bond, showing she was still extremely upset over the revelation of her being used. Ryan knew the fairy's pride would ensure she did not forgive the Cult of Chaos, nor the God of Chaos, for what had happened. Which was why he could trust her now. As for Erin, well, she had a heart of gold, even if she was naïve. He was sure he could trust her, and also just felt bad in general for having been mad at her.

"Right, then how about I give you a tour?" He summoned a clacker in the air in front of the two fairies, the sudden arrival of the skeletal eagle causing them both to drop a few feet in the sky from surprise. They were both able to alight themselves quite quickly, and Ryan hadn't been worried about them falling too far. They were about 200 feet above the ground of his fourth floor, after all.

Normally, they would have come out into the floor within his Boss's lair. After all, his core room was always connected to the boss room of his lowest floor. However, shifting his entire core room downwards wouldn't have been subtle, meaning he would have informed his fairies that he was up to something, while he'd been crafting his fourth floor in secret. His solution then, had been a tunnel from his core room downward, exciting out of the massive ceiling, just in the center of his fourth floor.

More appropriately, the tunnel came out just beside the towering spiral structure he had placed in the very middle of his fourth floor. It was a large construct that housed within it a staircase which wound its way, over and over, down from the third floor until it ended in a single opening which would allow the adventurers to step foot onto his fourth floor. The walls of the tower were lined with crystal skulls, allowing Ryan to chat with them in any way he deemed fit. He could hold conversations with adventurers as they descended to his next level. Or... he could mock them, taunt them, or do anything else he wanted to as they descended. It really depended on what type of adventurers they were, and how he was feeling.

The spiraling structure also had various traps laid throughout. For instance, if he were threatened, he could simply drop the adventurers out the side of the structure. Adventurers were tough, Platinum-level ones even tougher. However, he was pretty sure falling from such a height down onto mana infused spikes, which Ryan could summon in a split second now, would kill even a Platinum-level adventurer. Heck, it might even be able to bring down someone of Diamond Tier. Might being the key word there, because Ryan hadn't actually encountered anyone of the Diamond Tier yet.

Either way, Ryan had done his best to not only ensure he had time to prepare for anything making its way down to his fourth floor, but also wanted to enhance the shock and awe factor for when adventurers did finally step foot on his fourth floor. For when they did, they wouldn't be greeted by a single ornate room. No, Ryan had stepped it up a notch. If his third floor was a work of art, his fourth was a masterpiece. His fourth floor was a complete recreation of his town and the area directly around it from his human life. It was circular, with a diameter of close to two miles by his best estimation. Which, considering his returned knowledge and the books he had absorbed, were rather accurate. When adventurers stepped foot out of the tower, they would freeze and wonder if they were even in a dungeon anymore.

Chapter Three

"And right here is the town square." Ryan had been guiding the fairies through his fourth floor, using his clacker as a guide. During his time with his skeletal mobs, and even more so the Bone Zone, Ryan had mastered his control over his creatures. He wasn't directly possessing them, but he could make them do essentially whatever he wanted on command. As such, having his clacker act as a tour guide was a simple feat.

"And that?" Hel pointed towards the structure in the center of the town square. "A little dark humor, Darling?"

"Would I truly be a Darkness dungeon without it?" Once his anger had subsided over his death, and he came to accept it, he turned to a darker form of humor. Gallows humor, one would call it. Or, in this case, perhaps it should be Guillotine Humor? Because sure enough, he had recreated the platform which had existed in the center of the town for his execution. The mechanism that had ended his life.

Hel sent an approving burst of feeling through their bond as she flew past the contraption of death. Erin on the other hand eyed it warily, giving it a wide berth. Ryan knew the

Celestial fairy still felt a lot of guilt over Ryan's death. Even though he told her it wasn't her fault. It was the Zealots, and by association, the Goddess of Justice's.

"So, Ryan." Erin looked down one of the streets of the town. Ryan's village hadn't been large by any means, with only a few hundred actual residents. The houses were simple, crafted from stone mined from the mountains the village nestled in, with thatched roofs overtop. With all the various items Ryan had absorbed during his time as a dungeon, recreating the village had been extremely simple.

Especially because now he not only had the knowledge he'd gained magically through absorbing books and ascending tiers as a dungeon, but also his memories of being human. Meaning everything he knew and understood as a human, he once again had access to. Which…had made him chuckle sadly as he'd been crafting this new floor, as he remembered how hard the concept of a 'door' had been for him to fathom earlier on in his life as a dungeon core. Seriously, the Goddess of Justice wiping his memories had really not made his life as a core easy.

"Have you thought about what type of mobs you're going to use?" The Celestial fairy motioned around the floor. "Don't you think this is a rather large area to try and populate?"

Erin wasn't wrong. While the size of his dungeon wasn't anything to scoff at for his first three floors, they were separated very nicely into rooms, which gave him a condensed space to spawn mobs in. Doing so allowed him to provide an ample threat to adventurers in a confined area, making the mobs even more dangerous. It also gave adventurers a limited amount of room to fight in. The exception was always his boss rooms, which were much larger. Boss fights, after all, should always been given more room for activities.

Now, with his fourth floor being as large as it was, there

wouldn't really be any areas to corner adventurers in. The expanse of the floor also gave adventurers the ability to scout out ahead. Scouting of course meant they could track down and ambush his mobs, or prepare themselves for attacks. Ryan, had already thought about that and come up with his own solution. He had not been idle these past few months.

"Now that I'm Platinum Five I have a total of four-thousand-eight-hundred mob points." He mentally scanned over his triangles, checking his mob points with his experience. "Though I am certain after we open back up I will quickly be Platinum Four. Meaning six-thousand mob points total."

During the down time he hadn't been able to gain experience off of adventurers diving and dying within his dungeon. The frequent demonic attacks though had actually served to provide a nice side source of experience for Ryan as he worked. While he got a lot less experience from the mobs he was killing, likely due to their status as mobs and their lower rankings, it still added up over time. Additionally, the cultists he managed to kill during the attacks were usually led by a Gold member, even if the others were Silver or Bronze. While Silver and Bronze Tier beings barely even gave him a trickle of experience, the Gold Tier ones still provided a fair amount to his Platinum experience pool. Which meant he was nearly to Platinum 4 without having even opened his dungeon up.

"That's a lot of mob points." Erin looked from Ryan's clacker to Hel. The Chaos fairy was grinning eagerly.

"From here on out, Erin, Ryan's strength is going to grow in leaps and bounds. As will ours." The Chaos fairy flew to the guillotine, landing atop the wooden structure gently. Her childish frame ensured she wasn't heavy enough to topple it, but it still rocked slightly. Just enough that the blade dropped free, falling rapidly towards the ground. Hel just barely managed to avoid having her tail severed by the blade.

"Not if you get yourself killed first." Erin commented, a

grin washing away the slight worry that had been creeping over her face over the whole situation. Hel returned her smile, letting out a slight purr as she did.

"Trust me, Darling, I have too much to live for to let myself die." Hel flexed her wings behind her in an exaggerated way, to show just how large they had become. "At this rate we might even assume our true forms at Platinum Four."

Because of Hel's memories from her original self, the Chaos fairy knew a lot of what actually happened between a dungeon and a fairy. She had proved extremely knowledgeable on all things dungeon, even helping Ryan create his first ever mini-boss, appropriately named Mini Steve. She had shared the knowledge that normally when a dungeon hit Platinum 5 it's fairy would assume their true, final form. Because Hel and Erin were currently sharing Ryan's power though, they had not evolved when he ascended to Platinum 5. Still, they had grown a considerable amount. It was very likely they would soon be evolving into their final form, which Ryan was extremely excited for. He was also slightly worried though.

Hel would become a Succubus, a type of demon that could apparently manipulate and control living things. And because she was a clone of the exact Succubus that had attacked Ryan's dungeon and been seen by Marcus, Blake, and Cane, Ryan was afraid of the reactions people would have to the presence of Hel in the dungeon. At the same time, Erin's true form, according to Hel, was that of an Angel. A large, winged Celestial humanoid thought to only be found in high level Celestial dungeons. Or, more appropriately, only thought to be found in the Goddess of Justice's dungeon.

The two of his fairies gaining their true forms was something that could potentially complicate and endanger his dungeon. Especially if word got out about either. However, he wasn't certain he would be able to keep them from flying about the dungeon once they had their true forms. They were already getting rather restless in his dungeon as it was. And Ryan knew from experience he couldn't actually control the two or make them do anything they didn't want to do. But that was a problem for the Ryan of the future to deal with. Currently, the Ryan of now was giving a tour of his new floor.

"Back to the matter at hand ladies. How about I show you some of the mobs I have planned out for the floor before I tell you how I will spread them out?" Ryan ordered his clacker to move further away from the town center and the spiraling tower, towards what had to be the most out of place structure on his fourth floor. And while neither Erin nor Hel knew it, the structure was completely out of place. His village, so small and nestled in a mountain pass, would have no reason for such a structure. After all, a remote village was no place for a coliseum.

Chapter Four

Ryan couldn't take all the credit for the introduction of the coliseum to his dungeon. He had a smaller version functioning as his fighting arena for skeletal fight club after all. This was the reason it existed on his fourth floor. While he had been hard at work creating his fourth floor, he had wanted to keep track on his skeletal fight club progress as well. Though it wasn't difficult for him to split his attention across different areas of his dungeon at the same time, with his focus already partially split towards the Bone Zone, Ryan had decided to make his life a little simpler.

The end result was a massive coliseum that existed on one end of the town in the circular expanse that was his fourth floor. Across from that, two miles away, was another structure, the only other one that hadn't existed in his hometown. His boss mob's den. But he was going to show that to Erin and Hel at the very end of the tour.

"Is this the skeletal fight club arena?" Erin zipped ahead of the clacker as they drew nearer to the massive structure. It stood nearly a hundred feet in height, with a diameter of close to one-hundred and fifty feet. Within, rows and rows of seats expanded out across the structure, providing a perfect vantage point of the circular, hundred-foot battleground. He may have made the structure a little larger, for reasons.

"It is indeed." Ryan chuckled, flying the clacker towards the larger observation area that existed closer to the ground floor. From his understanding—not just of his human knowledge, but also the books he had absorbed—royalty or individuals of importance often resided in this area, giving them the premier view of the battle below. Apparently, Dungeon Core Ryan, pre-return of his human memories, had not been the most original in creating a fighting pit for his mobs. Humans had been doing it for hundreds of years, watching individuals of various rank take on monstrous creatures found and captured in the wild, or even other sentient creatures. It seemed a common trend at one point to force various prisoners of war, from a wide range of races, to fight for the amusement of the masses.

And of course the royalty didn't have to worry for their own safety because they were almost always the strongest individuals in the area. For special events, if the battles were thought to become too dangerous or deadly, the price of admissions was simply increased so those putting on the battle could afford to hire mercenaries or adventurers of appropriate rank to ensure the captives had no chance of injuring anyone of import. The policy had come about after a captured soldier managed to assassinate a cocky royal who had been taunted to come down to the battlefield and face off against the prisoner.

"Darling, please tell me you've plans to use this as more than just an area of interest." Hel was scanning the entire area hungrily, her tail swishing in a way Ryan had noticed it only did when she was truly excited. Excited and plotting something devious. "We could create a fight club between adventurers and mobs. And once I assume my true form...we could even have the adventurers fight each other down here." She licked her fangs, her eyes hungry.

"Trust me, Hel, I do intend to make use of it. Look down below." At one of the entrances he had created one of his loot boxes, with a skull implanted above it, glowing slightly. "I'll allow adventurers the chance to upgrade or duplicate treasure cards here, depending on the type of card and the challenge they wish to face." As he spoke he triggered the strings of mana he'd laid out over the building. As he had learned with his traps, he could trigger these strings to create different effects. In this situation, the mana strings caused all of the entrances into the bottom floor of the coliseum to seal off with mana infused crystal, nearly three foot thick. He was tired of watching individuals break through his mana infused stone. Crystal was stronger and could hold more mana in it.

"Once they agree, they will be sealed within until they have completed their challenge, or fallen in battle." He let his trap fade away, unsealing the entrance. "And don't worry, they are only allowed to do it once per arena token." Ryan was aware that creating an opportunity for individuals to simply farm mobs would not be ideal. It would create an unfair advantage, a chance for adventurers to safely grow rapidly in strength.

"Arena tokens?" Erin asked the question Ryan had been waiting to answer. His unsealed memories, combined with what he had learned over his time as a dungeon, had really led to some groundbreaking revelations on how to run his dungeon.

"Tokens that parties can gain from killing boss mobs." He made one appear atop the loot box, a Dungeon Mob's card that had a skull stamped on the middle of it with two swords crossed behind it. He summoned the various versions of them he had created. A common one, to be dropped by Steve, an uncommon one, to be dropped by Buttercup, a rare one, to be dropped by his skeletal mages, and an ultra-rare form, to be dropped by his fourth-floor boss.

"Technically, they are just like my other treasure cards, but arena tokens sounds better in my opinion." Sure enough, he had written those very words across the top of the cards.

The idea of the token had come from his human life. Villagers would receive weekly ration tokens, which they could utilize to access various features in the village. Because of the limited resources in the town, and the scarcity of merchants, the system had been introduced to make sure no one person was overusing any of the resources. Of course, it just led to people stealing each other's tokens or trading and buying them from one another. Which led to the exact problem the village had been trying to prevent, but on a somewhat controlled and limited scale. After all, the tokens existed in a controlled quantity, and once collected, couldn't be handed out again until the next week.

"The tokens have a slim chance to drop, meaning adventurers won't just be able to come in here and challenge the Arena whenever they want, or over and over. No, this arena exists as a way to reward and challenge the strong. If they've made it to this far, and are willing to take on the challenge, I will not stop them." While Ryan's returned memory had revealed to him that he was a human turned dungeon core, he found he was still the same individual at heart. His thoughts, his moral code, all of those seemed to have been deeply engrained into him. As such, his progress over the past year, his growth, his understanding of what it meant to be a dungeon, what it meant to grow more powerful, had not been undone. If anything, it had cemented his resolution that he would do what needed doing to grow stronger.

While he may have been a human at one time, that was no more. Now, he was a dungeon core, and he would become the greatest dungeon core in existence, merely aided now by the time he had spent as a human.

"You're amazing, Ryan," Erin exclaimed, flying rapidly towards the clacker, before stopping herself short. In her excitement, the fairy had intended to hug the clacker. It seemed for a moment she had forgotten that Ryan was still confined to the core room, all by his lonesome, trapped within a diamond.

"If you think that's amazing, just wait till you see what I've got planned. Behold, the mobs that will face off against the adventurers who dare take on my fourth floor. Allow me to introduce the two of you to my Bone Enforcers."

Chapter Five

Ryan let the name hang in the air. He took pride in it, and he could tell his fairies were excited too. But he couldn't help but draw the moment out a little longer. These were new mobs with a mechanic unique to his fourth floor, after all. They warranted a little extra explanation.

"Now then. I created a total of five different Bone Enforcers," he said, "which I can release into the area at any given moment. I've also set up various points around the town they can spawn from. I wanted them to be a surprise encounter, but also to make a situation that adventurers could at least slightly prepare for."

On his previous floors, adventurers had always had to worry about being ambushed at any and every point of his dungeon. This was because he had connected every single room to a vast expanse of hidden tunnels and underground networks.

He wanted to change it up a little in his town. Instead of making it more random, he wanted to give adventurers a certain level of expectation. To that end, there were key buildings in the town he had created that could serve as spawn points for Bone Enforcers. Once adventurers caught onto the spawn patterns, they would become more cautious when around these specific buildings.

This would play a little more with the adventurers. From his human memories, he could recall multiple situations where the knowledge that something bad was about to happen, that an area was dangerous, had actually made him feel more tense and worried. Adventurers were used to getting randomly attacked, they almost expected it. What Ryan was incorporating now, was the emotion, the fear, of the immediate expected attack. It would wear them down in a different way than the one they were used to in his dungeon. It could also lead to some amusing interactions, considering Ryan had no intention of always summoning his enforcers during the dives, nor of summoning the same enforcer at each location.

"There are a total of six locations the Bone Enforcers can be summoned from. The church, the cemetery, the blacksmith, the Mayor's office, the guillotine, and the local baths." Each of these locations was easily noticeable in his town. The church was stereotypical: a building with a large steeple, stained glass windows, and doors adorned with the Goddess of Justice's balanced scales. The blacksmith's shop was a two-part area: a storefront from which the town's blacksmith, Jon, had sold his wares; and the forge. Ryan had given the smithy a massive anvil, and a well-defined stone forge, complete with smoldering coals. A large chimney rose away from it, billowing dark smoke.

The Mayor's Office was the second largest building in town and had a different, more refined build to it when compared to the regular houses. It was the only three-story building in the village, with most houses having only the single story. The guillotine in the town center was a no-brainer.

The baths were a very simple building to spot, a large open courtyard instead of a single building. It led into three open-air baths, filled by Ryan with water and heated from underneath by one of his latest discoveries, molten rock. He had managed to adjust the temperature in the baths to make them similar to the mountain hot springs he and his friends had used to visit.

Within the bathhouse, he incorporated the separate baths, or privacy baths. Those had been more expensive in his town, but allowed individuals their own bath area, or even an area for a small group that decided to rent it out. The private areas had also included options for scented water, and special drink selections. Ryan had done his best to mimic that effect, adorning the area with various perfumes he had absorbed off adventurers. It was amazing, the value of items nobles carried around. With his memories of being human restored, Ryan had realized quite quickly how much wealth he actually had absorbed as a dungeon core.

The memory of his human life had also brought Ryan occasional pangs of longing. While he was glad he couldn't smell rotting zombie flesh...he couldn't help but miss the smell of the scented perfumes of the bathhouse. He also got occasional flashes of phantom hunger. These were alien to his dungeon core self, considering all he needed to survive was the ambient mana of the world.

"What type of mobs are they going to be?" Hel cut in before he could continue. "Are you going to use more of your soul mobs?" Soul mobs utilized soul fragments. Vampires, wisps, ghosts, and others were all creatures he discovered he could create following the mishap with killing A-a-ron and bringing the noble back—accidently, mind you—as a vampire lord. The soul mobs were extremely strong, and seemed to be immune to most physical attacks. They were a powerful tool for a Darkness dungeon, Ryan understood that, but he didn't like using them. Not only did they use a resource he had a finite amount of, the soul fragments, but he also couldn't get past the fact he was using leftover souls from living beings to create powerful mobs.

Ryan had managed to make it to Platinum without having to rely on them. The only time he'd resorted to using them was against the Light Enders—the vampire lord mobs were the only thing he had at Gold that could really take those Platinum-Tier demonic monsters down.

For adventurers and everyday dives in his dungeon, Ryan had shelved the idea of using soul mobs, though he did still have a few occasional ideas for them. Perhaps a monthly rare occurrence from one, with extra loot dropped? Or he could use them solely as tools to get rid of threatening intruders.

If an adventurer wanted to fight one, Ryan could make a soul-based mob for the Arena. But he needed to be careful with that resource. While he could see plenty of soul fragments all throughout his first three floors, as well as in the forest that surrounded his dungeon, it was not an infinite resource and it was not easy to replenish. Plus, he was the Bone Dungeon. Bones were kind of his theme, not ghosts.

"No. We don't need any more lifeless bloodsuckers in the dungeon." Ryan sent a burst of amusement through his bond to both his fairies. "Besides, we already get that with all the nobles diving through the dungeon." His memories had brought back not only his hate for the Church of Justice, predominately the Zealots of Light, but also for the nobles. His town had been small, but the noble who ruled over it had made the lives of his subjects miserable. The man had increased levies and taxes on the people as much as possible, all so he could throw lavish balls and treat himself with worldly possessions. Oh no, Ryan now had a renewed distaste for nobles.

"So then, what are they?" Erin piped up. He could tell she

was relieved he didn't plan on using the soul-based mobs. Even though he was only using soul fragments for them, the actual souls taken away by Death's reapers, it was still close to the taboo of desecrating life that Erin clung so dearly to.

"Why, they are skeletal mobs of course." Ryan tried his best to make his clacker flourish its wings. The result was awkward. *Someday*, he thought. His mind drifted back to the information the God of Death had given him when he ascended Platinum. The reason he needed to reach Diamond. A possibility of having his own body again. *Someday*.

Ryan pushed the thoughts from his mind, and turned back to the task at hand. He went through his mental catalog and selected the mobs that would be his Bone Enforcers. They weren't Platinum boss-level strong, even though he had been tempted to put a roaming boss in his floor. Instead, he had created his five Bone Enforcers, elevating them all to Platinum mini-boss status. Adventurers would have the potential to fight all five mini-bosses before they ever faced off against his fourth-floor boss. Meaning players had five new challenges and situations in which they could die. Making it to his fourth floor meant the adventurers were strong and capable. Surviving it would be a different matter. His fourth floor would truly test all who entered.

"Behold…My Bone Enforcers." And suddenly, the coliseum was no longer empty.

Chapter Six

As a Platinum 5 dungeon, Ryan had access to 4,800 mob points to utilize across four different floors and his Bone Zone. Growing to Platinum Tier had also given Ryan access to new classes of mobs. When it came to his skeletal beasts, he could now summon up to huge beasts for 30 mob points per beast. Meanwhile, huge zombie beasts cost him 35 points.

When it came to his human mobs, he had gained even more variety. He could now create enhanced versions of his armored skeletal and zombie mobs. These mobs cost 35 and 40 points, respectively, and not only came armored with Dark mana, but had their physical attributes enhanced by the Dark mana as well. In essence, they were harder, better, faster, and stronger than their previous forms.

At Platinum he also unlocked a new level for his mages. This new level, called "Archmages," cost 250 mob points per mob. He had only summoned one of those so far, against a small-scale assault force of demons. Ryan had dropped the 250 mob points to summon an Earth-based archmage. To his surprise, the skeletal mage had looked strangely similar to Rocky, one of his third-floor boss mobs, and wielded the exact same powers. Ryan could now produce generic skeletal archmages that were just carbon copies of his Gold-Tier boss. It was neat and piqued Ryan's interest as to what would happen if he used one of his archmages to create a new boss mob. The 1,250 mob point cost had dissuaded him from such an endeavor, though it was on his "to test out later" list. Now that he was on talking terms with his fairies again, he figured he should pass that on to Erin. He made a mental note to do so after he finished showing off the Bone Enforcers.

The five figures stood proudly in the coliseum, a strange, monstrous group of mobs that didn't look like they belonged in the same area together. The main reason for that was, they weren't natural. Ryan had wanted his Bone Enforcers to be unique. He wanted them to be the stuff of tales, of nightmares. Creatures that would cause adventurers to feel fear before they fought them in battle. Thanks to Ryan's returned memories, he knew exactly the kinds of things that could terrify a human. Because he had been one once. Before his soul had been trapped in a core, and he had been forced to become something different, something more, a dungeon core.

"What have you created?" Erin whispered as she looked over them. Normally, his Celestial fairy would rush to his new mobs, inspecting them excitedly, curious to see what they could do. This time though, she was staring at them wide-eyed, hesitant to approach them. Hel, on the other hand, was practically drooling at them, her eyes shining with pride. The Chaos fairy definitely liked these new creatures.

"Monsters, Erin. I've created monsters."

It had taken him only a month to carve out his entire

fourth floor and establish all of the buildings. Clearing out the massive expanse had proved mindless, but fruitful. During the time he had found even more skeletons; some complete, some incomplete. The deeper he went, the larger the forms he discovered. He had also been surprised to find that this far down he had come across another humanoid-type skeleton. Something his human mind remembered from ancient stories. Creatures once said to inhabit the land high in the mountains. Giants.

Ryan had added all these new skeletons to his collection and, after he meticulously recreated his town from memory, had begun the task of creating his monsters. He wanted these five Enforcers to be the most powerful and intimidating creatures he could make. Other than his boss, they were going to be the pinnacle of danger on his floor. Ryan had made the task more difficult for himself by deciding he wanted each one to be different and unique in its composition. Luckily, he had the bone sets to do just that.

He was quite happy with his ever-growing collection of bones. The only thing that upset him was that skeleton trapped outside of his reach, in the Dungeon Town's area of influence. But he had a new plan to acquire that one. And his human memories had already given him a hint as to what that particular skeleton could be. Something else from legend. Something that was supposed to reside near the mountains, not in the forest. *I'll get to that one soon enough.* No use pondering what he didn't have.

His bone collection, in order from smallest beasts to largest, now consisted of squirrels, rats, snakes, foxes, badgers, boars, owls, eagles, horses, lions, tigers, bears, dire wolfs, giant elk, and an elephant. He also had partial skeletons for large reptilian creatures, though most of their bones were fragmented or damaged beyond repair, and some had seemed to have eroded away into a murky black substance his mind called oil. Still, those that retained enough of their bone structure to be registered in his mental catalog via dungeon magic, were classified as massive or larger mobs. He knew instantly he could not summon these yet. He had even uncovered the body of a monstrous dragon. Now, someday, he would be able to have a Cynder of his own.

Ryan had also uncovered humanoid bodies that differed from the humans he was used to consuming. Judging from the amount of bodies he had uncovered during his excavation, the area had once been home to a massive battle, though nothing from his memories or the books he had absorbed mentioned a battle in the area. He now had skeletons of humans, elves, dwarves, and giants.

The elf and dwarf skeletons all acted as his human skeletons did. However, when he played with his giant skeletons, he noticed their cost seemed to have been increased by 1.5 times the normal human skeleton cost, rounded up. As such, a giant skeleton cost him 8 mob points to summon, instead of the 5 of a basic human skeleton cost. Which, given the 10-foot plus size of the mob, made sense.

With all of his new skeletons, nothing but time, and a need to get his mind away from his anger, Ryan had gone to work testing out what he could combine to create usable mobs. At first it had been a task of curiosity, but after a while, he had gone on his monster-making path that netted these five creatures.

The first was a combination of an elven skeleton, a snake, and an eagle. After combining two skeletons together and finding the combination worked, Ryan had tried adding another mob into the new hybrid. To his surprise, it had worked. That had sucked away even more of his time, as he started seeing what the limits to his combinations were.

"The first of my Bone Enforcers is my Slacker." That was the snake, eagle, elf combination, but for his naming reasons, he had just combined snake with clacker, making slacker. Trying to fit elf into the name had been a bit too annoying. It had the lower bone structure of a snake, the torso and arms of an elf, the head of a snake, and eagle wings spreading behind it. Sprouting from the lower bone structure of the snake were also clawed talons from an eagle. In testing, he had noted his Slacker could grab creatures with those talons and lift it before the elven torso, managing to still slither, or fly at a high speed, while the head and arms could attack the prey. It was…devastatingly effective.

Per the combination rules of being a darkness dungeon, the mob's base cost was the cost of the highest value base mob. This was the eagle as a medium beast, at 10 mob points. But because it had humanoid features, Ryan found he was able to upgrade it as he would a human mob. Meaning the base for the creature before it became a mini-boss was actually an Enhanced Slacker.

Following the transformation, he had a fifteen-foot Slacker, armored from head to tail in a dark, scale-like mana armor. Armed with a bone spear and sword, its wings had bone fragments floating all throughout. During testing, Ryan had witnessed that it could launch these as a hail of projectiles at enemies. Additionally, its fangs dripped Dark mana, which Ryan could only guess would prove quite dangerous to adventurers. All in all, it cost him 175 mob points.

His second Bone Enforcer was a combination of a skadger, a clacker, and a dwarf skeleton. The dwarf skeleton stood about as tall as Mini-Steve did, but had denser bones than humans and elves. The creation was a strange human-badger hybrid that, again, had wings sprouting from the back. The skull was badger-like, and the thick arms and feet ended in badger claws. Additionally, the skeleton grew an eagle tail, lined with deadly bones. Ryan empowered it into a mini-boss, this one at eight feet in height, with a sixteen-foot wingspan. Just like the slacker, it cost him a nice 175 mob points.

"This is my..." He trailed off for a moment "Badgerman." Alright, Ryan still needed help naming these. In fact, these two were the only ones he'd actually named. He was hoping his fairies would be able to help him out with what his Bone Enforcers should be called, before the adventurers faced them.

"Next up." Third was another snake combination. Based on not only his memories, but also what he had overheard, especially from Blake, snakes were terrifying. Their skeletons were unnerving, as well. They made for good nightmare fuel. This time he had combined a snake with a dire-wolf. When he had worked on this combination, the outcome had been more terrifying, and unexpected, than planned.

It still had the size, body, and form of a Dire-Wolf. That is, a wolf with shoulders standing about eight feet in height, and a body at close to fourteen feet, from nose to tail. On top of that, it had two snake heads, one on either side of the dire-wolf's head, as well as a long, coiling tail instead of its own. Ryan had combined the dire-wolf with his two-headed snek...for reasons. Because the dire wolf was a huge beast mob, its base cost was 30 points, making it a 150-point mini-boss.

"Fourth." As Ryan spoke, he used his clacker to draw the fairies' attention to the next mob. Ryan had gone back to his human combinations for monsters. He took his giant-elk, which was a huge creature, and combined it with a human. It created a monster straight out of a horror tale. It reminded Ryan of something. He was pretty sure he had heard about such a creature when he was human. But it was just a vague notion lingering in his mind, and searching his memories didn't prove fruitful.

The creature retained the body of an elk, with the human

torso sprouting up in the middle of the elk's back, almost as if the human were riding it. The torso was combined with the elk's back, and the human part did not have legs. Because of the size disparity of the two creatures, the human skeleton elongated in a strange way, giving it a grotesque, stretched appearance. It hung backwards kind of limply, its fingers stretched and pointed, almost trailing the ground.

From the human's head, a set of elk antlers sprouted, which could be used as extremely effective defensive tools. The hybrid cost him 30 mob points as a base, because the giant elk was a huge creature, bumping the cost to 150 for the mini-boss variant. Given its massive size of nearly twenty feet in height and thirty feet in length, Ryan had no doubt it would easily crush adventurers.

Erin shuddered as she looked over Ryan's elk-human combination, moving quickly to the final one. Even as Ryan flew his clacker closer to the fifth and final Bone Enforcer, he noticed Hel's eyes lingering on the beast. It seemed to interest her.

"Something on your mind, Hel?" Ryan asked. The Chaos fairy's head snapped towards the clacker. She shook her head and flashed him a smile.

"Nothing at all, Darling." She left the mob without another word. Ryan could tell something was up, and he was going to address it later. For now, he had one last mob to showcase.

"And last, but not least, my Giant." Alright, maybe he had decided to name this one as well. But that was because he saw it as a way to be witty. Ryan had taken the "Gi" from "Giant," and the ant from "Elephant," to make it... "Giant" again. Even with his human memories back, Ryan knew he wasn't the cleverest when it came to jokes. Still, the mob was nothing to laugh at. Hel did snicker for a brief second at the name, though. He took that as a win.

Standing at thirty feet tall, it had the already massive bones of a giant seemingly infused with even more mass and girth from the elephant bones. It was covered in Dark mana and heavy plate mail, with the head of an elephant atop its form, large tusks protruding outwards from the skull. A large trunk made of Darkness mana extended from it, which the creature could use quite effectively.

The bipedal mini-boss (which wasn't very mini), was armed with a large bone battle axe in one hand, and a bone club that Ryan had fashioned out of a dragon leg bone. He couldn't summon the dragon as a mob yet but that didn't mean he couldn't play with its bones to make items. The club had been enhanced, size-wise, to fit the Giant, though Ryan had resisted arming the Bone Enforcers with too strong of weapons. That seemed a little too overpowered.

Because of the increased cost of the giant mobs, Ryan had begun work on it as an armored giant instead of an empowered one. That put the base cost of the mob at 38 points. As a mini-boss, the massive, towering creature cost the most, at 190 points.

"So, what do you two think?" Ryan was beaming with pride. While working on these, he had found himself eager to share them with the two fairies more and more. His anger had kept him from doing so. Now though, here they were, enjoying the fruits of his labor in all their skeletal glory.

"I think you've really outdone yourself, Ryan." Erin commented, tearing her eyes away from the creatures to look at the clacker. "Though," *Of course there's a though,* "You really are bad at naming things."

"I must agree with the little one, Darling, those names are a bit…uninspired." *Everyone's a critic.*

"Well they were just place holders."

"Uh-huh" Erin and Hel both responded. They both had smiles on their faces. Everyone knew he wasn't the most creative at naming mobs. To be fair, Erin was terrible at it too. He had Steve and Buttercup thanks to her.

"Fine, how about we come up with their actual mini-boss names?" And with that, they got to work. It was good to finally be back. It was good to once again be working as a team.

Chapter Seven

"Right, now that that's settled." It had taken them a little over an hour to decide upon fitting names for the five Bone Enforcers. At the end, they were ones Ryan was pleased with. They were fitting names for the monstrosities he had created. It also meant he didn't have to worry about his half-hearted names ever being known outside of his little circle of trust.

"What are you going to show us next, Darling?" Ryan had just dismissed his five Bone Enforcers, leaving the two fairies alone on his massive fourth floor with just his clacker.

"Well, now that we've got the Bone Enforcers out of the way, I was going to show you some of my thoughts for the regular mobs on the floor. After that, how about the boss mob?" Ryan had thought long and hard on what he wanted his fourth-floor boss to be. It was something he had been planning for a long, long time, and it was finally ready. But, as excited as he was to share it with his fairies, he figured he should showcase the regular mobs that would inhabit his fourth floor first. He was saving his boss for the final reveal.

"More…combinations?" Erin still seemed shaken up from Ryan's Bone Enforcers. Their dark, twisted forms were definitely different from what he normally created. The Celestial fairy seemed to be rather perturbed by them.

"No, not this time. Just some upgraded mobs from previous floors, and a few new skeletal creatures to offer the adventurers some challenge." Because of the open expanse that was his fourth floor, Ryan found he had a lot more freedom with how he could spread out his mobs. On top of that, he had more mob points for his fourth floor than he had ever had to spend before. And with the tricks he had learned about optimizing his mob points, he could create an even greater challenge for adventurers. No longer did he feel constrained by his mob points. No, 4800 was enough, and everything past that was just going to allow him to create even more challenging obstacles for adventurers.

And eventually, they will meet the horde. The skeletal horde was an interesting option he had unlocked at Platinum Tier. Unlike all of the mob types he had unlocked previously, the skeletal horde was perplexing. First, the cost of it was outrageous. 2,500 points for a single mob option. That was the same as if he summoned ten of his skeletal mage bosses, or skeletal archmages. Or five hundred regular skeletal mobs, or two thousand and five hundred skrats. When he thought about it, that would likely have been a terrifying event. Ryan had put the idea on hold, wondering if he could do something like it later on, just to mess with a group such as Blake's. That many sneks, all rushing towards Blake and his party, would likely result in quite the reaction.

But pranks aside, Ryan couldn't fathom what type of mob would cost that many points. So, of course, he had summoned it, just to see what exactly it was. The short answer: it was terrifying. He also realized it was quite literal. It was a horde of skeletal creatures, a mismatch of all sorts of skeletal mobs he could create. Each one was an individual mob, but Darkness mana snaked through all of them, hundreds of them, combining them all with some sort of a link. The mass seemed to move as a single unit, and Ryan had watched bones actually shift from skeleton to skeleton in the mob, to best overwhelm and attack any and all targets that crossed the horde's path. It reminded him somewhat of ants, which would swarm over a single target whenever their hive was threatened. This was the same but on a much larger, and creepier, scale. Especially with the horde's constant clattering, droning sound that reverberated all throughout the massive empty chamber.

Sadly, while he really did have a ton of mob points now, he couldn't really justify 2,500 points for a single mob. Not yet, at least. Ryan did plan to try and utilize the skeletal horde on his fourth floor a little later on, once he was closer to Diamond. It could change things up for adventurers and would make it easy to repopulate the floor after every encounter. For now, though, it was his normal array of mobs. A mixture of human ones, mostly his upgraded skeletal fighters and archers, which had evolved into rare varieties during their time in skeletal fight club, and his new beast mobs.

Ryan also planned to throw in zombie versions of his beasts, though they were going to be few and far between. As much as he loved his theme as a bone dungeon, discounting the effectiveness that were his zombie mobs, or more importantly, his infested zombie mobs, was foolish. He was already hindering his own power by not using soul mobs or resurrecting fallen adventurers. There was no reason for him to further impede himself by stopping the use of his zombie mobs. Especially since Ryan wanted to reach Diamond as soon as he could. Without just slaughtering adventurers, of course. Because the last thing he needed was the Church or the Adventurers' Guild coming in and killing him.

No matter what, he was going to reach Diamond.

There was another reason he wanted to avoid mass murder. Ryan cared about his dungeon town. He cared about the adventurers within, and now that he had received his human memories, he felt a newfound connection to them. They were like a family, of sorts, and as long as it was within his power, he would keep them safe. Outside of dungeon dives, of course. If they accepted the risk of diving into his dungeon, and it wasn't some completely pointless or obnoxious form of death, he wasn't going to stop them. Adventurer deaths were his fastest path towards Diamond Tier. That was just the way of the world.

"I was thinking I could dedicate fifteen-hundred mob points to my first three floors and one-thousand to skeletal fight club. That would leave me with two-thousand three-hundred mob points to spread across my fourth floor, and to use for the Bone Zone if needed." Not only had his mana spiked when he reached Platinum, but he'd increased his influence by quite a bit during this downtime. Now, it spread over ten miles in all directions from his dungeon, meaning he regained his mob points and mana at an extremely fast pace. Even if he only used 1,000 mob points for his Bone Zone, he could keep quite the force going, thanks to his increased regeneration rate. It was going to be much harder for any force to attack him, or his dungeon town.

"That's a lot of mobs." Erin said.

"It's about time you got to see what a true dungeon is like, little one." Hel was practically radiating pleasure. While she was just a clone of a Chaos fairy, she held centuries' worth of memories of being a dungeon fairy. The actual Hel had served in countless dungeons and existed in a time when dungeons were viewed as demigods. Hel had memories of a time when dungeons as powerful as Ryan were widespread. Before they were hunted down and systematically culled.

"I was worried about using that many mob points at first,

Erin." Ryan added, addressing the Celestial fairy's concerns. It was quite the leap from his third floor. "But these mobs will be spread across the entire floor. That means adventurers can encounter them in smaller or larger groups than they would while diving the other floors. The difficulty of the fourth floor really depends on how the party chooses to go about the actual dungeon dive."

Ryan had thought long and hard on that. He could mentally command all 2000 or more mob points worth of mobs to converge on a single point. However, he wouldn't do something like that unless it was in order to protect his very core. And if that was the situation, he was going to be doing a lot more than sending those mobs at the threat. Ryan had new tricks to play with for any situation like that. His fourth floor was filled with new and devious inactive traps he could personally trigger, on top of the ones he had created for adventurers.

"Plus, if my power grew this much, just imagine what the adventurer's power will be like." During his time as a dungeon he had encountered only a handful of Platinum adventurers. Of those, Ryan hadn't seen a single one in action. At least, not to the full extent of their abilities. Judging by the short examples he had seen, such as the chaos users Xander and Samuel, Ryan was quite confident an adventuring party of five Platinum users would have no trouble taking on groups of mobs.

Therefore, Ryan figured from Platinum and on the challenge for adventures would be more a war of attrition, which meant throwing increased numbers of high-level mobs at them and an ever-changing environment to keep them on edge. If the brave explorers were uncomfortable with that, they could always choose to leave or rush to his boss mob. All in all, Ryan was creating a more dynamic experience, to challenge and reward them for their improved strengths, as well as to show off his own growth in power.

"I suppose..." Erin trailed off, looking from Hel to the clacker. Ryan could tell she was still hesitant. "It's just...what if something bad happens? What if they come after us?"

"Trust me, Erin. I will not let anything get close enough to ever hurt us again. And don't you worry about Marcus and the others. I've already thought of a way to ensure we can continue living together with the dungeon town." Ryan sent her over a rush of reassuring emotions, calming the doubt he could feel growing within her.

"Stop being such a tease, Darling," Hel interjected, flying higher as she spoke. "I want to see what you've been up to these past few months. It better be worth the wait." She winked at his clacker. "Otherwise you'll have to pay for keeping us in the dark so long."

Ryan didn't respond vocally to her comment. Instead, in an instant he brought his fourth floor to unlife. The ghost town he had created filled up with 2300 points' worth of mobs, the likes of which Ryan doubted any adventurer had ever imagined.

"Alright, Darling," Hel said as she looked out over the town. Beside her, Erin's eyes took in everything below her. Ryan couldn't help but notice the celestial fairy's mouth was slightly agape, a look of wonderment on her face, as Hel continued. "Consider me impressed."

The Exalted One

The Exalted One sat atop the Throne of Chaos, feeling the Chaotic energy swirl within him, reacting to the legendary artifact. It had been crafted by a group of Diamond Chaos users, intended to connect whoever sat atop the throne to the God of Chaos. They had been partially successful. Whoever sat on the throne was indeed able to speak with the Lord of Chaos. However, prolonged exposure to the God's Chaotic powers tended to irrevocably change the user's form, twisting them into a demonic being. That made it easier for the Church of Justice to hunt them down and kill them. He didn't need to worry about such changes though. He was the only being alive who could keep these changes hidden and his identity secret. Though, very soon he would no longer need to operate from the shadows. It was almost time for his plan to finally come to fruition.

"What news do you bring me?" The messenger before him flinched at his words, shaking visibly in his prostrated position before the Throne of Chaos.

"Exalted One —" The man's voice quivered. It really was getting harder and harder to find good messengers. The latest batch were under his control thanks to his recently acquired Diamond-ranked Succubus, Marissa. They were completely under her demonic powers, though their fear in his presence still shone through her...compulsion. Fear was a powerful tool he always enjoyed using. If people were terrified of him, they wouldn't betray him, even if they weren't completely under Marissa's control.

"Speak clearly, child," Marissa's voice cooed from beside him. The Chaos priestess-turned-Succubus stood in all her demonic glory, a terrifyingly beautiful creature. With her powers, she could bend any among the living to her will, given enough time. Creatures below Platinum could be instantly overcome by her powers. Those of Platinum Tier and above had the ability to resist, for a time. But eventually, they would succumb too. After all, a Succubus's "persuasion" was too enticing to resist.

"Yes, sorry." The messenger cleared his throat, a calmness washing over him after hearing Marissa's words. "The demonic forces are still conducting their raids as instructed. So far, the King's Army has managed to keep the fighting at a standstill, but they are losing more and more soldiers as the days wear on. However—" The messenger

glanced up at him, the fear evident in the poor man's eyes. "It seems the Church of Justice has begun sending groups to the dungeons, accompanied by adventurers from the Guild, to destroy the dungeons we have corrupted."

"It was only a matter of time." He knew how the Adventurers' Guild worked. Still, he was surprised at how quickly Alice had summoned her forces to go dungeon hunting. After all, dungeons were the livelihood of the Adventurers' Guild. They tried their best to keep dungeons from being destroyed. He figured the Guild couldn't ignore the fact these dungeons had all been corrupted by Chaos. Everything was playing out as planned.

"How are the people reacting to this situation?" That was the part he really cared about. It had been months since this part of his plan had been set into motion. He had ordered the Cult of Chaos to begin launching demonic attacks all across the human kingdom, attacking every small town and settlement they could. At the same time, a massive demonic army, fueled constantly by his corrupted dungeons, was to keep the King's Army at bay. His intention was to wear down the resources of any group that could oppose his ascension.

"They're terrified. More and more are running to the Church for protection."

"And the Church?"

"The Chaos across the land, the turmoil spreading, seems to have allowed for their more radical branch, the Zealots of Light, to rise in power. They've begun recruiting individuals from the towns to create defensive parties to help hold off demonic attacks. Their numbers swell daily."

"Goooood," he drawled. The more radicalized everything became, the easier it would be for his plot to come to fruition. "What about the Bone Dungeon?" That dungeon was the one thing that kept thwarting his plans. It should have been an easy tool to acquire; Darkness and Chaos had fought together back during the last Great War. However, this particular dungeon had resisted the calls of Chaos at every turn.

Even more perplexing, the dungeon had actually been protecting adventurers from the demonic forces sent to assault the dungeon town.

"It remains closed."

"Very well. We will use this time to get our forces in place. When it awakens, I want that dungeon removed." He dismissed the messenger. The man practically sprinted out of his presence.

"It seems the time is ripe for our next task." He stood, the whispers from the God of Chaos leaving his mind as he did. The Exalted One stepped away from the throne, his body brimming with Chaotic energy. He needed to make certain the last few parts of his plan were carried out perfectly. He had waited centuries for this. He would ensure nothing, and no one, stood in his way.

Chapter Eight

BLAKE

Blake had been away from the dungeon town ever since the day his father had died. Ever since the day the Cult of Chaos had attacked. He'd left his party, abandoned his friends, and fled to the Adventurers' Guild Headquarters. There, he'd found a sense of solace, a way to keep his mind occupied. There, he worked together with Alice, the leader of the Adventurers' Guild, to try and stop the Cult of Chaos. Now, it was over. Alice had decided it was time for him to leave. But Blake wasn't ready. There was still so much to do, and he wasn't going to up and leave it all without saying something.

"You can't —" The Guildmaster stopped him before he could even finish his statement. She narrowed her ever-swirling eyes, freezing him in place with her powerful gaze. It wasn't as strong as before, likely because of his growth in power. He had come a long way from the Bronze adventurer that had first stood before her. Still, she was Diamond 2, with dual affinities, and even at Platinum 4, Blake couldn't fight her overbearing power. In other words...he was going to leave without putting up as much of a fight as he'd thought.

"It is for the best, Blake." She sat behind her desk at the

Headquarters, a massive building situated in the heart of Valta, the human capitol. It was the seat of power from which she kept track of all the comings and goings of the Adventurers' Guild, and where Blake had spent his time during the past few months. A lot had happened since that fateful day…

…Blake had raced to the Adventurers' Guild Headquarters the moment he teleported away from the Bone Dungeon, immediately after his parting words to his party. He knew there was only one person that could help him answer what was going on. If there was anyone who could help him sort out what had happened to his father, it was Alice.

He found himself barging into the Adventurers' Guild, not taking no for an answer. The receptionist, as well as a few of the adventurers who were milling about tried to stop him, leaping up to bar his way. But Blake wasn't in a state of mind to care. He drew upon all of his power and caused the demonic sword in his hand to blaze with a Celestial glow. As the mana crackled over it, it took on a strange flicker, with reds and blacks coursing through it. He knew the sword was something special, something powerful, but he wasn't sure how. The appearance of it, pulsating with power, as well as the Dark mana swirling around his shield was enough to cause more than a few of the adventurers to back away.

However, every group has a wannabe hero. In this case, a Platinum Sentinel, the head of security in the location, stepped forward to challenge him. At any other time, Blake would have been intimidated, even fearful… or at least hesitant about practically breaking into the Adventurers' Guild Headquarters. However, all he felt now was a dull nothingness tinged with waves of grief. There was no room for fear or hesitation.

All his anger had burned out of him. Beating up that cultist, Samuel, had helped with that. His sorrow rushed through like a wave. He was still in disbelief over everything that had happened. He needed answers. And he wasn't about to be stopped.

The Sentinel's own body glowed with a blue light. He was a Water affinity user, and Blake knew what was going to happen next. The blue mana rushed off the man, and the ground between him and Blake began to frost over. The mana caked over Blake's form, freezing his feet in place, threatening to encase him in ice. It was a powerful move that Sentinels had, an upgraded mixture of a taunt and a crowd control effect. Depending on how much mana they pumped into it, they could hold an opponent frozen indefinitely.

Blake wasn't an ordinary opponent though. He could care less about a physical skill like that. After all, you can't freeze that which doesn't have a form. Blake turned his mana Ethereal and activated his Spectral form. The skill, costing only 75 points to trigger, was like a drop of water compared to his mana pool at Platinum 5. As a dual affinity user, he had a combined total of 9,600 mana. Eighty percent of that went to enhancing his physical traits, which left him still with an impressive 1,920 mana points to use on skills. Meaning he could activate his Spectral form easily and had plenty of mana left over to keep it up, considering it only cost him an additional 3 points of mana per second to use.

It wasn't perfect, considering every time he had to toggle it on and off increased the cost of the skill, and would eat through his mana quickly. Plus, the stronger his foes—well, they could wait out his ability.

"I've no time for your games," he growled as he floated past the stunned Sentinel. To the man's credit, he did call out a warning to the guards upstairs as Blake passed through him. Little good that did. Thanks to his permanently active visual ability, Blake could see the mana, the souls, of the guards above him. So, he simply moved through the walls, bypassing them even as they rushed towards the stairs.

His assault on the Guildhall ended as quickly as it had begun. He passed through the doors and was frozen in place by Alice's powerful gaze. Even in his Spectral form, even with his power burning through him, the strength of those magical swirling eyes bound him in place. With him frozen there and powerless before her, she demanded to know what was going on.

He was more than happy to oblige. He told her everything, how the demons had stormed the dungeon town while the cultists invaded the Bone Dungeon, his encounter with his demon-possessed father in the Dungeon of Ashes, defeating Marissa, all of it.

"There must be some mistake." Alice looked away, finally freeing Blake from her gaze. He'd already released his Spectral Form, as he knew there was no way he could escape from Alice's gaze. When the Diamond 2 locked her eyes on you, there wasn't anything you could do. Blake had wondered, more than once, what it was that gave her gaze such power. Whatever it was, it didn't seem natural. Of course, Alice wasn't natural, that was for sure. In fact, looking at her with his eyes, which could see the mana type and power of a person's soul, was painful. She was Diamond 2 and had dual affinities for Fire and Water mana. Her soul burned brightly, the fiery red and icy blue swirling in a never-ending mirage. Only sheer willpower kept him from looking away from her.

"No, there's no mistake." His voice dropped as he spoke, the emotion of the entire situation at last overwhelming him. Everything was laid bare before Alice—his emotions, too

"My father is dead. I couldn't do anything to save him," he repeated.

Alice stood from her desk then, walking swiftly towards

Blake. She reached him in mere moments. Her glance darted for a brief second to his new sword, and then to his eyes. Her eyebrow raised in interest. While she was obviously intrigued, she didn't comment on them. Instead, she placed a hand gently on his cheek, turning his head lightly down towards hers, so that he was staring directly into her eyes. For once, they stopped shifting, and a look of pure sympathy, of understanding, flowed through her into him.

"I have no words to offer up to you. I know all too well the pain of losing a loved one." Her eyes hardened, and began swirling again. This time, blue and red mana began to crackle around her as well. "However, I can offer you something else. It won't bring your father back, but perhaps it will give us both something we need. After all, your tale gives me the final evidence for what comes next."

"And what is that?" He asked her hesitantly, his voice cracking, his throat suddenly dry.

She grabbed a crystal around her throat, clutching it firmly in her hand. "Vengeance."

Suddenly, they were no longer standing in her office. Instead, Blake once again found himself in the town outside the Dungeon of Ashes.

Chapter Nine

Unlike when Blake and his party had arrived at the Dungeon of Ashes, mobs were present this time around. Demons were teeming around the entrance, cackling and laughing as they ran free. Something was wrong. This was not the same dungeon he had visited before. Something had changed, and for the worse. The Succubus was no longer in control. The dungeon was going wild. It was lucky they had arrived so quickly after the Cult invaded the Bone Dungeon. So many demons running loose would have been a major threat to nearby towns.

"I trust you can keep me safe, yes?" Alice seemed completely unconcerned about what Blake's answer was, but he gave it regardless.

"You have my word." He channeled his mana into his shield once more, the Darkness mana completely coating it. At the same time, he projected out a burst of Celestial energy, enacting the Paladin barrier that his father had used, what felt like a lifetime ago, to keep Blake safe from the eruption of Ryan's entrance.

"Very well. Now that there is clear evidence this dungeon

has been corrupted…" Alice rose a single hand towards the mass of demons that was stemming out of the dungeon entrance, like water breaking free from a dam. A serpent made of blue mana rushed forth from her hand, letting out a torrential roar as it blasted through everything in its path.

Any mob unfortunate enough to be in its path was instantly destroyed, leaving behind torn bits and pieces. Those that didn't outright vanish from her attack, erupted into a small explosion of Chaos mana. Blake's glowing golden barrier kept any debris from reaching the Guildmaster and him. "Let us avenge your father and my son, and destroy this corrupted dungeon once and for all."

"Are you coming, Blake?" Her words startled him. He had been so fixated on her destructive power, he hadn't realized she was already moving into the entrance of the Dungeon of Ashes. He caught up, placing himself in front of her, as was the duty of the tank. Still, he wondered if she needed him here at all. Blake had never seen power such as hers. And even more terrifying, she had done it with such ease. That thought, was followed by the next, even more sobering fact. Because of her dual affinities, Alice was the strongest living being in existence. Other than the Gods, and perhaps some dungeons. He recalled the rumors that she had destroyed multiple Platinum-Tier dungeons singlehandedly. After this small display of power, he realized those weren't just stories.

They made quick time moving through the dungeon. Unlike before, they had to traverse each floor of the dungeon. The pathway that had appeared before, funneling Blake and his party directly to the third floor, was no longer there. Still, nothing the dungeon threw their way could stop them. The deeper they dove, the more Blake got the feeling that some-thing else was amiss. The dungeon's attempts seemed almost halfhearted. Like the final struggles of an already defeated and dying creature. Very little sentience seemed to remain.

"What's going on?" Blake asked Alice as they finished clearing the second floor. While they still faced random demon mobs, they had also come across Fire-related mobs. The second-floor boss had been a large fiery golem, though Alice had decimated it before it could even attack the two of them. Blake seemed to be there to keep random bursts of flame and falling debris from hitting the two of them. Alice had only been using Water mana so far. She hadn't used any Fire mana, which made sense, but she also wasn't using the combination the two mana types. Meaning, she hadn't even started to use her true power yet.

"You mentioned the Succubus was teleported away after the battle, yes?" Alice spoke as they made their way down towards the third floor. She wasn't even breaking a sweat. "Without the Succubus in the dungeon, the connection between the dungeon and its fairy has been broken. Doing so usually causes a dungeon immense pain. And while dungeons can exist without fairies, they tend to become mindless. Feral. Once a dungeon has lost its fairy, it often longs for death itself."

The way she said those final words hinted at some hidden understanding of how dungeons worked. Blake was already surprised she knew the dungeons had fairies, but her knowledge seemed to go much deeper. Which made sense for the strongest adventurer and the leader of the Adventurers' Guild. Still, if she had all this knowledge, why hadn't she shared it? Why did she keep it secret?

"How do you know all this?" he said without thinking. He had been through a lot. His mind could only process and handle so much. Now, he wanted answers. She hadn't mentioned much about the Cult of Chaos yet, and he had let that slide. After all, they were about to take down the dungeon that had been the deathplace of his father. However, this knowledge about dungeons intrigued him far more.

"When you live as long as I have, Blake, you pick up a few things." She turned and offered him a sad smile. "These eyes of mine have seen a lot. I've seen more death, devastation, and suffering than I ever wanted to. And the worst part is, I'm sure I will experience much, much more before my end finally comes."

As she finished speaking, they stepped out into the third floor of the Dungeon of Ashes. It was just as Blake remembered, the massive expansive of rock, the lake of lava, and the strange island in the middle. There wasn't a single sign of his father's body. It was gone. Blake didn't know why he expected it to still be there. He knew from Ryan that the dungeon could absorb anything, and everything, it wanted to, as long as there wasn't a living creature to stop it. Sean's corpse would have been an easy thing for the dungeon to absorb.

A wave of rage washed over Blake, and he stepped out into the middle of the room. "Give him back," Blake growled, looking around for any sign of life. "Give my father back."

"You took her from me," A low, hoarse voice spoke from the furthest depths of the room. It almost sounded like it was sobbing. "She was here, but now she's gone." The voice continued, "bring her back. Bring her back. Please. No, not her. The other one. Bring her back." A wall of lava falling down the side of the room split open to reveal a massive, gleaming diamond, floating effortlessly, glowing a faint red. "Without her, why live? If she's dead. Can we be together when I die? We die? All there is left is death." The diamond stone had the symbol of the God of Flames emblazoned on it, glowing a bright crimson. It flashed red and a moment later a massive form began to rise from the lava.

"You poor thing," Alice said as she stepped past Blake, and he watched as her mana swirled and condensed around her. "You've been used, and yet you don't realize it. You've caused more pain and suffering than you could understand, yet you aren't to blame." A cloak of blue and red mana seemed to appear around her, and two massive serpents erupted from her form. The two mana beasts twisted and coiled outward, growing nearly twenty feet in height as they spread out. Then, without warning, the two rushed towards the core, twisting together and combining as they did. The mana took on a strange purplish hue as it condensed, and the serpents combined, a massive purple creature of pure destruction.

"Allow me to put you out of your misery. It's the least I can do." While she sounded sincere for the most part, there was rage and sorrow in her voice. She may have felt sympathy for the dungeon, but she still blamed it for her son's death.

As she finished speaking, the very air in the room, the very world, warped around that crackling snake as it obliterated the massive form growing out of the lava. With impossible speed it then connected with the dungeon's core. On impact, a blinding light erupted between the purple mana and the glowing diamond. For a moment, everything seemed to stand still. Then, a deafening sound ripped through the dungeon, a shattering, and a pained, wild roar. The final cry of the dungeon. A second later, the room grew dark, Alice's purple mana faded away, and the core was gone. In its place, a small gem, swirling with energy. A gem that looked extremely similar to Alice's eyes.

"And just like that..." The dungeon around them was shaking violently, with large pieces of stone falling around them. "The Dungeon of Ashes is no more." She took a step forward, and her form was wrapped in a purple light. A second later, she appeared beside the gemstone she had created. She picked it up and placed it atop a ring she wore on her hand. The gem disappeared as the ring flashed, and

Blake realized she was wearing a ring of holding—a magical ring that stored objects in an extradimensional space.

"Now that we've exacted vengeance on the initial dungeon, let us move onto the next task. Now that we know the Cultists have the power to corrupt dungeons, we must do all we can to try and stop them before they corrupt all the dungeons. Those that are already corrupted, though it pains me to say, must be eradicated." She wrapped herself in her purple mana again and appeared beside Blake. The air around her crackled for a split second before the mana faded away. "Tell me Blake, can you lend me your aid for the next few months? I would understand if you wish to go back to your friends. But," her eyes went soft for a moment, her entire complexion seeming to change as she took him in, "I could use you by my side as we move forward."

The thought of returning to his party, after the way he'd left them, scared Blake. He couldn't go back, not now. Not with the Cult still out there. As such, Blake didn't even hesitate as he responded, "Of course."

And so, for the past few months, he had worked with Alice to root out any information they could on the Cult of Chaos. She sent out other adventurers to investigate further into what Sean had been doing prior to his disappearance. All they had to go on was that he had been working to take down the Cult of Chaos for the Church. What had happened between that mission and his appearance as a demon was unknown, and troubling. Especially because, according to Alice, there should've been no way for someone without Chaos mana to be possessed by a demon. Even more startling was Blake's account of the dual mana he had seen within

Sean. The Celestial Paladin having Chaos mana was impossible.

"We've reached the end of what we can do together for now. We've managed to locate all of the corrupted dungeons and are assigning teams to take them out." That had been a big part of their work together. They were trying to track down all the dungeons that had been corrupted, without spreading too much alarm. This had been a difficult task, as they hadn't found a single uncorrupted dungeon. All except the dungeons of the Gods had fallen to Chaos.

It had been a secret they needed to keep as more and more dungeons were added to the list. If word got out that all the dungeons of the world had been corrupted, it would have been problematic for the Adventurers' Guild. As such, Alice had needed to keep up a pretense of normalcy. She couldn't directly go into each dungeon. Instead, she sent adventurers under the guise of dungeon diving, to destroy the affected dungeons. Discretion was paramount– the Cult might act if it knew the Guild was going after the corrupted dungeons. And while Alice was powerful, she was also cautious. Whoever was controlling the Cult had to be danger-ous. Meaning the Guildmaster needed to plan and prepare appropriately.

"With any luck, we will be rid of the Cult of Chaos within the fortnight. And with the corrupted dungeons taken out, we should see the end of the demonic army." There was sadness in her voice. They both knew that destroying the corrupted dungeons, and the Cult of Chaos along with them, would leave the Guild with very few places to increase their skills.

She walked towards him, her eyes full of kindness, compassion. "It is best for you to return to the Bone Dungeon and to your team, now."

I truly am thankful for your help over the past few

months, Blake. With your father gone, I found myself missing a dear friend." She held out her hand towards Blake. A gemstone, the gemstone from the Dungeon of Ashes, appeared in her hand. "Take this, as a token of our time together. Be safe, Blake." She closed his fist around the gem. The colors within it swirled, and he could feel a faint heat from it.

"What is it?"

"Something special. Keep it close for now. Once you reach Diamond, I will show you how special it is." Her eyes swirled mysteriously. "'Till then, please take care of yourself." She brushed a lock of hair from his eyes, her face softening even more. For a moment, she seemed like she wanted to say something else. She opened her mouth slightly, closed it again, and shook her head with a sad smile. "You look so much like your father," she whispered before lowering her hand.

Blake stared at her, searching for answers. Her face was an unreadable mask, and he could tell she wasn't going to give him any more information. She loved doing that. Giving just enough information to cause someone to further question things was a personal pastime of hers. She'd say the added mystery, the seeds of further knowledge, were what best helped people grow. If there was one thing Blake had learned about Alice over their time together, it was that she wasn't wrong in any of her assumptions. It was almost like she could see people's futures, or at least extremely detailed parts of them, with a single glance.

"If you ever need me again, Alice—" he started, but she raised her hand, silencing him.

"Go," she said.

Blake offered her a sad smile and let out a heavy sigh. There was another reason he was hesitant to leave, and she knew it. He had abandoned his party, hadn't spoken to them since that fateful day. Blake was scared about how they would react to his return.

He took another deep breath, before he clutched the pendant around his chest. He closed his eyes, picturing his destination in mind. He sent a small trickle of mana into the pendant, activating the crystal, willing it to teleport him back to the dungeon town outside of the Bone Dungeon.

As the magic swirled around him, he heard the faintest whisper from Alice.

"Your parents would be so proud of you."

Chapter Ten

Blake had to blink a few times as he appeared in the dungeon town. Or, more specifically, what used to be the dungeon town. What he saw as he appeared there, next to the giant crystal that allowed everyone to teleport freely into town, was not the small town he once knew. It was something more, something grander. It was more akin to a dungeon city.

The streets were filled with countless individuals moving to and fro, crowding the streets and making it impossible for those with carts or horses to pass. The stalls that used to litter the streets were gone, replaced with permanent structures. Which, speaking of the structures... there were a lot more, and of a much higher quality than before. The town had been busy these past four months.

In the past, the dungeon town had been comprised of hastily constructed buildings, with most adventurers and visitors living in a large open expanse filled with tents. The structures put up during that time were quick and easy to create, made of available materials such as wood from the forest the dungeon existed in.

When Blake had last been in town, a year after the

dungeon had been found, the buildings had a temporary feel, even after they had built a sturdier wall following Viktor's attack. They had reinforced the fortification when news of the demon attacks had reached them, though Ryan's wall of bones had made their own attempts feel rather pointless.

Now everything had been upgraded. It seemed there had been extensive construction throughout town while Blake was gone. Now some of the stores were constructed of stone, not wood. Those still made of wood, seemed to have received a little extra love and care. Some shops had gone so far as to paint their stores different colors, and many had wooden or even decorative metal signs hanging above their doors. Blake had known from his time with Alice that the town was going to see an upgrade. After all, it was extremely rare for a dungeon to reach Platinum Tier and still be deemed safe enough to dive for the masses.

That, plus the rumors over the past few months that the Bone Dungeon was one of the only dungeons not to spawn dangerous demon hordes, made the demand for Ryan's dungeon skyrocket. The Bone Dungeon was now the only dungeon under the jurisdiction of the Adventurers' Guild in existence that could serve as a training zone for adventurers, royals, and all others. It was now the only place to grow stronger outside of engaging in actual war and battles.

"Welcome to Boneville, please record your name and reason for visiting here." A man dressed in official Guild attire stepped forward the moment Blake had appeared. In his hand he held a ledger, and at his side were a few other individuals. Judging by their looks and gear, Blake figured they were Gold Tier, at least. It seemed Marcus had stepped up security for all individuals coming and going into the dungeon town as well.

"Bone…Ville?" He stared at the man. Was that really what Marcus had named the town?

The man with the ledger shrugged. "We left it up to a vote. It was either that or Boner-ton. That freaking Duelist paid off the entire tavern to try and vote for that name."

At that, Blake couldn't help but smile. Considering how rare of a class that was, and given the type of humor associated with the name, he knew exactly who the culprit was.

"Let me guess, Jack?"

The man nodded, flashing a grin. "Ah, so you know him?" He paused, taking a moment to look Blake up and down. His eyes lingered on Blake's shield, the shield Blake had presented to Ryan when he ascended to Gold, the shield that Ryan had 'accidently' turned into an ultra-rare item.

"You, you're Blake." The man bowed his head slightly towards Blake and handed the ledger off to one of his guards, before extending a hand towards Blake. "Name's Ollie, I've heard the stories about you." His voice dropped to a hush. "Is it true you can bring back the dead?"

"Er," Blake took the man's hand and shook it, but found himself at a loss for words. He had hoped his actions that day, when he brought Matt from the grave, would have been shrugged off by now. After all, the town had been attacked by demons, and there was an entire Cult of Chaos running around, corrupting dungeons, and launching demonic attacks all across the world. Unfortunately, it seemed his feat had not been forgotten, despite that.

"I'll take it from here, Ollie." A familiar gruff voice caused the Gold-Tier adventurer to glance backwards in the direction of the largest building in the area. The Guildhall created in the dungeon town had undergone an upgrade too. It seemed the Guild had spared little expense when further establishing its permanent location in the town. From the double doors of the stone building, Blake saw a welcome grizzled face. The Platinum 2 rogue, Marcus. The man appointed by Alice to run the town. It appeared he was now Platinum 1. Another reminder that things had changed while Blake had been gone.

"Understood, sir." Ollie offered a bow to Marcus, and then took one last look at Blake, his eyes once more lingering on the shield. He departed as another person appeared at the Port Crystal, off to collect their information and confirm the purpose for their visit.

"It seems the town has…grown." Blake glanced at Marcus as the rogue made his way towards him. Blake's disappearance had been sudden, and Marcus was one of the few who knew what had happened to his father.

"Unfortunately, in more ways than size." Marcus shook his head, running a hand through his hair. The man's hair had greyed further. The rogue had aged a few years since Blake last saw him. That was telling of the amount of stress the man must be under, considering you essentially stopped aging once you hit Platinum.

"Let's take a walk, Blake." The rogue motioned down one of the streets, which Blake knew lead out of the town, towards the dungeon. Without waiting for a response from Blake, the rogue walked away. Blake followed. He could feel his emotions swirling inside. Again he wondered if he was ready to return to this life. Was he really ready to begin his life as an adventurer again? Could he go back to diving in the dungeon with his party, his family, after all that had happened?

Chapter Eleven

Marcus didn't say a word until they exited the dungeon town and walked a small distance away from the walls. The guards stationed at the entrance—something new to the town— simply nodded to Marcus as he left. Once the two made their way down the newly paved road to the dungeon entrance, Marcus slowed his pace.

"Blake, about your father."

He knew from Marcus's tone what was coming next. And honestly, he didn't want to hear it. The wound was still too fresh.

"Don't," Blake whispered. His throat caught as emotions he had buried fought to surface once again. Being an adventurer, Blake was used to death. It happened all the time. It came with the territory. People died daily in the dungeon. But this was different. His father was supposed to be invincible. Sean had been a Platinum 1 Paladin and had been one of the strongest adventurers alive. His death would have been a shock even if he had died within a dungeon.

What made it even worse was, no one knew what had happened to him, nor how he had been corrupted. Even worse, the way his father had died, the once invincible Paladin killing himself before Blake's very eyes…all because Blake had been too weak. That was so much worse than if his father had died in a dungeon, doing what he loved.

"You're right." Marcus pulled out a flask. The rogue took a heavy drink, closing his eyes for a moment as he did. "Some things are best left unsaid." He took another long swig and offered the flask to Blake.

"Thanks." Blake grabbed the flask and took a drink. Or tried to. The fiery liquor was nothing like what he was used to drinking. And that was saying something—the ale at the tavern wasn't all that great. Whatever Marcus was drinking was much harsher, Blake found his throat burning, and eyes watering, as he finished swallowing what little he hadn't spat out.

"Oh, should have warned you about that." Marcus flashed him a wicked smile. The rogue knew exactly what would happen. "I make it myself. There's a special kind of wheat that grows near the God of Fire's dungeon that makes for a strong drink. Plus, it's pure enough that if you were to ignite it, it would erupt in a rather large fireball. Which is why I call it 'fireball whiskey'." He took another drink. Blake figured the rogue had finished about half that flask in the span of the conversation.

"I think I'll stick to whatever the tavern has to offer." Blake could still feel his mouth burning, but he was noticing some rather interesting flavors of spice lingering on his tongue. If only that drink wasn't so…overwhelming.

"Probably for the best." Marcus pocketed the flask and they resumed walking in silence for another few minutes. As they drew ever closer to the dungeon's entrance, Blake could feel his apprehension growing. His memories were flashing back to that day, to the battle within the dungeon against the Cult of Chaos. There was another reason he had been hesitant to return. He still had nightmares about the Chaos mana rushing through him. The madness, the hunger, the intoxication that had pulsed through his body as the mana had begun to twist his very form. It had been terrifying yet exhilarating. And in that moment, on the heels of his father's death, Blake had lost himself to it.

"I'm sure you're wondering why I've led you out here, Blake." Marcus stopped and looked at the younger adventurer, a serious expression on his face.

"I'm assuming you're going to tell me." Blake had gotten used to just going with whatever Alice had planned for him. Seemed that had carried over to his ready acceptance of following after Marcus. Asking questions only prolonged the path towards the truth.

"I see your time with Alice has taught you a few things." The rogue chuckled darkly. "And you are correct." He took in a deep breath. "I need you to keep an eye on the dungeon."

"What do you mean?" Marcus was one of the few people that knew of Blake's relationship with the dungeon.

"I'm sure you saw that smaller Succubus in the dungeon during our fight against my sister." Marcus's voice dropped at the last part. The leader of the Cult of Chaos had been his sister, Marissa. A Platinum Chaos user.

"Briefly." Blake really hadn't seen much during that fight. Everything was still just a blur, a cloud of red.

"The dungeon also created demonic mobs. But I haven't mentioned that to anyone, not even Alice." Marcus paused. "I don't trust our lines of communication anymore. I know I can trust Alice…But these cultists, the attacks…even Viktor. Something is going on, and I have to be extra cautious about what is known."

"You could always send Alice a secure—" Marcus raised a hand, stopping Blake.

"Neither Alice nor I truly trust these magic systems

anymore. There is something larger going on. Which is why I've raised security in the town. It is also why we're out here, having this conversation in person."

"You can't really believe Ryan has been corrupted?" Blake knew his relationship with the dungeon was unique. His ability to raise in tiers and ascend not just to Gold, but also Platinum, was connected to the bond he shared with Ryan. He owed his life to the dungeon and had helped it out on a few occasions as well. The two used to converse through a special pendant Ryan had made for Blake, a secret few knew about. Blake also knew that Ryan had a secret of his own. The dungeon had a Celestial fairy, and a link to the Goddess of Justice.

"I don't." Marcus shook his head. "But I've been wrong about things before, and those errors were fatal. The dungeon has been closed ever since that night but has been keeping us safe against any attacks. Still, you and I both know dungeons are cunning and unpredictable creatures. The stronger they get, the wiser they become. I want you to keep an eye on Ryan, and I need you to give me a warning if anything feels amiss." The rogue put a large, scarred hand onto Blake's shoulder. "Can you do that for me?"

"I-"

"Really now, you know I can hear you, right?" Ryan's voice echoed out from the pendant around Blake's neck. Both adventurers jumped.

"What the actual—" Marcus started.

"Calm down. I'm not going to hurt you," Ryan's voice echoed, not from Blake's pendant this time but from a skull-shaped crystal that had grown out of the ground in front of them, about twenty feet down the path. "Now then, how about we all have a talk?"

Chapter Twelve

RYAN

The silence that hung in the air was palpable Everyone was focused on Ryan, waiting on the core to speak. He relished that. It was a moment of complete control.

"I'm sure you've got a lot of questions," Ryan broke the silence after another brief moment, figuring he should move on with the topic at hand. He had been eavesdropping, as was his new norm, on Marcus and Blake. Because Ryan had now spread his influence all throughout the area, including the very top layers of soil, he could sense whenever adventurers stepped foot into his territory. He still couldn't spread his influence into the radius around the dungeon town, which annoyed him, but that was something he had gotten used to. The moment they were out of that protective area, he could "see" and "hear" everything the humans were doing and saying. It was a great way to gain a lot of information on the goings on outside of his dungeon.

"You could say that." Marcus was slow in his response, the rogue's entire body tense. The Platinum 1 rogue held his attention. Ryan had been waiting for a good time to reach out to the man. Marcus was, after all, the main voice of the

Adventurers' Guild in the dungeon town. Meaning Marcus was the person Ryan needed to ensure was on his side. Having just Blake on "team Ryan" wasn't good enough anymore.

"Feel free to ask a few, before I discuss what I wish to speak with you about. What's most important to me right now is honesty." Not just with his fairies, but with Blake and Marcus. He was done with secrets. They all needed to be on the same page so Ryan could grow without any fear, worry, or hinderance. He needed to hit Diamond Tier. Especially considering what he could do once he did.

"Right." Marcus glanced for a quick moment to Blake, before turning his attention back to the crystal skull. The Platinum 4 Specter of Balance, because apparently Blake had grown a little stronger during the past four months, simply shrugged. He was no stranger to interacting with Ryan. Blake and his party had gotten used to Ryan's... quirks? Ryan also hadn't spoken with Blake in a long time, meaning Blake was as caught off-guard with the whole situation as Marcus was.

"First, what do you mean 'you can hear' us?" It was a valid question. From what Ryan knew from Hel and Erin, people didn't know all that much about Dungeons, nor what they could actually do.

"Well, that's simple." A momentary flash of annoyance crossed from his bond with Hel. The Chaos fairy could tell Ryan was about to spill some dungeon secrets, and she was not a fan of that. But to her credit, she held her tongue. Ryan was in charge of this situation. He had given her and Erin a stern warning not to interrupt any of his conversations with others.

"Do you see the faint glow on the ground all around you?" It really was faint, and in the forest it was easy to miss. One could almost mistake it for the gentle glow of sunlight in the area. Even at night, it could be mistaken for moonlight reflecting off the grass or ground. Only on nights of a new moon, when it should be completely dark, would someone be able to discern the unnatural glow without being made aware of it.

"I —" Marcus stared hard at the ground, his brow furrowing. After a moment, the rogue nodded. "I do. —"

"Anything that light touches is mine. It signifies what has been created by my mana and I have a direct influence over it. Through such objects, I can hear and see everything." Ryan's comment caused Marcus to pale. The rogue grasped the implications of his statement: Ryan had eyes and ears practically everywhere.

"Well, that's not information I wanted to start my day with." Marcus rubbed his temple. "So, you can see and hear everything. Nice. Second, what is it that you want?" The rogue was getting straight to the point, Ryan liked that.

"Honestly, I want the same things I've always wanted. I want to be allowed to continue to grow." It really was a simple request.

"Well, it's not like I'm stopping that —" Ryan cut Marcus off before he could continue.

"You're not right now, and you haven't in the past. To your credit, the adventurers of the town have tried, in their own ways, to help keep me safe. Though we can both agree your defenses have been a bit...lax." The threats to Ryan's dungeon had to pass through the dungeon town. If they'd done a better job of keeping themselves safe, Ryan wouldn't have had to deal with that necromancer, or the Cult of Chaos.

"My job is to protect the town, not the dungeon," Marcus growled. Ryan knew from observing the rogue that he was always straightforward, passionate about his duty and his efforts to keep his people safe.

"Well if something happens to me the town goes away, yeah?" Ryan glanced between the two. "Besides, who do you think has been keeping the demon hordes away from the town over the past four months?" Not the adventurers, that was for sure. Ryan had been efficient in stopping any and all attacks that came into his Bone Zone. It was easier for him to just take care of the adventurers rather than gamble on their abilities. He didn't have much faith in them, other than a few parties such as Blake's.

"I appreciate the efforts you have been going through to keep the town safe." Marcus bowed slightly towards the crystal skull. "But don't think I haven't forgotten what I've seen in your dungeon. I know you have the ability to summon demonic mobs as well. I've been taking your efforts into consideration, as proof that you haven't completely turned…yet." Marcus let the final word hang in the air, the threat implied. Ryan's anger flared.

"Listen here, Marcus," he growled. Ever since he'd gotten his memories back, he'd found himself a little more emotional, at times. It was almost as if his memories of being human had brought a variety of emotional responses that he previously hadn't tapped into. Either that, or his fairies were rubbing off on him.

"I can promise you I have not been tainted. I am still the same Darkness dungeon I have always been. I am here to ensure there is a complete understanding between you and I, and to make sure we have a clear line of communication in the future. As long as both of those conditions are maintained, we can continue as we always have."

Ryan wanted to add in a threat of his own, but he stopped. He was still scared of what the Adventurers' Guild could do to him if they were angered. After all, he hadn't seen a Diamond adventurer yet and was worried about just how powerful such an individual might be.

"Information and communication, are always important in building trust." Marcus placed hands into the belt at his side. Blake stood there, glancing between Marcus and Ryan's crystal skull, the same as Ryan's fairies were doing. They were in uncharted territory here.

"I'm glad we can agree on that." Ryan found himself mentally nodding towards Marcus. "Onto why I've decided to speak with you here. I will be reopening my dungeon entrance in a week's time, and I want to make sure you've got the proper information and preparation in place for when I do."

Blake's eyes lit up at those words, and even Marcus's stoic expression shifted a little. They were both adventurers and a dungeon opening up was always a reason for excitement.

Marcus's eyes focused on Ryan's crystal skull. "I'm listening."

Chapter Thirteen

"I can't believe you did that, Ryan," Erin said. Ryan had completed his meeting with Marcus and Blake just moments before. Erin broke the silence immediately after. "It, it goes against everything I've ever been taught."

Ryan glanced at the Celestial fairy. Soon she would be an Angel, a Platinum-Tier Celestial mob. Something Ryan was still trying to process. Her growth, and Hel's, was something he couldn't discount.

"It needed to be done." He said simply. This was all part of his plan. He needed to make sure he could trust everyone around him. His fairies, the adventurers. This understanding and line of communication with Marcus was much more proactive than sitting around, waiting for something bad to happen.

"I wish you hadn't been so forthcoming, Darling." Hel was sitting atop his core, which had grown large enough that the adolescent-sized fairies could perch comfortably atop him. "It does seem counterproductive."

During his conversation with Marcus, Ryan had given the rogue a full breakdown of how his fourth floor was going to work. He had gone so far as to give Marcus its layout and the location of the boss. He hadn't, however, told Marcus what the mobs would be like. That was something adventurers could discover for themselves.

"It is no surprise that my dungeon is going to become more difficult now that I am Platinum-Tier. I wanted to make sure Marcus would be able to convey that message to the adventurers preparing to dive. Only those who are of an appropriate power level should venture into my fourth floor."

Hel purred, though she failed to completely mask the annoyance that crossed through their bond. "Yes, but that much? You're going to miss out on some easy experience now, Darling." She paused. "You're not letting your past sway who you are now, are you?" She leaned closer to his core. "You are no longer human, Darling. You are a dungeon core. A demigod."

Ryan's anger flared, and he let it seep across the bond to her, causing Hel to flinch. "I am who I have always been." Ryan stated simply. "I've not gone soft. I'm not going to go easy on adventurers just because I was once human. The past can't be changed."

Hel nodded, but remained silent, allowing Ryan to continue.

"I decided to give Marcus fair warning, so that when the deaths begin, it is not at an alarming rate. We need to ensure Marcus that we haven't changed. We are not corrupted, and we aren't growing as a threat to the people. The responsibility for the deaths needs to be placed solely on the adventurers. If they die in the dungeon, it is because they either make a mistake, or they aren't strong enough for the challenges they choose to face."

The Chaos fairy pursed her lips, her eyes looking into Ryan's core. "You've certainly grown in this short amount of time, Darling."

"That's because he is going to be the greatest dungeon core around," Erin added in, her face beaming. While she had been against Ryan sharing all the information, and was still shocked he had, Erin had been happy with some of the topics he brought up with Marcus. Mainly the promise from Ryan that he wasn't going to animate any adventurers who fell in his dungeon, and that he wouldn't summon any demonic undead mobs. Both were high points in Erin's book. And both were necessary for Ryan to mention. It was obvious demonic mobs would be a huge issue at this time, and he refused to go through another A-a-ron fiasco with regards to animating fallen adventurers.

"That's obvious, little one. He's got me to guide him, of course he will become great." Hel flashed a smirk towards Erin. In response, Erin simply stuck out her tongue at the Chaos fairy. During their time trapped in solitude together, while Ryan was busy with his fourth floor, the two had moved past their animosity towards each other...and their efforts to score physical and emotional wounds on one another. Now their relationship had evolved into antics that reminded Ryan of a sibling rivalry. Though if that were the case...was Ryan the older brother or the dad core in this situation? He glanced at the two and decided that wasn't a line of thinking he really needed to get into. Too weird, even for him.

"I've got two great companions, and as long as everything goes according to plan, we'll hit Diamond in no time." Ryan was already flipping through his dungeon, ensuring everything was prepared for him to open within the week. Technically, he could have opened right that moment, but he wanted some extra time just to double check everything. He needed Marcus to share the information to the adventurers, in order to try and ensure foolhardy adventurers didn't get themselves killed. The weaker the adventurers were, the less experience Ryan gained from their deaths. And he needed to optimize his experience gain if he was to grow quickly.

"If something goes wrong, I want to make sure we are strong enough to handle whatever happens." That was the most important piece. While Ryan was pretty confident in his strength at Platinum, especially considering the jump in mob points he had received from Gold 1 to Platinum 5, he needed to make sure nothing, and he meant nothing, could threaten him. Which was why he was wracking his brain, his fairy's brains, and all the information he had at his disposable from his absorbed inventory, to ensure he could set as many contingencies in place as possible.

He was looking forward to the final payout he should be receiving from his open communication with Marcus. His memories now intact, Ryan grasped more than he could have hoped to, before. The adventurers would have a much easier time getting the books, materials, and unique objects he coveted, even those tantalizing bones under the dungeon town. Ryan wanted them all to increase his growth. The final bit of information he passed on to Marcus had been about his latest addition to his dungeon's mechanics. He was going to assign quests to the rogue to post for adventurers. And anyone who completed a quest Ryan had assigned would receive an appropriate reward. Ryan was a just dungeon, after all.

"You just wanted those bones." Erin giggled as she sat next to Hel atop the core. He had discussed the bones with the two fairies prior to his conversation with Marcus, when he had been brainstorming ideas on how to get them. Hel had been the one to mention dungeon issued quests.

Prior to the time of the dungeon-killers, dungeons had chosen individuals who would serve them. These dungeon followers would be tasked with going out into the world and acquiring rare and mysterious objects to provide the dungeon. In return, the dungeon would craft unique equipment and magical gear for those followers. Unfortunately, some of those followers had led to the first of the dungeon-killers

Ryan wasn't too worried about that part of history repeating itself. He had no intention of ever crafting anything for adventurers that could prove a threat to his existence. No one would be getting the Crown of Sorrows, nor would he ever produce something similar to the Subjugation Crystal. Adventurers would get rewards appropriate for the quest they completed. He would be coming out on top with these quests, growing both in knowledge and power with the newfound items and gear he could add to his loot inventory.

All of that aside…Erin wasn't wrong. He really wanted those bones.

Chapter Fourteen

Word travelled quite quickly about Ryan opening within the week. He was sure there were some questions to Marcus about how exactly the rogue knew when the dungeon was going to open. But that wasn't Ryan's problem. Plus, once adventurers resumed their dungeon dives, they would be quick to learn just how sentient Ryan had become.

Eavesdropping had taught him that people viewed dungeons as strange, feral types of animals. Only the stronger adventurers, or those who had been around for a long time, had an inkling as to the intelligence a dungeon could possess. It wasn't common knowledge that a dungeon core was a trapped soul. Adventurers were in for a wicked surprise when he started interacting with them on a larger scale, something Ryan was excited for.

While he was doing his best to focus on the finishing touches of the dungeon, he couldn't help but notice the increase in activity around "Boneville," as the town was apparently now called. Overnight, the population of the town had at least doubled, and eager adventurers came to Ryan's entrance constantly, anxious to see if his dungeon was once again opened. They all met with the same sight: the skeletal wolf maw that led into his dungeon closed, barring any attempt to enter his dark depths.

What bothered Ryan about the increase in activity was the startling number of low-ranked adventurers. Because of the spread of his influence, he no longer needed to wait for them to step foot within his dungeon to see their rank, class, and affinity. Instead, as long as they stepped foot out of the protective ring of influence of Boneville, he could see all their information. Most of them were Bronze and Silver. The vast majority of them, in fact. More so even than when he had first opened his dungeon to the world over a year ago.

More worrying—or more appropriately, annoying—was the increase in nobles. Most of them had left following the unfortunate death of A-a-ron, but it seemed that shock was now over. The richly dressed, arrogant aristocrats were easy to spot and they flocked to his dungeon like moths drawn to a flame. Many ordered their guards to establish tents outside his opening in order to try and 'claim a spot' for when he did open. Ryan guessed they hadn't yet heard of the system Marcus had in place for determining who got to dive into his dungeon.

They would learn. Just as all of the new adventurers would learn. Everything had a way, a process, and as long as the rules were followed everything would work out. If they weren't… Ryan no longer had any qualms about deaths in his dungeon. Sure, the longer they survived and the stronger they got, the better for him. But as Marcus had said the very first time the dungeon opened up; "Those foolish enough or careless enough to fall in this dungeon early on, are doomed to die." It took wits, teamwork, and a little bit of luck to make it in the world. Ryan's dungeon was the proving ground for that.

"That's a lot of new adventurers." Erin's comment pulled

Ryan from his musings. His mind had begun drifting back to his own death. He'd been a simple villager, too poor to actually travel to the city in order to have his abilities "unlocked". The process that everyone who joined the Church, the Army, the Mages' Guild, or the Adventurers' Guild underwent, which attuned them to the mana of the world around them and granted them access to their level and experience triangles. While every living thing in the world innately had them, humanoids had to have their powers unlocked to allow progression.

"Mhmmm." He turned his focus fully to what she was talking about. They had been watching Boneville's entrance absentmindedly, to spy on any batches of adventurers coming to check out his dungeon. He may or may not have also been messing with the noobs, spawning the occasional pile of bones, or making strange sounds out of the occasional hidden crystal skull, just to cause panic and confusion. It was an easy way to pass the time while he waited to open up.

"I don't think those are new adventurers." Hel's voice was hushed as she spoke, and she gestured towards them. They moved in an organized, almost militaristic manner, even though they were clad in simple white robes. It was their lack of defining gear, and simple clothing, that had likely made Erin consider them new adventurers. However, as they drew closer to his influence-infused terrain, Ryan felt his anger raise.

He had seen these individuals before. Not all of them, mind you. But the man in the center, the one in charge, Ryan had seen that one before. His face was forever burned in Ryan's mind. The final face he had seen before his death. The man in the center of the group was the leader of the group of Zealots of the Light that had visited Ryan's town and not only condemned him to death but executed him.

"Darling?" The Chaos fairy was the first to take note of

Ryan's rising anger. Which made sense. The soon-to-be Succubus was a creature of emotion, extremely apt at controlling and manipulating it.

"Ryan." Erin wasn't far behind as the Celestial fairy picked up his sudden rush of emotion. Ryan's focus had narrowed in on the priest in the center of the group as they all walked into his domain. Now that they had gotten close enough, he could see the image of the Goddess of Justice on their clothes, denoting them as members of the Church. To those unaware of their existence, it was nearly impossible to differentiate Zealots of the Light from regular members of the Church of Justice. They wore the same robes, worshipped the same Goddess, and carried the same symbols.

The difference though, once you knew it, was plain as day. Zealots of the Light, to show their "complete devotion" to the Goddess, burned her sigil, the scales, onto the palms of their hands. They claimed to do this so that their hands, "blessed" by the Goddess, could bring justice to the world.

"Remember your conversation with Marcus." Erin was speaking quickly now, panic in her voice even as she tried to soothe him. "We need to continue proving we haven't been corrupted."

Ryan was half-listening, his mind racing with ideas. He could open a pit beneath them. He could summon a wave of skeletons. He could simply make them disappear. No one would have to know...

"As much as I hate to agree with her on this point, Darling..." Hel joined into the conversation, touching his core lightly as she sent a conflicted batch of emotions through their bond to help enhance the impact of her words as well. As a Chaos fairy, she was against the Goddess's followers as much as he was. "Killing them right now would be counterproductive to the plans you have already laid."

"You don't understand," Ryan growled. "He's the man who killed me."

Erin stiffened at that remark, her already pale skin going nearly translucent. Her eyes darted from the man back to Ryan's core, sorrow flowing through their bond.

It was Hel that broke the silence following Ryan's statement. "Well then, Darling. How about we come up with a proper plan to get revenge on him? One that won't ruin all you've worked for. Killing him now would be letting him ruin your life twice over." She leaned closer, her fangs showing as she smiled devilishly. Her tail even swished back and forth in excitement as she did. "Trust me, Darling. I'm sure we can come up with something more than appropriate for this man."

"What do you have in mind?" Ryan asked, doing his best to calm his anger.

"I've nothing just yet —"

"—I think I've got some ideas." Erin's voice cut Hel off even as the Chaos fairy spoke. Ryan's Celestial fairy was practically shaking with rage. It seemed she had done a complete one-eighty from sorrow to anger. Of course the Celestial fairy wouldn't like the idea of Zealots killing innocent people in her Goddess's name. That this man had killed Ryan probably didn't sit well with Erin either.

"Oh, I'm all ears," Hel purred as she draped an arm around Erin, prompting the normally passive, peace-loving fairy to begin revealing all her violent ideas. As she spoke, Ryan made a mental note never to get on Erin's bad side.

Chapter Fifteen

"I'm sure there are many of you out there who are tired of this speech." Marcus was standing in front of Ryan's entrance with what had to be hundreds of adventurers. Many more than Ryan had ever seen at his dungeon. Marcus hadn't been kidding when he mentioned the dungeon town had been growing. From what Ryan had learned from the Platinum adventurer, his dungeon was the only remaining one deemed safe to dive into. The constant threat of demon attacks also had something to do with the influx of brand-new adventurers. *Ugh.* He really disliked the noobs. But he knew they had to start somewhere.

"Get on with it," a voice from the crowd called out, and a group of veteran adventurers started chuckling. Marcus shot them a stern look, though the rogue's eyes betrayed his good humor. The main adventurers of Boneville, those who were ready to dive into Ryan's depths, had been a part of the town since day one. They had been there right beside Marcus, helping the town grow for over a year. They had been there defending the town against the skeletal horde summoned by Viktor. And they had been there to stand against the demonic forces. They were like a family, a tight-knit community. They had a bond that went deeper than blood, one that could only be formed by those who had fought together, time and again, with their lives on the line for something they cared about. And yet, their family, their community…kept getting interrupted by real-world events and all the newcomers.

"If you keep that up, I'll make sure you don't even get a chance to dive this week, Jerry," Marcus called back, causing the veteran, a Gold 1 Centurion, to flush. Jerry let out an uneasy chuckle. Whether or not Marcus was joking, the rogue did have that type of power. Ryan had watched Marcus ban A-a-ron, a royal, from the dungeon for an entire week. In hindsight, maybe Marcus should have banned him for life… then A-a-ron would never have met the unfortunate end he did. It would've saved everyone no end of trouble.

"Now, as all of you know, the world is in a chaotic state. The rise of the Cult of Chaos is in full swing, and the cultists have corrupted the rest of the dungeons spread across the continent. Their demonic forces continue to swell, and they are raiding towns left and right." A murmur spread through the crowd as Marcus spoke and Ryan could tell more than a few of the grim-faced hopefuls had experienced a demon raid or two. That was another perk of Boneville: Ryan kept the demons away.

"The Adventurers' Guild is setting out, along with the Church of Justice, to destroy all the corrupted dungeons. Our strongest members have been rallied and sent off with teams of appropriate size and power to take on these threats." There was cheering from the crowd even as Marcus's eyes hardened. It had been a directive from the leader of the Adventurers' Guild, a Diamond 2 Archmage named Alice, that the dungeons must be destroyed. Which meant, other than Ryan, the only remaining dungeons in existence would be the dungeons of the actual Gods.

"While these dungeons are unlikely to go down without a fight—as long as the cultists have anything to say about it—I am confident this mission will be completed within the month. And with that, the demonic hordes should be stemmed, as well." More cheering.

"Because of this, it is imperative that all of you understand things will be changing around here. I am sure you have noted the extra security we have put into place." Ryan had been extremely insistent with Marcus that the rogue ensure there was always ample security around the port crystal into town. While that magic crystal served as the main way to get into Boneville, it also served as a prime tool for evildoers to make their way into the area, past Ryan's Bone Zone. And while he was much more powerful now than ever before, he did not need any more surprises showing up.

"Along with the implementation of our increased security forces, travel to Boneville from the port crystal will be restricted. You are all encouraged to make sure you know the proper procedures for porting back into town, to avoid unnecessary screening and confrontation." Marcus smiled coldly at the crowd, as winds swirled around his form. "I've personally seen to these new measures, and you do not want to experience them."

According to Marcus, part of the perk of hitting Platinum Tier was that all classes came with magical means of perceiving their surroundings; a passive trait that had to do with the amount of mana coursing through their bodies at all times. Depending on their affinity, they had means of knowing when anything living or empowered by mana entered within a certain proximity of them. The higher rank they were, and the more mana they had, the more powerful this passive trait. The rogue claimed his wind mana allowed him to perceive when anything entered an area within twenty-five feet of him, even if it was invisible. In a world of magical abilities and skills, Ryan doubted these passive traits would suffice. But it was better than nothing.

"Furthermore, a curfew will be set in place. I do not need any of you doing anything stupid late at night, nor too early in the morning." Groans, hundreds of them, echoed out from the crowd of adventurers. Marcus silenced them all with a raised hand. "Don't worry, the curfew is reasonable. I just need all of you out of the taverns, and in your homes, tents, or whatever sad excuse you call for a home, by midnight. And don't leave your homes till the strike of dawn." The rogue flashed a smile at a few members of the crowd. "Some of you could benefit from actually having to get reasonable amounts of sleep."

Marcus turned to look back at Ryan's entrance and gave the darkness that was the start of Ryan's dungeon a nod. Ryan was watching from many different angles, but the rogue must've felt it easiest to direct the nod into the heart of Ryan's dungeon itself. They had discussed this portion as well. Marcus had his set speech that he intended to give all of the newbies, but before then, Ryan wanted to add in a little extra flair. A little something special, to get the adventurers excited and prepared for what lay ahead.

"Ready for this?" He whispered to the fairies. He had spoken with them long and hard about this plan of his, after they had finished making their plans for when the Zealots finally stepped foot in his dungeon. He was satisfied to see they were amongst the groups of adventurers preparing to face him. He hadn't been certain if they were actually in Boneville to dive into his dungeon, and Ryan would have been upset if his chance at vengeance disappeared before he had the opportunity to enact all he had prepared. After all, it was only right he issue out proper justice to those who had murdered him.

"I'm still not sure we should be doing this," Erin

mumbled. She had been hesitant about this part of the plan. She was pretty much anti him interacting with anyone outside of the dungeon. Hel, on the other hand, was surprisingly supportive, at least to a degree.

"Show them just how great you are, Darling," the Chaos fairy purred. "Reclaim the existence of dungeons as demigods." That was the bit she really had been excited about. She figured if he went through with this plan, he would attract followers the way the dungeons of old had. Borderline religious, almost cult-like, groups had once worshipped dungeons because of their amazing powers and abilities. According to Hel, these groups had offered up sacrifices to their dungeons in order to increase their power and garner their favor. While Ryan wasn't about to allow people to sacrifice anything living to him—he had already been there once before with the Chaos cultists Xander and Samuel—he was happy to receive their stuff. That was the whole point of this.

He focused his influence into the darkness that was the entrance of his dungeon. He had been preparing for this for ever since his initial conversation with Marcus. He knew the rogue had already placed the quest board in town, which had likely caused some confusion and interest among the adventurers. But now…now was his time to shine.

"Greetings, mortals." His voice, which he was trying to deepen, echoed out from the darkness. He had created one of his crystal skulls on the ground of the entrance, masked by a layer of dirt and the darkness within. He made it large enough that, as he spoke through it, his voice reverberated around the dungeon mouth, and echoed out, loud and fearsome, from the wolf skull that was his dungeon's iconic entrance. "I am the Bone Dungeon."

Chapter Sixteen

The silence that rolled out across the adventurers was deafening. Everyone seemed to pale as their eyes widened. They stared into the darkness that was the mouth of Ryan's dungeon, and he was certain they felt something staring back.

"Seriously?" A voice echoed into Ryan's core room, breaking the silence. Blake was whispering into the pendant around his neck. His favorite adventurer stood at the very back of the crowd, accompanied by Jack and Karan. Oddly, Emily and Matt were not present. Ryan planned to chat with Blake about that later.

"Just stand there and listen, buddy," Ryan whispered back. He blocked out any messages coming to his core from Blake's pendant, turning his focus back upon the adventurers fanned out before him.

"For over a year, I have allowed all of you to enter my domain and traverse through my dungeon on your quest for riches and power." Oh, he had totally been practicing this speech.

"Once again, I have decided to allow all of you to enter

within my vast expanses but know this…I am watching you. I am judging you." There was a murmur throughout the adventurers, and he noticed more than a few had started to step away from him. They were scared and he didn't blame them.

"I know the world is chaotic and death lurks around every corner. But I want you all to know, I have not changed who I am. I am still the same Bone Dungeon you all know." This was the most important part. Ryan wanted everyone to be clear that he was not a corrupted dungeon. He wanted to prove to them all that he was on their side. For the most part.

"As is the natural course of the world, as I grow stronger, my dungeon becomes ever more dangerous. That has not changed, and I warn all of you: strongly consider your abilities before you step foot in my deepest layer, my newly completed fourth floor." The veterans in the crowd began whispering excitedly at that.

"It is more difficult than any floor you've encountered before. At the same time, the treasures it holds will more than reward you for overcoming the challenges within." That caused even more excitement. Ryan didn't want adventurers to be terrified of his dungeon. He wanted them to have an appropriate amount of caution, built from the respect of his strength and the dangers within. He also wanted them to be excited because he had been hard at work improving the type of loot he could create.

"For those of you who are not yet ready, do not worry. Those who have come before you can attest to the fact that my dungeon is one in which you can grow, you can learn, and you can evolve. However," he deepened his voice even more, trying his best to sound intimidating and solemn, "foolish mistakes can, and will, result in your death." This time, the murmuring came from the new adventurers. Their excitement prior to Ryan's speech had faded and they all seemed nervous now. *Good.* Ryan really wanted to cut down on the amount of pointless low-level deaths in his dungeon.

"One last thing, before I allow Ma-...er...your leader to continue." Ryan was abuzz with excitement about this part. "I have spoken directly with him, and the quests he has posted are personal quests from me. If you complete one of the tasks I have issued, you will be greatly rewarded." He let the words hang for a moment. "I am a benevolent dungeon, as many of you know, and I will do all I can to ensure those who aid me are properly rewarded." This set the crowd alive with excitement. Before Marcus could stop them, about half a dozen adventurers began rushing back towards Boneville. Ryan just barely caught the word "excavation" before he turned his attention back to the crowd.

"Thank you for that, oh mighty Bone Dungeon." Marcus seemed hesitant as he completed the last part. Ryan had obviously told Marcus his name, but the rogue thought it important that Ryan kept his name a secret. That, as well as his prior existence as a human. Only Marcus, Blake's group, and whoever else Marcus had told would know the full truth of Ryan. To everyone else, he was simply the Bone Dungeon.

"As you have all witnessed, this dungeon is not a wild, destructive force as the world has been led to believe." That was another thing Ryan had learned from Marcus. Apparently, it was taught that dungeons were wild, magical creations that simply appeared in the world. Adventures could gain immense power and wealth from them, but dungeons eventually became too powerful and dangerous for any but the strongest to enter. It seemed the age of dungeons as demi-gods had ended during the time of the dungeon killers.

"The Bone Dungeon has been fighting to keep us safe from the demons and has allowed us time and time again to dive within his vast depths, killing his creations, and claiming the riches he has dropped for us." Marcus stepped away from Ryan's entrance, moving closer to a group of excited, young novice adventurers. "Do not take the Bone Dungeon's kindness for granted. If you make a mistake within his dungeon, you will die. Just because he is sentient, just because he protects the town from outside threats, does not mean he will not hesitate to allow you to fall within his domain." The noobs paled and flinched away from Marcus's words. "Because just as we get stronger from killing his mobs, he grows stronger by killing us."

Marcus stepped back up toward the entrance, pulling out the very familiar circular disk with which he would be able to track the status of adventurers within the dungeon.

"Anyone foolish enough, especially after the Bone Dungeon's revelation, to put themselves in a situation in which their death is likely, would be better off absent from this world, anyway." Karan, who was making her way towards Marcus with Jack and Blake in tow, flinched slightly at the rogue's harsh words. The rogue was callous. It was survival of the fittest when it came to dungeon diving and adventurer life, and fools either died young or got those around them killed. Ryan had seen more examples of that truth than he wished he ever had. Though, he had to admit, the extra experience was nice.

"We will begin assigning diving positions to all who have gathered. Those who will only be diving the first and second floor, please form one line. For those either prepared or foolish enough for the third floor and deeper, form another."

As he spoke, Blake and Jack reached the front of the crowd, glanced at Marcus, and then headed off to the start of each of the lines. It seemed they were Marcus's helpers for now, a role that had belonged to the twin Darkness affinity assassins, Sasha and Rasha, before they reached Platinum and began training their small pack of wolfkin.

"If you need healing upon exiting the dungeon, Karan here will be able to assist you. Otherwise, the Church has set up a healing station at the town port crystal, for those who are unable to exit the dungeon by the main entrance." He looked at the group, grinning slightly. "Though, word of advice. The Adventurers' Guild and Karan here will charge a much smaller price for healing than the Church 'requires' in donations."

With that the group began to form into the appropriate lines as the air outside of Ryan's dungeon began to practically vibrate with excitement. Ryan had spoken with Marcus about his plans for allowing adventurers to dive within his dungeon. They had agreed Ryan would be fine with two sets of groups exploring at a time, but only if one set was limited to the first and second floor and the other was limited to his third and fourth. That way Ryan could easily manage the mobs on both floors and keep extra mob points available for any situation, including a random demon attack. It was also the best he could work with for now, until one of his other quests was completed. That quest had been specifically assigned to Marcus, who had passed on the request to the Adventurers' Guild. If it were completed, Ryan would have an even easier way for adventurers to go through his dungeon. Something that would make his—and the adventurers'—lives easier. And Ryan was just curious what he could convince people to bring him.

"Looks like the first group of noobs is up," Hel whispered, turning Ryan's focus to the party of five walking hesitantly towards his entrance. They were all Bronze 11 adventurers, save for a Silver 1 Knight with an Earth affinity. If Ryan had to guess, the Adventurers' Guild was working on rapidly leveling some parties, even though their numbers were limited given the current demonic situation afoot. Power leveling, Ryan knew from the dives of nobles, was a very real thing in the world. It was also frowned upon because it meant adventurers didn't get the proper amount of actual experience using their skills, managing their mana, and acting as their class role demanded.

A worldwide demonic threat was probably a good reason for the Adventurers' Guild to start using such a tactic. Ryan wasn't about to complain, especially if it ensured Bronze and Silver adventurers had minimal deaths and a new influx of Gold and Platinum adventurers began diving his dungeon sooner.

"Good luck," Ryan whispered from a crystal skull he had created just before the downward slope towards the very first room of his dungeon. His comment, to his amusement, caused the entire party, including the Silver Knight, to jump. Oh yes, Ryan was so going to enjoy life as a Platinum-Tier dungeon.

It was good to be open again.

Chapter Seventeen

"Well, that was underwhelming." Ryan stifled a yawn of boredom as he watched the latest group of newbies make their way out of the dungeon. Four of the five members had deep wounds and bite marks across their body, while the fifth, the Silver member of the party, was doing her best to keep a rather nasty wound on her neck closed. Ryan couldn't be certain, but he was pretty sure these new adventurers were a lot less prepared than the groups had been a year ago. Either that, or perhaps his floor was more difficult than he thought it was?

He watched the group flinch at the sound of clattering bones as they made their way through the first room of his dungeon, heading toward the sloping path that would lead them outside. Nope, they were definitely a softer breed of adventurers than Ryan remembered.

"Pay up, little one." Hel was grinning as she extended a hand towards Erin. While everyone had initially been excited about opening the dungeon back up, the day had been rather dull. So dull, in fact, that his two fairies, at the prodding of

Hel, had begun placing bets on how the new parties would do on his first floor. Ryan had given them each an equal pile of gold coins, though Hel's was considerable larger now than Erin's. The Chaos fairy seemed a much better judge of these adventurers' capabilities than the Celestial fairy was. Probably due to Hel's vast memories of being a dungeon fairy, and because Erin seemed to be way too optimistic about the adventurers. She did think the best of each of the groups. Which led to her overestimating the skills of those who stepped into the dungeon today.

"I don't understand." The Celestial fairy shook her head as she handed another gold coin to Hel. "I was sure they would have been able to make it to Steve.' To Erin's credit, the group *had* been doing decently. They had gotten through the first room quick enough. However, the chaos of the second room, with mobs ambushing the adventurers from within the foliage and undergrowth, had been the team's undoing. Their Silver leader had put herself in a precarious position, trying to protect her weaker allies. The rest of the party, in their inexperience, had failed to protect her in turn. A nearly fatal mistake.

Ryan wondered if that was more the party's fault than his own. While he did his best to avoid changing his floors as he grew stronger to ensure a constant, proper increase in difficulty, Ryan had tweaked his first floor, albeit only slightly. Partially because he wanted to test out a new mob, and also because he figured it would help better prepare the adventurers for the boss fight against Steve. He had previously noticed a lot of adventurers were caught off-guard against Steve's ranged attack. The flying bones had killed more than a few adventurers before they were prepared to react, so Ryan had decided to give the adventurers a taste of ranged attacks prior to Steve. And he wanted them to be proper ranged attacks...not just the random stalactite falling on an adventurer. Though, that was still a personal favorite of Ryan's.

Luckily, mob evolution had provided him with the perfect candidate for the task. A creature that wouldn't overwhelm adventurers and would offer a taste of what was awaiting them later on in the dungeon. It had been a win-win, or so he'd thought. The new adventurers, all of whom seemed completely unprepared for the dangers of the dungeon, were proving otherwise.

"Should I remove the Skuirrelshot?" That was the name of the mob Ryan had created, or rather, discovered and nurtured to fighting strength. And by nurtured, Ryan meant thrown into skeletal fight club for the past few months until it reached an appropriate evolution. Initially the skuirrelshot had grown from the discovery of a skuirrel which had evolved to the point it could launch its tail bones at enemies. When Ryan first absorbed it, it had been a 2 point mob, very similar to his victorious skuirrels and skrats. During the training regime in skeletal fight club, the skuirrelshot had grown to a final form—a 5 point mob that counted as a medium beast.

It was about the size of a dog, consisting of lean, fragile looking bones. The tail on the skuirrelshot pulsated with extra Darkness mana, and it was able to whip its tail forward towards an enemy to launch deadly bone spikes at its foe. Ryan had replaced the two victorious skuirrels, which cost a total of 4 mob points, with one of his skuirrelshots. He had also added in a plated skrat, removing the 2 champion skrats that had existed prior, in the second room of his first floor. Which increased the mob point cost of the room by a total of 2 points, even as it decreased the number of mobs by 2 as well.

"It's probably for the best you leave it in." Hel was toying with her pile of coins as she spoke, a look of satisfaction on her face. She enjoyed the amount of gold she was winning off of Erin. Technically the two had an endless supply of gold, and Ryan could make them whatever they wanted, as long as he had absorbed it before. The betting really was rather pointless, but was a fun way for them to pass the time, and so Ryan obliged. He'd done his own bit of gambling back when he was human, specifically with dice and cards. But betting on how adventurers did in the dungeon was fine as well.

"Any particular reason? Other than your growing pile of coins?" Ryan asked. The party had made their way to the exit, handing a few of their loot cards to Marcus at the entrance of the dungeon as Karan went to work healing them. She headed to the Silver member first, her hands glowing with golden light as she healed the slowly congealing mess. It was a nearly fatal wound, a gash across the neck that had to be a hair's length away from an artery. The skuirrelshots had excellent accuracy with their attacks, and a Silver Tier adventurer did not have the mana enhancements coursing through their body to keep such an attack from cutting through.

"It's doing what you wanted it to do, Darling," the Chaos fairy replied. "It's keeping them from dying to Steve."

"She's right," Erin said as she glared at the Chaos fairy's pile of coins. Erin was running low, and if her losing streak continued, she might not make it through the day. "Though, I don't understand why these parties are struggling so much." She shook her head, golden hair flashing in the light of Ryan's core.

Ryan wished he had an answer for her, but he was just as perplexed. He scanned the vast group outside his dungeon, racking his brain for the answer. Where had they all come from? Why had there been such an influx now? It was almost like—*That's it*. Everything fell into place.

"I think these are brand new adventurers."

"That's kind of obvious Ryan." Erin's tone told him she

didn't understand what he was getting at. Hel, on the other hand, sent the slightest sense of approval through their bond. She had noticed it earlier but hadn't mentioned anything. And why would she? She was making a killing off Erin.

"No, like, these are brand-new adventurers," Ryan stressed and turned their focus from inside of the dungeon to outside, giving the fairies a better look at the first line. It was obvious, the more you looked at them.

When Ryan had first opened himself up to the world, adventurers like Blake and his friends had first begun diving. Sure, they had all been low Bronze, new and inexperienced, but they had still been skilled in their weapons. They had been trained to fight. They had been preparing for the time when they could dive into dungeons.

These new adventurers, this crop outside of Ryan's dungeon, looked extremely uncomfortable. Some seemed scared of their own weapons. Others had mismatched gear that wasn't even worn properly. The Silver members standing in line with all these Bronze newbs were doing their best to help them out, but there was only so much they could do. The new adventurers were plain old townsfolk who had suddenly decided to take the plunge to become adventurers, and Ryan had one guess why. Demons.

"Very good, Darling," Hel cooed as she shot a glance at Erin. Realization crossed the Celestial fairy's face.

"Because of the chaos the world is in right now, people are going to be flocking towards your dungeon. Individuals who have never wielded a weapon before in their life will align themselves to the Guild to try and grow stronger. Most of those people out there have likely lost loved ones, or perhaps even their entire villages, to the demon attacks."

"That's horrible," Erin whispered, her eyes filling with tears.

"That's life," Hel replied. Her voice was soft though, and

Ryan could feel a strange mixture of emotions swirling within the Chaos fairy. His normally bloodthirsty, cold, and calculating companion seemed to feel something, even if she was doing her best to hide it.

"Life shouldn't be lived in fear," Erin retorted. "Life should be enjoyed. Life should be lived. Your God of Chaos is the reason for all this death." Her voice grew stronger. "The Goddess of Justice would never…" Erin trailed off as she glanced at Ryan's core. He had, after all, been killed by followers of the Goddess of Justice.

"Life is not black and white, little one." Hel's voice stayed quiet, her eyes searching, pondering. "Perhaps my God has done some terrible things. Or perhaps his followers are doing terrible things in his stead. That does not mean he is evil." The Chaos fairy narrowed her eyes towards Erin, her voice hardening, "And I accept that. Just as you should accept your Goddess and her followers are not without faults of their own."

Ryan could feel Erin's emotions take a dangerous drop. The fairy was well aware now of the sins the Goddess of Justice's followers could commit. Ryan had been murdered in cold blood by them. Erin knew that. And who knew what else could be going on? Still, it was one thing for someone to understand these facts, and a different one for someone to have to work through, regarding their personal beliefs. Ryan could empathize with Erin on that aspect, and knew it was going to take the fairy some time to fully understand, and perhaps begin to move away from her unquestioning faith. It had taken Ryan a few months to come to terms with the realization that he had once been human. Was Erin going through something similar, but on an even deeper level?

"I know." Erin's voice cracked as she spoke, her eyes filling with tears. She was on the edge of having a breakdown, Ryan knew it, and the Chaos fairy knew it too.

"Just remember, everything isn't black and white, Erin." Hel tossed a coin back towards Erin as she spoke, offering the Celestial fairy a fanged smile as she did. "Now, how about we get back to the real important matters at hand?" Hel turned back to Ryan. "Has the other party finished their descent?"

Chapter Eighteen

Ryan had not expected to see any groups take on his fourth floor that first day. There were only a handful of groups capable, in his mind, of exploring his fourth floor. Blake's group was one of the obvious choices. An all-female group with a strange speech pattern, which Ryan knew hailed from a coastal region of the continent, was another. That group had stood out to Ryan the first time he'd seen them because of their fierce attitude and their strange gear. They had proven themselves to be fierce warriors—highly skilled, and extremely efficient. They were treated as outsiders at first, but it didn't take long before they began interacting with the veterans outside the dungeon. After all, it didn't matter where you came from, or who or what you were. An adventurer was an adventurer, and they all recognized each other as that. Besides, they had handled a few uppity nobles who'd insulted them without issue, which had helped the others warm up to the strange party.

The first group making their way down the massive staircase to his fourth floor was neither of those groups. Instead it consisted of adventurers from a few different parties Ryan had watched grow over the last year. Parties which had lost members not only to Ryan's dungeon but also, from what he could overhear, to the demon attacks and a change of priorities. Some had left to seek their fortunes elsewhere—as the real-world events were causing an influx of new dungeon divers seeking to grow stronger, so too was there a high demand for strong adventurers to be hired out as mercenaries and guards to protect against the Cult. Some had left the dungeon town for the promise of a steady, well-paying job. In fairness, it was probably safer than the constant challenge of diving Ryan's dungeon.

"I've got two gold coins that say they wipe." Hel flashed them towards Erin as they watched the five-man party near the end of the staircase. Because Ryan had been busy observing the newer parties as he tried to figure out the high failure rate puzzle, he hadn't messed with this party the way he'd intended to with the tower. Still, the party was on edge. Good—Ryan wasn't going to pull any punches the moment they hit his fourth floor. Their party may have been untested with regards to their teamwork, but four of the five members were Platinum 5, making them the strongest party in the area that day. Especially since Karan and Jack were still Gold 1. If Matt and Emily returned to Blake's party, it would still only have 3 Platinum members.

"Hmm." Erin looked over the party appraisingly. Ryan could tell the fairy didn't like the idea of betting on whether or not the whole party would die in the dungeon. But, at the same time, she was running low on coins and needed to make a comeback. "I'll raise you to five gold coins that they retreat after defeating a Bone Enforcer." Erin pushed all five coins, the remainder of her coins for the day, towards Hel. The Chaos fairy flashed a devilish smile, matching the bet.

"Deal."

"You're a bad influence on Erin." Ryan piped up as he

pulled up the information on the party, which was now fanning out at the base of the massive tower. They were awestruck at the size and magnitude of his fourth floor—exactly what Ryan had wanted.

The party leader was named Brook, a war mage with a Fire affinity. War mages, the Platinum upgrade of your run-of-the-mill mage, generally specialized in destructive magic. In the instance of Fire related war mages, that usually involved massive fireballs or condensed white-hot beams of fire. Ryan had noticed parties were often wary around Fire-related mages because of how destructive and, for lack of a better term, explosive their magic was. Other affinity mages had much better control over their powers, but Fire consumed all.

Next in the party, the leader from a now-disbanded group, was an Earth sentinel named Dirk. Sentinels were extremely efficient at their role of tank, and able to masterfully stand their ground against any and all foes before them. They specialized in single or small group tanking, which meant Ryan's fourth floor may prove an interesting challenge for Dirk.

Past him was the party's healer, their Gold-level member. At Gold 4, their cleric, named Alfred, was much weaker than the Platinum members and Ryan could not help but wonder at that. Alfred did have a Celestial affinity, which was the one preferred for healers. But Ryan was curious why the party had chosen such a low-ranking healer. Was the situation with the Chaos cultists pulling away healers? Ryan knew the Church of Justice had called back many of their members. Perhaps that was why there seemed to be a shortage of high-level Celestial healers? Either way, it was clear they were trying to power level Alfred. Taking on his fourth floor with their healer as their weakest member was definitely a bold move. Ryan was curious to see how it would play out.

After Alfred, the party had a Platinum ranger, which Ryan remembered was the class Matt had originally wanted to take. Rangers were extremely skilled, and when a marksman became a ranger at Gold Tier, they were assigned an animal companion. This animal acted similar to Emily's summon, Cynder, in that the ranger was able to bond with them through their mana and could empower their animal companion. Rangers were proficient not only with their bows, but also with a short-ranged weapon, often a sword. To top it off, rangers could set basic traps and excelled at hunting down foes. They were a versatile class, which was why they were highly sought after for roles outside of dungeon diving.

The ranger with this party, a female by the name of Danielle, had a Wind affinity and a magnificent golden eagle as her companion. Ryan remembered the eagle had been so small and fragile-looking when she had first gotten it. Now, at Platinum tier, her eagle had grown in both size and strength.

Last, but certainly not least, was the most…unique member of the party. Beth, a Platinum 5 Grappler with a fire affinity. Now, Ryan wasn't often one to judge life choices, but Beth's made him question her thought process. The path to Grappler went: fighter at Bronze, warrior at Silver, and Grappler at Gold. The class itself focused on hand-to-hand combat, often with a variety of throws, grabs, and various other techniques. Because they focused on such close-range fighting, Grapplers didn't wield weapons or use shields. Furthermore, they only wore tight-fitting cloth armor with extra protection in the form of metal pads on their knees and elbows, along with fitted gloves that stopped after their first knuckles, which were also reinforced with metal protection.

In essence, if a Grappler wasn't in the process of flipping an enemy or choking them out, or some other violent, personal manner of attack, they would strike with their elbows or knees with an explosive amount of force. The class was a strange mixture of speed and power combined with martial arts abilities that allowed them to overcome a variety of foes.

It was a strange choice for Beth, first and foremost, because she was the only Fire affinity Grappler he had seen. The Fire affinity users more often went Blade Dancer, such as Blaine Dragnov, or occasionally Berserker, the other option for warriors. On top of that, Beth did not have a slim build, unlike most of the Grapplers he had seen. Instead she was stocky, built with large, heavy muscles. The results, Ryan was sure, of a very hard upbringing. She looked like she should have been a Berserker. But instead, she had made it to Platinum 5 as a Grappler—no small feat. Ryan would be lying if he didn't claim he was more than a little interested to see how she fared against the massive foes he had on his fourth floor.

From where the party was, at the heart of the town that made up his fourth floor, they could not see all that surrounded them. The skies above revealed the occasional greater clacker, which was an evolved version of his clackers. The greater clackers, at a cost of 15 mob points per summon, had a wingspan of nearly fifteen feet. On top of their larger size, they had the devastating ability to launch bone "feathers" towards enemies when they swooped down towards them. Plus, they were big and sturdy, always helpful in the intimidation factor.

Other than the ten greater clackers he had placed on his floor, Ryan had filled the rest of the floor with a mixture of skeletal fighters and archers, skeletal mages, plated skrats, snakies, and a brand-new mob, the skelephant. The skelephant, stood about ten feet in height, with a length of roughly twenty feet. Its dense bones were covered with swirling Darkness mana, and the mob had a trunk made out of Darkness mana as well. Given the size of the mob, it was the first of the huge tier of basic beast mobs that Ryan had summoned now that he was Platinum. Each one cost him 30 points. Because of the cost, he kept the number of skelephants low, and only had two of the huge beasts roaming about his fourth floor.

Altogether, as planned, Ryan had spent exactly 2,300 points on his fourth floor. The greater clackers cost him a total of 150 mob points, the skelephants 60. His mixture of skeletal fighters and archers, of the armored variant, cost him a total of 1,000 mob points across the forty he had summoned. Additionally, intermingled with those armored versions, were ten uncommon armored skeletal fighters and archers. The ten of those cost 380 mob points total, as each cost him 38 mob points, instead of the normal 25 mob points. After those, Ryan had positioned five empowered skeletal mages in a few key positions of the fourth floor town, worth a total of 500 mob points. Empowered skeletal mages being the 100 mob point version of skeletal mages, making them stronger than basic skeletal mages, but weaker than the Platinum archmage variant of skeletal mages.

Lastly, to round out the "feel" of his town, Ryan had inserted eighteen Plated Skrats, and fifteen infested snakies, because every town had to have some sort of rodent infestation. Ryan's hometown, having been located within the mountains, had been known to have a rather potent version of rattlesnake. His inclusion of the infested snakies was a call-out to that childhood danger he had grown up with.

The inclusion of so many infested snakies on the floor was also in line with Ryan's belief that, when it came to Platinum-Tier adventurers and above, he was offering more of a war than a battle. A test of endurance, of stamina of resilience. Meaning additional threats, rather than just traps and attacks from mobs, were needed.

Snakie venom was always a unique, dangerous threat. Especially because even at Platinum, if an infested snakie landed a bite and the party didn't have the antidote or a way to cleanse the venom from the adventurer, they would have to retreat from the dungeon to seek treatment, ending their dive.

And of course, on top of his 2,300 mob points, there were the Bone Enforcers. He needed to start figuring out which one he was going to summon. The party members had finally gotten over their awe at his fourth floor and were making their way towards the town center. They would be coming up on one of the spawn points for his Bone Enforcers, the guillotine. While technically there was only a chance a Bone Enforcer would spawn at that location, for this instance, the first time a group of adventurers would set their eyes on the reminder of Ryan's fate, he was going to summon one. If he was going to have the guillotine forever in his mind, he might as well create a new, lasting memory with the first group to stumble upon it.

Chapter Nineteen

The adventuring party took their time moving towards the town center. This was a combination of cautiousness, checking the different buildings for loot and traps, and checking around every corner for mobs. The slow, methodical approach to the floor was extremely important for adventurers because not only had Ryan changed up how his floor was designed compared to his previous ones, he had stepped up his trap and loot game as well.

Ryan's new set of traps across the floor included many different trip wires within buildings, which could result in a variety of deadly occurrences: from his classic bone spikes erupting from the ground, to actually bringing an entire building down upon whoever stepped foot inside it. While such a trap was bound to cause damage, Ryan figured Platinum-level adventurers would be able to shake off having a building fall on them. Ryan's plan for his fourth floor had never been for instant death.

While the traps would make adventurers wary about entering any of the rooms, Ryan ensured the rooms were furnished in such a way that the adventurers would want to investigate them. These buildings, decorated on the inside to look like actual, lived-in homes, courtesy of Ryan's human memories, had little hints of treasure hidden throughout. And because Ryan's treasure came in the form of loot cards, it meant he could hide such things in a variety of wonderful places. Granted, he still went with the treasure chest option here and there. It was a classic and surefire way to spark the loot-chasing adventurer trait. These would just lead to them spending more time searching in his rooms, putting themselves at greater risk of his traps, and allowing more mobs to reach whatever area the adventurers were located in.

Outside of the houses, the pathways, the road, everything could potentially be hazardous. The road had hidden pressure plates which could open pits beneath the party, dropping them onto spikes, into bone maidens, or, one of Ryan's newer…inventions. A trap that had actually sparked inspiration from his excavation efforts for bones outside of his reach. In other words, Ryan had figured out, through a lot of trial and error, and some frustration, how to create explosive, in a sense, traps.

The traps, activated by a pressure plate, would trigger a mass of Dark mana that Ryan had prepped. When a trap was triggered, all of the mana would be launched at a certain point, usually underneath the adventurer who had stepped on the pressure plate, though Ryan had made a few of them trigger from behind, so it would hit the other party members instead.

This mass of Dark mana would crash against the underside of the road, just beneath the adventurers, hitting another bit of Darkness mana-infused material. The force of the collision would break the ground apart in a fearsome eruption and send the adventurer flying backwards at least a dozen feet or so.

Ryan had initially tested these traps out on skeletons…

but his test dummies had simply ended up blasting apart in a shower of bones. So, he had tested it out on his zombearie… though he was careful to ensure his fairies were nowhere nearby when he did that test. He was not about to go through the whole "Do you have any idea how hard it is to get zombie flesh stench out of your hair?!" spiel again. He was certain Erin still hadn't fully forgiven him for that one. Traumatized fairy aside, the zombearie, when it triggered the trap, had been sent tumbling through the air, its massive, rotting form cracking one of the stone buildings as it smashed against it. That made the trap a roaring success.

All of these new features gave his dungeon a brand new, unfamiliar feel. He had gone from a rough, basic dungeon, to sophisticated, elegant floors - and now, he had an entire town. Now, with this latest upgrade, he had taken adventurers out of their element and thrown them into a new world; ironically, his old world. And it was working.

"Should we head back?" Alfred, the Gold 4 cleric, asked nervously. He was shaking beside Dirk. The group's sentinel had led the group through the floor, but after Alfred had taken a decent chunk of damage, courtesy of one of Ryan's explosive bone traps, the sentinel had made the call to switch positions. Now Danielle, the ranger, was leading the group, her eagle doing its best to scout the area from above, while avoiding the occasional clacker attack. Ryan's skeletal birds were doing diving runs on the party, with the massive chamber giving his mobs the space they needed to escape ranged retaliatory attacks from the ranger and war mage. For the most part, at least. Three of his clackers had been blasted apart by a well-aimed fireball from Brook. Judging by the size of the flaming sphere, Ryan was fairly sure he had pumped it up with quite a bit of mana in order to ensure he hit his targets. An act of desperate frustration after his first four flame attacks fell short. Ryan had added to that frustration by taunting the mage from one of his strategically placed crystal skulls. He really loved those things.

"It looks like we are coming up to a clearing," Danielle called back to the group. "We can rest there, and regain some of our mana. After that we should be fine to keep exploring." The party had already been assaulted by a handful of Ryan's groups of mobs. The back-to-back skirmishes, intermingled with trap-triggering, was starting to wear on the party. Still, the loot they were gaining, and finding was spurring them on. Ryan's fourth floor was set up to pay out if adventurers were willing to take the risk. His mobs were dropping loot cards with hefty amounts of gold listed on them, and all the loot cards that pertained to items were rare. The party was in for a good payday, if they made it out.

Ryan heard the members of the party talking about farming down on this floor as much as they could, in an effort to collect the necessary number of loot cards to create an ultra-rare item for each member. The adventurers had figured out, before Ryan had closed his dungeon, that they could combine the cards using the loot boxes to create new, higher level loot. While the party was only speculating, Ryan had indeed put a loot box in his fourth-floor boss room which could combine rare cards to create an ultra-rare one of the same type.

What they didn't know was that it would take sixteen rare cards of the same type to create one ultra-rare item. So, while Ryan was going to give them kudos for farming up early, they were going to have to farm for quite a while to get the necessary number of cards. They had a better chance hoping for an ultra-rare drop from his Bone Enforcers or the fourth-floor boss. While small, that was still a higher chance than normal mobs. Ryan made sure harder mobs had a higher chance of dropping better loot. More danger, more reward.

"Did you hear that, Darling? Your plan's working. They're

going to stop in the clearing to rest, just like you thought." Hel motioned towards his core and at the party as they neared the town center. They had slowed their already cautious pace as they neared the large expanse. It was empty, save for the raised podium in the middle upon which sat the replica of the guillotine that had ended Ryan's life.

"I most certainly did," Ryan responded, excitement rising within. Just as the full party entered the empty space, Ryan activated the final new feature of his floor. Walls of Dark mana, swirling with tiny bone shards, erupted behind the party, and across every pathway which led into and out of the town center. These walls would make any adventurer or other living thing think twice about passing through. While Ryan no longer had flesh of his own, he could imagine the hesitation an adventurer would have about rushing through a multi-foot thick wall of rapidly flying shrapnel. That...would definitely leave a few cuts. On top of that, because it was just Darkness mana and swirling bones, Ryan's skeletal mobs could pass through practically unscathed. It would be difficult for adventurers to leave the area, but easy for Ryan's mobs to join in.

He had devised this final method after he set up his coliseum. It was an attempt to keep the adventurers engaged in the fight at hand and, secretly, an effort to make sure party members did not abandon each other out of fear. Something Ryan doubted would happen with Platinum-level adventurers, but still, a "friendly" precaution. If there was one thing Ryan really disliked, it was gaining experience from betrayal or cowardice. He preferred to grow stronger through his own efforts, not reap the benefits from less than savory actions and events.

At the end of the day, a death was a death in Ryan's dungeon, each one leading towards his goal. But Ryan wanted those to be proper deaths, not pointless ones, not sacrifices, not betrayals. In his mind, those deaths cheapened his accomplishment as he grew stronger.

"Behold." Ryan's voice echoed into the town square where the five adventurers stood, their eyes glancing around cautiously. The sound caused them all to jump. Definitely on edge. "One of my five Bone Enforcers." As he spoke, Ryan willed the ground before the guillotine to break apart. From deep below, a platform began to rise. Ryan had created summoning chambers underneath all his key Bone Enforcer areas, allowing him to pre-summon the mob and raise it to the battlefield when it was time. A process he had automated, but was manually controlling this time around. It was the first time he got to play with the enforcers, after all.

"I'm sorry, little one, but you're about to lose." Hel grinned devilishly as Ryan's Bone Enforcer began to appear. While Erin remained silent, her eyes fixated on the scene unraveling before her, Ryan could feel her apprehension. He could understand it. After all, he had chosen the largest and mightiest of his Bone Enforcers for this engagement. His giant and elephant combination, lovingly named "Andre the Giant."

Chapter Twenty

"Why does Andre have a shield?" Erin asked accusatorily as Ryan's Bone Enforcer emerged. Clear as day, the Giant, who had previously been armed with an axe and a club, was now wielding a massive tower like shield, made from countless leg bones fused together, and his dragon bone club.

"I felt it was more fitting for him," Ryan replied sheepishly. While he had liked the idea of Andre using two weapons, the more he thought about it, the more it didn't make sense. Since the boss was already covered in heavy plate, Ryan figured a shield was only fitting. It did make the mob more formidable.

"They're doomed," Erin murmured as the three turned their focus to the fight at hand. The party was in for a tough fight, but he wasn't counting them for dead just yet. For one, Andre was just a mini-boss on his fourth floor. A party of four Platinum 5s and one mid-level Gold should be able to beat him. Still, Ryan understood Erin's concern. Even though the adventurers could clear his 250 point Gold boss, this 190 point mini-boss was far tougher.

According to Hel, as a dungeon grew in power, the mobs

it unlocked at higher levels were stronger than their lower-ranked counterparts, even if the costs were similar. According to the veteran Chaos fairy, the base Tier of the mob used in the creation of mini-bosses and bosses amplified the abilities of that creature quite a bit.

Ryan's third floor bosses were made from Silver-Tier mobs. While they were powerful, packing a deadly punch and proving themselves formidable creatures, they were crafted from a lower Tier base. Ryan's giant, on the other hand, was created using an elephant, which was classified as a huge beast mob. Which meant Andre had a Platinum-Tier mob as its base. And that, according to dungeon core logic, meant the Bone Enforcer's capabilities were amplified to match the expected difficulty of a Platinum-Tier mob. The more Ryan thought about it, the more he realized this was the first time he actually had an amplified mob appropriate for the floor level running about as a miniboss.

Suddenly, Ryan's confidence in the party's survival diminished.

"They've still got a chance," he replied weakly, before his focus turned to the fight at hand. While he said the words to be encouraging, his tone and emotions betrayed him. He may have just doomed this group. Part of him wanted to stop the fight, but he knew he could not do that. The adventurers knew the risks, and Ryan...he needed experience. Plus, as he knew from trial and error, showing kindness of any sort might lead to worse. He still remembered the bloodbath that had been his second week as an opened dungeon. He had pulled his punches the first week and shown kindness to the adventurers. That had led to a lot of unnecessary deaths the next. Many adventurers had died before they could really even begin to grow.

"Did we just trigger a boss fight?" The cleric of the party wasn't even trying to hide the fear in his voice as he asked his question. His eyes were darting from his party members, to Andre the Giant, and then the swirling, bone-filled mana trapping them in the town center. It was clear this was more than he had signed up for.

"There's no sign of a loot box. And while this floor is unique, the Bone Dungeon wouldn't just spring a surprise boss mob on us." Dirk's body was glowing green with Earth mana as he spoke, his eyes taking in the situation. The former party leader was the calmer one in this situation. Of course, he also had a lot more mana than poor Alfred did. "It's more likely this is a mini-boss."

"Sure, make the mini-boss a midget on the third-floor," Beth's fists were glowing with flames as she looked at Ryan's Bone Enforcer. The massive creature was taking in the situation. The swirling pits of darkness that sat where his eyes should have on the massive elephant skull of a head, seemed to look over the party. The mini-boss was figuring out the best way to take them down. "But make this one a freaking giant." Beth let out a dark chuckle. "You've sure got a twisted sense of humor, dungeon."

Ryan had not intended to be funny in this situation. While Mini-Steve was a joke about the whole mini-boss concept, Ryan hadn't sought to be ironic in making his fourth floor mini-bosses massive. Still, all five of his Bone Enforcers were on the larger side of things. And Andre was the largest mob Ryan had ever created, other than his fourth-floor boss...

"How about we don't antagonize the dungeon?" Brook's eyes were alight with crimson as flames raced across his hands and up his arms. A literal firestorm appeared to be brewing around his body. On the other side of the party, winds were swirling around Danielle and her golden eagle glowed with a faint silver. The party was serious. They were taking Andre on knowing full well that if they conserved anything, they could die.

"It doesn't look like he should have any ranged attacks." As Dirk spoke, his green mana continued to flare around him, chunks of earth and stone ripping from the ground, attaching itself all over his body. The sentinel grew until the large knight, who had already been over six feet tall, was close to ten. He was encased from head to toe in stone armor. Stone also formed around his shield and mace, to create large, rocky versions of his equipment. For a moment, the green mana seemed to glow brighter then suddenly faded, all of the stones changing into crystal.

"If I go down—" Dirk locked eyes with Andre the Giant as he spoke, the thirty-foot mini-boss seeming to feel the ten-foot adventurer was the biggest threat of the time, its Darkness mana trunk twitching towards Dirk. "Make sure you guys get away."

Even as Dirk finished his words, Ryan's mini-boss seemed to have grown tired of waiting. The mob lowered its head towards the ground, leveling its mighty tusks towards Dirk, and charged forward. The sentinel, embodying his role as a tank, rushed forward to meet the giant head on.

Ryan watched Dirk raise his crystalline shield to meet the approaching tusks as he swung his mighty crystalline mace. Bone and crystal met, the force behind the collision sending a massive wave of energy rolling off the two combatants. The rest of Dirk's party was forced backwards, fighting to stay upright as the shockwave of the collision washed over them. At the same time, the air shimmered with crystalline fragments, Dirk's shield showing damage.

"Let's do this." Beth was the first to recover, and the Grappler rushed forward, her limbs afire as she approached the two giant forms. Even as Andre, who had stood to his full thirty-foot height following the collision, wrapped his Darkness mana trunk around Dirk, Beth was there. The Grappler, leaving fiery portions of melted stone with each step, rushed up the condensed Darkness mana trunk. The flames around her feet tried to burn away the trunk, but the Darkness mana held. This was a fight where both sides were using Platinum-Tier mana, meaning the Darkness flowing through Andre would not be so easily severed.

"What does she think she can do?" Erin bemoaned as they watched Beth reach Andre's head. While the Grappler was muscular, her frame was still tiny compared to the giant. In fact, the elephant skull alone was nearly the same size as her.

"Just watch, little one," Hel said. Ryan could sense the excitement flowing through the bond from her. The Chaos fairy wasn't even trying to hide it. "Platinum fights are much more exciting than anything you've ever seen."

Beth's limbs, still alight with flames, burst with crimson mana as they grew even brighter. The heat, had she not had an affinity for Fire, would have killed her. That was part of the advantage for a Grappler with a Fire affinity when they faced off against living things. The intense heat of the flames they armed themselves with would be enough to kill any living thing that did not have a way to protect itself.

But Ryan's mobs were undead creations. Bones and Darkness mana did not burn easily. While he could see the mana flowing around Andre shift and shrink a tiny bit, merely turning up the heat on this mini-boss wasn't going to work. The party would need much more to bring Andre down.

As the flames grew even larger, seemingly increasing the size of Beth's limbs, the Grappler reached forward. Her fiery hands made contact with the Darkness-filled eye sockets, grabbing hold of the bone from the inside. As Andre shook his head violently, she began launching knee strike after flaming knee strike into the skull. Just before each strike impacted, Ryan saw a blast of fire erupt from her foot, accelerating her knee even more. Each impact sent a burst of flames outward from the zone she struck, and the Darkness mana protecting the bone grew thinner. Not only were her strikes powerful, but they were made with deadly precision.

Andre wasn't going to stand there and take that quietly. The Giant let out an inhuman sound and smashed his shield into Dirk. At the same time, Andre's trunk, which was wrapped around the sentinel, gave a great heave. The combined force of the impact and the strength of the trunk ripped the sentinel from his stony rooted position and sent him flying across the town square. Dirk had used some of his Earth mana to attach himself to the ground with stones, but that proved inadequate in the face of the giant's might.

With Dirk out of the way for a moment, Andre's trunk rapidly shifted its target. The dark, snakelike appendage grabbed a hold of Beth's waist. Mid-knee strike, Andre tore the Grappler free from his skull and threw her straight into Dirk. To Beth's credit, she fought as hard as she could, and instead of letting go of her grasp, ripped parts of bone free from Andre's face as she was sent flying into her friend.

The mini-boss shook its head, from pain or anger—Ryan wasn't sure—and turned its focus on the two. Dirk had caught the flying Beth with a wall of soft stone. The impact still took a toll on the Grappler, but much less so than if she had crashed into the crystal-covered sentinel. Dirk had probably done that in order to protect himself from the Grappler's flames too, considering Ryan could see some of the sand he had caught Beth with had been turned into glass from the intense heat.

So far, neither side had given any ground in the fight. But Ryan had a feeling the adventurers wouldn't be able to keep this pace up for long. Sure, Andre had been injured, but the mini-boss still had a lot more fight in him. And it seemed to

Ryan that his boss was just now getting used to his own skills. The Giant cracked its head from side to side, its eyes focused on the duo as it lowered its tusks once more for another charge.

Dirk was almost standing, but his movements were hampered by his massive crystalline form. He'd had to use some Earth mana to help lift his frame up. At first he'd been stranded, almost akin to a turtle stuck on its back.

Beth had blood trickling from her mouth, showing the impact into the sand still caused a good chunk of internal damage. That, and Andre had cracked her ribs when the Giant grasped her with his trunk.

"I can't watch." Erin closed her eyes as Ryan's boss rushed forward. Part of him shared that sentiment, but the other part of him refused to look away. Judging by the feelings Hel broadcast through her bond, this fight was just getting started.

Chapter Twenty-One

Ryan knew adventurers at Platinum were formidable. He knew they had a vast reserve of mana to pull from as well as the unique and powerful abilities they unlocked from their classes at Platinum. He knew their bodies were significantly strengthened and enhanced. What he had failed to realize was just how powerful they could be when they worked together.

When Brook's party had defeated one of his skeletal mage bosses on the third floor, opening the path for them to the fourth, Ryan had not been surprised. It was kind of a given that a party with four Platinum 5 adventurers would be able to take down the third-floor boss. After all, Samuel and Xander, the Platinum-Tier Chaos users who'd entered his dungeon to set the Seed of Chaos that had turned into Hel had taken down his third-floor boss with ease.

Outside of the Chaos duo, Ryan hadn't gotten to see many Platinum Tier individuals going at it. Even when Marcus and Cane had shown up to save Ryan from Marissa, it hadn't quite been a fair fight. For one, Blake had been beating the crap out of Samuel, and Xander had been trapped trying to hold the portal open. Marcus and Cane were both highly skilled, powerful physical classes. Marissa, the leader of the Cult of Chaos and Marcus's sister, had been a support class. That put her at a disadvantage, even though she had been Platinum 1.

Now, as Ryan watched the battle unfold, he was reminded of the one time he had seen a Platinum individual go all out. And it hadn't even been within his dungeon. Instead, it was the time he had watched Blaine Dragnov, the Platinum 1 Blade Dancer, take down a Light Ender while Ryan was under siege from the Cult of Chaos. Blaine was outfitted in extremely high-quality gear and was using cursed weapons capable of greatly enhancing his powers at the risk of his own life, but the way Blaine had fought, the way he had brought down his opponent, had been impressive.

And here, now, Ryan was watching a party of five take on a Platinum Tier mini-boss. These five adventurers, whom Ryan had thought might have some difficulty working together because they were from different parties originally, meshed surprisingly well. They must have been working on their teamwork before they had dived into his dungeon. Either that, or they had simply gotten used to knowing what their roles were, and how to best fill them, no matter what the situation.

"Flames that burn." Brook's voice was strangely deep as he started chanting, the words filling the area even as Andre the Giant charged headfirst toward Beth and Dirk. "Flames that yearn," he continued. His body glowed crimson, the flames swirling around him changing from red to orange, growing even more intense. Fire raced around his form, crackling, the heat enough to distort the air surrounding him.

"Heed my call." the flames changed hue again, blue joining with the other shades, "And consume it all." His hand's spread outwards towards Andre. The mini-boss was roughly five feet away from Beth. The Grappler, upon hearing Brook's chanting had begun pumping a ton of mana into her body. From head to toe she was wreathed in blue flames. The portions covering most of her body were translucent, but all Ryan could see from her hands to her elbows, and from her feet to her knees, was dense flame.

Meanwhile, Dirk had stopped trying to stand. Instead, he had smashed his crystalline shield into the ground in front of him, embedding it in the earth. Now he was crouched behind it, green mana pulsing from his form into the earth. Because Ryan was connected to it all, he could see the mana grasping at the earth, sprawling through it till it reached its destination. As a beam of white-blue fire blasted into Andre the Giant, massive stone walls erupted from the ground in front of Dirk and all-around Alfred.

"My turn," Danielle called out as the beam of fire impacted against Andre. The attack hit him from the side, knocking him off course mid-charge. The bone enforcer, caught off guard by the attack, stumbled, toppling to one side, barely managing to catch himself with his trunk and bone club. And, while he had managed to avoid completely collapsing to the ground, the attack had done damage. Where the fiery attack had hit him, Ryan could see a clear hole. The attack had burned clear through the mini-boss's armor, bones, and exited out the other side.

With Andre stunned for a moment as he took in the damage done to him, Danielle pointed towards the mob. From above, her golden eagle let out a screech, making its way toward Andre. As it did, Danielle nocked her bow, drawing from her quiver a set of arrows previously untouched.

"What are those?" Ryan asked as he looked at them. Normally, archers used basic arrows in his dungeon. Some even resorted to using his bone arrows if they ran out of the ones they had brought. What Danielle drew from her quiver were arrows he had never seen before. They seemed to have shafts made not of wood, but instead of metal, fletched with large feathers that Ryan was certain came from an eagle. What caught his eye was the arrowhead. The arrow seemed to have six metal spikes, all strung together, connected to a clear stone affixed to the shaft of the arrow. Ryan recognized the stone as smokey quartz, which enhanced Air mana.

"That's a very good question, Darling. I would like to see for myself." Hel licked her lips as she looked at the weapon. If there was one thing he knew the Chaos fairy loved as much as experience, it was learning new things. What impressed Ryan most was, the adventurers were using something Hel had not seen before. She had centuries worth of memories, though Ryan could not help but remember none of the dungeons she had been in had survived for long. He had to wonder how many adventurers she had seen in Platinum and above.

With slow, calculated movements, Danielle launched arrow after arrow towards the stunned Andre. The arrows, each one seeming to pulse for a moment before she released them from her bow, flew high into the sky in a large arc. Ryan could tell their trajectory was sending them toward Andre, but he was curious as to why she had chosen such a strange flight path towards the boss. Not only that, but the arrows were descending slowly. As he watched them, he realized the stones on the tip of the arrows were releasing small gusts of wind to slow their descent. They had also begun to spiral in a strange way. What was going on?

Ryan's thoughts blanked out as the scene unfolded. As more than a dozen of the arrows began their downward path towards Andre, Danielle's eagle, which had been slowly circling above Andre, suddenly accelerated. The eagle circled rapidly, glowing with wind mana, as visible trails of air began to trace its flight path. The circling of the eagle, combined with the Wind mana oozing off the bird, created a funnel of wind, more and more visible as it picked up dust and debris.

As the funnel touched down, it created something Ryan had known vaguely about as a human, though he had never experienced one in the mountains. A tornado. A natural phenomenon people claimed could cause massive damage.

The arrows, with their strange make, dropped inside it, only to be claimed by the cycling winds. The tornado was going in the opposite direction to the rotation of the arrows. The metal blades were ripped from the spinning arrow and were sucked into the sides of the cyclone. At the same time, the feathers came free from the arrows, leaving just the spinning quartz stones and the metal shafts. Those continued their descent, seeming to gain speed as they punched through the eye of the tornado directly toward Andre.

As Andre stood, the metal shards, which had gotten lost in the debris and windstorm, smashed against the giant. Sparks flew as they scratched across his armor, the high winds giving them more and more force. Ryan could see his mini-boss tighten its grasp on his bone club, even as Andre's shield was nearly ripped from his hand.

Still Andre fought against the attack. Ryan's Bone Enforcer was tough. He was not going to go down without a fight. He took a step forward, but even as he did, the descending metal shafts and stones smashed into him. The spiraling stones seemed to drill into his form, piercing through him. Then, as the crystals shattered, small eruptions of mana, like what Ryan had observed happen when he accidently filled a crystal with too much mana, took chunks out of Andre's armor.

The mini-boss was affected by that. How could he not be? He had been assaulted by crystalline weapons, fiery fists, a beam of intense heat, and now, mana eruptions and a literal force of nature. Ryan was starting to wonder if he had overestimated his Bone Enforcers. Or, more appropriately, had he been underestimating Platinum adventurers?

"We need to finish this, quickly." A cry from Danielle, barely audible over the rushing winds, answered Ryan's question. It was not that he had underestimated his Bone Enforcers. No, the adventurers were just burning everything they could to take the boss down before the fight could drag on. In the war of attrition, Ryan's fourth floor would win for now. The adventures, while impressive, could not keep up fighting at the level they were.

"He's going to break through soon," she continued, her eagle slowing. The ranger was out of her strange arrows, and while she was launching more attacks towards the cyclone, her hands were shaking slightly. That skill was consuming a lot of mana.

"All or nothing." Beth was standing now, golden light fading from her body, wiping dried blood from her mouth. Danielle's attack had been meant to hold up Ryan's boss while the others prepared themselves. It was an attack meant to give their Gold Tier healer time to heal their wounds.

"On my mark then." Dirk was holding out a hand towards the Grappler. He had done his job in keeping the healer alive, and then Danielle had bought them time to regroup. Now, they were launching their final assault. Whatever happened here and now would determine if the party members survived this fight or became the first casualties of his fourth floor. He risked a quick glance toward Erin, wondering if she was watching all of this. The Celestial fairy had her hands over her face, but he could just make out her eyes behind them, opened wide, watching the final gambit of the party.

"Just like cornered beasts," Hel whispered, her euphoria flowing freely through their bond, "adventurers fight the hardest when they know they are about to die."

Chapter Twenty-Two

Their final attack started with Beth stepping into Dirk's enlarged crystalline fist. The Earth mana-enhanced adventurer lifted the Grappler up even as her flames continued to burn brightly around her. Then the sentinel threw Beth towards the slowing cyclone. Andre the Giant's form was visible now, as the winds were dying, and the mini-boss had managed to get himself partially freed from the attack. He was using his massive bone shield to part the tornado from the inside, even as more and more debris battered him. Ryan could tell the mini-boss was suffering. There were holes in his armor, his mana was wavering in places, and his face had already taken quite a beating from Beth.

As the Grappler was launched in an arc towards the massive enemy, Brook followed up with another attack of his own. Where before he had used highly concentrated Fire mana to launch the white-hot beam, he now activated a different, though no less impressive, attack. Crimson mana raced from the war mage towards Andre, drawing a circle of red around the tornado. From the glowing lines of mana, fire shot upward. The flames were instantly drawn by the spinning winds, changing the tornado from one of air to one of fire.

More and more fire rushed into the tornado. The flames, already emitting immense heat, grew in ferocity and destructive power as they continued to spin around Andre. Ryan's mob let out a loud roar as he smashed his shield into the ground, driving it deep into the rocky ground, splitting the very earth apart with the motion. As the entire area shook, Andre lashed out with his bone club, smashing an even larger swathe of rock and stone. The shockwave from the attack was strong enough to send debris flying in all directions, with enough force to actually keep the debris from being sucked into the fire cyclone.

Ryan winced as he watched a storm of rock shards rain down towards the adventurers. Andre could not see them, not with the wind, flames, and debris blocking his vision, and so the mini-boss had simply done an attack which would hit everything around him. As such, it did not give the adventurers any area to dodge or to safely take cover under. What's more, the rumbling of the earth from the shield smash had knocked Brook and Alfred off-balance, the magical classes having less physical enhancement to keep their stance amidst the attack. Fatal, had Dirk not responded when he did.

Even as Beth was flying towards Andre, even as this set of attacks was going on, Dirk was still doing all he could as a sentinel to keep the party safe. The moment he had seen the bone club raise and begin to come down, the adventurer had responded. Green mana had raced out from all around him, extending towards every one of his members, causing another round of stones to erupt from the ground as he did his best to protect them.

He wasn't quite fast enough. Brook, who was the farthest away from him, suffered as a result. Even as Dirk's protective stones began to form up around the war mage, a few shards of stone from Andre's attack connected with the adventurer. One piece of shrapnel, a sharp portion of rock about a foot wide, punched into the war mage's soft stomach. Another shard smashed into his shoulder, the force of the impact sending him flying against the stone walls that had been created to protect him. While Dirk couldn't see what was going on, his vision blocked by the stone he had summoned, Ryan looked on as the mage's head smacked against the wall with a sickening crack. In an instant, the fiery runes on the ground ceased and the war mage slumped to the ground.

"One down," Hel whispered, licking her lips. She knew how close Ryan was to Platinum 4, and the death of these adventurers could bump him to that next level. But he had not received the rush of experience he normally would from the death of an adventurer. It seemed the war mage had not yet died, but was merely unconscious.

Still, Ryan could see the form of a reaper already appearing by the mage. Ryan had been blissfully unaware of these reapers until he'd unlocked the soul mobs, after creating his first vampire out of A-a-ron. Ever since, he was able to not only see the soul fragments of those who'd fallen in his dungeon, but also the reapers come to collect the souls from fallen adventurers. In this instance, the reaper was waiting patiently by the body of Brook, its hooded face turned towards the man, watching the small, flickering red that was his soul. Judging by the diminishing state of Brook's soul amidst the chaos of the battlefield, the party was not going to save the war mage.

A burst of light above Andre drew Ryan's focus away from the dying war mage and back to Beth. The Grappler was above the giant, her entire body still wreathed in flames. As she descended, she somersaulted, her body twisting over and over itself as she rotated, gaining more and more momentum as she fell.

Andre, still held by the tornado, his shield now embedded in the earth, club lowered due to his attack, looked up at the Grappler, pausing for a moment as he tried to process how to respond. The Giant moved to try and get his bone club up to intercept, while he simultaneously sent his Darkness trunk against her approaching form. Or at least tried to. As the trunk of Darkness mana moved away from his body, trying to stop her approach, it was snagged by the dying fire-cyclone. Flames burned across the Darkness mana trunk, and even as Andre fought against the powerful winds, he couldn't respond in time to stop the Grappler.

At the last second, just as Beth neared Andre's skull, her final rotation completed. She had been rotating in a forward motion, as if completing rapid front flips. At the peak, her right foot extended, and in that final, rapid spin, she brought the flaming heel of her foot smashing directly into the center of Andre's skull.

An explosive sound, which reminded Ryan of a thunder-clap following a lightning strike, echoed through the massive cavern. A concussive burst of wind blasted around Beth and Andre, so strong it blew apart the flagging fire cyclone. Time, which had seemed to freeze for Andre and Beth, resumed as the Giant's skull shattered apart. Massive bones came apart in an instant as Beth fell the thirty feet to the ground. As if she needed any more style points, the Grappler managed to land somewhat on her feet, both hitting the ground at the same time as her right fist, in a sort of heroic, crouching moment.

As she hit the ground, the flames around her faded, and she tried to stand, only to fall to her knees. Her right boot was gone, and Ryan could see bone showing on her foot where the impact had blasted away her protective flames, causing her flesh and bone to take the brunt of the force. Her body may have been enhanced by a large amount of mana, but a human body, even at Platinum, wasn't meant to withstand that type of force.

"Alfred —" She started, her face contorted with pain, before she stopped. Her eyes, which had been searching for their healer, fell upon the sight that all the others were looking upon as well. The moment Andre had fallen, Dirk had released his protective shells around the party. In doing so, he had revealed what Ryan already knew. For in that same instant, even as the party had reigned victorious against the Bone Enforcer, Ryan had felt the all-too-familiar rush of energy signaling the death of an adventurer. And, out of a kindness to the party, he had left Brook's body there for them to see instead of absorbing it, as was the norm. A physical reminder of their fallen friend could serve as a sign to others above of just how dangerous his fourth floor really was.

"He knew what he was getting into." Dirk's voice was hard, his eyes looking at the party members as his crystalline armor faded away. His eyes were red, and Ryan could see blood dripping from his ears. They had all burned through more mana than they were likely used to utilizing at a single time. Up until now they hadn't pushed themselves, not at Platinum. They had not tested their own limits, and had, in the heat of the moment, all blown through their most powerful abilities without thinking.

It had been an impressive display of power, but also somewhat reckless. And as a result, one of them had died. This encounter had served not only the adventurers, in teaching them more about themselves and their floor, but also Ryan. He now knew how formidable his Bone Enforcers were, and he could not help but wonder what the future would bring. With the death of Brook, word would spread above, and adventurers would be much more cautious on his fourth floor. They may even resist heading to the fourth floor until their party was completely prepared. A choice Ryan would not fault them for.

As the party gathered up their fallen comrade and collected the loot from Andre—including his dungeon mob card—Ryan pulled up his level triangles. Sure enough, he had gained enough experience from Brook's death to advance to Platinum Rank 4. He summoned the triangles into the room, mentally grinning as he looked at both his fairies. Hel was handing the coins over to Erin, though the Celestial fairy was less than thrilled with her victory. She had won the bet, but Brook had died.

"Cheer up Erin," Ryan said, trying his best to send her a burst of enthusiasm. Even now, after over a year of his being a dungeon, the Celestial fairy, true to her nature, grew dismayed over the loss of life. That was something Ryan admired about her. While he didn't exactly feel guilt over deaths, especially when they transpired during evenly fought matches such as the one they had just observed, there was still a small part of him that felt a twinge of regret. No matter the cause, Ryan had accepted that this was the way of things. The path towards power for a dungeon came through the defeat of others. This was how the Gods had designed it. And he wasn't in a position to question Gods.

"Brook's death wasn't in vain." He focused on the level and experience triangles, forcing his experience into his level triangle. The two objects glowed for a moment, and as they did, Ryan felt the rush of power flowing into him, signaling his level up.

"Finally." Hel let out a purr. Even as Ryan's core rushed with new power, both his fairies' bodies began to glow as well. Erin's form became encased in golden light, as crackling red and black mana swirled around Hel. The mana burned brightly around the two, filling the massive chamber that was now his core room with the two contrasting types of mana.

As their transformation continued, a tingling, almost burning feeling, rushed through Ryan. As it did, the connection he had with Erin and Hel deepened, becoming even more intertwined. When the light faded and their transformations ended, all he could do was stare in awe at what had become of his fairies.

Finally, he was a true Platinum dungeon.

Chapter Twenty-Three

BLAKE

The party members were sitting around their normal table at the tavern, after spending their entire day helping Marcus out at the dungeon. On the plus side, since they were technically doing Guild work, their meals and drinks were covered by the Adventurers' Guild. They also got a small amount of coin for helping out, though it was nothing compared to what they could have made diving in the dungeon.

Still, it had been a long, long day. Blake sat there, his drink in hand, staring blankly at the table. His time away from Ryan had lessened, to a degree, his acceptance of death within a dungeon. Adventuring could be deadly, but it had been months since Blake had seen a death. In fact, the last death he'd seen, before heading back to Boneville, had been his father's.

When the party of Platinum members had exited Ryan's dungeon, carrying in their hands the body of their leader, wrapped gently in his bloodied, crimson robes, Blake had been taken aback. So much so, he hadn't been prepared for what was going to happen next, as his mind had raced back to his own father's death. Another Platinum adventurer, dead. Platinum adventurers weren't supposed to die, especially not like this. At Platinum, they should be practically invincible.

"I can't believe that dick." Jack's eyes shot across the room as he spoke. His comment pulled Blake from his thoughts, head looking up from the table in time to see whom Jack was referring to. The tavern had grown hushed, as a group of four walked into the dungeon. Dirk's group. The group that had just lost their Platinum 5 war mage.

"They were grieving. You can't really blame them." Karan put a calming hand on Jack's shoulder. The Duelist stiffened, but he didn't jerk away.

"Still." Only as he took a drink did he look away from the man. His eyes had focused solely on Dirk. "Not an excuse for what they did." Dirk, the man in question, was the tank of the party that had attempted the dive into Ryan's fourth level. His party, which had consisted of four Platinum 5 party members, and a Gold 4 cleric, seemed capable. However, Blake had been there when the light had gone out on the disc in Marcus's hands. He had been there when the party emerged, carrying the body of their fallen comrade. And because he had been there...the situation had worsened.

It was no secret that Blake had once before brought someone back from the dead. Just a few months ago, Matt had been assassinated in this very tavern, right before their eyes. A tavern full of adventurers had witnessed the tragic event. What's more, the assassination had been carried out in the trademark way of not just any member of the Assassins' Guild, but of their leader's. An individual clouded in mystery, known to *always* finish off their target with a simultaneous dagger to the throat and heart, ensuring there was no way to survive.

But no one, not even Blake, had known about his strange powers then. When Matt was killed, Blake had awoken to a brand new, unique ability that only he could wield. The ability to pay the toll, the weight of the individual's soul in mana, in order to bring them back from the dead. Of course, the skill had limits. As a Gold Tier Specter of Balance at the time, he shouldn't have been able to use the skill. However, his ultra-rare shield could be used to activate the skill, once a month. Now that he was Platinum, he could use the skill three times every month per his class rules, and an additional fourth, with his shield.

The skill was not free. Nor could it bring just anyone back from the dead. A skill as powerful as that had specific rules. He had to be there at the time of death to offer up the mana in exchange for the fallen adventurer's soul. Then, he had to provide the reaper with mana equal to the amount the individual could wield. Meaning the stronger the individual, the higher the toll. Blake had nearly died saving Matt, though he would have given his life for his friend.

The adventurers who witnessed the miraculous resurrection didn't know the rules and stipulations of Blake's ability. All they knew was he had two different affinities: something unheard of. Something he was supposed to have kept a secret. That was out of the bag though, and with it, people learned that he could bring people back from the dead. All of this had caused the situation to spiral out of control at the dungeon, earlier that day. Blake's eyes grew hazy for a moment as he took a drink, his mind going back to the moment...

"Blake." At the sound of his name, Blake turned, glancing back towards the dungeon. There, emerging from the dark entrance, covered in blood and signs of an intense battle, came the party that had lost their member. Everyone outside the dungeon already knew someone had died. Marcus had exclaimed as much the moment the crystal had gone dark. It was a rare circumstance for a Platinum individual to die within a dungeon. So rare, they had wondered what had caused that death.

"Blake." The man calling his name was Dirk, the sentinel that served as the tank for the party. Blake saw three of the other members of the party stepping slowly out of the shadows as well, their eyes dark, their steps heavy. Dirk carried, ever so carefully, the body of their war mage, Brook. It was gently wrapped in his crimson robes.

"Bring him back." Dirk's red-rimmed eyes met Blakes. He'd been crying, likely for the entire walk back. Loss was not uncommon. Everyone had lost someone they'd known to a dungeon. It was only a matter of time. But that didn't matter when it came to your party members. For the stronger teams, the party was family. And those losses never went away. Blake knew that all too well.

"Dirk." Marcus put a gentle hand on the sentinel's shoulder, trying to pull him away. There was a group forming around them, countless people offering condolences. Even the nobles in the area stayed quiet out of respect. They knew well how rare a Platinum death was. It wasn't something to make light of. "Come on, Dirk." Marcus's voice was soft, yet firm.

"Please." The sentinel ignored Marcus. He stepped from the rogue's grasp, as if he didn't even feel it. "I'll do anything." He reached Blake and held out the bloodied form of his party member. From what Blake could see of the poor mage, his had not been an easy or kind death. Just what had Ryan created in his dungeon? "We will do anything." Dirk's party members nodded solemnly towards Blake. "We'll give you all our loot, our armor, our weapons. Anything. You name it, and you can have it, Blake. Just...please, bring him back." Dirk's voice broke.

Blake looked down at the poor war mage. He opened his mouth to speak but couldn't. His voice cracked, and for a moment he saw his father's broken body before him. Then his mind flashed to Matt's bloodied body, the day he had watched his friend get killed before him. And even before that, another form flashed in his mind. Todd, the man who had wanted to pay his respects to his fallen party, murdered in Ryan's dungeon before Blake's eyes by the necromancer Viktor.

Blake was no stranger to death, yet, in that moment, he was speechless. Whatever he said wouldn't' be enough. And he knew he couldn't give Dirk the one thing he wanted. Blake wished he could. As much as he wanted to help Dirk, wanted to make sure this party didn't feel the loss of a family member, he couldn't. His skill was not all-powerful. It had rules and restrictions, and it wouldn't work on Brook.

"Dirk, I can't," Blake said gently. He shook his head, reaching a hand towards the sentinel. He lightly touched the massive man's shoulder. "I'm sorry, but I can't."

"But you can," Dirk said, shaking his head. "I saw you. I was there. You brought back Matt." He shoved the lifeless body of Brook into Blake's hands, dropping the corpse, forcing Blake to catch it, to hold the dead weight. Strange how a lifeless corpse always weighed more. As if the very air around it, the fact, the sorrow of the death, weighed it down. Blake wanted to drop the body, but he couldn't. He couldn't disrespect Brook in that way.

"I'm telling you, I can't." Blake looked past Dirk towards Marcus, pleading for help. What was he supposed to do here? What could he do? He knelt slowly to the ground, setting Brook's body down gently. Even though half his powers involved utilizing dead bodies, this was too fresh, too soon, too personal. Brook had been one of them. Brook had been one of the original divers of the Bone Dungeon. He was, in a way, a distant family member. He deserved respect. He didn't deserve this.

"You can't, or you won't?" Dirk's tone hardened. The man's gauntleted fists clenched. "Do I not have enough to offer you? Are we not good enough? Is that it? Tell me what it is you want. Anything, no matter how long it takes me, I will get it for you. Please. Blake. Just bring him back."

"That's not how this works." Blake shook his head. "I can't just bring anyone back. I'm sorry. But he's —"

Blake saw it coming, but he did nothing to stop it. As a Platinum 4 with dual affinities he had more mana coursing through his body than anyone standing there. He could see the punch coming towards his face. Still, he didn't block it.

The fist connected with his face, the metal mesh connecting with his skin, ripping flesh and cracking his jaw. Dirk had put a lot of force into that punch, but there was more to it. Sorrow, frustration, rage. As a tank, Blake could understand all of those. Having a party member die, someone you were entrusted with protecting, was the worst nightmare for a tank. That was why Blake let that punch land.

"Bring him back." Another punch, another strike against Blake's jaw. He winced as this one left a cut underneath his eye. As subtly as he could, he sent his Celestial mana to his wounds, healing them even as Dirk struck again. The sentinel was sobbing, each strike hitting with less and less force as his frustration flowed out of him. Even though each had less force than the previous one, Blake couldn't help but feel more and more pain. It overwhelmed him. If only he could do something...

"What if—" Dirk's tone changed as his tears dropped. His eyes, filled with sorrow, shifted ever so slightly. Blake didn't like that change. "What if I forced you to do it? What if your only choice was between bringing him back and dying?" Green mana flowed around Dirk, the earth responding to his call, covering his fists. This was getting out of hand. "Would you do it then? You're selfish, aren't you? You only do what's in your best interest. So then, it's in your best interest that you bring him back." His fist, now covered in a jagged stone blade, swung towards Blake's chest. The attack was aimed towards his sternum. It wouldn't kill him, but it would inflict a grievous wound.

Before Blake could respond, Marcus intervened.

Winds suddenly wrapped themselves all around Dirk, catching his movements, freezing him in place even as his eyes, filled with a crazed look, bore into Blake's soul. The look on his face in that instant reminded Blake of all he'd felt when that Chaos mana had flowed through him. Even though he'd been partially affected, he was certain, at that time by the mana, he knew that emotion too. It was that emotion that had enveloped him as he abandoned his party and sought his revenge against Samuel and the Chaos cultists. In that instant, Blake was staring at a reflection of himself from four months ago. That moment hurt the most.

"I can assure you, Dirk, if Blake could, he would bring your party leader back." Marcus's voice was stern. "However, his skills have limits, just as all of ours do. He is not a God. You should know better than to treat a fellow Guild Member the way you have." His winds swirled for a moment longer, before fading around Dirk. As they did, the sentinel's mana released the stones around his fist, and his arms dropped to his side.

"Now then. Brook would not want you to act like this," Marcus continued. "You and your party members should take him back to the Guild Hall. We will ensure a proper cere-mony is held for him. He will be remembered. Do not tarnish him or his death any further with your actions." And with that, Marcus sent them on their way.

As Dirk and the others left, carrying their fallen member back to town, Blake couldn't help but fight the renewed emotions flowing through him. That encounter had reminded him he'd never dealt with his father's death. He'd never dealt fully with the emotions of that night. And now, they'd resurfaced.

He decided he could really use a drink.

"I can understand what Dirk was going through," Blake spoke up, clearing his mind from the events of the day. When Ryan had first announced he was going to open back up, and mentioned his fourth floor, all Blake could think about was how excited he was to continue adventuring with his friends. For the past few days, after his reintegration with Jack and Karan, everything had felt...right, as if they were moving in the right direction.

He had been dismayed when Karan informed him Emily and Matt wouldn't be joining them until the day after Ryan opened back up. They had been the first ones on Ryan's third floor, and he had been hoping for a similar experience on the fourth. But now, after what had happened to Dirk's party, Blake couldn't help but feel doubt filling him.

Would he be able to truly keep his team safe on the fourth floor? Was his party strong enough to survive? Following today's events, he realized they needed to be as prepared as they could before they took on this new challenge. While Blake was battling with his emotions, he realized something else. He couldn't stand any further loss. Anything more would break him.

And that meant, not only did he need to be as prepared as he could be for the dungeon, but his party needed to be as well. They weren't going to set foot onto the fourth floor, not until the entire party was Platinum. From what Karan told him, Matt and Emily were both Platinum 5 now. That was part of why they weren't there yet. They were finalizing their ascension to Platinum and finishing up some additional training.

Karan and Jack were still Gold 1. They both had the experience to ascend to Platinum, but they hadn't, not yet. Something kept Jack from reaching Platinum, and Karan had refrained from ascending out of support for her companion. It was time for them to deal with that. Both needed to be Platinum, not just for Blake, but for the party and themselves. Jack, just like himself, would tear himself up if he ever brought the party down.

Blake took another drink, to prepare himself for what he needed to do. Dirk's party had taken a seat in the tavern, and Karan had turned Jack's attention back to their own table, convincing the Duelist to calm down and enjoy his hot chocolate. As the man before him took a long sip from the drink, Blake cleared his throat and prepared himself.

"Hey, Jack," Blake paused, his eyes focusing on the Duelist. He had already had this conversation, in secret, with Karan. She was on his side, and she had assured him that Emily and Matt agreed, as well. The one who needed convincing, the one who needed to make the decision, was Jack.

The moment stretched for a bit too long and Jack noticed. "Cat got your tongue, buddy?" The Duelist said as he flashed a grin towards Blake, but it barely reached the man's eyes. Jack had noticed the sudden shift around Blake.

"Something like that." He paused again, preparing himself. This had to happen, for the party to move forward. "Are you still able to get into contact with Sasha?"

Chapter Twenty-Four

Blake was up early the next day, his excitement and anxiety strong. Not only had he and Karen convinced Jack to get a hold of Sasha, but it seemed the wolfkin leader would be able to meet up with them the very next day. They were going to reunite with Emily and Matt, whom Blake hadn't seen in close to four months, and tackle the last obstacle in the way of the party's continued dungeon endeavors.

With nothing better to do, Blake started his day by gathering up his gear, and heading out for a training session. It was something he tried to do daily to better work on his mana control and practice with his skills to discover what powers he had at his disposal. Alice had helped him hone some of his abilities, but Blake was certain there was much more for him to learn. A huge downside of having a unique class like he did was that there were no records detailing all the skills available to him. He had to learn and unlock all of them on his own.

His early morning training also helped him clear his mind. When he trained, he would enter an almost trance-like state as he lost himself to his movements, to the feel of his mana rushing through him, the ebb and flow of power as he utilized his various skills. One of the benefits, if he could call them that, to his outing his dual-affinities nature, was he no longer had to worry about practicing in public. He could work through his skills, his power. Now though, he trained far away from town. He had no choice following the incident during the first week back at Boneville...

The first few days back at Boneville, before Ryan opened back up, Blake had gone to practice in the massive clearing set aside to that purpose. There, dozens of pairs of adventurers, mercenaries, and the occasional noble were practicing, doing their best to prepare themselves for the dungeon. Blake had met up with Dirk, whom he'd trained with before and had been on good terms with, and started sparring with him.

At first, everything had been fine. He started, as he normally did, training with just his Celestial power. The golden mana was what he normally utilized in public before Matt's attempted assassination. As they worked into the motions, he had called forth his Darkness mana as well, beginning to cycle through skill sets. At this, Dirk's face had grown grim, but the sentinel hadn't said anything. More than a few groups had stopped sparring by that point and had formed a ring around the two, watching with interest as Blake circled Dirk.

That was when Blake started feeling self-conscious. People weren't watching Dirk. They were only watching Blake as he used his skills, and even as he tried to keep his head clear, to focus on the sparring match, he could hear the thrown-around comments. More than a few of them negative. Darkness mana wasn't received well. Especially considering a necromancer had nearly destroyed the town. But they were just words, and Blake was able to ignore those for the most part.

What he couldn't ignore was a golden burst of Celestial mana erupting in front of him. The mana skill, an ability clerics had, was a type of cleansing meant to harm only the undead. As such, it was effective against Darkness mana. Not only did it instantly force away the mana Blake had been utilizing, but it also caused him to lose connection with his skeletal left hand. The weight of his shield, and the gauntlet that hid his skeletal hand, caused the now mana-less limb to fall to the ground.

Stunned silence followed, and the crowd around Blake began to separate, the whispers turning to those of horror. Furious, Blake had called forth his Darkness mana, once more forming the connection with his skeletal hand, lifting it back in place as he eyed the crowd. That skill, that attack, had to have come from a Platinum Tier Celestial user. Otherwise Blake's mana wouldn't have been affected. That, and he had been passively using the mana, out of habit, to keep his hand under control. If he'd been actively channeling the mana, exerting more force and control over it, he could have kept it from being completely dismissed by the attack even if it had come from someone of Platinum level.

"It seems we have an abomination amongst us, brothers." A voice, cold and cruel, spoke, and Blake snapped his head towards the source. There, as the crowd cleared even more, he saw him. A man clad all in white, with silver hair and cold grey eyes. Blake's eyes widened. Judging by the size of the man's soul, he was a Platinum 1 Celestial affinity user. Hard to discern, given his plain white robes. Behind him, over half a dozen others stood, all dressed in a similar fashion, though none as strong as the man who spoke.

"Behold, adventurers, a monster has found his place in our midst during these trying times." The man's body began to glow golden as he spoke, his hands rising up towards Blake. As they did, Blake noticed the sigil of The Goddess of Justice burned into the man's palms. His father had told him of the Zealots of Light before. A group his father had always despised, as the older Paladin always claimed they were doing more harm in the Goddess's name than good. They were deeply rooted in the Church, many now holding positions of seniority, and gaining considerable power within the congregation over the past few years. Any questionable acts attributed to them were quickly swept under the rug.

"I'm not a monster." Blake could tell the man was channeling a lot of mana into his palms, and he also knew whatever skill he was preparing wasn't going to be good. He also wasn't sure how he was going to stop the attack without being contradictory. Technically, he would be performing an act of self-defense if he took action against the man. However, as a Platinum 1 Zealot of Justice, the man likely had a high rank in the Church of Justice. Attacking him, no matter how Blake did it, would have repercussions.

"We shall see. Be cleansed in the light of the Goddess, monster, and pray she grants you mercy for your sins." The man raised his hands high, and a swirling circle of golden light appeared above Blake.

He knew what this skill was. He'd never seen it before, but he knew what it was. It was available to bishops, Platinum level clerics. The Celestial version, known as Divine Judgement, called forth a cone of blinding, powerful Celestial mana. Anything undead within the area would be destroyed in an instant. Any Darkness mana would be shredded apart and Darkness users caught within it would be burned alive as the mana within their very bodies and souls was 'purified' by the Celestial light.

Given the nature of his Ethereal mana, and the fact it contained Darkness mana, he wondered if his Ethereal State would protect him from the attack. Would he be able to avoid the "cleansing" if he used his Ethereal mana to go incorporeal?

Blake had no intention of experimenting with that. Almost everyone who had gathered around previously had dispersed the moment the man had started channeling his mana. Everyone knew to stay away from the Zealots. The Church of Justice, given its position as the main church in the area, held too much power. Even the Adventurers' Guild deferred to the religious organization. The Zealots were known to be quite…radical in the name of the Church. Their aggressive application of the Church's beliefs was never met with repercussions.

Blake was on his own for this one.

"Cancel the spell, Paul." Marcus's gruff voice came even as the swirling mana above Blake began to condense. That was the one thing about such a high-level skill, it took a while to channel. "Or I'll have to explain to the Church why their bishop ended up unconscious on the training field."

Blake saw a very angry Marcus approaching, his winds swirling around him. The Zealot, Paul, turned to glare at him. His hands stayed high in the sky, the skill still channeling.

"You would defy the work of the Goddess?" Paul smirked, and in his eyes, Blake saw something other than just cold hate. The man was cunning, but in a scary, crazed way. "None can escape her judgement."

Swirling winds wrapped around the bishop, tightening on him, cutting off his words as Marcus's mana seemed to deny the priest his ability to breathe.

"I will gladly send you to your Goddess, Paul. I'm not Sean. I don't believe in second chances." Marcus growled, and Paul's fingers twitched, before he lowered his arms. As he did, the mana above Blake dispersed. The moment it did,

Marcus's winds calmed, and the bishop let out a slight gasp. Paul shot angry glares towards his cohorts, none of whom had moved a finger against Marcus. Granted, they wouldn't have been able to put up a fight against the Platinum 1 rogue.

"Know that you and that monster will be punished by the Goddess. Justice cannot be avoided." Paul turned and moved away from the training grounds, leaving Marcus and Blake. With the exit of the Zealots, people began once again flocking towards the training grounds, though they all eyed Blake with more than a little caution.

Since that day, Blake had made sure he left the dungeon town when he went to train, practicing a good distance away from the town, close to the Bone Walls that formed what Ryan called his 'Bone Zone.' With the walls near him, Blake felt safer.

Perhaps it was his connection to the dungeon, but he could take comfort in the certainty that Ryan would help keep him safe. They'd saved each other's lives multiple times. Even if Ryan didn't come to Blake's aid, they were far enough away from the town that Blake was confident he could, at the very least, render Paul unconscious and escape back to town without fear of repercussions.

Short of surprise magical attacks it was very rare for a magic class to be able to take down a physical class. That was why parties existed, to cover the weaknesses of each class type and build on their strengths together.

Blake was faster, stronger, and sturdier than a bishop could ever hope to be. Blake also had more mana than the Platinum 1 bishop. Even if the bastard tried to hit him with another Divine Judgement spell, Blake would have been able to take the vulnerable bishop down during the channel time of that spell.

Blake prayed to the Goddess he never had to test that theory out. He really did want to make the Goddess of Justice proud. The memory of his father, too. He did not relish the thought of harming a bishop of the Church, even if he was a Zealot. They still, technically, served the same Goddess.

"Oy, are you trying to miss out on meeting up with Matt and Em?" Jack's voice pulled Blake from his training. He looked up, even as his body was filled to the brim with Ethereal mana, in time to see Jack and Karan moving towards him. The Duelist offered him a wave, but Blake could tell Jack was just putting on a show. The Duelist was still angry for what was about to happen. And if Jack's body language was any indicator, the Duelist was mad at Karan too. The look she gave Blake before her eyes returned on Jack confirmed it. Still, the excitement of regrouping with Emily and Matt had helped ease some of that friction. Even if Jack was upset at all of them, there was no way he could ignore or avoid them with their pending party reunion.

Which, judging by Jack's statement, Blake was about to miss. Had it really been that long? It was easy to lose himself to his training out in the Bone Zone. The massive trees in the area kept the sun hidden, making it hard to track the time of day. Jack's appearance and the sudden rumble in his stomach told him he had been training into —if not past—lunchtime. It was almost time for Matt and Emily to arrive.

"Sorry." Blake began putting away the blade he had been training with. That was the weapon he had picked up from his father's corpse, the black and blood-red hues mimicking the colors of Chaos mana. He wasn't sure what skills it held, despite being a legendary weapon. The demon possessing his father had said so, and when he questioned Alice about the blade, she had confirmed as much. She'd claimed she couldn't discern what it could do either. At the very least, Alice had recommended he not flaunt it in public. Walking around with a demonic weapon, given the current state of the world, might be received poorly.

For that reason, he now carried two swords on him. The demonic sword he kept sheathed and covered on his back, while he carried a rare, Celestial-class sword at his side. Part of him wanted to get rid of the demonic blade, to never see it again. But not only would that be foolish, as legendary weapons were—well, legendary—but it, along with the ring he wore around his neck, were the only two pieces of his father he still had. He wondered what had happened to the rest of his old man's gear. If there were any keepsakes of his father's he wished to have, it was the special gear the Goddess of Justice had bequeathed his father.

He finished wrapping the blade in its cloth and settled it upon his back. It was not unheard of for adventurers to carry multiple weapons. Dungeons were dangerous places, and weapons could sometimes be lost or destroyed. Having a backup was important. The more cautious the adventurer, the greater their chance at survival. One could never be overly cautious. Everyone always tried to be perfectly prepared for whatever they might face, which meant no one questioned him about the spare sword on his back.

"I'm ready to go." He nodded towards Jack and Karan, motioning for them to lead the way.

"Well, that makes one of us," Jack grumbled lightly as they began making their way back to town. Yup, the Duelist was definitely sore about the whole situation. Hopefully, after they met with Sasha, everything would be resolved. Hopefully, Blake hadn't made a mistake in his planning.

Chapter Twenty-Five

They met up with Matt and Emily as the siblings teleported into Boneville and helped the two go through their arrival process, in accordance with the new protocols at the dungeon town. Afterwards they moved out of the busy streets and away from the town itself before they began chatting and catching up.

Part of this was because Blake didn't feel comfortable talking in the middle of the streets, especially as he caught sight of Paul and a few of his Zealots. They also had agreed to get out of the town as quickly as possible once they regrouped. They had a good distance to travel to meet up with Sasha and her pack. The wolfkin wanted to meet up in a relatively private location, out of sight of prying eyes—human and dungeon alike.

The wolfkin queen was aware of all that had been going on in town, and also seemed suspicious about the relation-ship between Blake and Ryan. That made sense, considering her and her twin's involvement in the necromancer situation. They'd learned a fair amount about Blake and the dungeon during that time, while they were still part of the Adventurers' Guild and serving under Marcus.

"The next time anyone gets to go off on secret training, I want in," Jack grumbled as they exited Boneville. Blake was surprised the Duelist had kept his mouth shut this long.

"Why? You've got enough experience to reach Platinum Five," Matt responded. It was no secret to the party that Emily and Matt had been off training in the God of Fire's dungeon. What caught them all by surprise was the gear the two had returned in. Gear the Duelist clearly envied.

"It's not about the experience, man." Jack motioned towards Matt's form, the Duelist's eyes running up and down the man's armor. "It's about that gear." Matt, the group's Platinum 5 arcane archer with a Water affinity, had previously been wearing the sapphire-studded leather gear that was the norm for arcane archers. Now, Matt was wearing a blood red set of armor covered in overlapping crimson scales. Scales which looked incredibly similar to the scales Blake had seen on Cynder when she transformed into her juvenile form. Dragon scales.

The armor, which covered Matt from head to toe, looked really, really cool. Especially the open-faced helm, which had a set of dragon horns rising out of it. On top of that, Blake could see countless sapphires embedded in the armor, glowing a faint blue. Maybe that armor wasn't ultra-rare, but it was definitely rare, and far better than regular class gear.

"Oh, this?" Matt smirked as he looked over his form. "What's so special about this?"

"Dude. How lucky are you? You got full dragon scale armor, with a ton of gems embedded into it! Did you sacrifice Blaine to the dungeon?"

The group chuckled, though Matt and Emily's laughter was a bit strained at that. Blaine was their older brother and the heir to the Dragnov family. Their father, nicknamed the

Duke of Blood, was one of the strongest humans in the world, a Diamond 3 individual known particularly for his love of fighting and killing. He had tried, and failed, to have Matt killed twice now.

According to Matt and Emily, they had run into Blaine during the Cult of Chaos's attack on Boneville, after Blake had left the party following Marissa's defeat. Blaine had come to the town's aid and had been pivotal in helping keep it safe. Apparently, their elder brother had been intrigued by Matt's ability to continually escape death. Blaine had informed the two he would leave them alone, as long as they could continue to grow stronger and stay away from their father. And, of course, they didn't use the family's name. The two were quick to agree, but neither trusted Blaine.

"Actually, it was just rare gear when it dropped." Matt looked from Jack to Emily. "I had to commission some craftsman to put in the sockets and inlay the sapphires into it. Which was not cheap." The arcane archer pointed to Emily. "If there's anyone you should be jealous of, it's her."

At this, Emily offered Jack a smirk. The once shy Emily had grown bolder and more confident, both as a result, Blake figured, of her time spent with the rest of the party and her ever growing powers. It probably also didn't hurt that she was now a Platinum 5 summoner with a dragon at her beck and call. A dragon was the rarest, most powerful Fire summon someone could ever receive. It was quite obvious she had the favor of the God of Fire, especially considering he continued to allow her to train within his dungeon—something unheard of.

"I don't know what you're talking about." While Matt's armor was impressive and made Blake more than a little jealous, Emily had undergone an even greater change. She had previously been fitted with typical Fire affinity mage-class gear: Crimson silk robes, fine quality boots, a ruby pendant, and a special ruby circlet designed for her by Ryan. Now…she was, in something on a whole different level.

Gone was her fine silk cloth. In its place was something Blake could only describe as a mixture between a dress and a robe. It was scarlet in color, and yet Blake couldn't guess at the material it was made of. As Emily walked, the colors shifted just right, making her form seem to be ablaze. Around both her forearms she had fine golden metal, twisting and turning, forming the visage of flames. Each of these metal pieces had a perfect ruby fitted in the middle. Around her neck she had a large piece of golden jewelry in the shape of a dragon in flight. Its entire form was adorned in small rubies imitating scales. The only piece of original gear she'd held onto was the circlet Ryan had made for her.

"Uh-huh. So, you're telling me, finding a random chest with *all*," her brother motioned once again towards her as he spoke, "of that in it was just luck?" Matt had a point. Emily definitely seemed to be favored quite highly by the God of Fire.

Emily looked like she wanted to say something. A twinkle in her eyes said she knew something about that chest, but she held her tongue. Instead, she smiled sweetly towards her brother as they continued on their way. Whatever secrets she had about the God of Fire's dungeon, she wasn't sharing.

"It's common for dungeons to only drop gear of their own affinity. You should be grateful the Bone Dungeon has given you an ultra-rare scimitar with your affinity despite being a Darkness dungeon," Karan said aloud, drawing the topic away from Emily. As she said that, Jack flinched, and shot a glance towards her.

"Oy, don't tell the dungeon —"

"Is that so?" Ryan's voice came from the pendant around Blake's neck, causing the party to flinch. Of course Ryan was eavesdropping on them. Why wouldn't he be? They were still walking over portions of land under his influence. "I'll keep that in mind."

"Well, now you've done it," Jack grumbled, his hand tracing along the wolf-head scimitar he had received from Ryan. Before Emily's arrival, Blake and Jack had been the only two members of the party with ultra-rare gear. And now it seemed they may have lost their chance at additional ultra-rare gear; at least the kind tailored to their appropriate affinities.

Luckily, there were ways to change the affinity of gear. The process was costly though, and had a chance of failure, which would destroy the gear. Few people ever actually pursued that route. Instead ultra-rare and above items were more often traded with one of the large organizations, such as the Adventurers' Guild or the Mages' Guild, whose members would swap around gear that didn't work with their affinity.

Still, such gear was, well, ultra-rare. Just because you had an ultra-rare piece, didn't mean the guild would have one suited for you. Considering Ryan's dungeon was now the only one still open, save for the dungeons of the Gods…if he stopped dropping gear of different affinities, many adventurers may begin to have a hard time getting ultra-rare gear appropriate for their affinity and class. The supply chain was going down, but demand was about to get way up.

"I'm sure Ryan won't just stop dropping gear of different affinities. He's a different type of dungeon, after all," Blake said aloud. He had the best relationship with Ryan, and he knew the dungeon was constantly trying to prove how it was exceptional. Maybe he could guilt Ryan into keeping his loot drops the same? It was worth a shot. But if Ryan heard, he didn't acknowledge Blake's statement.

"Gear aside." Emily cleared her throat as she spoke, the party now far enough away from Boneville that they couldn't see it. "Do you want to see something that will really make you jealous, Jack?" As she spoke, Cynder, who up till then had been resting lazily along Emily's shoulders in her baby form, let out an excited cry and spread her wings.

"What could possibly —" Jack's words caught in his throat. Cynder, who moments before had been perhaps the size of a large cat, or a small dog, had taken flight and begun glowing red. As the dragon climbed in the air above them, her form began to grow. This wasn't the first time they had seen her transform. When Emily had hit Gold, Cynder had gained the ability to transform into a juvenile dragon, the size of a large horse. Now, Cynder was continuing to grow, far larger than her juvenile form.

"Okay. I quit," Jack grumbled. Cynder let out a triumphant cry. It was no longer a high-pitched, cute sound. Instead it was fearsome. The roar of a powerful, magnificent beast of destruction. Cynder's form had to be at least twenty, perhaps thirty, feet in length. And if she were on the ground with them, Blake would guess her shoulder-height would have been at least ten feet. What's more, her wingspan now was fifty feet across, casting a large, ominous shadow on the ground. Her form had not only grown in size, but her entire body was covered in large, magnificent scales, which looked like palm-sized flames. As she flew above them, the sunlight filtering on her, the dragon's entire body appeared ablaze.

"Allow me to introduce you to Cynder's adult form." Emily's voice was filled with a mixture of pride and amusement. This transformation, the dragon that was now at her command, explained where her newfound air of confidence came from. With Cynder at her side, Emily felt invincible.

Chapter Twenty-Six

It was nearing dusk as they reached the planned meeting place, a valley deep within the woods. They had passed by Ryan's Bone Zone hours before and had stepped past the last bit of strangely glowing land, which marked Ryan's influence, about an hour ago. They were, for all intents and purposes, completely on their own and far away from any known allies.

"No matter what happens," Blake started as his party glanced around. So far, there were no signs of Sasha and her pack. "We leave here together."

The last time Blake had seen the twins, they had both been Platinum 5, and were working to rebuild their wolfkin pack. Sasha and her brother, Rasha, were wolfkin royalty and, if Blake was correct, Sasha was working to create her own wolfkin tribe. If they were still Platinum 5, this would be a lot easier. However, Blake doubted that would be the case. Even though Sasha and Rasha had left the Adventurers' Guild, he'd heard word they were working as mercenaries to help fight against the demonic forces. There was a good chance they'd gotten a lot stronger.

"If we leave here at all," Jack said, his voice dark. "You

know their terms. I either join them, or I die the moment I go Platinum, Blake." The Duelist looked over at Blake, desperation and fear clear on his face. The closer they had gotten to the meeting place, the more withdrawn the easy-going man had become. "Seriously, why are we even doing this? So what if I stay Gold One? Find someone else, replace me. Don't risk your lives just for —"

Karan stopped Jack with a sudden embrace. In a move completely out of character for the reserved cleric, she planted a kiss on his lips. Everyone watched in stunned silence as the embrace continued for a moment before Jack's shoulders slumped in defeat.

"You're bound to me, Jack. Even if it weren't for this—" Karan touched the earring she was wearing, which formed the Duelist bond between her and Jack. The loophole that Jack had come up with when he'd chosen his Duelist class, in order to get around the frenzy a packless wolfkin would undergo otherwise. "I love you. And I need you by my side."

Jack was speechless, his eyes showing the conflicting emotions running through his mind at Karan's display and words. Their relationship had been deep before he had bonded to her. Now, they were inseparable.

"Besides, we need you and Karan to keep getting stronger with us, so we can keep diving the dungeon," Blake added. It may have sounded selfish, but it wasn't. They weren't just a party. These four—Jack, Karan, Matt, and Emily—were his family. And he wanted—no, needed—to do everything he could to keep them together. They were going to deal with this, and deal with it now, so they could keep moving forward.

"I'll make sure Sasha agrees to leave you alone after you reach Platinum, even if I have to use—" Blake's voice caught in his throat, words faltering as his eyes picked up movement in the distance. Massive, dark forms racing with inhuman speed towards them. By his count, there had to be over a dozen of them, though what stood out the most were the two forms in the lead. Before they even got close enough for him to see their souls, he knew who they were, and knew they had gotten stronger.

The rest of the party turned, and watched as the forms approached, the air around them seeming to grow cold, not just as the sun drew lower in the sky, but as the very real potential for conflict made itself clear. They had already discussed that there was a chance Sasha and Rasha would refuse their request. If that happened, they would be forced to clash with the ultimatum Sasha had issued once before. Either Jack joins her pack, or he dies. They would not allow either to happen, meaning the situation would come to blows if the wolfkin refused to hear reason.

"Two can play at intimidation." Blake barely heard Emily's whisper, the words so faint he at first thought he had imagined it. The sudden, excited cry from Cynder proved otherwise. It turned into a deafening roar as the dragon took flight above the group and reassumed her adult form. At the sight of the massive beast circling overhead, the approaching wolfkin pack slowed, then halted. It happened so quick, some of the smaller wolfkin, Bronze Tier by the size of the souls, stumbled, falling over themselves.

The two figures at the front of the pack began to shift back into their human forms, the deadly forms of the twins, Sasha and Rasha. Behind them, their pack followed suit. As the wolfkin began making their way toward Blake's party, they began walking as well. The groups met in the middle of the valley, Cynder's shape casting a growing shadow as she circled above. The approaching pack had been intimidating... but Blake had to hand it to Emily, the adult dragon was downright terrifying.

"I cannot tell you how happy it makes me to once again

see you, Jack." Sasha was the first to speak as the group met up. She was still dressed as she had last been, in her dark leather assassin's gear, the strange circlet with the opal inset atop her head. Rasha was wearing his gear too, the leather armor with the wolf's head on the chest piece inlaid with onyx. If it weren't for the fact Blake could see the large mass of Dark mana swirling within each of them, he would have assumed they were still Platinum 5.

"And—" Sasha's eyes moved from Jack to look Blake over. Her eyes traced along his form, pausing for a moment on his chest, where the wolf-head ring from his father rested. The wolfkin Queen licked her lips and smiled sweetly at Blake. "It is an even greater pleasure to see you've continued to grow, Blake." Come to think of it, Sasha had shown interest in him during their last encounter. With everything that had gone on, and his worry over Jack's situation...he'd forgotten the Duelist wasn't the only one Sasha had her eyes on.

At her words, Rasha let out a low growl. The male assassin now glaring at Blake. While Sasha claimed she was happy to see him, Rasha most certainly wasn't. Then again, Rasha didn't like anyone. The male assassin almost always seemed to ooze bloodlust.

"Now then, we have met as was requested." Sasha pulled her gaze from Blake so that she could look over their party. It seemed she was doing her best to ignore the circling dragon overhead, though Blake could see the rest of her pack, a mixture of Bronze, Silver, and Gold wolfkin, glancing up cautiously at Cynder. "Have you come to hand over Jack? Or is there another reason for this meeting?"

The tone of her voice shifted from pleasant and sweet to low and threatening. She knew exactly what the point of the meeting was. Blake had no doubt she had been gathering information on him and the others even while away. She'd made it no secret in the past she was interested, for wolfkin reasons and traditions, in Jack's fate. And, while Blake still didn't know why, she had an interest in him as well.

"I think we both know why we're here." Blake tried his best to remain calm, keeping his tone as neutral as he could. He respected Sasha and Rasha. They had saved his life in the past and had played a huge role in keeping the dungeon town safe when Viktor the Necromancer had attacked. It was no secret that during the demon attack on the Bone Dungeon, their pack had been the one to overcome the cultists and close the portal that was launching demons towards the Bone Zone, while Blaine and the adventurers fought against the demon horde. Because of this, Blake really didn't want conflict with them. He wanted to keep this as civil as possible.

Sasha looked him over, her eyes flashing golden, taking on their lupine aspect as she grinned. "I've got more than a few reasons to be here. All of which should prove to be..." She let out a growl. "Entertaining."

For a moment Blake had to fight the urge to reach for his weapon. The way she said that, the way she looked at him, the hunger there, it made him uneasy. Her mana showed she had to be at least Platinum 3 by now, as was Rasha. Blake was stronger than either of them, one on one. He didn't know what their wolfkin forms would do for their powers, nor did he know what they had planned. Either way, though he may technically be the strongest one among the three, he couldn't help but feel uneasy. Something was going on, something his instincts were trying their hardest to warn him about.

"I've asked Jack to set up this meeting so that you will allow him to become Platinum without forcing him to join your pack," Blake responded, even as the hairs on his neck began standing up.

Sasha smiled, her fangs growing in her mouth. It was as if

she were beginning her transformation without even realizing it. Unsettling, to say the least.

"As I said before, Blake. The old laws must be followed. Jack Silverfang must join a pack and must bond to an Alpha, else he will be killed the moment he becomes Platinum Five." She licked her lips, her smile widening. "As Queen, I must uphold our ways. My hands are tied." The group of wolfkin behind her began letting out howls; long, mournful howls.

"Unless." She raised a hand, silencing the howling behind her. Sasha let the silence hang in the air for a moment. "As Queen, I could forgo this decision, if it were for the betterment of the pack. I could allow Jack to continue on his way, despite the danger, if the pack gained something greater out of it. But it would need to be something *quite* valuable," Her eyes bore into Blake. "Would you join the pack and stand by my side in his stead?"

Everything seemed to pause for a moment, even as Blake felt an immense amount of bloodlust roll towards him from Rasha. The male twin glared daggers at him. If looks could kill, Blake would have died many times over. To his credit, or perhaps, to show the amount of control Sasha now wielded over the pack, Rasha remained silent.

"What do you say, Blake?" As she spoke, Sasha closed the last few feet between the two of them, her golden eyes glowing with excitement. As she reached him, she placed a hand gently on his chest, just over the wolf-head ring, and looked up at him. Her next words came out in a quiet whisper but echoed the loudest in Blake's ears.

"Help me rebuild the clans your bloodline slaughtered."

Chapter Twenty-Seven

Blake stood there, dumbstruck, as he looked at Sasha. What in the name of the Goddess was she talking about? What did she mean by the clans his bloodline had slaughtered? What was going on?

"I —" Blake paused, trying to find the words. He glanced around at everyone, wondering if they'd heard what she had said. If they had, no one was saying anything. Everyone was just looking towards him and Sasha. Jack was staring at Sasha, his face a mixture of disbelief and rage. Karan and Matt looked surprised, and Emily had covered her mouth, eyes wide with shock. None of it was helping Blake at all with the situation.

"What?" He reached up and grabbed Sasha's hand, trying best he could to gently pull it away. She tugged for a moment on the ring, flashing him a wink, before she let go and stepped back.

"Is that a no, then, Blake?" Her voice, her features, spoke of legitimate disappointment. Sadness, almost.

"Of course it's a no," Blake started. He was caught off-guard, out of control, and he didn't like it. Sasha knew something about his family that he didn't. That made this situation even more unsettling. "I could never leave my party, my family. And while I would do anything I could to keep them safe, I also know I cannot keep them safe if I leave them behind." His eyes narrowed on Sasha, who was watching him carefully. He couldn't get a read on her. "And speaking of family, what do you know about mine?"

"Perhaps if you join me, I will tell you." She turned her head slightly, watching him. When it was apparent he wasn't going to change his mind, she let out a heavy sigh. "Still no?" She shrugged. "I can respect keeping those you care about safe, Blake. You've always been so honest. So straightforward. Even without your past, it's part of what makes you so..." she grinned back at him, "intriguing. In fact, as the leader of my own pack, I share a similar sentiment. I must do everything I can to keep my pack, my family, safe. Trust me, I understand."

"Sadly," Sasha continued as she stepped back to stand beside Rasha, who was practically shaking from bloodlust. "That means we are at an impasse. I know the dungeon has reopened and I heard of Brook's fate. Obviously, this meeting is to ensure Jack can ascend to Platinum so that your party can begin diving the dungeon and grow stronger. Am I wrong?"

"No," Blake stated. Now was not the time to worry about the link between the wolfkin and his bloodline. All that mattered was leaving here alive and as a full party, with the freedom for Jack to become Platinum. "You are correct. All we seek is you allow us to continue as we have, and allow Jack to ascend. Surely he's proven he will not be a threat, he will not tarnish the wolfkin- —"

Sasha held up a hand, stopping him short. "I don't need you to detail his actions to me. I've kept quite the tab on our young pup there. As such, out of respect for him and your urge and passion to keep your family together and safe, I will offer you one final chance. Though I warn you, you may not like what it entails."

"What is it?" Blake knew he wasn't going to like whatever it was. But a part of him had known he wouldn't be able to settle this matter simply. Sasha had been dead serious when she warned them, back when she gave Jack the earrings to bond to Karan, that she would not be able to turn a blind eye to his actions if he were to ascend to Platinum. The earring, the pass for him at Gold, was for his actions and efforts in the past, and because of a debt Sasha felt was owed to the party. This time, Blake's side didn't have any bargaining chips to sway events in their favor, other than Sasha's strange obsession with Blake. But that option was not on the table.

"There is a wolfkin tradition." As she began Blake noticed Rasha's demeanor completely change. The male twin suddenly seemed to calm as a satisfied look crossed his face. "Which was established to settle matters between differing clans."

"I'm listening," Blake responded, prompting her to continue.

"In an effort to keep casualties down, the leaders of various wolfkin packs devised a tradition. The leaders of the packs, those with a royal bloodline, along with a chosen ally, would fight, two versus two in a duel. The two from each side would represent the entire pack and the outcome of the duel would be respected by both sides. Jack, having the blood of Silverfang running through his veins, can partake in this tradition."

Rasha was now grinning towards Jack, and Blake didn't even have to guess what had the assassin so excited. The idea of fighting against Jack in a duel was bringing Rasha no small amount of excitement. Jack, on the other hand, had paled. The Duelist was glancing wide-eyed from Blake to the twins.

"What does Silverfang have to do with this?" Jack's voice was hoarse. The first time Blake had ever heard the name had been when Sasha mentioned it the last time they met. Afterwards, Jack had informed Blake and the party that Silverfang had been his father's name. Apparently Jack's father had been a wolfkin who abandoned his pack after falling in love with a human woman. Jack hadn't told the party anything else on the matter, other than the fact both his parents were dead.

"Silverfang was a prince. He carried in him the royal blood of one of the original wolfkin clans. You too are a royal, though your half-blood nature has diluted some of the additional powers wolfkin royalty would offer you," Sasha responded coolly.

Now, everyone went from staring at Blake to staring at Jack. The Duelist was caught off-guard by that, plain as day.

"If I'm royalty...then can't I be my own Alpha?" He looked at Sasha, his eyes hopeful. That would make their lives easier. If Jack could be Alpha to his own pack, then they wouldn't be in this situation. It wasn't going to be that easy, though.

Sasha shook her head, and this time, she really looked sad about her response. "Your father tried to argue the same point. He even took on the same offer I'm going to offer you; if he won the duel, we would have let him live free, allowed to stay with his family and his young son. However, he didn't have the strength to stand by his convictions...and he was put down."

"But," Sasha continued even as a strange set of emotions rolled over Jack's face. If Blake had to guess, the Duelist hadn't known the cause of his father's death. And from the sound of it...the cause was standing before them. "If you and your chosen ally can defeat Rasha and I in a duel, in accordance with wolfkin laws, you would prove your power and your ability. You would show you are worthy of being an Alpha and I, as wolfkin Queen, will then permit you to live your life as you see fit."

While a duel against the twins wasn't a favorable option, they didn't have any other choice. "If he accepts and we lose, what happens?" Blake asked. Jack was working through a torrent of emotions, so Blake took the lead on the negotiations.

"If Jack and his ally lose, then, per the tradition, I may make one demand of the losers, which they must agree to, no matter what" She looked hungrily at Blake. "I'm sure you know what that means. If he and his ally lose the duel, then I will demand both of you join my pack."

"There's no way." Jack looked from Sasha to Blake. His eyes were practically pleading. "Blake. Let's just drop it. I'll," he paused and looked back at Karan, his throat catching for a moment before he continued, "join the pack, and then the four of you can leave. There's no reason for us to do this. There is no way we defeat the two of them. Maybe if I were Platinum, it would be fair. But I'm only Gold One."

Blake looked from his friend to Karan. The cleric was looking at Jack, her eyes filled with love. Through their bond, they could feel each other's emotions, and Blake could only wonder at the turmoil that was going on through both of them. He was feeling his own fair share of emotional turmoil as well.

Still, this was the only way. It was more of an opportunity than he had expected, and he was going to take it. He couldn't help but feel the doubt slowly creeping into his mind; what would happen if they failed?

If they lost this battle, it would be the end of everything he'd worked so hard to achieve. Regardless, being an adventurer meant living life on the edge. It was taking gambles and risks. Besides, it wasn't as if Blake was powerless. He was stronger than either of the twins. At Platinum 4, he was technically stronger than a regular Platinum 1 adventurer. Surely, he could take them both on, even if Jack was only Gold 1.

"Let's do it, Jack." He looked Jack dead in the eyes, doing his best to bolster his friend's confidence. "I'll be your ally in the duel. Together, we can do this."

"But —" Jack started, but Blake held up his hand.

"You're not just Gold One, Jack. You heard her. You're Gold One wolfkin royalty. Besides, you know how capable I am."

"Right." Jack took a deep breath before he turned to Sasha, his face set with determination. "Blake and I accept your duel."

As Jack said the words, the wolfkin standing behind Sasha and Rasha began howling once again and started to change into their wolfkin forms. Now that Blake looked over them, he could see they all had forms that, while larger than Jack's wolfkin form had been at Bronze and Silver, were smaller than Jack's form at Gold. While Jack may not have been aware of his bloodline, he had been reaping some of the benefits that came with it.

"Very well." Sasha's eyes twinkled with excitement even as her form began to ripple. Silver fur began sprouting from her body as her muscles began to grow larger. Beside her, Rasha transformed as well. While they did, the rest of their pack began spreading out, giving the group a large berth.

"Once your friends have gotten a safe distance away, we can begin this fight." Sasha made a motion towards the rest of Blake's party, signaling for them to step away just as her pack had. Blake offered a nod of assurance towards his party members, and they started walking away, albeit with a lot more hesitation and reluctance than Sasha's pack. Karan lingered for a moment, whispering something to Jack.

"Your dragon, too," Sasha called out as Emily and Matt

neared the tree line. Karan was halfway to them as Cynder let out an annoyed roar, before Blake watched the dragon begin shrinking as she flew back toward Emily

"So, what are the terms of this duel?" Jack asked. He had assumed his seven-foot wolfkin form, his body covered in brilliant silver fur. As he spoke, he slowly drew his two scimitars.

"It's really quite simple," Sasha stated. She, like Rasha, didn't wield physical weapons. The assassins seemed to prefer to craft their weapons purely from Darkness mana. Even without that, they both had formidable and deadly natural weapons thanks to their teeth and claws. After all, they both stood nearly twelve feet in height, dwarfing Jack and Blake.

"The first side to have both their combatants unable to fight, loses," Rasha picked up where his twin had left off, his eyes raised, mouth drawn back to show his teeth. "Anything and everything goes. Though I promise I'll try not to kill either of you." Oh yeah, he wanted this fight. The male wolfkin was more than a little excited about this. Beside him, Sasha seemed amused. What went on in her mind? Blake couldn't get a read on the wolfkin Queen.

"What's the signal to start?" Blake asked as he prepared himself. He readied his shield in his left hand and drew the rare sword he kept at his side. He thought about drawing his legendary sword, but decided against it. He still didn't know what powers it had, which meant that other than being extremely sharp and durable, it didn't offer him any additional perks.

Sasha pointed towards one of her wolfkin followers, a brown-furred, Gold Tier wolfkin. The wolfkin leaned back and started a long howl. "When the howl stops, the fight will begin."

As she said that, Darkness mana began swirling around

the twins. It was well into dusk now, the diminishing sun casting long shadows across the valley. Even as the howl continued, their forms seemed to begin to fade; a mixture of the low light and their assassin abilities. With their Darkness affinity, and the skills granted to them by their class, a dimly lit or dark battlefield was ideal. It was too perfect. Blake's suspicions were confirmed: this had been Sasha's plan all along.

"Let's do this, Jack," Blake said to his friend even as he called forth mana, covering his shield in darkness as the rare sword burst to life with golden light. No matter what, he wasn't about to lose. Not here, not now. He had his family to protect, and that was exactly what he was going to do.

The howling stopped, and the fight began.

Chapter Twenty-Eight

During his time with Alice, Blake had been doing more than just helping the Guildmaster and researching the Cult of Chaos and its demons. He had been practicing, training with Alice and others whom she trusted, to hone his abilities. On top of that, Blake had spent his free time reading about the various classes. As a party leader it was his job to fully understand the ins and outs of different classes, as well as their abilities. Luckily, the Adventurers' Guild had a vast amount of resources at its disposal. And even as he looked up information on his teammate's classes and their abilities, there was one other thing he put a lot of focus into. Following the assassination attempt on Matt's life, Blake wanted to know everything there was about assassins.

The first thing he knew about them was that theirs was a class built on speed and precision, similar to Jack's Duelist class. Considering they both stemmed from the thief class, it made sense. Because of that, Blake knew that, in general, assassins would always be faster than he was, even if they were of an equal level and mana. His class, stemming from the knight tree, amplified his strength and overall constitution more than his speed. He wasn't slow by any means, but the assassin class would have the advantage. Just as he would be able to overpower them when it came to tests of strength or endurance.

Second, Blake knew assassin skills and training focused much more on operating from the shadows and striking from your enemy's blind spots than other classes did. The whole purpose of the class was to bring enemies down without being seen or noticed. To get to an enemy's weak spot and kill them before the fight even began. They were highly skilled in their lightning-fast strikes, and always struck with deadly precision. Their class, therefore, had abilities that worked to allow such attacks to be made. It depended on the type of mana affinity an assassin had, to determine how the assassin would accomplish their goal.

For instance, all assassins could form weapons from their mana. The favorite type of weapon was a dagger. The less gear and equipment an assassin was utilizing, the easier it was for them to fade in and out of combat. Those with Wind affinity could utilize Wind mana to make their form fade away, as if their body were made of air. Fire affinity assassins could distort their physical forms utilizing intense heat, causing mirages to appear on a battlefield, enhancing confusion and allowing them to strike unnoticed. Darkness mana assassins were the deadliest. As long as there were shadows in an area, a Darkness mana assassin could sink into the shadows, completely disappearing. It was a skill known as Shadow Step.

Because he knew this, he was not surprised when the two wolfkin in front of him completely disappeared. At least, their bodies did. Jack couldn't see any sign of the two, and the Duelist was grasping his swords tightly as his wolfkin eyes scanned around the area. Because Jack was still Gold, he didn't have the Wind aura that he would have at Platinum.

Meaning he didn't have the, near-supernatural ability to detect approaching enemies, like what Marcus continually displayed. Luckily for Jack, he wasn't fighting alone because if he were, he'd be dead. Blake, with his constant ability to see souls, could easily track the twins even as they moved from shadow to shadow.

"Behind you," Blake called out as Rasha's form erupted from Jack's shadow, twin daggers in hand. The assassin was striking with deadly speed, and even with Blake's warning, the Gold 1 duelist was barely able to block the attack, even with his lightning fast reflexes. Had Jack been any other class than a Duelist, he would have fallen right there. But Duelists excelled at one-on-one combat. Their forte was the exchange of blows, rapid strikes, parries, and dodges. Long as Jack knew where the attacks were coming from, he would be able to survive...if only just. There was a small line of crimson on his silver fur, showing the shadowy dagger, aimed for his back, had managed to score a cut, albeit a shallow one.

"You should be more worried about yourself." Sasha's voice came from behind Blake even as the wolfkin sprang from his shadow. He'd known where Sasha was, and wasn't terribly worried about her attack. Afterall—

"Why? Can you even strike me?" As Blake spoke, his mana converged within and he spent the 75 mana points to make himself go ethereal. At the same time, he stepped backwards, passing harmlessly through Sasha as the wolfkin Queen and her dagger burst through his incorporeal form. It was a strange sensation, a tingling over his entire body, as she passed through him. He knew, from painful trial and error, that if he dropped his ethereal form while within something solid, he would be painfully expelled. It was agonizing and destructive, for not only himself but whatever he was within at the time. His left hand, which he'd tested the process out with, had been shattered, his gauntlet mangled, when he tried it for the first time. And when he tried it with a common sword, the blade had been shattered.

Sasha let out a growl, both annoyed and amused, as her form dove back into the shadows. He watched her soul move seamlessly from shadow to shadow as she pulled back to plan her next attack. Just like his Spectral Form, shadow stepping took mana to not only activate, but utilize. That was the one area the wolfkin had an advantage on Blake. Utilizing his ethereal mana, which needed equal parts Dark and Celestial mana, meant his skills cost him double what they normally would. If they kept toggling abilities back and forth, he would run out of mana before they did. He needed to be careful about how he used his mana.

"To your right," Blake called out as he rushed towards Jack. The Duelist spun effortlessly, the Wind mana whipping around him and accelerating his spin, as Rasha appeared from the shadows, striking at Jack's side. Again, Jack parried the blows, but again, he was left with a set of shallow wounds. Rasha was a deadly assassin, Platinum Tier, and had his already impressive physical abilities amplified by his wolfkin form. If Jack had been human, even as a Duelist, he would have been incapacitated already. Even if he were a normal wolfkin, he would have fallen. According to Sasha, Jack had enough royal wolfkin blood to give him some sort of an edge. If only Blake knew what type of edge that was. Mysteriously, there wasn't much information on the wolfkin at the Adventurer's Guild.

"You know you can't win this." Sasha' voice came from the shadows once more, the wolfkin having again approached him, though she remained in the shadows. He had his Ethereal mana ready, prepared for her next strike. But she waited, whispering from the shadows. He was almost next to Jack, his intention to help the Duelist take down Rasha so they could work on Sasha together.

"Losing isn't an option," Blake replied. It really wasn't. There was no way he would let Jack and himself become Sasha's prey. No matter what the wolfkin Queen thought, they would win this fight.

"Sometimes, losing is inevitable." Her soul, a swirling bit of darkness, seemed to pause. A second later, it was no longer by Blake's side; instead, it was directly underneath Jack. At the same time, Blake saw Rasha's form erupting from the shadows, charging directly at Jack. The Duelist was grinning, his weapons swirling with Wind mana, as he readied himself.

"Jack, no —" Blake wasn't going to get there in time. Sasha's assassin abilities gave her a huge mobility edge on Jack. Of course, that was why he had started rushing towards his friend. He needed to be by Jack's side, to act as best he could as a tank.

"Wha —" The Duelist glanced out of the corner of his eye and saw that Blake was looking at the shadows underneath Jack. Even as he processed what was going on, it was too late. He had prepared himself for Rasha's attack, the male assassin already just a few feet away. It would be impossible to avoid Sasha's attack now. Already, Blake could see the hints of her clawed fingers emerging from underneath Jack, reaching for his ankles. She was going to pin him in place, so that Rasha could take him down. And then it would be two versus one, a fight that Blake was certain he couldn't win.

Think. The world seemed to slow as Blake rushed forward, adrenaline pumping through him. There had to be something he could do. *Think.* His Celestial mana shields wouldn't work well against Darkness attacks. His taunt wouldn't be able to get both wolfkin in time, still leaving Jack in danger. He had one other option. A skill Alice had helped him develop. Without another thought, he sent a massive rush of Ethereal mana from his body.

The grey mana rolled off him, moving at the speed only mana could. Faster than the twins or Jack could react. Everything the mana touched became colorless and distorted. Just as Sasha's hands gripped at the Duelist's ankles, as Rasha brought both his shadow daggers down in an overhead arc towards Jack, just as Jack brought his own scimitars up to block, even as his footing was about to be ripped from him, Blake's Ethereal mana reached his party member.

In that split second, Jack's entire form faded from existence as his body became Ethereal. Rasha's two daggers passed harmlessly through, and Sasha instantly lost her grip.

Blake skidded to a stop as an intense focus of hatred suddenly rested upon him. Rasha hadn't stopped. The wolfkin reacted instantly, showing his extensive amount of experience in fighting. The wolfkin spun, landing on all fours, and leapt towards Blake. At the same time, Sasha soul reappeared underneath Blake, ready to strike. They had failed their attack on Jack but were already launching a new double strike against Blake.

"Oh no, you —" He planted himself and prepared for their attacks. The moment they turned their attention away from Jack, he dropped the Ethereal mana on the Duelist. The ability, which he called his Spectral Zone, cost him twice as much per person he applied it to, as when he did it on himself. Meaning a skill that normally only cost him 75 points of mana, had just cost him 150 points of mana to activate on Jack. The cost to maintain it, which was normally 3 mana a second, was also doubled, per additional person.

"Don't?" Sasha's voice was low as Darkness mana sprung towards Blake from all sides, countless daggers of darkness launching themselves towards him from the ground all around. Another assassin tool, the ability to create a nearly endless rain of attacks to overpower an enemy's defenses. It was a skill that let the assassin attack from 360 degrees, launching attack after attack on their foe. From what Blake had read, each dagger only cost a single point of mana. They weren't overly powerful, but they weren't meant to be; it was a quantity over quality tactic, as the daggers were still potent enough to inflict a wound. And while one or two wouldn't do much against a physically sturdy class like Blake's, dozens or hundreds would.

The twins had him figured out. As he flickered his form back into its ethereal state, Sasha once again shifted herself. Her barrage of attacks stopped on him and the shadows around Jack began launching attacks as well. The Duelist began moving in a blur as his scimitars worked around him, his form twisting and turning in an elegant dance to block the rain of daggers. Additionally, his Wind mana swirled around his wolfkin form, intercepting Darkness daggers as they neared his fur. Still, the twins, at Platinum 3, had a lot of additional mana to spend on these abilities. And because Blake's Ethereal skills cost double the mana, he was limited to the mana pool of a Platinum 4 adventurer. He couldn't keep Jack and himself safe at the same time. He didn't have the mana to do so.

Besides, he was fighting with a handicap. Death knights, the standard version of a Darkness affinity elemental knight, normally specialized in defensive abilities. Their abilities to block attacks, absorb damage, and deal with their enemies, were some of the best among the elemental knights. However, that was only because of what they could do with their Darkness mana. Or, more so, what they could normally do. Death knights specialized in manipulating bones and portions of fallen enemies or mobs, to create a never-ending supply of defensive and offensive material. Out here, on this field, Blake was without access to these resources. That was why Cane, his death knight mentor, had insisted on layering his armor in bone fragments and carrying around a bag full of bones.

Blake didn't have access to the full range of his Dark mana abilities. While he could make Celestial shields and barriers, they wouldn't do much against Darkness mana. Celestial mana and Darkness mana were opposites, which gave them advantages and disadvantages against each other. Darkness mana could cut through Celestial mana, and Celestial mana could cut through Darkness mana. Creatures of the opposing type took more damage due to this...which was why Blake's Holy Smite skill worked so well on Darkness mobs.

Sadly, that didn't help in this situation. His Ethereal skills had the inherent weakness of costing him too much mana. The biggest downside of using a dual affinity mana, was the skills took equal parts of his Celestial and Darkness mana to utilize. Making them too draining to spam for this fight. As much as he thought about it, he started to realize if he and Jack didn't do something drastic now, they were going to lose this match. They needed to go on the offensive.

"Holy Smite!" Blake let out a loud roar of frustration as he drove his sword into the ground. The Celestial mana he'd shrouded his blade in burst outwards, chasing away all of the shadows for a moment. Sasha's rain of shadow daggers disappeared as she emerged from the shadow she'd been hiding in, the shadow having been pushed away by the blast of light.

Rasha let out a howl of pain and surprise as the world suddenly lit up. Jack knew to close his eyes the moment Blake had yelled out his ability, having learned from being blinded himself in the dungeon, just how bright the skill was. Rasha, who had been watching for Blake to drop out of his Spectral form, had launched an attack even as Blake activated his skill. When Blake's sword dug into the ground, his form had become corporeal, allowing Rasha to strike across his chest. It was then that the blast had struck his eyes in full.

The blinded wolfkin was atop Blake, grasping him tightly, his claws searching for traction over Blake's plate chest piece. Blake caught the wolfkin in the chest with his shield and pushed with a grunt. The wolfkin was twice his size, and had managed to cut deeply into Blake, though Blake's Celestial mana was already healing the wound. Trying to fling the wolfkin off him was awkward, the beast clawing and snapping at him as he tried.

"I'll kill you," Rasha growled as he snapped towards Blake's neck. Blake responded by instinct, his reactions honed from countless life-or-death situations courtesy of adventuring in the dungeon. He sent a burst of Darkness through his shield, causing it to enlarge, creating a massive shield of mana in its place. At the same time, he ripped his sword from the ground, plunging it into the wolfkin's stomach. As he did, he unleashed another Holy Smite. That, combined with a strong shove, freed him of Rasha.

"I'll kill you," the wolfkin snarled weakly as he landed a few feet away from Blake. The male wolfkin had managed to keep himself from tumbling to the ground and had landed on three of his four limbs. His fur simmered with smoke, blood flowing freely from the wound. It wasn't fatal, yet...but Blake had unintentionally struck the wolfkin with lethal force. Untreated, it was a deadly wound.

In Rasha's right hand, Blake noticed a flash of silver. The wolfkin was holding the chain that held his father's ring. It glinted strangely in the dusk light. Blake leveled his sword at the wolfkin. "Give it —"

"Blake—!" Jack's muffled cry ripped Blake's attention away from Rasha. His eyes widened. The Duelist was pinned on the ground by Sasha, his body covered in countless bleeding wounds. In the few moments it took Blake to deal with Rasha, the wolfkin Queen had launched her attack on Jack. The Gold 1 Duelist, unable to trace her movements as the shadows returned, had been overcome by the Platinum 3 assassin.

"It seems you're going to lose." Sasha grinned and released her grip around Jack's neck as he went limp. A glance at his soul told Blake the Duelist was still alive, but unconscious.

"You won't win this," Blake said. He hadn't turned completely away from Rasha, aware the wolfkin wasn't out of the fight yet. Rasha may have been gravely wounded, but he was still a threat.

"I'll kill you," Rasha growled again, blood and spittle erupting from his mouth as he spoke. A frothy crimson foam was forming around his maw as he stepped toward Blake. Rasha wiped the blood away from his mouth with his right hand, the ring on the chain dangling, taunting Blake. Blood covered the silver ring, painting it red. As it did, Blake noticed something...impossible. Something he was certain no one else could see.

Somehow, someway, a soul seemed to be emerging from within the ring.

And it was powerful.

Chapter Twenty-Nine

"Wha —" was the only warning Rasha gave that something strange was happening to him. The wolfkin froze mid step, his eyes going wide as they stared past Blake. Sasha froze as well, her eyes darting from her twin to Blake. She could tell something was amiss, but only Blake saw what was happening.

The moment Rasha's blood had coated the ring, Blake had noticed the light of a soul springing to life within the ring. Which, completely baffled him. Blake had carried that ring for a long time, and never had it been anything more than just a ring—a keepsake—from his father. Something his father had passed down to him, an item that once belonged to his grandfather, and his father before him. All it was, was a family heirloom.

And yet, as it was bathed in wolfkin blood, a soul appeared. At first, it had been a faint light, but then it had burst into a brilliant emerald, denoting an Earth affinity. As it flared to life, Blake recognized that the size of it implied a being far stronger than anything he'd ever fought against. The size of the soul signaled it was in the Diamond level of strength. And as quickly as it appeared, it leapt from the ring and into Rasha.

"Rasha?" Sasha's voice was hesitant, questioning, as she looked from her twin back to Blake. Jack was still unconscious on the ground behind her, meaning this was supposed to be the culmination of their duel. Blake was certain Sasha had tasted victory. He was certain she and her twin could have brought him down, given their combined might, even if Rasha was gravely injured. But that had been before. Before whatever this was that had sprung to life. Before the soul had taken over Rasha's body.

"Hmmmm." The mass of green mana seemed to pulse from within Rasha's body. Green light began to dance around Rasha's form, crackling and darting around the wolfkin's body like lightning. "Interesting." While it was coming from Rasha's mouth, the words, the very voice, sounded different. "Very interesting." The energy danced along the wolfkin's form, pausing for a moment at the wound. A substance that appeared to be clay appeared around it, stemming the blood flow and patching it up. It wasn't full-on healing, but it was enough to make the wound no longer fatal.

"What did you do to him?" Sasha's voice came out as a growl as she fixed her full gaze on Blake. For the first time ever in his time dealing with Sasha, her gaze was pure rage. As he locked eyes with her, all he could see was murderous intent. The Queen was furious. And it was evident she thought he was the cause of whatever this was.

"I —" Was all Blake got out before Sasha disappeared. Her form melted into the shadows and he saw her soul flash towards him as she erupted from the shadows at his feet. Even as he made his body go Ethereal, preparing himself for the sensation of her passing through his form, the move turned out unnecessary. Sasha was stuck. Vines had sprung from the ground, wrapping themselves taut around her. Even as she had begun to erupt from the shadows, the very ground around her liquified, pulling her back into its clutches, solidifying around her.

"Now, now," the creature that was previously Rasha said calmly. He was still standing there, his eyes calmly watching the events going on. Which was strange in and of itself. Rasha was normally full of anger and rage. Whatever had taken him over was calm and collected. To an almost emotionless degree. "Wolfkin royalty must never lose themselves to emotion," the voice said. If the situation wasn't so dire and confusing, Blake might have laughed. Sure, Sasha was often collected, but Rasha was nothing but emotion.

Sasha turned her head towards Rasha, her ears going back slightly even as she barred her fangs towards her brother. While she couldn't see the creature's soul like Blake could, the power radiating off his body was evident. They were both outclassed. "Who are you, to speak of wolfkin royalty?"

Blake watched the possessed Rasha's eyes light up, the first sign of anything other than calm. He smiled, before responding to Sasha's question. "Mikal Stoneclaw."

Sasha fell silent at his statement. The name didn't mean anything to Blake, but as soon as Sasha heard it, the fight left her completely. Her eyes went from rage to fear. Every bit of her body not covered in vines or stone went slack.

"Impossible," she whispered. She looked at her brother. "You cannot be the original Wolfkin King. He, along with his entire clan, was slaughtered. Your bloodline was wiped from the world by the Church of Justice during the purge."

Mikal nodded toward Sasha. "You are correct. My clan, my family, my pack. All of them, were killed by the followers of the Goddess of Justice. However, it wasn't because of the purge." He blinked and his voice fell. "I was betrayed. My second turned from the path of the wolfkin and sought to overthrow me. He sold out the pack and committed the very crimes that brought about our demise. Through his actions, he singlehandedly doomed my clan and the wolfkin race." Part of Mikal's lip curled up, as the green mana flowing about the wolfkin flashed, the earth at his feet cracking as it did. "But I was given a single chance, so that I might tell my tale to the future wolfkin. So that I might right the wrongs done to the wolfkin."

His eyes turned from Sasha back to Blake, looking him up and down slowly. For a moment, his nostrils flared, as if he were taking in Blake's very scent. "I'm not sure how much time has passed, nor am I aware of the situation going on here. But this young man's ancestor beseeched the Gods to grant me one opportunity at justice. And for that, I owe his family a great debt."

Mikal bowed his head towards Blake.

"Now then." He looked back at Sasha. "Tell me, niece, what is going on? My time is short, and there is much to be discussed." As Mikal spoke, Sasha was freed from her earthly prison.

"I —" Sasha paused. It was rare for her to ever be off-guard, yet here she was, completely unbalanced. This was impossible to follow. What was this Mikal talking about? How long ago did he live? And what did he mean, Blake's ancestor had helped provide him a chance at righting a wrong? Did this have something to do with Sasha's interest in him? Did this all play into whatever she claimed his bloodline had done?

Sasha swallowed hard and then seemed to muster up enough of her old self to continue, in a more formal, wolfkin Queen, manner. "We were in the middle of a duel. In order to settle a matter of dire importance, in accordance with the wolfkin ways."

"And what, may I ask, were the terms of this duel?" Mikal glanced over the rest of the battlefield, taking everything in, including Jack's unconscious form. At that sight, Mikal raised his lip slightly.

"A wolfkin wishing to ascend to Platinum while refusing to join a pack." Sasha said simply.

"Oh?" Mikal's eyes lifted as he smiled, as if amused. The facial reactions were so out of character on Rasha's face. "Go on."

Sasha paused, caught off-guard. From how she spoke of the subject to Jack and Blake, it was a taboo which called for death or an equal type of payment. And yet, this Mikal thought little of the matter.

"As per our laws, he would have to join a pack, or be slain." Sasha's voice turned less certain as she spoke.

"Those weren't my laws," Mikal commented simply. "Those weren't the original laws of the wolfkin."

Sasha stared blankly at Mikal. "But the bloodlust. Without being a member of a pack, a wolfkin is cursed to lose control of themselves."

"Aye. And we deal with those ourselves. But," Mikal held up a clawed finger, "I never made it a law that you had to be in a pack. There were countless solutions towards dealing with the bloodlust. Some swore away their wolfkin forms. Others," he pointed towards Jack's form, "such as that one, took on classes that bound them to individuals, which stopped the bloodlust from taking hold."

"As wolfkin Queen, I —"

"As wolfkin Queen, you are expected to care for all wolfkin, whether they are of your pack or not. As wolfkin royalty, it is your duty to ensure wolfkin are thriving instead of causing trouble in the world. So, tell me, dear niece. Was that half-blood causing the world trouble? Was he bringing shame on the wolfkin race? Because if he was," Mikal's voice deepened, though he didn't seem to lose his composure, "then you should have taken care of him before he ever got this far."

"I —"

"Answer me."

"No," Sasha said quietly. "He's never caused any problems to the wolfkin…But—"

Mikal interrupted once more. "Then why is this a problem? Dear niece, you've been led to believe the wrong laws of our kind. Either that, or you're interpreting them in a way that best fits you and your own clan." He let out a low growl. "But you wouldn't be doing that, would you?"

Sasha stayed quiet, her eyes drifting towards the ground. It was clear who the Alpha was in this situation.

Mikal turned toward Blake. "Tell me young one. What were the terms of the duel?"

Chapter Thirty

Blake didn't like the attention being back on him. But, while he was still uncertain of what was going on, he could tell, at least for now, Mikal was an ally. And the lull in the fighting at least allowed him to replenish the mana he'd been exerting during the fight. However, he also noticed a figure was approaching the group. A figure Blake had hoped to never see again. A reaper was coming for a soul, and if Blake had to guess, it was here to collect Mikal's. They were running out of time.

"If my friend Jack and I defeated Sasha and her twin in the duel, we would be allowed to continue on without fear of repercussions from Sasha and her clan Jack would be allowed to climb to Platinum without needing to join their pack." As Blake responded, he could feel Sasha's glare directed towards him.

"And if you lost?"

"Then Jack and I were going to join Sasha's pack." He held eye contact with Mikal, not daring to look towards Sasha.

"Typical of a Shadowclaw." Mikal's voice was calm, but as he said the name, there was an inflection he placed on it that signaled he wasn't fond of that clan name. "While I can tell you truly do care for the wolfkin race, niece, you seem to have inherited that nasty streak of your namesake...the one that put our kind in such dire straits to begin with. The selfish trait that only seeks what is best for yourself and your clan, not the wolfkin as a whole."

He turned and looked over at Sasha and narrowed his eyes. As he did, Blake saw the reaper had finished his approach and was holding out a lantern. Already a small trickle of green mana was flowing into the lantern from the body Mikal was possessing. "After all, your namesake, my younger brother, was the one who brought the Church against the wolfkin in order to get rid of me so he could rule over all the clans."

Sasha shook her head, eyes going wide. "No. Dante Shadowclaw led the wolfkin against the Church following their unprovoked slaughter of the Stoneclaw clan. He vowed vengeance on the Church in response to your death. He aligned the packs under his name to fight against the oppressive Church. It was only through his efforts that our race survived the purge, even if our numbers were broken and we were scattered across the land."

Mikal started laughing. A deep, dark, sad laugh, even as more of his mana flowed from his form and into the lantern the reaper held. His eyes turned from Sasha to Blake, and he tilted his head, noting the direction Blake was looking in. "Can you see him? The reaper? Come to collect my soul after all this time."

Blake nodded in response. He doubted Mikal could see the reaper, but perhaps the powerful creature was able to feel his strength waning.

"My time draws short and I've not the time to regal you

with the full story of what happened. Just know my younger brother framed my clan members because he was not strong enough to defeat me, and he needed me gone, so he could take on the mantle of wolfkin King."

Mikal looked from Sasha back to Blake. "I found out too late about my brother's betrayal. Before I could clear the name of my clan, before I could declare our innocence, we were attacked. The Warriors of Light, as they were called at the time, brought down the swift justice of the Church. Their leader was a man of not only devout faith, but kindness and reason. Before I died, I beseeched him to hear my plea. I could already feel the God of Death collecting my life, but I could not let myself die there. I could not let Shadowclaw get away with his plot."

Mikal's eyes went distant even as more of his soul flowed into the reaper's lantern. "I called out blindly to the God of Death, and the man before me went to pray to his Goddess. He returned, shortly after, with a silver ring." He held up the ring that was still clutched in his hand. "This ring. It would house my soul, locked away in a place not of this world, suspended in time, until the moment when the blood of wolfkin royalty was shed atop it." Mikal chuckled darkly. "Though, I did not expect this to be the situation I was brought back in." He looked at Blake for a moment. "That man was your forefather. It is his blood I sense running through your veins."

"Why–?" Sasha started. "If that was the case…Why was your life not spared? If you were innocent? If your brother was the true culprit behind all of this, why did you die?" Sasha shook her head. "You had powers nearly rivaling those of a God. Why did you let yourself be killed?"

Mikal smiled sadly at Sasha. "That, you already know the answer to. As King, all actions of our kind were ultimately my responsibility. It was my fault that my brother was able to do what he did. It was my fault, my failure, that brought about the death of so many of our kind. And as King, I had to take on the full weight of that blame." More of his mana flowed away from him, and Blake could tell his time was nearly up. "Know this, my niece. The mantle of royalty is a heavy one. Your responsibility now is to all wolfkin, even to those not in your pack."

With those words he fell to one knee, and Blake saw nearly all of his soul was now in the lantern. Mikal coughed and blood came from his lips. The Earth mana he'd been keeping the grievous wound at bay with was gone. "I trust, wolfkin Queen, that you will do what is right." He coughed again and turned back to Blake. "And you. I can already tell, you are doing your bloodline proud." His eyes closed then. The rest of the Earth mana, his very soul, slipped from Rasha's body and into the lantern. The reaper closed the lantern door and began to fade away, taking his prize back to the God of Death.

"Blake," Sasha started, looking from Blake, down to Rasha. Her eyes furrowed, and he could tell she was conflicted. Sasha looked at her unconscious brother, his breath coming in shallow gasps. Now that Mikal was no longer possessing him, his injury was continuing to take its toll. Blake stood there, not quite sure what had happened. Had he not been there, had he not seen what he'd just seen, he wouldn't have believed it had happened.

"None of this makes sense," Sasha said silently. She looked around, her eyes frantic. "Was he really betrayed?" She shook her head. "No, I know he was speaking the truth. I could feel it. But...that means—Things need to change." Her form shifted, changing from that of fierce wolfkin to human. Instead of a proud Queen, Blake saw a different side of her. She seemed lost, uncertain. A single woman, with the weight of an entire race on her shoulders.

"Sasha." Blake couldn't help but feel for her. What they just experienced, what they'd just heard, he couldn't help but feel it drew them closer together. His heart told him he should comfort her, help her. But what could he say, what could he do? Mere moments before, he'd been in a fight for his very life and freedom against her.

He did the only thing he could think of. He walked over to Rasha's collapsed body, his hands glowing with golden mana.

Without another word, Blake healed the wounds he had inflicted on the twin. His mana flowed through the massive creature, healing the internal bleeding, sealing the wound shut. After a few moments, it was as if Rasha had never been injured. And once he'd finished healing the man, he reached down and picked up the silver wolf-head ring, placing it around his neck once more.

"You're free to go," Sasha said, not even looking at Blake. "You and Jack. You're free." Her voice was faint. "Do whatever it is you want." She stood up slowly and walked over towards her brother's unconscious form. "Just, make sure you don't cause me, or the wolfkin, any trouble." At that, she turned her head towards him, her eyes, still conflicted, settling on him for a moment. "Otherwise, I might have to come after you again." At that, she offered him a small smile, and knelt beside Rasha. She gently placed a hand against his massive, wolfkin head. "We've got a lot to think about and uncover, brother," she whispered.

"For what it's worth," Blake said sheepishly. "I've always thought you were doing what was best for your clan. I've always respected you as a leader." He didn't know what else to say. This whole situation had gone from a violent life-or-death fight to awkwardness. Blake wasn't the best in these situations.

Sasha turned back to him and offered him a small smile and a single wink, even though her eyes seemed on the verge of tears. "My offer still stands if you ever want to join the clan. Before, I wanted you for the power you would bring, and as a way to atone for the sins of your predecessor. But now, hearing what your ancestor did for Mikal, I want you in the clan even more."

"Maybe someday," Blake responded jokingly. He didn't really know what else to say, and the awkwardness of the situation had him completely out of his element. Still, he'd accomplished what he'd hoped to. Jack was free to ascend. They could move forward. The final obstacle between his party and their path as adventurers had been cleared. And, it seemed, he'd carried out a legacy of his family line he hadn't even known about.

In the end, everything felt right in the world. After all the bad that had happened in the past year, finally, things were looking up for Blake and his new family.

The Exalted One

"Are you ready for your next task?" He watched the man before him carefully, searching for any sign of doubt or betrayal. His plans were nearly complete. He was in the last phases, the final steps before his goal, his dream, was finally reached.

He needed to be extremely careful about what happened next.

"Being prepared is part of my job description," the cloaked figure responded. He was the only Death's Breath currently living, a Diamond 3 title applied to those with a Wind affinity who had taken on the assassin class. He was also the head of the Assassins' Guild, and one of the deadliest living individuals in the world.

"True. Though I've heard tales lately that your skills may be slipping. Your guild has failed to kill the same individual twice." He smirked at his statement, though the helm he wore would keep the

Death's Breath from seeing it. Still, he was certain the action could be shown through his eyes. He was trying to get a rise from the man. Testing him.

"The first individual who accepted the bribe has paid the price for his failure. As for the second attempt, he was killed." The man shrugged. "The life was gone from his body. Not even a Celestial feather could've brought him back. I take no responsibility past death. A job's a job, and mine was done fully and perfectly." The cloaked man's voice was hard, and while he was doing his best to shrug it off, it was evident that failure was not taken lightly by him. Still, that was a situation outside of his control. The power to bring someone back from the dead was unheard of. It was a power that intrigued the Exalted One to no end. A power he'd never seen before, and he had lived to see Diamond Tier individuals of all affinities and classes. It was a power he intended to claim for his own. But before then, he needed to remove a few more…obstacles…from his way.

"Very well. I expect the same level of professionalism as always from you for the next target." He pulled out a piece of parchment and slid it across the table towards the Death's Breath. The man grabbed the paper and unfurled it, his eyes only showing the slightest hint of surprise at the target. The Exalted One had been using the Assassins' Guild over the years to kill of key individuals, when he needed to, to clear the path for his plans. However, this final target, would go down in history as the most powerful person ever assassinated. Dependent, of course, on the Death's Breath's ability to complete the task. If anyone could do it, it was the man standing before him. And if he failed…that would be troublesome, but the Exalted One was confident he could handle the target in person if he needed to. He just preferred to avoid open combat when possible. Besides, he would have qualms over fighting a fellow Diamond Chaos user. Sadly, the Duke of Blood was an obstacle that needed to be removed. The man would stand against him, if only for the sake of facing off against a powerful foe. The man was bloodthirsty to a fault.

"This is the last one, then?" The Death's Breath looked at him, his eyes searching.

"Indeed. Kill this target and your life will no longer belong to me." He chuckled darkly. "Complete this task, and I will fulfill my promise to you." He had been putting pieces of his plans into place for a long, long time. The Death's Breath was just one of the pieces he'd created a long time ago. Finding an ambitious assassin who longed for power, longed to be at the top of the Assassins' Guild. It had been simple for the Exalted One to help orchestrate the removal of those that stood in the ambitious man's way. With a few pulled strings, he had ensured when the slot of a Wind affinity human to ascend to Diamond was open, The Death's Breath got it. Those slots, three allotted per race, per affinity, were key to controlling the power of the world. It had taken the Exalted One quite a bit of time to secure the power to put those plans in motion. But it had been well-worth it. The Assassins' Guild had served him well for over a decade now.

The cloaked man bowed slightly and disappeared. The Exalted One stood there for a long moment, standing in silence as he congratulated himself for how smoothly everything was going. Now that he'd set everything in motion, it was only a matter of time. Soon, he would have his revenge. Soon, he would stand atop the world. It had been worth taking all this time, all the precautions and preparations, to put himself in the position he was in today. It had taken centuries, but now, he had all the pieces he needed. It had just been a matter of getting the proper…leverage, set up, to have such powerful "allies" in place for his plans.

Speaking of, he grinned and held a hand up in front of him. With a thought he activated the ring he wore on his hand, pulling out a crystalline globe from within his ring of holding. The globe would allow him to see everything that was going on around the crystal attuned to the sphere. The crystal was worn by Marissa at this time, the Succubus out on her latest mission for him. He grinned as he took a seat in his throne, the globe floating before him. From it, he could see Marissa was in place, hiding in the shadows of a dungeon as a party made their way into the heart of it.

The Adventurers' Guild, along with the Church of Justice, had begun sending teams to eliminate all the dungeons which had been corrupted by his Seeds of Chaos. Those teams had met with misfortune of late. A misfortune named Marissa. His Diamond 3 Succubus was making sure his plans ran smoothly. He looked closer into the globe. The party members were making their way past her hiding spot. She was using a variety of legendary and ultra-rare items, gifted by him, to ensure she could complete her task. The mission was the thwarting of the Adventurers' Guild's attempts to destroy the corrupted dungeons, as well as the accumulation of some additional pawns to add to his swelling forces. The Succubus was quite skilled at that particular task. As he scanned the party sent to this dungeon, seeing how many new recruits he was about to have at his disposal, he found himself sucking in a breath.

"Well played, Alice," he said aloud, frustration welling up as he recognized one member in this latest party. It seemed the leader of the Adventurers' Guild was taking extra precautions following the Guild's loses within the dungeons. It really had been helpful that bodies were never expected to be found when someone died within a dungeon. It was the perfect place to make people disappear, without raising suspicion.

It seemed Alice had decided to step up the forces she was sending into the dungeons, to make sure the corrupted dungeons were destroyed. After all, there was no other reason why Monica, the Diamond 3 Death Lord, a Diamond Tier version of an elemental knight with a Darkness affinity, would be accompanying the party on their mission to destroy the dungeon.

"Change of plans, Marissa," he thought, sending the message through the bond they shared. He could feel her dismay, her Succubus nature having been more than a little excited about what she was about to do to the party. Still, her bond to him was absolute, and she had no choice but to obey him. He sent her a small reassurance,

though. They would deal with the Death Lord, soon enough. In a different way, at a different time. After all, he couldn't allow any Diamond Tier individuals to exist who may stand in his way. And Monica would stand against him. However, removing Diamond Tier individuals required a special level of attention.

This would take a little more preparation.

But time was something he had more than enough of.

Chapter Thirty-One

RYAN

"Just go over it one more time." Ryan was looking at his two fairies, his voice stern, as they prepared for another day of adventurers. It had been almost a month since they opened back up, and at last adventurers were going to step foot onto his fourth floor again. Following the death of the Platinum mage, Ryan had overheard countless groups confirming they wanted to train a little more on his third floor before they descended to the fourth.

He couldn't fault them for it. They didn't want to die. And for the most part, Ryan didn't wish any of them ill. Other than a few here and there, such as the man who'd killed him. Sadly, the Zealots of the Church of Justice hadn't yet stepped foot within his dungeon. Meaning he couldn't go about with Operation Justice, as Erin called it, until they did. Sooner or later, though, he would get his revenge.

"I'm not to reveal my presence," Hel started, her voice conveying what she thought of his "rules". Now that the fairies had gained their full mob status they looked completely different. "I'm not to do anything that would result in a pointless party wipe." Hel crossed her arms underneath her chest. She was now a full-fledged Succubus and looked exactly like the demon formerly running the Dungeon of Ashes. Which made sense because she was a clone of that demon.

"And?" Ryan prodded. As a Succubus, she now looked like a full-grown woman, but still had her accompanying black leathery wings, tail, and the slight horns atop her head. As an added bonus, she now had swirling red and black lines spiraling around her body in intricate patterns like some sort of tattoo. They glowed and could be used to enthrall adventurers.

"And, if you call me, I'm to come back immediately," Hel finished the last portion with a heavy sigh. She may have changed outwardly and gained all the powers of a Platinum Tier boss mob, but she was still fragile. As a Succubus, her powers came from manipulating mobs and adventurers. She had the ability to control living things, to enchant them, and bind them to her will. She could make them susceptible to gentle suggestions, further allowing her to toy with her prey. But if she were to be put in the middle of a physical conflict, Ryan and Hel both knew she wouldn't last long. The Succubus was a lover, not a fighter.

"Good, glad we've got that covered." He looked over to Erin who had assumed her final form. Erin too was no longer a mere Celestial fairy. Instead, she had evolved into an angelic form. While Hel had developed a physical appearance that emphasized her traits as a temptress, Erin's transformation had been different. Apparently, Angels were Celestial beings of great power from the Goddess of Justice's mob list. Angels served as an enforcer type of mob for the Goddess of Justice. A mix between a paladin and a cleric.

Erin, who was also now the size of a grown women, had gained more definition and muscle than Hel, and the mana reinforcing her granted her not only increased magical abilities but also increased strength, speed, and physical endurance. The Celestial fairy was now physically stronger than Hel, even though they were both equivalent, mob-wise, to a Platinum Tier Boss.

"How about you, Erin?" Both his fairies were eager to finally take a more active part in the dungeon. But Ryan had made sure to establish some ground rules for the both of them. The last thing he needed was to have either of them— more likely Hel—cause trouble that would bring unwanted attention to his dungeon.

"If the criteria are met, I can offer my aid in the form of healing or a protective barrier on the adventurers for a short amount of time." She started, smiling sweetly towards Hel. The two of them, based on their clashing personalities, had come up with different roles for themselves within his dungeon.

"I cannot, however, intervene if they have not met the appropriate criteria. Nor can I help a party more than once a dive." Erin had wanted to act as a sort of Guardian Angel; a divine figure brought forth to bless the party on behalf of the Goddess of Justice. Ryan wasn't opposed to the idea. Sightings of an Angel within his Bone Dungeon might help keep the Church at bay.

"And...?" Ryan prodded.

"I'm not to allow any adventurer within physical reach of me. And if I am threatened, I am to return immediately."

"Aaaand?" Ryan had placed a few extra regulations on her because of the special nature of Erin's wings. As he'd learned long, long ago, Erin, as a Celestial fairy, and now Angel, had special, legendary feathers. Known as Celestial feathers, they could heal almost any wound, and could save someone from the brink of death. That made it imperative that no one got too close to Erin.

"And, I have to accept responsibility that if one of my feathers is taken, the adventurer in question will be killed." That was the final rule he had applied to her. Partially because it was difficult for Erin's feathers to fall out. The only reason Ryan had them in the first place was because he accidently blasted a part of her wing when they had first met. Her transformation to Angel made it even more difficult to acquire a feather. The only way for one to be removed was through severe damage or extreme force applied on her wings. If an adventurer somehow gained a feather from her, it was through force or malicious means. And Ryan could not excuse any excess force towards his fairies, especially considering Erin was there to help them.

"Very good." He sent them both approval through their bond. They were both full of energy and excitement, though he could tell Hel was doing her best to hide her feelings. Considering he was keeping her more restricted with regards to what she wanted to do in the dungeon compared to Erin, the Chaos fairy was bound to be upset.

Her request, now that she had her true form, had been a lot darker and more problematic. Succubi had a plethora of unique skills, including some that would allow them to put adventurers into a deep sleep and then interact with the adventurers' dreams. She had begged him to allow her to create a secret space, where she could hold adventurers captive so she could utilize these Succubus skills there. Doing so allowed her to steal mana and life force from her victims, which could turn into experience for her or the dungeon.

However, considering Ryan was currently on the "no Chaos association" list, he needed to keep her blatant actions to a minimum. He couldn't very well have her putting herself into adventurers' minds and dreams, no matter how she begged. Even if the idea of extra experience without having to kill adventurers, was tempting.

Which was also why she was to do all of her tasks while hidden. That limited her, and he knew it wasn't quite fair, but that was sadly the world they were in currently. He did promise her that once they were Diamond, he would give her more freedom. Once he became a Diamond Tier dungeon, nothing would be able to stand in his way. He just needed to get there first.

He had been making good progress, having reached Platinum 4 shortly after opening, thanks in large part to the continued demonic attacks taking place in the Bone Zone. The Cult of Chaos had continued its attempts to take down Boneville until recently. When those attacks had stopped, they'd cut Ryan off his free experience train. And with adventurers playing it safe in his dungeon following Brook's death, there wasn't much experience rolling in. That was another reason why he, like his fairies, was excited for the adventurers to begin once again diving into his fourth floor. It meant the chance at high levels of experience. It also meant he would finally get to see adventurers explore his fourth floor. He'd put in all of that hard work, it was a waste not to have adventurers going through it.

"Right. Well then, I think we are ready," he said. With that he turned his focus to the large crystal skull that he'd erected just outside his dungeon entrance, next to which Marcus stood by. Now that Ryan had declared his intelligent nature, the leader of the town had taken to waiting for Ryan's permission each morning before allowing adventurers to enter.

"You may begin," Ryan said, doing his best to make his voice deep and powerful as it echoed from the skull. He grinned internally as a few of the younger, weaker adventurers flinched. Even after a month, they weren't quite used to this. After all, from what Ryan knew and had learned over the past month, he was something completely unheard of in current times. He was unique, the last untainted dungeon. An intelligent one, at that.

And those were just the aspects of Ryan's dungeon that they knew about.

Chapter Thirty-Two

Ryan was going to have a very good day. Not only were adventurers finally going to reach his fourth floor again, but his efforts with regards to assigning quests were about to be rewarded as well. It was about midday when Ryan noticed something out of the ordinary. A party of noobs had just completed his first floor, barely managing to defeat Steve without a casualty, and another group was making their way to his third-floor boss. Boring, all of it, except....

"They did it," Ryan whispered, drawing the attention of Hel and Erin. Hel had been in the process of testing out the whip Ryan had made for her at her request, while Erin had been sleeping or praying to the Goddess of Justice. Sometimes she claimed she was offering prayers up to the Goddess while secretly taking a nap instead. Essentially, the fairies had been growing bored and were trying to keep their minds occupied while they waited, anxiously, for the sign that someone was approaching his fourth floor.

"They did what, darling?" Hel coiled her whip as she walked towards his core. While his core was still suspended in the air, Hel's full size enabled her to lock deep into his core from the ground. Granted, that didn't stop either of his fairies from taking their preferred seat atop his core when something truly interesting occurred.

"Look for yourself." He turned the image in his core, his full focus towards what he had seen. A party of humans, dressed in fine robes, making their way from Boneville. Half a dozen of them, all mages. Ryan didn't need to look their information up to figure that out. Not just because of how they were dressed, but because of what they were doing. Between the six of them, a large crystal with runes etched into it floated magically. Ryan had no doubt in his mind as to the object's identity. His request for a teleportation crystal had been answered.

"Praise the Goddess," Erin mumbled. She had definitely been asleep. Slowly, she moved towards his core to look as well. She blinked, her sleep-addled mind taking a few moments to process what was happening before her mood soared, excitement flowing through their bond.

"I—I can't believe it." The Celestial fairy was awash with emotion. "You—How—I've never heard of a dungeon ever getting a teleportation crystal!"

"It used to be a common thing, little one," Hel replied. The Chaos fairy knew how dungeons used to be. She was the one who'd mentioned to Ryan that he should see if they would bring him a teleportation crystal. Hel was constantly giving him old knowledge to try and help him improve, even if sometimes they disagreed on how the dungeon should be run.

"Maybe in ancient times. But when I was getting taught, something like this wasn't even mentioned as a possibility." Erin looked into Ryan's core. "This, this is huge."

"Honestly, I'm a little surprised." Ryan looked at the group, judging their distance to his entrance. Given the pace they were traveling, it would take them another 30 minutes to reach his entrance. *Ugh.* His excitement was going to kill him before…*Wait a second.*

"Well, humans are greedy creatures…and you did promise them quite the set of rewards in exchange for one," Hel purred slightly. "It's so easy to manipulate a human if you know what makes them tick. I'm glad I was able to help you with this, Darling."

"Yup, because I totally wouldn't have been able to figure out how to get what I want from humans. It's not like I was one once, or anything," Ryan said sarcastically. He couldn't help himself. Perhaps it was his excitement at the whole situation? Or the surprise that it had actually worked? Either way, he wanted his crystal, and he wanted it now.

Without another moment to waste, he created one of his elegant crystal skulls and pushed it out of the ground about a hundred feet ahead of the approaching party. He then instantly dug out a good portion of ground appropriately sized for the teleportation crystal, just in front of his crystal skull.

"Do I assume you've accepted my terms?" Ryan projected his voice through the crystal skull. The mages, who'd already stopped their approach the moment he'd created the crystalline skull, stayed quiet for a moment. They glanced around at each other, before the mage in the lead, wearing the finest robes of a rich, emerald color, moved confidently towards Ryan's crystal skull. The closer he got, the more Ryan was able to make out of the man, and not just his large array of emerald-coated bracelets, rings, and pendants.

The man looked older than most adventurers Ryan had seen. His hair, pulled back in a long ponytail, was silvered like the moon. His eyes, the way he carried himself, showed he felt little of his age. In fact, at this moment, at Ryan's sudden appearance, the man had even gained a burst of energy. His eyes shone with excitement and intrigue as he moved closer towards Ryan's skull. The way he walked, the way he held himself, the way the others looked at him, made Ryan more than a little interested in who this man was.

Let's see how strong—Ryan paused as he looked over the man's information. For a brief second, Ryan felt a rush of fear flow through him. A moment of panic as his mind processed who he was looking at, who it was that had accompanied—or more appropriately—who was leading this exchange. Zacharias, Diamond 2 Archmage, Earth affinity. From what Ryan knew of the world (courtesy of eavesdropping, and all of the countless books, notes, and reports he'd absorbed), this man was the head of the Mages' Guild. Not only that, he was one of the strongest humans currently living.

"Allow me to formally introduce myself, oh mighty dungeon." The man's voice was soft yet held a unique tone to it. While Ryan was no stranger to the arrogant manner in which plenty of mages and nobles spoke and acted, this was different. This man spoke with confidence. He was comfortable in and certain of his power, of the might he wielded. And that assurance just carried over through his voice. He wasn't arrogant. Merely confident. "I am —"

"Zacharias, correct? I am humbled by your decision to come personally." Ryan purposefully interrupted the mage, trying to regain control over the situation.

Zacharias was ridiculously powerful. As a Diamond 2 mage the amount of mana he could wield, and the powers he could call forth, were immense. At Diamond 2, Zacharias alone had as much mana as a five-man party of Platinum 5s. And that was regular mana, it didn't count the skills he'd unlocked, as well as all the bonuses his gear must offer him.

But Ryan was a dungeon core. And even though he respected and feared what such powerful individuals could do to him, in his mind, he was safe. They were a fair distance away from his entrance, and even further away from his core.

He was…ninety percent certain that even if Zacharias tried to destroy him for some reason, Ryan could survive the attack. The ten percent of uncertainty was what was keeping him on his toes, so to speak, and why he was doing his best to offer up a similar air of power and confidence.

"It seems the rumors about you are indeed true," Zacharias continued, walking closer, pausing once he reached the pit Ryan had created for the teleportation crystal. "You cannot fathom, dungeon, how many reports have landed across my desk in regard to you." He held a hand out in front of him and green mana danced across his palm. A split second later, he'd created for himself a stone pipe, which he promptly filled with tobacco he pulled from his robes. As he lit the pipe, he continued, "The first time I heard of you was when I learned of the death of a promising Fire mage that belonged to my Guild. A Gold Fire mage, dying in a dungeon that had just opened itself to the world. Unheard of."

Ryan knew all too well who Zacharias was talking about. That same Fire mage had tried to hold Blake hostage in order to get his hands on the Celestial feather Ryan had unwittingly given to the group that first investigated his dungeon. In Ryan's defense, he didn't know how important a Celestial feather was at the time, and it had been an attempt to keep Sean, the late Platinum Paladin and Blake's father, from killing him. Ryan had killed that greedy Fire mage, not only protecting Blake but also ensuring his early survival. Ryan didn't regret it… after all, that mage had given him a good chunk of experience.

"Of course, you were still a fledgling then. And well, deaths in dungeons do occur," Zacharias continued, his eyes inspecting the crystal skull Ryan had created as he gently puffed on his pipe. "I didn't think too much of it. A simple fluke. But then there was the situation with the necromancer, and more rumors began to spread about you. Again reports made their way to me, of your unique loot, the development of these 'dungeon mob cards'. Another first when it comes to dungeons." He took a step into the pit, though as he did, the stone underneath seemed to react to him, creating a pathway leading directly to Ryan's crystal skull.

"After that, you created an even more intriguing loot system. Most dungeons lack… creativity. Most act as wild, barely intelligent creatures. But you, I must say you are quite the enigma. Something the world hasn't seen for a long, long time.

"If that wasn't enough, you then began protecting this town. You actively went out of your way to keep the people here safe against demonic attacks." He reached the skull, crouching so he could look into its eyes. Ryan stared back at the Archmage, searching the man's face for anything. His gaze was drawn into Zacharias's eyes, which seemed to hold within them an infinite array of thoughts and emotions.

"I'm sure you cannot blame me for accompanying the members of my Guild here, given your most surprising action, to date. Your request for a teleportation crystal…" Zacharias smiled ever so slightly. "Of all the dungeons I've been in, all the dungeons I've explored, all the dungeons I've researched, all the lore I've uncovered…you are the most reminiscent to those of ancient times. The dungeons that exist now—save for those of the Gods of course—are little more than animals. The occasional Platinum Tier dungeon may offer some semblance of understanding, may even interact, rarely, with a degree of intelligence with adventurers. But you. You flaunt yours. You innovate, you create things never before seen, and you are constantly moving forward. And it has not been lost on me, how you interact with those who dive within you. You not only have a consciousness, but a sense of humor as well." Zacharias chuckled as he took another drag on his pipe.

"I've heard about the randomly appearing bone piles, as well as the names of your mobs. Steve is a personal favorite of mine." He grinned at that last part, before his face went somewhat serious again. "Everything about you, everything I hear, and even now, as I speak with you, I just get this strange feeling. You're not just some creature. Nor a simple dungeon. Instead... it's almost as if you're human."

Ryan sat there in silence as Zacharias spoke. For once, Hel and Erin were quiet as well, as they all took in what was going on. The Archmage was correct in his assessment. Ryan had indeed been human once. And he was definitely not just a wild creature, despite that being the narrative that had been spread across the world, according to Hel, to justify the killing of dungeon cores back in the day.

The knowledge of what a dungeon core was, had been lost through time and the greed of humans. What had once been common knowledge, that dungeons were human souls given a second life within a dungeon core, had disappeared. Following the mass destruction of the dungeons, and the shortage of dungeon fairies as a result, Hel had informed Ryan that all the new dungeons were seen as mere empty shells of their former glory. No surprise that Ryan stood out as something special. But he wasn't about to let the secret out to this mage, even if the brilliant man had already deduced the truth. And so he said nothing.

The two stayed there in awkward silence for a long moment. Zacharias kept his gaze deep on the crystal skull, as if his eyes were searching for something within Ryan's creation. As if he were trying to get Ryan to spill some unknown secret. Ryan simply kept quiet. He didn't know how to respond and figured it was best to remain silent. He couldn't give anything away if he stayed silent.

Perhaps his silence could be interpreted as an air of indifference. All Ryan wanted was that teleportation crystal. He wasn't about to share anything else with Zacharias. While the Archmage seemed intrigued by Ryan, the powerful man hadn't done anything to earn himself a spot within Ryan's circle of trust.

"You are either foolish or wise to hold your silence." Zacharias stood tall again, put away his pipe, and motioned towards his group of mages. As one they began making their way towards Ryan and the Archmage. "I do hope, in the future, we might have a moment or two to speak on more familiar terms." The Archmage offered Ryan a smile. "After all, this is the first time I've ever gotten to meet a dungeon whom I could learn something from. I can only imagine the possibilities you present to the world—and more importantly to my Guild."

"How intriguing," Hel chimed in, her eyes flashing with excitement. Of course the Chaos fairy would become more invested in the situation the moment it turned to an opportunity to fulfil her desire for power. She thrived on such things.

"If I can think of anything else your Guild might have which could be of interest to me, I will pass the message along," Ryan responded. He suddenly wanted this conversation done with and Zacharias gone. He really, really didn't like it when people took this much interest in him. Such interest was what led to near-death experiences at the hands of overly powerful individuals. And Zacharias fit that description only too well. Ryan couldn't help but be reminded of Viktor. Still, if the Mages' Guild had objects of interest to him on his quest for power, Ryan wouldn't handicap himself by not trying to obtain such things.

"I'm sure we could arrange an agreeable situation." Zacharias offered another small smile before he stepped away from Ryan's crystal skull. "For now, allow us to complete this simple trade." He held out his hand expectantly. "I believe it was five hundred platinum pieces?"

"That is correct." Ryan had learned, via correspondence he'd absorbed off a fallen noble, that teleportation crystals could be purchased from the Mages' Guild by anyone who had the right amount of gold. The going rate had been one hundred platinum pieces for a teleportation crystal to be purchased and installed in a town. Platinum pieces were the highest form of currency, and each platinum coin was equal to a hundred gold coins. Generally only nobles and large organizations such as guilds would utilize the currency, because everyday individuals and shops or places of commerce in towns couldn't handle the change needed to utilize platinum pieces. Unless you happened to know of a dungeon you could dive in constantly that had good coin drop rates, there was very little chance of ever having more than a hundred gold coins at any given time in your life.

Ryan was a dungeon core gifted with the ability to create at will anything he'd absorbed. So, one of the earlier quests he passed out to the people of Boneville had been to acquire a platinum coin. The bank, which had been established by the Merchants' Guild in Boneville, had accepted that quest. It was a good deal; Ryan had been offering two hundred gold coins in exchange for a single platinum coin.

For the deal at hand, Ryan knew what the proper price for a teleportation crystal was, and he was sure he could have bought one at the normal price, or posted a quest for someone to buy one for him and give it to him. However, for something this important to him, something he was this interested in, he'd decided to take a safer route. To that end, he offered five times the going rate for the object and sent the offer, through Marcus, directly to the Mages' Guild.

"Once I've acquired the teleportation crystal, I will give you the full amount." Ryan said as he spawned a single treasure card in front of Zacharias. The card flashed in the sunlight, the images of coins atop it inlaid with platinum. Across the top read, "Platinum Coins – one hundred".

"You really are quite the unique dungeon." Zacharias grabbed the card and turned away, signaling to his mages to place the crystal in the pit Ryan had created. After they did, Ryan directed them to move a slight distance away before he closed the earth around the crystal and absorbed it. The moment he did, his mind raced with the newfound knowledge, the ins and outs of the crystal. The greatest perk of being a dungeon core was that instantaneous knowledge and understanding of anything he absorbed. A trait he was certain wasn't common knowledge. Otherwise, he was sure people would have been much more hesitant about what offerings they made to the dungeon.

Ryan fought back the urge to begin experimenting with his latest toy long enough to summon four more of the treasure cards for Zacharias. The Archmage seemed to know how Ryan's dungeon worked, so he must know how to redeem the cards for the appropriate amount of coin. It was also common knowledge, at least around Boneville, that you could redeem the cards at the bank for actual coin if needed.

The bank had a party of adventurers on staff who would head into Ryan's dungeon at the end of each week to redeem the treasure cards. It was quite the tactic, because they would wait until they had the appropriate number of each tier of treasure card to combine within Ryan's dungeon and increase the amount of coin they received from the cards.

A tactic likely learned from the adventurers who had begun buying and trading their treasure cards to collect the amount they needed of the same card, to upgrade it to a higher rarity. Ryan's cards had created quite the submarket amongst the denizens of Boneville, to his great amusement.

"I look forward to hearing how you put that crystal to use," Zacharias called back towards Ryan's crystal skull as the Archmage grabbed the other cards. "I'm certain you've got some unique intentions for such a thing." He motioned at his followers, and they all made their way back towards the dungeon town. Likely to cash out their cards and head back to Valta, the human capitol city where the Mages' Guild was centered.

"Oh, I do." Ryan had been dreaming about this moment ever since Hel mentioned the idea to him. And now, he had the crystal, he had the knowledge, and he had the power. Now all he needed was for night to come so he could begin his upgrades.

Ryan loved being a dungeon.

Chapter Thirty-Three

"Better luck next time?" Ryan said as he watched the final high-level party leave his dungeon. Contrary to his hopes, the adventurers outside his dungeon that day had not ventured into his fourth floor. Or rather, those that had made their way down to the fourth floor thought better of their actions and left the floor before going more than a hundred feet into it. The worst of it was Erin and Hel hadn't gotten to have any fun. They'd been so excited in the morning—as had Ryan—because it meant the parties who'd been talking about venturing into his fourth floor the week prior would finally be able to do it.

They had been full of hot air, it turned out, still too intimidated to venture to the active parts of the floor. Frustrating, considering these parties all consisted of Platinum 5 members. Ryan's fourth floor couldn't be that impossible, could it? He was certain a five-man party of Platinum 5 members would be able to explore most of it in relative safety.

Brook's death had been an unfortunate accident. If the

party's healer had been Platinum 5 and able to manage the injuries the party had received, they would have walked away without any deaths. Besides, it had been a series of unfortunate events that led to the death. And accidents, such as shrapnel impacting at the worst possible time and the healer being unaware of the injury until after a party member bled out, happened sometimes in a dungeon. It was just the way things were.

Still, Ryan could feel the disappointment flowing through his bond from Erin, and Hel was more than a little annoyed. They'd waited all day for a chance to act. More, they'd been waiting a month for this. Ryan could understand how they must feel. Waiting so long for something, just to find you have to wait even longer. That would be terrible. On the plus side, the last adventurers making their way out of his dungeon meant something exciting was about to happen. He could finally outfit the dungeon with his latest and greatest acquisition. Of course, some testing would be needed…

"I can't believe no one wanted to try out the fourth floor." Erin shook her head. "Even with the altar to the Goddess there…even with the instructions on how to summon my aid. They still choose to leave." Ryan had added a pedestal similar to the one with the riddle on his third floor; it vaguely described how to gain the Goddess of Justice's favor. That favor, of course, would be a blessing from Erin. Her "summoning" involved tracking down various objects he'd hidden across the floor, and then presenting them back at the pedestal.

"We know Blake's group is going to come through, eventually, this week." Blake's group had not only all reached Platinum 5, but Blake, the Specter of Balance, was Platinum 4. They'd already made it clear during their last dive that they would be visiting Ryan's fourth floor the next time they entered the dungeon. Unfortunately, they hadn't drawn a spot for the first day of the week for dives.

"I cannot wait," Hel purred. The Chaos fairy, and Erin for that matter, had some strong feelings for Blake and his party. Ryan wasn't one to judge; he viewed Blake as something akin to a friend and he enjoyed the party Blake had as well. They were the epitome of an adventuring party, and Ryan was looking forward to watching them explore his fourth floor.

"You better stay away from Blake," Erin called back towards Hel, the Celestial fairy's emotions spiking. Erin was really protective of Blake.

"Or else what?" Hel taunted, turning to look fully at Erin. The Chaos fairy let one hand rest on her hip, while her other hand traced along the handle of her whip. "I'm sure he could entertain me."

"Pretty sure showing yourself to Blake would be a bad idea," Ryan cut in. He didn't want the two starting a fight over a guy, even if it was Blake. He had things to do in the dungeon, and breaking up a fairy fight wasn't one of them.

"I'm sure I could give him good reasons to forgive me, Darling," Hel said playfully, sending a wink towards Erin as she did. "Though, I suppose I'll behave. For now."

"How about we focus on something a little more exciting?" Ryan turned his attention inwards as he went over his knowledge of the teleportation crystal. In theory, teleportation crystals allowed anyone who'd linked their crystal pendant to the teleportation stone, to teleport to it instantly. Often times adventurers would use their pendants, which he knew they'd linked to the stone in Boneville, to teleport out of Ryan's dungeon once they'd cleared their boss fight.

Ryan figured he could create teleportation crystals at the entrance to each of his floors, allowing adventurers to instantly teleport to the appropriate level of his dungeon once they'd unlocked it. It was a way, in his mind, to speed up the dungeon runs. He knew that the more parties that could enter his dungeon in a day, the more opportunities for experience gain on both sides.

"Are you certain this is going to work?" Erin asked as Ryan turned the focus of his core to his first floor. There he began readjusting some of the layout to create a large, empty area near the trap door which led down to his second floor. In the cleared-out space he created an exact replica of the teleportation crystal he'd absorbed from the Mages' Guild.

"I don't see why not," Ryan replied. "It seems simple enough. They have to link to the crystal, and then they can teleport to it. I know the runes are tuned to allow the crystal to absorb ambient mana from the area around it, to empower the crystal and activate the teleportation magic. Each crystal has a unique signature that allows people to teleport to that specific..." Ryan trailed off as realization struck him. He could create exact copies of what he'd absorbed. Meaning... each teleportation crystal he created would be the same. Would that be a problem?

"Um, Hel."

"Yes, Darling?" The chaos fairy had a twinkle in her eye showing she already knew what Ryan had just realized.

"What happens if all the teleportation crystals in my dungeon are exactly the same?" he asked.

"Whatever is trying to teleport to the crystal in question will be torn apart, their being split as the magic tries to teleport them to all the crystals at once. It's actually a really easy way to gain some fast experience as a trap," She responded, the disturbing twinkle in her eyes brighter. He was guessing she'd seen that happen before...and had liked it.

Ryan stayed silent for a moment as his mind processed that. Sometimes he forgot just how cold-blooded and twisted Hel could be. For the most part, she was extremely helpful and supportive, doing everything in her power to help him grow stronger. The idea of purposefully creating a trap to literally tear apart unsuspecting adventurers in such a way crossed more than a few lines in Ryan's mind.

"Yeah…We're not going to do that," Ryan responded. He left the crystal on the first floor but held off on summoning the ones on his other floors. He'd been creating the spaces for them at the same time and had just been about ready to create them on his second through fourth floors. However, Hel's revelation meant he needed to work through this problem in a different way.

"Of course we aren't." Hel let out a sigh. "And I suppose you don't want to know how to create teleporting mobs either?"

At that, Ryan's attention turned completely to Hel. "Teleporting mobs?"

"Yes. Dungeon cores of the past would use teleportation crystals and crystal stones attuned to them to teleport their mobs across their dungeon. It was a work-around, similar to your underground summoning chambers, to allow them to add new mobs to a room already filled with adventurers." She shrugged. "But I figure that's not something you would really want to do."

"No. That, I could use." If he could create a way to rapidly teleport mobs throughout his dungeon, including into areas where adventurers already were…There would be so much he could do. He hated the fact he couldn't summon mobs in an area with adventurers occupying it; something to do with their own individual mana zones of influence and the magical laws related to dungeon cores. There was a range, Ryan had found, that existed when it came to summoning mobs around adventurers. And it could be decreased, if something such as stone, or a wall, was in the way.

"But," Ryan started, even as Hel began to smile. "First,

how am I supposed to get that many different teleportation crystals? It took me a month to just get this one."

"You're a dungeon, Darling." Hel let out a little laugh. "Crystal isn't really that hard to find in the ground. Just enlarge individual pieces of crystal you've absorbed over your expansion period and then apply the appropriate runes." She shook her head. "Sometimes you can be so brilliant. And other times…"

To Ryan's credit, even as his anger flared at the retort, a combination of both her insult hurting him and the rage that suddenly flowed through his bond from Erin, he remained silent. She had a good point. Ryan had absorbed countless crystals during his time as a dungeon core. Crystal was more abundant the further he delved into the ground. Sure enough, when he pulled up a mental catalog of the resources he'd absorbed and focused on the crystals, he was met with an astonishing amount of varieties. This task had suddenly gone from impossible to super simple, all in the span of a few minutes.

"Oh, and, Darling?" Hel started as Ryan turned his focus to his second floor. He summoned a crystal, enlarging it until it was similar in size to the teleportation crystal he'd made on his first floor. Ryan went to work carving the runes into it, using his mana to etch them into the crystal.

"Yes, Hel?" He asked, half-paying attention as he focused on his task.

"Please be careful. If the runes aren't perfect when you activate the crystal, then it will —" Ryan learned what Hel was trying to warn him of before she even finished. He'd accidently drawn the wrong line across one of the runes without realizing. Once he finished the runes and pulsed mana into the crystal to activate it, the entire thing erupted in a blast of magic and crystal shards. Not only that, but for a split second, Ryan sensed all of the mana in the room get drawn into the crystal, depriving the room of all mana before it erupted. The devastation to the room was immense. But that momentary void of mana in the room, when mana was normally constantly abundant in the air, the world, at all times, was terrifying.

Oops.

Chapter Thirty-Four

"So, how do I make these teleporting mobs?" It had taken Ryan two or three hours to craft the needed teleportation crystals to establish stones at the entryway to each of his floors, as well as a healthy amount of additional crystals for the purpose of the teleporting mobs.

It may have taken him a little less time, but he'd accidently blown up a second crystal. Even as a dungeon core, he wasn't perfect, and these runes were intricate. Which meant he'd had to fix not one, but two rooms after he'd completely destroyed them.

"It is quite simple, Darling," Hel said as she left her game with Erin to stand beside him. The two fairies had been left to their own devices while Ryan was tinkering with teleportation crystals. Partly because it was slow, tedious, and rather dull work, and partly because Ryan blew up the second crystal. After that, the fairies had retreated a safe distance away to play "Dungeon Mobs." They'd picked up the rules of the game from Blake and had Ryan craft copies of all the cards for them, so they could start playing around with different deck types. Apparently, the card game was enjoyable.

"How simple?" Ryan was hoping it actually was simple. He needed something simple. His mind was not up for more intricate work. Not right now. It had been fun and invigorating the first few crystals, but after that, it had grated on him.

"Extremely simple." Hel flashed him a smile. "After all, every single adventurer in your dungeon has carried the appropriate tool on them when they entered your dungeon. All you have to do is give your mobs adventurer-like crystal pendants and link them to the teleportation crystals."

"That's it?" Ryan asked, disbelief evident in his tone. He knew the pendants she was talking about. He'd even made some before, first for Blake and later for Marcus. The adventurers used them to teleport away from the dungeon, he'd seen them do it countless times. But he'd thought there was at least something more to it.

"Pretty much." Hel's fangs shown as her smile widened. "The crystals themselves do all the work. The mobs only have to pulse mana into them to activate the teleportation. It's just like using any magic item."

That really was simple. The crystal pendants were all exactly alike. Every single one he'd absorbed was the same. A simple little crystalline stone, wrapped tightly with gold and silver wire. Just as with the teleportation crystals, the pendants had runes within the stone. Additionally, the wire on the pendants had magical properties which amplified the crystal's powers and enabled the abilities of the pendants. These included communication with other pendants, teleportation to crystals, and enabled the creation of parties. The magic of the crystals even went so far as to affect how much experience was gained by each party member. Ryan had done his best not to try and fully fathom this last one, leaving it up to the vagueness that was the magic of the world. Not all things needed to be understood in the world.

"Does it have to be the full pendant, or can I incorporate the crystal into the mob?" Ryan had already summoned one of his basic skeletal warriors and was looking it over. The pendants, small enough a human could hold one completely covered in their hand, would fit rather nicely in the middle of the skeleton's skull. Plus…Ryan could link the crystals to his core, which would allow him to speak out of them from the mobs. Something Ryan felt would be extremely amusing.

"Depends on the dungeon. Normally Dungeon Cores opt to embed the crystal into their mobs, with the forehead or the chest being the favorites After all, if the crystal is embedded in a mob, you don't have to worry about the pendant falling off. Plus, you can save that mob, with the crystal embedded into it, as a mob type, so you can mass summon them later." Hel paused, before grinning wickedly. "I'm sure you know how much time that can save."

She'd added on that extra portion because Ryan had a bad habit of micromanaging his mobs. Or at least, he had earlier. When the demons were attacking in the Bone Zone day in and day out, he'd been constantly focusing on how his mobs were armed and armored with their basic bone equipment. He'd even tried out different weapon combinations and toyed with different dual-wielding options for his mobs. All of this he'd been doing individually. Summoning the mob, and then the equipment afterwards. It…had taken a lot of time before Hel's off-hand comment that he could save each type of mob to mass summon later.

That was then, and this was now. Those were basic bone weapons, simple objects he gave his mobs to help them fight against the adventurers. He hadn't been sure if the crystal pendants would be different. After all, they were a magic item, and he'd never…

"Hey, Hel?" Ryan had stopped mid-experiment, the skeleton's skull on the ground, the crystal partially embedded in it. Something important had just crossed his mind.

"Yes, Darling?" As she spoke, Erin left the area they'd been playing Dungeon Mobs in, and came over as well. Ryan's swirling emotions and tone seemed to have gotten her attention.

"Can a dungeon's mobs use magic items?" He went back to his task, setting the crystal nicely in the center of the skull's forehead, almost appearing as a third eye. "I know you mentioned they can use these pendants. But is that unique? Or can they use any type of magical item…?" He trailed off as he felt a momentary rush of excitement flow through his bond even as the faeries' eyes lit up with excitement.

"Have I ever told you how glad I am that you are my dungeon core?" Hel purred slightly, stepping towards his floating core as her clawed hand gently traced along his glowing surface. Her hand paused at the sign of the God of Death, the dark skull engraved on his orb, showing his affinity for Darkness mana.

"Not recently," he replied, enjoying the praise, as much as he could. Erin's excitement was quickly fading, to be replaced with what felt like jealousy and sorrow? He knew the Celestial fairy felt inferior to Hel, which was understandable. While Erin had been able to help him with his early development, Hel had access to much more knowledge than Erin could hope for. Ryan was more reliant on Hel with his later developmental parts than he was on Erin.

"Well, Darling. You are definitely my favorite dungeon core, ever." She drew her head closer to his core, her eyes looking deep within them. "And yes, you can arm your mobs with magical weapons, items, and gear."

"Alrighty, then." Ryan quickly put his skeletal mob back together, then absorbed it, noting mentally that a new summon option appeared in his mental mob catalog. The cost was the same, but he now had the option to summon his skeletal humanoid mobs with, or without, an embedded crystal. *Neat.*

"Teleporting mobs are done. How about something a little more exciting?" He shifted his focus from one fairy, to the other. "I think our next set of experiments is going to require a visit to skeletal fight club."

Chapter Thirty-Five

Ryan had created some great things in his time as a dungeon. His loot system was one of them, and the Bone Zone was another. However, one creation stood above all the others. One creation just kept giving, and it was the greatest of them all.

Skeletal fight club.

Not only had it helped him with his mob evolutions, but it had led to the discovery of different rarities of mobs and given Ryan a proving ground for all of the mobs he created.

Every time Ryan gained a new rank or Tier, he did his best to allocate mob points to skeletal fight club to maximize his potential of developing new and unique mobs. At Platinum 4, this still held true, and Ryan had actually put all of his mob points from his rank up, all 1,200 points of them, into skeletal fight club. Meaning there were now over 2,000 mob points worth of mobs taking part in skeletal fight club spread across all four levels.

Level one of skeletal fight club, underneath his first floor, was where he worked on evolving his smaller mobs. He used it on his skuirrels, skrats, and sneks, and had even begun using it for some of his infested mobs. Skeletal fight club level 2, which was a massive, underground coliseum, still saw his skeletal fighters and archers training hard against each other. Level 3 involved his larger bestial mobs, and he had his skeletal variants of bears, foxes, badgers, eagles, tigers, and wolf mobs all fighting in it, waiting to see what evolutions may occur.

His newest version of skeletal fight club, which existed underneath the expanse that was his fourth floor, was where most of his mob points had gone. That was because, while the others had large areas allotted to them, his fourth version of skeletal fight club dwarfed the previous three. It existed underneath the largest floor he'd ever created. It was also much deeper, giving it a higher ceiling; he had much larger mobs to test out, after all. His skelephants, for example, were over twenty feet in height.

What made it different was that his fourth floor wasn't just a one-on-one, or even small-scale brawl. It was a full-on, never ending battle. It was where his mobs fought as armies, working against each other, until one side came out victorious. The winning army would be healed, their fallen ranks resummoned, and then Ryan would create a new opposing force to attack the victors. He was working on figuring out what mobs worked the best together and seeing if he could force any further evolutions from his mobs. During his time as a Gold Tier dungeon, he'd discovered uncommon mobs. At Platinum, skeletal fight club level 4 had given him rare mobs.

Ryan was hoping for even more.

"You can't be serious," Erin spoke through her pendant to Ryan as the two fairies entered the fourth level of skeletal fight club. She was, of course, referring to his latest experiment: mounted skeletal warriors.

"What can I say, they're effective," Ryan responded dismissively. The mobs were a variant of his skeletal warriors, which had been trained to ride atop mounts in battle. Honestly, it had been easier to get the mobs to transition riding upon other mobs than it had been to create freaking saddles and proper riding equipment for the appropriate mobs.

It was a problem he hadn't expected. In his mind, he'd imagined the mobs would work flawlessly together; or at least could be linked with Darkness mana. But doing that always started a fusion process which he wasn't after. In the end he'd found he needed actual riding equipment for the mobs, which presented its own problem.

He didn't have access to any saddles, for any type of creature. And while he was sure asking for a horse saddle, while strange, wouldn't cause too much concern, asking for riding gear suited for an elephant would raise some concerns. Which meant, he'd had to get creative, and craft the riding gear for himself.

His solution for the skelephants included bone platforms which rested atop their backs. He'd found he could fit three skeletal archers atop the platform, with one additional skeletal rider commanding the mounted mob. That was the name Ryan had given his new mobs, skeletal riders. There was a training area for them on his fourth floor, and he'd managed to create variants capable of riding all of his bestial mob types. For humor's sake, Ryan had used dwarven skeletal fighters for the larger badger skeletons. He also had a giant skeleton that could ride atop skelephants, though the platform with human-sized skeletal archers was more efficient. Most of the time, Ryan knew where to draw the line between efficiency and humor.

"When would you ever use something —" Erin was cut off as a shrill sound pierced the sky. Even though he had his fairies heading towards a specific area on the battlefield, Ryan hadn't stopped the war going on at skeletal fight club. The battle raged all around his fairies. That shrill sound signaled one of Ryan's newest, most prized skeletons. Its value was amplified by how long it had taken him to acquire the blasted thing.

"What in the name of the Goddess?" Erin cursed as she flew backwards. Hel swiftly moved out of the way, and just in time. A massive, bony creature passed through where they stood moments before, shooting downwards with unnatural speed towards the skeletal armies. The creature, which had the head and wings of an eagle, with the body of a lion, was the skeleton he'd found underneath Boneville.

The adventurers, incentivized by his generous reward, had been rather prompt in collecting the remaining bones for him. Once he'd gotten all of them, he'd learned it was classified as a Huge creature called a gryphon. At Platinum tier, he could use it immediately, unlike a certain monstrous dragon skeleton that was taunting him and the fact he couldn't summon it yet.

Another thing he noticed about the gryphon skeleton, which both perplexed and intrigued him, was how natural it felt. It was a combination of different creatures, no question about it. However, all the bones, the structure, everything about it *worked*. It didn't have that monstrous, unnatural feel to it inherent to the creatures Ryan created.

"That would be a gryphon," Hel said simply.

"Obviously, I knew that." Erin responded quickly. Ryan had already shown the mob off to them, the moment he'd gotten the bones delivered. There was no hiding his excitement for new mobs.

"I meant, what is going on with it?" She pointed towards the gryphon, which was strafing the line of skeletal fighters and archers. As it did, the skeletal wings launched bone shards down upon the enemy forces. From its back, sitting behind a skeletal rider, was a skeletal mage launching fireballs. The devastation was more than a little impressive.

"Too much?" Ryan asked sheepishly. He was known to go a bit over the top with some of his experimentations. Sure, he didn't need a mage flinging fireballs from atop the already formidable gryphon. Points-wise, it wasn't the most efficient use of mob points…But it was so awesome.

On top of being an inefficient use of mob points, it wasn't practical. This collection of mobs required a gryphon, a skeletal mage, and a skeletal rider. If he wasn't directly controlling his skeletal mobs, they adopted some of the traits inherent to the species they had once been. And gryphons especially, weren't fond of letting people ride them. Which meant a skeletal rider was needed, then, to keep the gryphon in check so the mage could launch his attacks.

Even that didn't stop the gryphon from occasionally jerking about wildly, in an attempt to throw off its riders. Which was also why Ryan had lashed his skeletal mage and rider to the back of the gryphon using even more summoned gear. A tactic that was a terrible idea for living beings, but perfectly fine for undead creatures. Fine or not, it was needless and impractical. Meaning there was a good chance this combination wouldn't be utilized in the dungeon. But hey, Ryan could at least enjoy watching the craziness.

"It, just feels a little over the top, huh?" Ryan prompted. The fairy had gone quiet, watching the gryphon and skeletal mage mow down another line of skeletal warriors with their joint fire and bone shard attacks. For the current war, Ryan was doing a quantity versus quality test. The quality side, armed with the skeletal mage and gryphon combo, was going to win.

"It's, uh, definitely unheard of," Erin responded. She was less than impressed with his shenanigans, it seemed.

"If you keep experimenting like this, Darling, you'll be

invincible." Hel, on the other hand, seemed all for the death and destruction that was the gryphon-mage combo. Pure pride flowed from the bond he shared with her.

"I doubt adventurers will get to see that combo any time soon," Ryan responded with a chuckle. As deadly as it was, it felt like too much. Plus, as he watched the combo do another run of fiery death, he figured it might be too agile and deadly for his current difficulty. It was one thing to attack adventurers from up high with his greater clackers…but chucking fireballs at them from way up high just seemed like overkill.

"Tease," Hel said under her breath, her emotions fading as she resumed complete control over them.

"Speaking of teasing." Ryan mentally nudged the two of them. "Hurry up and get going. I sent the two of you down here for something much more exciting than this battle." He sent a silent command to all the mobs on the fourth level of skeletal fight club. Instantly they froze, stopping their attacks and going lifeless…er, more lifeless. The battlefield became a frozen scene, stopped mid-combat. He would have them resume once his fairies were safely away from the battlefield.

"How are we supposed to find the correct mobs, again?" They were flying in roughly the right direction, but skeletal fight club level four was rather large. There was a lot going on, it was easy to get distracted and lost. Ryan sent them a mental image nudging them in the right direction.

"I've put them next to the Tiger Queen. She's impossible to miss."

Chapter Thirty-Six

"Let me guess, Ryan." Erin and Hel had made their way towards the end of the massive battlefield. The Celestial fairy had pulled up short and was pointing towards a very prominent figure that stood out over everything else. "Is that the 'Tiger Queen'?"

"Obviously, little one. Or were you expecting an even more...obvious sign?" Hel retorted before Ryan could even respond. The Chaos fairy let out a laugh as the two continued on their way, descending until they touched down on the ground. Appropriately, they kept their distance from the figure in front of them. Even though Ryan's mobs were his own, they often acted based on whatever instincts and drives had been a part of their species as if embedded somehow in their very bones. Ryan had noticed as much in the past, with his skuirrels and skrats and their actions, but had never paid much attention to it. With his human memories returned though, it became even more obvious. Somehow, the magic that gave life to these mobs gave to them also certain quirks and characteristics reminiscent of their living counterparts.

Ryan figured this was another of the long, mysterious

ways in which mana and being a dungeon worked. It was the only way to explain how his mobs worked It was also the only way to explain how they adapted to their skeletal forms, and how they instinctually knew how to act and use their powers.

Steve, after all, shouldn't have been able to randomly shoot bone spikes at his enemies right away. Nor should Buttercup have been able to use her Dark mana-clad antlers the way she did. Neither of those were "natural" and Ryan obviously had no idea, back in the beginning, how to manipulate mana and bones in those instances.

He'd been learning new tricks from his mobs since the very start. The more he summoned and the more he observed, the more he learned. Ryan wondered sometimes if the God of Death was somehow embedding in these mobs certain actions to help Darkness dungeons learn all they could do with their powers.

Ryan was totally fine with that, if it helped him to grow stronger he would take all the extra knowledge he could. Nothing about it said he would have to use all of the knowledge he gained. But he would rather have it and not need it than go without, and never realize he was missing out on something.

Case in point, what they were here to do. Giving mobs magical items. He had gone all the way to Platinum 4 without that type of knowledge. Now that he had it…it felt kind of obvious and he hated the fact he hadn't realized it sooner. That would be taken care of once the fairies finished admiring his latest creation. He'd created his Tiger Queen out of a random urge to try and make something a little more exotic.

"That is indeed my Tiger Queen." He focused on the mob, giving her a basic command. Instantly she rose up from the throne she'd been sitting atop of. A throne that seemed crafted from the bones of tigers, their massive tiger heads creating the back of the throne, the paws, the arms and legs of the throne. The tail bones, draped down elegantly, to almost rest atop the shoulders of the Tiger Queen as she sat there. "Behold, the newest mini-boss of the fourth floor."

The skeletal humanoid stepped away from the throne, her eyes glowing with a dark power. Her movements revealed her true form to the fairies. For a base, Ryan had used an elven skeleton. As a human, he'd heard stories of elven rangers who used tigers in battle. He'd decided to play off that story and create something similar all on his own. Elven bones were thinner and more graceful in appearance, and the skull had sharper angles, giving it a more feminine appearance without any necessary augmentation.

She was going to be a mini-boss, and so Ryan had given her enough mana to make her an enhanced armored skeleton with a basic cost of 35 mob points. With that, her form was covered in Dark mana armor. Ryan had utilized the ranged skeleton class, giving a light, leather pattern to her armor. At her waist, a bone sword hung loosely, connected with Darkness mana. She held a bone bow in one hand and had a quiver of bone arrows on her hip.

Of course, her just being made from an elven skeleton didn't make her all that special. Nor did being an enhanced armored skeleton. What made her special was what was about to happen. Ryan, on his quest for greater power, had learned something new about making mini-bosses.

Without warning, Darkness mana pulsed from the Tiger Queen, running from her body, across her arms, and into her wrists. There, coils of Darkness mana twisted and turned, creating twin bracelets on her wrists. From these bracelets a long trail of mana flowed into the throne. The Darkness mana traced across the throne, to rest around what would have been the necks of each tiger, forming into glowing, pulsing collars.

A moment later, the collars flashed once more, and Darkness mana raced through the throne. Both tiger heads opened their mouths and let out terrifying roars as their bones shifted, pulling away from each other, breaking apart and reassembling to resume their original shape. That is, the shape of two skeletal tigers. This was why the elven enhanced skeleton standing there was called the Tiger Queen.

The two skeletal tigers were covered from head to claw now in Darkness mana, which condensed enough to give them an almost completely solid form. As they moved away from each other, it was apparent the leashes connecting them to the Tiger Queen were still there, lines of Darkness mana linking the two mobs together. Without prompting, the two tigers stepped towards the Tiger Queen, only to stop on either side of her. There they each sat, their eye sockets looking lazily towards Erin and Hel as the Tiger Queen looked them up and down.

When he'd first started creating his mini-bosses for his fourth floor, Ryan had been combining skeletal mobs together to see what he could create. He'd eventually started to wonder if he could combine them in other ways. Part of that idea had come from the skeletal horde mob, the massive 2,500-point mob that consisted of countless mobs, all of them connected to a single point by Darkness mana.

After some trial and error, and a disturbing zombie creation he didn't want to think about involving mushrooms and parasitic spores that he was pretty sure would create additional zombies from whatever they landed on, he'd found he could link mobs together with strands of Darkness mana. Doing so combined the mob cost of the included mobs, creating a single mob.

For instance, binding his enhanced armored elf skeleton, which was normally a 35-point skeleton, with the huge beast skeleton that was a tiger skeleton, cost him 50 points. Doing so with two tigers brought the cost to 65. From Ryan's understanding it kept the base cost of the primary mob, aka the elven skeleton mob, and then added half the mob cost of the mobs being bound. In this case, the tiger skeletons were normally worth 30 mob points, but when bound to the Tiger Queen, each cost 15 points instead.

Ryan figured out why this was, in the early stages of testing. If the link binding them was severed, the tigers would run rampant, attacking everything in the area, whether it be friend or foe. By being bound, they lost any of the embedded instincts and mannerisms normally put into them by the Darkness mana. They could only function properly when bound to their skeletal counterpart. That flaw kept Ryan from creating any other such combinations for basic mob purposes. However, through some testing, he had found that as a mini-boss that downside was partially removed.

By turning the 65-point trio into a mini-boss which cost 325 mob points, Ryan found that the mana linking the two tigers to the Tiger Queen was much denser, making it extremely difficult to sever. If it were severed, instead of going on a rampage, the mob would freeze where it was. Sure, this left it vulnerable to attack, but it also meant Ryan wasn't creating a possible danger to his mobs by making these bound mobs. Even better, the Tiger Queen could reattach the bond with her severed tigers; unless adventurers killed her, or destroyed the tigers completely, they were in for a long fight.

Finally, what made the Tiger Queen so fascinating were her abilities. The leash on each tiger could go out to about fifty feet in one direction. It could extend past that point but doing so made the bond weaker and easier to sever. As long as the mobs were bound to the Tiger Queen they could be healed. The Tiger Queen could also pulse Darkness mana into the tigers, almost similar to the bond a ranger had with its bound animal companion, thus enhancing and healing them in order to keep them in the fight. Such an ability justified the steep cost for this mob.

As awesome as she was, Ryan didn't plan to reveal her just yet. Andre the Giant and the other Bone Enforcers were enough of a challenge for whoever stepped foot onto his fourth floor. For now.

But the adventurers were going to get stronger. He figured he needed to make sure he had stronger mini-bosses lined up for when it became time to step up the difficulty. He also figured she would prove a good test run for adventurers to see if they were ready for the boss on his fourth floor. If the adventurers couldn't defeat her, Ryan had little faith in their ability to overcome his fourth-floor boss.

Even Ryan's fairies agreed there was only one way to describe his fourth-floor boss. Only a single descriptor, for what awaited the adventurers within the boss's lair. And that was *monstrous*. But Ryan was certain there was quite a bit of time before any adventurer made it to his boss. Meaning, it was time for something a little more…appropriate.

Chapter Thirty-Seven

Ryan allowed the fairies a few minutes to inspect the Tiger Queen and even had her showcase some of her skills and abilities for them. While she wasn't their main reason for coming down here, he couldn't help but let the new mob take up some of the glory and attention. Ryan loved getting praise from the fairies, especially for his moments of brilliance. The Tiger Queen, of course, being one of those.

Once he'd felt he'd answered enough of their questions and sufficiently showcased his exotic boss to them, he turned their focus to the real task at hand.

"Now that you've met my skeletal royalty," Ryan said through the pendants they wore. This was cheesy and he knew it. But he couldn't resist. "Allow me to introduce to you...the new...improved...Skeletal knights." As he spoke, six forms, which had been standing about fifty feet back from the Tiger Queen, began moving forward.

"The N.I. Knights?" Hel looked at them, her voice rather dry. "We really need to work on your naming skills, Darling."

Ryan let out an exasperated sigh. "That's not—I'm not

naming them that." Seriously, did she really think he was that bad at—

"Yes, you're terrible at naming things, Darling. It's just the unfortunate truth."

"She's got a point, Ryan. Your mobs generally end up with some ridiculous names," Erin cut in, and it was her interjection that really got under Ryan's...er, core. She was even worse at this than he was. She was the whole reason he had a freaking Steve and Buttercup.

"They aren't the N.I. Knights, or whatever craziness you are imagining." He calmed himself for a moment, "I was thinking of calling them Skeletal Knights of the Bone Order."

"Skeletal Knights of B.O.?" Hel looked towards Erin, and both started laughing. "Still not any better."

"I hate the two of you..." Ryan grumbled. He turned back to the six mobs, pushing the fairies' ridicule out of his mind. "Would you just...look at their actual names and stop making fun of me?" Technically, he hadn't assigned new names to them, yet. Currently they were just listed as Skeletal Fighters, though instead of the dull white that depicted a regular mob name, these had their names listed in a shimmering blue. The magical color depiction for things of rare quality.

These were rare mobs.

"They're rare," Erin exclaimed, clapping her hands together. "You didn't tell me the skeletal fighters had increased in rarity again." Ryan could feel the pure happiness and excitement flowing through the bond from the Celestial fairy to him. She was elated, as she should be. It had taken a long time to get his uncommon skeletal fighters to evolve. Lots and lots and lots of skeletal fight club matches had taken place.

It had been much harder to get the skeletal fighters and

archers to increase in rarity than his other rare mob. The only other mob type he'd managed to get to increase in rarity had been his sneks. Those mobs, apparently, increased in rarity based on the number of heads they had, and their size. Case in point, when he hit nine heads total the mob had become rare and was classified as a huge beast...he loved it.

"It's a new development." He'd noticed their rarity increase a few days ago and had forgotten to mention it to the fairies. Mainly because they'd been so busy about planning for the arrival of adventurers and the roles they would be able to play. Because of the rules he'd had to establish for his fairies, and the preparations he'd put into the fourth floor for Erin's plans to interact with the adventurers, he'd forgotten to mention it.

"You continue to impress, Darling." Even though Hel wasn't in his core room, he could practically feel her finger tracing along his core, as she often did when she was excited by something he'd done. "You truly are going to become one of the greatest cores in existence." That praise caused an even greater feeling of warmth to flow through Ryan.

"I'll become the greatest, for all of us," Ryan responded. He would. He would become a dungeon greater than all the others before him. He would become a dungeon that could rival the Gods. Because then, and only then, would he truly be able to free himself from the chains he felt bound him. Given the fact the Goddess of Justice had locked away his memories of being human, he couldn't help but be a little suspicious of her. And whatever she was planning, whatever was being plotted behind his back, Ryan wanted to make sure he was strong enough that he would no longer worry, whether justly or not, that he was being used.

"I won't put too many of these in the dungeon just yet," Ryan started. "After all, while a basic skeletal mob costs five points, a basic version of these, at rare, costs me twenty points. Common-rarity enhanced armored skeletal fighters cost me a total of thirty-five points, while a rare version would cost me a whopping one-hundred and thirty-three points."

"Points well spent, Darling," Hel added in. "Surely you could afford to take away some points from all of," she looked back towards the battlefield spreading her arms wide, "this. In order to add some rare mobs to your fourth floor."

"I can. But I need to be careful. Because they are much more potent than the common and uncommon mobs." Ryan had tested them out already. They not only had greater strength and speed than the uncommon variants, but they were able to utilize more Darkness mana skills. To Ryan, it seemed like the rare version of the mobs were able to use skills and abilities similar to those of Gold Tier adventurers. So, when you combined the mobs' enhanced traits, access to such abilities, and then magical gear...they quickly became very potent.

"Fine," Hel let out a sigh. "I suppose the less you have up above, the more you can have down here in Fight Club, anyway. Now that you've got rare mobs, I can practically taste ultra-rare versions." She licked her lips. "And then, legendary mobs."

"Before we get to either of those," Ryan stopped the Chaos fairy, who was practically drooling at the thought of legendary mobs, "how about we arm these skeletal knights appropriately?" He looked them up and down. At the moment they were clad simply in bone armor and armed with bone weapons.

"Can I give them any rare items I want?" Ryan's mind went to one of the legendary items he had at his disposal. The Crown of Sorrows. That legendary Item had been used by the necromancer Viktor to summon a lich to attack his dungeon. Could he give such an item to his mobs and have them summon powerful creatures as well? That seemed tempting, yet dangerous.

"Hardly," Hel commented. "Mobs are able to equip weapons equal to their rarity or below. You can arm your rare mobs with rare items and below, your uncommon mobs with uncommon items, and your basic mobs—well, those can only get common gear."

"Simple enough." That would make outfitting his mobs a lot easier. If they were limited by their rarity to their gear of choice, then it was a matter of crafting gear of the appropriate level. Conveniently, all the class gear Ryan had absorbed from fallen adventurers was rare gear. Meaning he had at his disposal a very, very large collection of rare gear to start with.

"Sometimes, Darling, the simplest things are the deadliest." Hel smiled. The way she said that sent chills down Ryan's spine. He decided to ignore whatever she may have meant with that statement and focus on the task at hand. They had the rest of the night to arm these rare mobs and get them placed on his fourth floor appropriately before the adventurers returned. On top of that, he needed to officially rename them. If they were going to arm them with rare gear, and they were rare creatures, he felt they needed names appropriate for their awesomeness.

"Right, well then. Erin, Hel. Would you two like to help me outfit these knights of mine? And after, shall we name them?"

"I've got the best name already planned," Erin exclaimed as Ryan's words echoed out of their crystal pendants. It happened so fast that Ryan groaned aloud. Luckily, he was alone in his core chamber and he hadn't sent that groan through to their pendants. He really hoped Hel could come up with a good name. Knowing Erin, he would end up with something silly.

"I'm sure you do, hun." Ryan replied as he turned his focus to the main part of the task. "But first…What type of gear should we give them?"

Chapter Thirty-Eight

BLAKE

"I can't believe we took them all down." Blake was breathing heavy as he looked at his friends. They'd just completed the boss battle on Ryan's third floor and were now looking at four different loot chests. One for each of the bosses they'd slain.

"Neither can I." Ryan's voice came through the crystal skull that appeared in front of the Loot Box in the room. That was Ryan's new thing. He really loved making his crystal skulls. In fact, Blake had noticed Ryan really seemed to have a new crystal fetish ongoing. The dungeon not only had crystal skulls planted all over the dungeon, but now each floor had a teleportation crystal in the entryway. Blake knew no adventurers would ever complain about a faster way to travel through the dungeon. But Ryan's continual rate of growth was, while not alarming (considering his nature), still unsettling. What would happen if someone angered Ryan? What would happen if something pushed him over the edge like the Dungeon of Ashes?

"I knew you guys were strong," Ryan continued. As he spoke a fifth box rose from out of the ground to sit with the other four. "But I really was worried you guys were about to die."

"Ah, look, he really does care," Jack commented before he let out a raspy, pained cough. He was still in wolfkin form, silver fur singed and covered in crimson. The Duelist had countless cuts and wounds spread across his body, courtesy of the chaos that fighting all four skeletal mage bosses at once had brought on. Blake couldn't shield everyone from all the attacks at once, so Jack had filled in the gaps, to the wolfkin's detriment. Even now though his wounds were being healed. Karan, now a Platinum bishop, was using her larger mana pool and more powerful healing abilities to get the party back up to fighting shape.

It had been a little over a month since their battle with Sasha. In that time, Karan and Jack had ascended to Platinum Tier and the party had begun diving the dungeon once again. With Blake already Platinum 4, and Matt and Emily close to leveling up to Platinum 4 as well, the magic in their pendants had ensured Karan and Jack received most of the experience from their dungeon runs, to help the party even out again.

Blake and his group had decided to take on all four bosses this time around, because everyone was nearly at Platinum 4. From their quick estimations, killing all four bosses would ensure they had enough experience to hit Platinum 4 before stepping into Ryan's fourth and deadliest layer. Considering the loss of Brook on Ryan's fourth floor, every adventuring team was cautious in their preparations to explore that floor.

That being said, the fight against all four skeletal bosses had been anything but easy. His party had worked their way up over the past month, gauging their strength, and were confident at the start of the battle. After all, fighting three of the skeletal mages had been manageable, while somewhat tricky.

During the fight against three of the bosses, they'd used

Cynder and Emily to keep Frosty, the ice skeletal mage, at bay, while Blake squared off with Rocky, the earth skeletal mage. Meanwhile Jack had gone toe to toe with Breezy, the wind skeletal mage. Matt provided ranged cover and attacks for the party, while Karan kept everyone healed up and provided a magical barrier. A new ability courtesy of her ascension to Platinum.

Success bred confidence, and so this time around they'd been certain they could take on all four. Granted, they didn't have much choice, as they needed to kill all four in order to get the experience they required. The fight though had gone differently with four bosses. With the fourth mage added in, and without a proper way to occupy that fourth boss's attention, there was a lot more chaos.

It was all Blake could do to keep most of the aggro drawn to himself while his party members worked frantically to burn the skeletal mobs down. In the end, they'd won by focusing their fire on single targets while Blake tanked the others. With Jack covering any attacks that got past Blake's efforts, they overcame the hardest fight any of them had ever faced. And it seemed the fruits of their labor came not only in the experience that allowed Blake's party to all climb to Platinum 4, but also, additional loot. Extra loot was always a nice perk.

Having healed his own wounds with his Celestial mana, Blake walked over to the chests, inspecting them as he did. There was one for each of the elemental mobs they killed, meaning a fire, a wind, an earth, and a water chest. The fifth chest was larger and more artistic. Instead of the classic, wooden chests Ryan seemed to favor, this one was made completely of bone. It was about three times the size of the normal ones, and instead of having a normal padlock, there was a grinning skull. Furthermore, the hinges of the chest were made from human spines. It was a lot darker than what Blake was used to from Ryan.

"So, Ryan." Blake moved closer to the chest. Lately the loot from Ryan's dungeon hadn't really been all that great. Which wasn't really Ryan's fault. His party was well-outfitted, considering Emily and Matt had their gear from the God of Fire's dungeon, Jack had his special scimitars, and Blake had his ultra-rare shield and the legendary sword he carried on his back. "What's in the chest?"

The crystal skull lit up, burning more brightly than normal. When that occurred, it meant Ryan was interacting directly with the skull. The dungeon core was watching Blake and his party intently.

"It's a reward for being the first party to fully clear my third floor." Ryan's voice was filled with excitement. "And personally I think you'll find what's in the chest will really help you with the next floor."

Blake glanced at his party members. Their healing was done, Cynder was in her Juvenile form, and everyone was moving towards the chests. They were essentially ready to begin their dive on the fourth floor once they collected their hard-earned loot. Apparently, there was a massive staircase, over a hundred feet in height, that descended to the fourth floor. That descent would give his party enough time to recover the rest of the mana they'd expended on the fight before they reached the bottom.

"And what exactly could —" Blake opened the chest and paused. Often, Ryan made the chests for show and simply put treasure cards within them. This would require adventurers to head to the nearest loot box in order to redeem the card for the treasure. The object sitting in the bone chest though was not a treasure card. Instead it was whole. The increased size of the chest suddenly made sense. Sitting inside, waiting for Blake to remove it, was a massive chest piece.

"Oh man." Jack, back in human form for now, stepped up beside Blake, looking into the massive loot box. The Duelist's eyes looked over the armor before he turned towards the crystal skull. "What do I have to do to get something like that but for a Duelist?" Even as he finished his statement, Karan punched Jack in the back.

"Show the dungeon some respect," she whispered, even as she fiddled with the pendant around her neck, the one Ryan had made for her. Other than Matt, every one of Blake's party had received a special, unique piece of equipment from Ryan. But what was in the chest, what the dungeon had just given Blake, had to take the cake. At least in terms of artistic value.

The chest piece itself was made of a mixture of bone, plate mail, and blackened leather. The bones affixed to it in a way as to mimic the rib cage of a large creature, complete with a spinal column running down the back of the armor. Holding the armor, Blake could tell the bones weren't there just for show. His Dark mana could sense every one of the bones, meaning he would be able to use them for his bone-related skills. Additionally, he could tell each of the bones had been reinforced with Darkness mana, making them sturdier than steel.

The dark metal of the plate mail was also infused with Darkness mana, making it more durable and sturdier than the current gear Blake wore. More appealing to Blake was the trim running across half the armor. Half of the armor had golden trim running through it. The other half had a silver trim. And on the center of the chest piece, where the two trims came together, were the Scales of the Goddess of Justice.

Though they weren't alone. Interlaid with the scales was

the skull of the God of Death. Ryan had somehow crafted the symbols to line up so the scales and eye sockets matched perfectly. On the left half, which was silvered, sat a perfect onyx. On the right side, a perfect opal. Ryan had put the gems on the sides of the armor that Blake favored for each of his mana types, so they would coincide with his normal efforts.

As Blake focused on it, the name appeared before him, shimmering in a ruby light. This chest piece, the **Breastplate of Judgement**, was ultra-rare. Blake could hardly contain his excitement as he began to remove his current chest piece.

Normally, Blake would have shied away from embracing his Dark mana side. In public, amongst adventurers and the Church, he did his best to keep his dual affinity a secret.

At least, the old Blake had. The run in with Paul, the Zealot of Light, had soured that mindset for Blake. Furthermore, Blake knew he would need to cast aside such trepidations if he truly were to become what he wanted to be. If he were to reach his goal and become powerful enough to forever protect those he loved. Without another thought he donned his new breastplate, feeling the flow of power rush through him as he did. With this ultra-rare piece of gear, Blake was taking another step forward.

"Alright." Blake looked towards his party and towards the exit leading down to the fourth floor. "Everyone ready to see what the fourth floor is all about?" Blake's party let out cheers and gave him nods as they moved towards their goal. They'd looted the other treasure chests while he'd put on his new armor and already pocketed the treasure cards. They would split the loot at the end of the dive, as was their norm.

He tried his best not to imagine how much the guild tax was going to hit on their dungeon run this time around. Whatever it was, he knew he would gladly pay it. With his new chest plate on, Blake couldn't help but feel invincible.

What would it feel like, to be armed and armored with Ultra-Rare gear from head to toe?

"I guess you like it?" Ryan's voice came out of the crystal skull as they passed it.

"I love it," Blake responded. In his mind, he was imagining how jealous Cane would be of his new gear. The thought came with a pang of guilt. He hadn't contacted his old teacher in a long time.

"Good, then you won't be mad about this." As Ryan spoke, Blake could just make out the sound of metal rustling. He looked back just in time to see his old chest piece get absorbed by the dungeon. In his excitement over his ultra-rare loot…he'd forgotten about the chest piece he'd left behind. Sure, it wasn't as good as what he was now wearing, but he would have been able to sell it for a good amount of coin. Now, it was gone. Blake let out a low growl even as Jack started laughing, which was soon followed by the rest of the party. Blake had made one of the oldest noob mistakes in the book. You never let your gear get too far from you in a dungeon, otherwise it was bound to go "missing".

"Right." Blake cleared his throat. While the loss of the armor was upsetting, the embarrassment over such a rookie mistake stung even more. "What are the chances of you giving that back?" He asked aloud. The only response Blake got, as his party reached the pathway towards the next floor, was Ryan's laughter.

Chapter Thirty-Nine

Ryan's fourth floor was breathtaking. It was unlike anything Blake had ever seen, and as he and the others stepped out of the large spiraling staircase onto the streets that made up the fourth floor, they had no choice but to pause. Ryan had definitely evolved. This floor was not the creation of some random instinct-driven creature or monster. This was so much more.

If not for the fact they were underground and within a dungeon, Blake would have thought he was in a normal town. All around them, streets went to and fro between rows of houses all cut from stone. The craftsmanship and detail Ryan had put into the design was more than just his normal mimicry. It was as if he were crafting this floor from something much more intimate.

"Welcome, brave adventurers, to my fourth floor." Ryan's voice pulled the group out of their silence. Blake had to give it to the dungeon core. Ryan must have waited at least five minutes before he turned the attention back to himself. That was an aspect Blake and the others had noticed about the dungeon. He liked for things to revolve around him. Which, considering they were in his dungeon, kind of made sense. After all, in a strange sense, within a dungeon, the dungeon core was God, and they were at his mercy.

"You've really outdone yourself," Blake commented. The others quickly agreed, commenting on the masonry and the layout of the floor. All of which the dungeon core seemed to greatly enjoy hearing.

"Right, well —" before Ryan could continue, he went silent. A few tense moments later, with Blake's party left standing there awkwardly, his voice returned. "—Without giving too much away, let me inform you this floor is unlike any you've ever explored."

That was a no-brainer. They could already tell his fourth floor was much more complex and almost human feeling than any of the ones before it. And if they'd learned anything from diving in the Bone Dungeon, it was that the more refined and sophisticated a floor of Ryan's was...the more dangerous.

"As you can see, this floor has been designed to mimic the layout of a human village." Again, an obvious statement. Blake could tell Jack really wanted to make a comment. Karan, linked mentally with Jack, seemed to sense it as well. Blake noticed her hand grabbing hold of the Duelist's arm, squeezing it tightly.

"I would encourage you all to fully explore this floor, though do be careful. The mobs, well, they've evolved." Ryan chuckled. "And I feel even your group will find this floor to be a rather intense challenge."

Blake didn't need Ryan to tell him or his party that. They'd been adventuring in the dungeon for over a year now. They knew just how dangerous he was. And they'd seen the strange types of mobs Ryan had created on the floors above.

Blake could only imagine what weird creatures they would run into on this floor. His first encounter with the zombearie flashed through his mind, and he nearly gagged at the remembered stench. Hopefully Ryan would stick to his bone theme and limit the number of zombies on this floor.

Looking around, Blake was relieved to notice there didn't seem to be any signs of sneks or snake-like mobs anywhere. They kind of made sense on the other floors, and Ryan loved using them against him. Surely, in such a pristine town, Blake wouldn't have to deal with the blasted things. He hated snakes.

"Anything else you'd like to tell us?" Jack was walking away from the party towards the teleportation crystal that hovered next to the stairway they'd just exited. He held his pendant up to the crystal, touching it gently. It glowed brightly for a moment before it dimmed back down. He'd attuned his pendant to the teleportation crystal, meaning he would now be able to teleport directly to the fourth floor. The rest of Blake's party followed suit as they waited for Ryan's answer. Blake knew any time Ryan went silent for these long periods he was usually discussing things with Erin. However, he couldn't mention that to the rest of the party. He'd sworn to keep Erin a secret from the party.

"Uh, have fun? And try not to die?" Ryan let out a dark chuckle. "Oh, and before I forget. You asked about how to get some armor like Blake's." At that, Jack's eyes shot towards the crystal skull. "I think you'll find a way to do just that on my fourth floor. If you can survive the Arena."

"Arena?" Jack turned, taking in the area. He pointed with one of his scimitars to where a massive, circular structure seemed to rise out of nowhere, dwarfing the buildings around it. Even though they appeared to be in the middle of a town, the structure was large enough to stand out. Next to the spiraling staircase they stood besides, it was one of the few noticeable structures. The other appeared to be a town-hall, in the opposite direction.

"That's the one." As Ryan confirmed Jack's question the Duelist's eyes lit with excitement, and he took a few steps towards it.

"Come on, guys. First stop, the Arena," the Duelist said excitedly. Blake had no objections. They were here to explore the floor, and it didn't matter where they started. Still, they did need to exercise caution. The last thing they needed was to make a fatal error early on. Blake had a feeling this floor was going to be a long one.

"Before we do," Blake said, halting Jack in his tracks. "How about we take in everything around here, and then proceed carefully?" Blake motioned above them, where massive clackers were visible soaring through the air. He'd also heard a few strange sounds other than just the distinct clattering of skeletal fighters and archers. This floor was full of mobs. That much he was certain of. And he was willing to bet it was filled with even more surprises. Traps, for one.

"Probably for the best," Ryan piped in. "Besides, you have to get an Arena token, which is a rather rare drop, before you can even take part in the Arena," Ryan said it nonchalantly, but Blake could tell the dungeon core was enjoying this. "If I were you, I'd start by checking out what the note on that pedestal says. Then start exploring."

Karan was the first one to the pedestal. It mimicked the one on the third floor, a stone pillar with a wide flat surface at the top. Affixed to the surface, was a piece of parchment. Just as Ryan had done on the third floor, he was giving adventurers clues. However, while the third floor note detailed, in rhyme, how to activate the boss battles, this note covered something else. As they all gathered around, Blake couldn't help but stare, wide-eyed, as he began to read.

For those who seek light in the dark,
Have no fear, be ye pure of heart.
Go forth and complete these simple tasks,
Then the Goddess shall send aid when asked.

Chapter Forty

As Blake expected, the fourth floor was massive and dangerous. Following the inscription, his party had talked it over
and decided they would try to activate the Goddess's blessing
on the floor and see if any of the mobs would drop an Arena
token for them. They still weren't sure how the Arena would
work, but Jack wanted to visit it. The Duelist was a sucker for
gear, everyone knew that.

According to the hints Ryan had given the party, the main
task necessary to receive this "blessing" involved clearing out
the houses in the area. Because the fourth floor seemed to be
a mimic of a massive town, there were a lot of houses.
Hidden amongst them, according to the dungeon, were five
golden feathers. Returning all five to the pedestal, along with
killing at least thirty creatures of darkness…which everyone
agreed were skeletal mobs, would result in them gaining the
Goddess's boon.

The "killing creatures" part was an easy task. Ryan had
filled the fourth floor with mobs, and it felt like they couldn't
go ten feet without seeing some sort of hostile creature.
Alright, maybe Blake was exaggerating. Perhaps it was more

like fifty feet, but the feeling of dread and danger hung in the air. Combine that with the increase in traps on the floor, and Blake and his party were very quickly getting worn down.

Mobs, and even bosses at times, weren't the most dangerous aspects of being an adventurer. The ever-present threat of death was a common companion. What scared them, what truly posed a threat to adventurers, however, was a mixture of encountering the unknown and exhaustion. Ryan's fourth floor seemed to have both of those in a large amount, and Blake was starting to understand how Brook's death had occurred. The thought of that death also had Blake and his team on edge.

Blake's party had been making their way slowly through the town, heading toward the Arena first. Information-gathering was important, after all. A lot of houses stood in the way to their destination. A large building, its unique architecture causing it to stand out from the rather uniform houses, made the party slow their advance. Brook's party had been ambushed and forced into a fight against some sort of boss mob after they'd come to a unique clearing with a gallows in it. Would this unique building trigger a fight as well?

"Is that…a bathhouse?" Jack, in wolf form, was just a few paces behind Blake. The Duelist had been using his winds and keen senses to keep an eye out for any of Ryan's plethora of traps. As the party's tank, Blake walked in the front, ever ready to put himself in the path of any and all attacks. In the vast expanse above they could hear the occasional roar, followed by a blaze of fire, as Cynder took on the giant clackers to keep them safe from aerial attacks. These giant clackers were massive forms of Ryan's usual skeletal birds, but against Cynder in her adult form, they really didn't stand a chance. She was, after all, an adult dragon. Blake turned back to Jack, eying the building ahead.

"Looks like a bathhouse to me," Blake agreed, scanning

the structure. His eyes, capable of seeing the souls of living creatures as well as the mana-filled centers of Ryan's mobs, were checking for any sign of an enemy. As he'd gotten stronger he'd noticed the range on his skill had increased. Also, he found if he pulsed extra Ethereal mana into his eyes, he could enhance the visual prowess of the skill to the point he could see through solid barriers. However, the mana cost to increase it past fifty feet as well as to enable it to penetrate through solid objects quickly became wasteful.

"See anything?" Winds billowed around Jack as he asked. Just like Blake had his eyes, Jack, finally Platinum, had an ability to passively keep the winds around his form active, which helped him recognize disturbances such as nearby creatures or traps.

"Another blasted snakie hanging out by the entrance...but otherwise nothing just yet." Contrary to Blake's previous assessment, Ryan had put many of his snake mobs on the fourth floor. At this point in time, Blake was suspicious Ryan was doing it just to mess with him. Ryan's laughter when a snakie had fallen on Blake from above as he walked into one of the houses had seemed to partially confirm Blake's suspicion.

"Man, someone needs to call in pest control on this town." Jack chuckled, a strange, deep rumbling sound. His wolfkin form, now that he was Platinum, had grown even larger than before. He wasn't as massive as Sasha and Rasha, likely due to him being only a half-blooded wolfkin, but he was still larger than the non-royal wolfkin Blake had seen. On top of that, Jack's silver fur now seemed to glow ever so slightly with its own light. His eyes had taken on a rich golden color, and his fangs and claws had all grown more formidable as well.

Blake chuckled at Jack's joke. Not only did the town have infested snakies, but it seemed there were a good amount of plated skrats running about. Blake had to admit, all this did give it the feel of a real town. Even when he'd been in Valta, Blake had seen more than a few rats running around the massive city. Along with stray cats, dogs, and various other critters. "Do you think Ryan would pay us to clear out the town for him?"

"Maybe. Though my services aren't cheap. I'm royalty, after all." Jack grinned, and pointed past Blake, back towards the bathhouse. "So, what do you say, shall we give this one a check?" The wolfkin made a sniffing sound. "You and the others could probably use a bath."

While they were able to heal their wounds, that didn't erase the blood staining their clothes. Nor did they have an instant, magical way to clear off the sweat, bone fragments, and zombie pieces that got caught on them as they did battle against the undead. Luckily for everyone, Blake and Jack received the majority of the undead showers during battle. Even after over a year of diving in Ryan's dungeon, the stench —and the longing for a quick rinse and change after a dive— was strong.

"Oh yeah, and then we can walk around with you smelling like a wet dog." Blake let out a laugh and cautiously started walking towards the bathhouse. He caught Matt's attention and motioned towards the entrance, signaling to the arcane archer that there was a snakie there. Matt nodded and drew his bow, pulling back an arrow.

He closed his eyes and slowly breathed out. The air leaving Matt's lips seemed to cool, and Blake watched as the arcane archer used the faintest amount of mana to cool the air around him, causing the water in the air to chill and almost frost. That string of frost reached the entrance to the bathhouse, stopping where the snakie lay in wait. With blinding speed, Matt opened his eyes and launched a single arrow towards the bathhouse. The missile flew true, and a second later the snakie's mana disappeared from Blake's field of vision.

"Alright, let's be careful about this. I wouldn't be surprised if there's a feather hidden here." So far they'd only found one, even though they'd searched a dozen houses. Ryan had furnished the insides of the houses, making them feel like humans had been living in them up until just recently, which made the searching even more difficult. On one occasion, they had found a treasure chest that contained a couple coin-based treasure cards. And, they had found a golden feather underneath a pillow in another house.

With the snakie dead, Blake began once again moving towards the bathhouse. As he approached it, he couldn't help but appreciate the size and grandeur of it. Ryan had crafted it, like all his other structures, from clean, white stone. However, the dungeon hadn't stopped with just making a bathhouse. Instead he'd decorated it with ornate sculptures and drawings across the walls. Nearing the entrance to the bathhouse, Blake could make out a sprawling courtyard where a few open-aired baths sat.

A small bit of steam came from the water, showing Ryan had gone so far as to even heat the water. There were also two buildings further within the courtyard of the bathhouse, which Blake figured were separate bathing areas for male and female bathers. In essence, Ryan had created a high-class bathhouse fit for royalty…in the middle of a literal dungeon of death.

"Well, I don't see anything just —" Before Blake could finish, a voice interrupted him.

"Blake. Pick a number from one through five." Ryan's voice caused the hairs on Blake's neck to stand up. He knew it. Ryan had something planned.

"Uh….four?"

"Drat, I was hoping you'd say one. Oh well." As Ryan

finished speaking, Dark mana erupted down all sides of the street, blocking Blake and his party in with nowhere to go but into the open expanse of the bathhouse. There, in the furthest portion away from them, rising from the ground between the two separate bathing buildings, was a monster Blake had never seen in his life. Fear rushed over him, and for a second, panic filled his veins.

"What in the name of the Goddess is that?" He whispered, mustering his strength to step forward, keeping himself between his party and the monster. The others were stepping cautiously into the clearing as well, their eyes fixated on the monster before them. Its body, seemed to be that of a massive, skeletal elk. Yet on its back, melded into the bones, was a humanoid figure, though the hands, the proportions, were all wrong. Atop the creature's humanoid head, a set of massive antlers. What was this thing?

"That, Blake, is my —" This time, Ryan was cut off.

"It's a Nuckalvee," Emily said. Blake, even with all his training, couldn't help from looking back at Emily, disbelief crossing his face. She knew what this nightmare-fuel was?

"Er. That's right. It *is* a Nuckalvee…" Ryan went silent for a long moment. Apparently, the dungeon core hadn't expected his creature to be recognized. Emily, suddenly aware of everyone's looks, and the fact she'd spoken out loud, shrugged her shoulders.

"The Nuckalvee is the strongest summon available for summoners with Darkness mana," Emily said, matter-of-factly. "I saw a statue of one once."

"Well, yeah… Behold my Nuckalvee." The creature had nearly risen from the ground, its empty eye sockets turning to focus on Blake and his party. Somehow, Emily's interruption of Ryan's grand explanation and entrance had lifted the some of the fear from the party. "He is one of five mini-bosses you may find on my fourth floor. One of five Bone

Enforcers." Ryan started cackling darkly, maniacally, as if he were trying to make the mood tense and dark once more.

"Ha." Jack started chuckling to himself. A moment later, the Duelist seemed to realize all the attention had now shifted from Emily to him. After all, this didn't seem like a laughing matter. Jack shrugged as Blake raised an eyebrow in his direction. "Seriously? Bone Enforcers…Bon-ers…" The Duelist shook his head as he moved to stand besides Blake.

As he did, Blake couldn't help but chuckle. Jack's statement erased the fear and trepidation that had crept across Blake at the creature's appearance. After all, it may look terrifying, but Blake was confident in his party. There was no way they were going to fall to Ryan's…Bone Enforcers.

Chapter Forty-One

The Nuckalvee was terrifying—that had already been established.

The creature seemed a strange, impossible combination of an elk and a human. Of course, Ryan had made combined creatures before. Heck, the howlers and Buttercup were combinations of deer and wolves. Still, those were two creatures completely fused into one. This, Nuckalvee, very much so retained both its original forms. That was because the whole elk remained, albeit on a massive scale. And then, fused into the middle of the creature, rising out from the Elk's back, was the torso and upper body of a human-like creature.

However, the "human" had the horns of an Elk atop its head and its dimensions were off. Like, way off. From hoof to top of the human head, the Nuckalvee was close to twenty feet tall. Somehow, the bony arms and hands of the creature descended all the way down towards the ground, elongated in an unnatural, impossible way. Not to mention, the human body fused to the elk seemed, ironically, boneless in how it slumped and shifted about – despite the fact that Blake could see the bones flowing about in the Darkness mana.

Creepy appearance aside, Blake could already tell it was going to be a strong foe. The enormous mass of the creature's mana gave that much away. The creature was enhanced, its body covered head to hoof with Darkness mana, creating a false version of flesh and fur on its body, granting the creature a whole extra layer of armor.

If that wasn't enough, Ryan had also seemed to find it funny to give the Nuckalvee an overly massive bone sword, which the creature held loosely in one of its disproportionately slender hands, dragging behind its form. The sword's girth and size, compared to the almost snakelike, unnaturally long and thin arms, was ridiculous. It would have been comical if this weren't a life and death situation.

The fight started with the sound of thunder as the Nuckalvee came charging towards Blake. The speed with which the creature closed the gap between the back of the bathhouse and where Blake was standing, probably two hundred feet away, was amazing. Still, Blake was a tank. He had at his disposal a wide variety of skills to ensure he could block any attack thrown at him within reason. He was pretty sure he wouldn't stand a chance against attacks launched at him by say, Alice. But as Ryan had said, the Nuckalvee was a mini - well, not so mini, mini-boss.

As the Nuckalvee neared him, Blake readied himself, ensuring he had a steady footing. He then summoned before him a massive shield of Darkness which hung magically in the air before him. He pulsed a healthy amount of mana into the skill from his vast mana pool to ensure it could withstand the oncoming attack. At Platinum 4 he had access to a total of 2,400 mana for his skills, split evenly between Darkness and Celestial mana. His physical traits, specifically his physical fortitude and strength, were empowered by 9,600 points of mana. He was physically already stronger than even a Platinum 1 tank class. And he was going to make sure he used that advantage to win this fight.

The mini-boss didn't even slow as it neared the massive shield of mana Blake had created directly in front of him. It lowered its elk head and crashed into the shield with such force that a shockwave sent the water from the baths in the courtyard erupting upward, raining warm droplets down across the entire space.

Blake only had a second to appreciate the force of that impact as the Nuckalvee unnaturally twisted its human torso with impossible speed. With the rapid motion, the Nuckalvee's long, strange arm cracked towards Blake and his party like a whip. Because of how large Blake had made his mana shield, the Nuckalvee's arm found itself impeded by the shield. However, instead of stopping, as was expected, the arm twisted and bent around Blake's defensive shield.

In a human, that would have signified a broken arm. For Ryan's mob, the bones just seemed to shift magically, as if they were free-flowing objects suspended in the shape of an arm formed by Darkness mana. In doing so, the Nuckalvee, with its sickening arm and its large bone sword, whipped around Blake and headed towards Karan and Emily.

"Jack," Blake cried as he pulsed Darkness mana into his shield, sending the mana roiling into the Nuckalvee. Part of Blake wanted to use his Ethereal mana to cause Karan and Emily to go incorporeal. However, using so much mana this early on in the fight would be more detrimental. Instead, he put his trust in the Duelist. Blake wasn't alone and he knew he could rely on his party. They weren't going to drop, even if the Nuckalvee had gotten them with a surprise attack.

"Worst tank—" Jack's voice was lighthearted as he spoke, his form disappearing in a rush of wind, only to appear before the Nuckalvee's sword. The wolfkin caught the massive weapon with his own scimitars, which he'd crossed in an 'X' before his chest. "—Ever," he grunted as his massive wolfkin form was forced backwards, muscles straining against the Nuckalvee's blow.

A normal Platinum 5 Duelist would have been knocked flying by such an attack, but Jack's wolfkin heritage gave him an additional bonus to his physical attributes while he was in his wolfkin form. As such, Jack was much tougher than a normal Duelist. Still, Blake could see the claw marks tracing across the ground from where Jack had dug in, and still been pushed back by over ten feet. The Nuckalvee packed a punch.

"Karan, we'll need auras." Blake turned his focus back on the fight. The Nuckalvee's human skull was staring down at him, its mouth agape as its elk front legs kicked against his massive Darkness shield. At the same time, it was winding its arm back, preparing for another attack. The taunt Blake had sent against the Nuckalvee was having less of an effect on the mini-boss than Blake hoped. He had been afraid of that. The stronger the creature, the more quickly it could shake off the effects of a taunt. To make matters worse, mobs gained a resilience to consecutive taunts.

Crap.

"Matt, try to take away its mobility." Even as he issued orders to his party, Blake was preparing for what was coming next. He knew how his party would react, and he knew what was going to be needed of him as the party's tank. In preparation, he began preparing a mass of Celestial mana for his next skill. Karan was able to give them Celestial auras which could mitigate the damage they took and heal their wounds for a set amount of time or until she ran out of mana. It was a helpful skill, to say the least, but also less effective, given they were fighting against creatures formed from Darkness mana. And, while Karan now had access to some offensive Celestial skills as well, they couldn't risk her using mana on offense, not when she was the party's main healer.

He needed to make sure they could keep the Nuckalvee at bay to ensure Karan could maintain her healing abilities and the rest of the party could get to work. Matt, with his Water affinity, had a knack for slowing enemies down…literally. Then, of course, there was the party's other ranged DPS.

A loud roar echoed through the massive chamber as Cynder descended from the air. As an adult dragon she dwarfed the humans of the party, her size similar to that of the Nuckalvee. If they were going to be facing off against the strongest of all Darkness mana summons, well, it was only fair to use the strongest of all Fire summons.

"Em, just, try not to burn us, yeah?" Blake released his Celestial mana, enacting a powerful golden barrier around his teammates. The defensive shield would only hold against one, maybe two blasts from the mini-boss, if the force it had struck at Jack with was any indication. This creature was meant to take foes down with single, powerful attack. However, the golden barrier he'd erected for his allies wasn't really to protect against the Nuckalvee. Instead… its purpose was to keep any accidental damage from say, a certain dragon's fire attacks, from hitting the party. That dragon had circled around from above, swooping down behind the Nuckalvee, and her eyes were sparkling with fire, flames licking across her maw.

"I would never burn you guys," Emily said, smiling at Blake as he shot her a sideways look. She had specifically burned him on multiple occasions. She'd never been the most…precise with her magic. And the more powerful she got, the more accidental burns Blake had suffered. Friendly fire…was not friendly. But Blake would gladly take on a few burns in exchange for the amount of damage Emily dished out to the enemies. Such was the life of a tank.

"Let me remind you how bad singed fur smells," Jack called out. He was already dashing past the Nuckalvee's massive arm. During the prep, the Nuckalvee had managed to launch another attack that Jack had intercepted. Even prepared this time for the force, Jack had been pushed backwards; he had even busted a blood vessel in his eye from straining against the force of the attack. Was the Nuckalvee increasing the strength of its blows?

Blake didn't have time to ponder that, and began moving to the other side of the Nuckalvee, trying to flank the creature with Jack. With the wolfkin on one side, Blake on the other, and his massive, Darkness shield blocking the Nuckalvee's path towards the rest of the party, he figured they could fight the boss with minimal damage. Just as he got into place, a golden glow appeared around him and the rest of the party, denoting Karan's protective aura was now up on the party.

"Shouldn't you guys be focusing?" Emily smiled sweetly at Jack as she pointed back towards the Nuckalvee. Jack had looked away from the creature for a moment to shoot a wink towards Karan. In that instant, the Nuckalvee's arm had once again twisted about. Instead of whipping forward like the previous two attacks, the appendage was snaking across the ground. The mini-boss had dropped its sword and seemed intent on catching Jack instead.

Most disturbing of all was that the arm was literally stretching. As it chased after the wolfkin it was growing thinner, and the fingers were becoming snaking tendrils of darkness, intent on catching their prey. Emily's comment had managed to just barely keep the wolfkin from being caught.

"Man, this thing is going to give me nightmares." Jack's scimitars flashed downwards, sending blades of air cutting into the dark tendrils. They made cuts but didn't have enough force to completely sever the mini-boss's mana.

"Who would create something like this?" He sent a flurry of slashes towards the approaching finger-tendrils. Darkness mana was blasted away by Wind mana, and irregularly shaped finger bones were blasted apart into shards from Jack's attack. Still, the Nuckalvee continued.

Jack had a good point. Up until now, Ryan's dungeon hadn't really been horrifying. At least, compared to how it could be. Sure, the dungeon used skeletons and zombies, but they were all pretty basic. The only strange combination they'd seen before now had been Buttercup and the howlers. And compared to the Nuckalvee, Buttercup was an adorable thing. This Nuckalvee was the embodiment of horror.

To make matters worse, Blake could almost sense some sort of underlying emotion stemming from the creature. Most of the time, mobs just felt like mobs But this creature radiated a sense of anger and agony. As if it was aware of its own unnatural existence and was taking that out on everything around it. Just what type of creature had Ryan created, and what else did he have waiting for them in the dungeon?

Blake's train of thought shifted back to the present as the humanoid body atop the Nuckalvee twisted around to face Cynder. The dragon had opened its maw, preparing to release a blast of fire now that Blake and Jack were out of the way, on either side of the Nuckalvee.

As the cone of fire erupted from Cynder's mouth, the antlers atop the Nuckalvee's elk and human head flew off, spinning rapidly, just as Buttercup's had. The spinning bones and Darkness mana stopped the flames before they could reach the Nuckalvee, pushing against the stream of fire, closer and closer to the dragon's mouth.

The mini-boss was somehow forcing Cynder's flames back towards herself. And while that was scarily impressive, it caused a new problem for Blake and Jack. For as the dragon tried to blow past the Nuckalvee's spinning bone defense, the deflected flames were forced outward, flowing past the spinning bones, past the Nuckalvee's body, to the left and right, and towards Blake and Jack.

Jack dove into one of the baths, submerging himself in water as the flames danced over where he had been. Luckily for him the errant flames did at least burn away some more of the Dark mana which made up the Nuckalvee's arm tendrils which had still been chasing him. As for Blake, he took a trick out of the boss's own book. With a thought and a pulse of mana the bones that covered his chest plate sprung forth and began spinning before him, creating a protective barrier of Darkness mana and bone fragments.

The flames flowed around him, just in time for him to notice the Nuckalvee's elk-like body had begun to turn. Apparently, the humanoid torso and elk body operated separately of each other. And while the humanoid form was dealing with the dragon, the elk had decided to do something about the shield blocking it from its prey by taking out the source of the shield. In other words, it was focusing on Blake.

As the fire attack from Cynder ceased, Blake had just enough time to see the flash of hooves coming towards him. If skeletons could smile, the Nuckalvee's elk mouth definitely was. Knowing he couldn't get his actual shield up in time, Blake did the next best thing, even if it cost a little more mana. The hooves crashed through his now Ethereal form, shattering the stones he stood on, creating massive craters as the boss tried to pummel him to death beneath the massive hooves. He was immediately thankful he hadn't tried to intercept that normally. Judging by the damage, those hooves would have caused some serious injury to him, even with all the mana strengthening his body.

With the creature trying to pound him into dust, Blake moved swiftly towards its underside. There he reached into the beast, and with his Spectral Grasp, drained some mana from it. He had hoped he might be able to cause some serious damage to the mini-boss with this skill. He'd once used the skill to win in a boss fight on the third floor. However, the Nuckalvee's massive mana pool was much more than he could siphon, even with all the mana at his disposal. Still, siphoning even a small amount could cause the creature to panic. And panic could cause an opening.

Sure enough, as he spent 200 points of mana to draw 100 points of mana from the Nuckalvee, replenishing thankfully the 100 Darkness points he put toward creating the 100 points of Ethereal mana needed for the Spectral Grasp, the entire mini-boss shuddered. The elk head looked about frantically, letting out a horrifying sound. Meanwhile, the humanoid body atop instantly withdrew its arms, bringing them closer towards its body as its eyes searched for the threat. But Blake was Ethereal and underneath it; the creature could neither see nor feel his presence.

This backfired a moment later, as the confused mini boss, unable to find the source of its discomfort, panicked and launched a large-scale attack on everything around it. The humanoid torso began spinning rapidly above the elk's body. Around and around it rotated, like a top, picking up speed. As it did, its arms, one of which was once again holding the giant bone sword, began to spin. Winds and debris began swirling around the mini-boss, and Cynder was forced to retreat outside of the range of the frenzied boss.

"Great job, Blake," Jack called out as he poked his head just above the water of the bath he'd been taking solace in. "I think you made him mad."

The elk head, unable to locate Blake, had turned its attention back towards Emily, Karan, and Matt. Emily had been using her mana to buff Cynder. Karan was using hers to keep the party safe. Matt, on the other hand, was standing there, seemingly doing nothing. At least, that was how it likely seemed to the mini-boss. Blake knew better. While the Nuck-alvee had been busy with Blake, Jack, and Cynder, the arcane archer had been preparing his skill. He'd picked up quite a few new tricks at Platinum, one of which was really, really handy in a boss fight. It just took a lot of time and mana to prepare.

"Ready Matt?" Blake called out. He could feel mana draining from him. Not only was he being drained three points of Ethereal mana per second to sustain his Ethereal form, but he was using Celestial mana still to keep up the barrier on his teammates, as well as Darkness mana to keep the massive mana shield erected in front of Karan, Emily, and Matt. Needless to say, he was losing a lot more mana than he was regenerating per second, and constant consumption like this wasn't something he wanted to keep up, especially not in a boss fight.

"Eight more seconds," The arcane archer called back. That wasn't going to do. The Nuckalvee had reared back and kicked the Darkness mana shield. Even with all the mana flowing into it, Blake felt it waver, cracks appearing on the solid black surface.

"Alright. Here goes nothing," Blake let out a grunt and dropped his Ethereal form. As he did, he sent a rush of Celestial mana into his sword, causing the blade to erupt with a brilliant light. "Holy Smite." he called out as he drove the sword into the monster's underbelly. The Celestial mana-clad blade cut cleanly through the Darkness mana that formed the stomach of the creature. The blade sank all the way to the hilt, the Celestial mana causing a lot of internal damage to the Nuckalvee. The Nuckalvee stopped its charge, unable to ignore what had just happened to it, and leapt backwards. This time, it was able to see the cause of its damage. This time, Blake felt the full attention of the boss focus on him.

"How's that for a taunt?" He grinned, bracing himself. The boss was charging at him, full force, and he knew he couldn't move out of the way. To do so would put the party at risk. So instead he held his ultra-rare shield out in front of him, sending Darkness mana into it. At the same time, he erected three more massive shields, made purely of Darkness mana, in front of him, creating a layer of defenses. Just like his other skills, using this one multiple times over increased the mana draw for each additional shield. However, he could instinctually sense that he needed this many shields to stop this attack. The Nuckalvee had previously been testing out its own strength. Now the boss, which Blake was certain had been created to simply overpower its enemies, was serious. And Blake was about to taste the true force of its attack.

The Nuckalvee crashed into the first shield and blasted it aside without even slowing. On the second one its momentum paused for a moment, before it ripped through that as well, coming in contact with Blake's third mana shield as it did. Again it blasted through this shield, allowing its lowered head to finally connect with Blake's own shield. Judging by the amount of agony that ripped through Blake as the creature blasted into him, he'd made the right choice. If it had this much force after going through those three shields, any fewer would have likely allowed the creature to hit him with enough force to knock him unconscious. At least that's what he thought as he found himself flying through the air, the bones in his arm shattered, aware of the fact he may have broken some ribs too. Still, he'd done what he needed to.

As Blake flew backwards, a twinkling blue light appeared above the Nuckalvee. It started as five points, sparkling brightly. While he continued on his trajectory backwards through the air, the mana spread across the five points, creating a star. Then, more mana branched out around them, over and over again, to create the shape of a snowflake high above the Nuckalvee. The snowflake pulsed with blue light before thousands of tiny arrows formed of ice rained down on the Nuckalvee. The mini-boss's entire body halted as frost overtook its form, freezing it perfectly in place.

"Finish him," Blake said in-between coughs as he smashed into the ground. Blood erupted from his mouth as one of his broken ribs punctured his lung, making his vision waiver. Being a tank class, the mana helped dull some of the pain, but this really hurt. Thankfully, his role in the fight was over.

Cynder let out a mighty roar. The dragon dug her claws into the frozen Nuckalvee, lifting the massive boss off the ground with her powerful wings. Up and up she flew, the frozen boss trapped, unable to react. The arcane archer's skill couldn't permanently freeze the creature. It was an effect, just like a taunt, and the stronger the creature, the quicker it could break free. Cynder got about a hundred feet into the air before it seemed like the Nuckalvee began regaining its movement, at which point the dragon promptly dropped the mini-boss.

Then, Cynder's entire form erupted in crimson light. With mana flowing into her from Emily, the dragon opened her massive jaws and launched her strongest breath attack. The flames met the frosted body and the sudden change of temperature, from being super chilled to super-heated, made the Nuckalvee's form crack in a thousand different ways. To the credit of Ryan's mini-boss, it managed to retain its form until it crashed into the ground. The Nuckalvee's own weight, combined with the force of Cynder's blast and the damage it had received caused the Nuckalvee to erupt into thousands upon thousands of pieces.

In place of the fallen boss, a massive chest appeared. They'd done it. They'd defeated Ryan's monstrosity. But as Blake picked himself up, slowly, from the ground, his Celestial mana and Karan's healing aura both working to repair his wounds, a thought crossed his mind. Ryan still had four more of these on the floor. And they were just mini-bosses. What was the boss on the floor like? Judging by how this fight went, his party wasn't going to be taking on the boss this dive.

To do so would be utter suicide.

Chapter Forty-Two

With Cynder watching from the skies, Blake and his party rested long enough in the crumbled remains of the bathhouse to heal their wounds and regain a large portion of their expended mana. Cynder, in her adult form, was able to do more than an ample job in the skies against the enlarged clackers, keeping Blake and his party safe from aerial attacks.

When she wasn't occupied with those massive forms, she could communicate locations of ground-based roaming mobs to Emily. It wasn't perfect, as they'd found some mobs liked to hide within the houses or under cover, but it helped keep them a little less stressed, while they were resting.

What finally prompted them to head out of the bathhouse and continue on with their journey of the fourth floor had been a less than subtle nudge from Ryan that they'd sat around long enough. The dungeon wasn't the bloodthirsty type, but Blake had known Ryan to be impatient. It was generally a good rule of thumb not to dawdle within the dungeon for too long. Sometimes Ryan would drop stalactites on people who waited too long. Or at least, that had been his old go-to. For his fourth floor, for some ungodly reason, he'd come up with an even more terrifying way to encourage adventurers to keep moving...Teleporting sneks.

One minute everyone was relatively relaxed, chatting about the mini-boss and speculating what other mini-bosses would be like on the floor. The next, flashes of light within one of the private bathhouses alerted the party to new arrivals.

About ten sneks came rushing out of the bathhouse, moving rapidly towards the party. To make matters worse, they weren't Ryan's normal sneks. They instead had four heads each, were roughly eight feet of unnatural bones held together by Darkness mana and moved a lot quicker than the previous variants. Ryan had been upgrading his sneks.

As the party dispatched the unwelcome intruders, Ryan's chuckling voice turned their attention back to the center of the large courtyard of the bathhouse, a crystal skull now rising up from the crater that had been the impact point of the Nuckalvee. Ryan informed them, bemusedly, that if they lingered much longer they would be getting more than just sneks for a surprise, and also tipped them off to the simple fact he could now teleport his mobs around at a whim. Nowhere on his floor would be safe.

Of course, this was the same Ryan who had created underground passages all throughout his other floors to ambush adventurers with roaming mobs. They weren't terribly surprised he'd planned new ways to attack adventurers, though the concept of teleporting mobs was alarming. After all, if a mob could teleport, it meant it could be any size of mob. The roaming ambush mobs had always had to be small enough to fit in the underground tunnels; all of them, save for mini-Steve, were relatively weak.

With new motivation, the party checked over their gear, making sure there weren't any major damages to their equipment that could cause problems during the dive, and continued on their way. While Ryan was being forthcoming with information, he'd also let slip they could stop looking for Arena tokens. Apparently Ryan had set those up to only drop from bosses and mini-bosses, meaning Jack really didn't have much chance of securing one during this dive. Jack took the news as well as expected. He was moping as they moved towards the Arena. Even though they couldn't enter today, that didn't mean they shouldn't at least check it out.

Luckily, after a short amount of time, they managed to make it to the Arena, without running into any more surprises. They even managed to find a second golden feather on their way. The dive was starting to look up.

Of course, Blake knew better than to allow himself to relax in Ryan's dungeon. Even though he couldn't help but consider Ryan a friend—the two had a connection—, he knew with relative certainty the dungeon would kill them if they dropped their guard. They'd come close enough to death a few times too many to hold that in doubt.

Still, he couldn't help but let his guard down a little in stunned awe as they reached the Arena. The coliseum dwarfed everything in the town. Its massive stone structure was impossibly large, making even Cynder appear small. All around it, entrances could be seen through stone archways, welcoming all who would go inside and face whatever challenges awaited. Jack and the party were sans an Arena token, meaning they wouldn't be able to activate it. But that didn't stop Ryan from telling them just how it worked.

"Once you acquire an Arena token for yourself," Ryan pipped up from a crystal skull sitting just before an entrance to the Arena, "you will be able to step inside and offer it up to me via a set of different stone altars. Depending upon the altar you place the token on, you will activate a different kind of challenge."

"What kind of challenge?" Jack asked as he licked his lips. This sounded like gambling. And the Duelist loved gambling.

"Well, each Arena token has a rarity, which will affect the tier of challenge you can choose. For instance, Steve drops a common one, which will allow you to choose up to three fights. A rare arena token, possibly dropped by my third-floor bosses, and the Bone En —" Ryan had to pause as Jack started chuckling again, "—Enforcers, will allow you to fight up to ten enemies in total. These enemies will vary in strength as well, depending on numerous factors. At the end, your rewards will be based on the rarity of your token, the types of mobs you faced, and how many rounds you decided to participate in."

"Sounds like a great way to farm some experience too." Jack was already rubbing his hands together, imaging the experience and loot he could earn.

"Right?" Ryan piped up. "I thought so too." The way Ryan said that, and the fact everyone knew the dungeon got stronger by gaining experience from killing adventurers, caused everyone to go quiet for a long moment.

The silence was broken by a chuckling Ryan. "I'm joking, mostly. Though, be careful. Once you start a challenge, you will be sealed in there until you either complete your challenges or die."

"Oh." Jack seemed subdued for all of a second, before a sparkle appeared in his eyes. "So…how many waves, and what type of token will I need to get awesome loot?" He asked.

"No gambling with your life, Jack," Karan said as she stepped besides Jack and hit him gently on the back of the head. "You're going to have to do this slowly. Trial and error." She shook her head. "I'm not about to let you get yourself killed after everything we've been through together, gambling in a dungeon."

"If you cleared all of a rare ticket's waves, Jack," Ryan prompted over Karan's scolding. "Trust me, the rewards would be worth it."

Jack looked from Karan to the crystal skull, and back to Karan. Blake could tell the Duelist was wondering if it would be worth it. However, after a moment he shook his head vigorously, as if solving an internal conflict. "You're right Karan. But what if —"

"No buts," Karan scolded, causing everyone, including Ryan, to laugh.

"Right, well," Blake started, looking around at his teammates. They'd gotten the info they'd come for on this side and still had a large portion of the floor to explore. No need in hanging around at the Arena anymore. Plus, Blake really didn't want Ryan to teleport any more snakes on them. "Shall we get going?"

"About that," Ryan interrupted again. Blake had a feeling Ryan was quite excited to finally have a group exploring his fourth floor. And in that excitement, Ryan was being a lot more hands on than normal. "I've one last thing for your party, while you are all here. Check it out."

The party turned around, drawing their gaze away from the Arena and Ryan's crystal skull, back to the street they'd walked down earlier. The previously empty street was no longer empty.

Five skeletal mobs stood patiently, as if waiting for Blake and his party to notice them. Blake could practically see Ryan's hand in this little gathering. But he couldn't help but be more than a little intrigued, especially as he focused on the mobs, and pulled up their assigned names. They were called Skeletal Champions and their names shone with a blue light.

They were rare mobs.

Chapter Forty-Three

The fight against the rare mobs escalated quicker than Blake anticipated. They'd fought uncommon mobs before in the dungeon. Those mobs had been tougher and faster than the regular skeletal fighter and archer versions, and could use basic mana abilities.

Depending on what type of skeletal variant Ryan used as the base, as it seemed Ryan could create differing levels of skeletons, denoted usually by the amount of Darkness mana within and around them, they could become quite powerful. The first time Blake's party had run into the uncommon mobs they'd struggled quite a bit. As such, they were more than a little cautious starting this new fight. That extra bit of caution stemmed not only from the blue color of the Skeletal Champions' names, but also from how they were equipped.

Normally Ryan's mobs were armed with simple bone weapons and armored with Darkness mana armor. The stronger the mob, the more solidified the Darkness mana flowing around them, and the tougher they became.

These Skeletal Champions were immediately different. The three in the front were covered in full sets of plate mail, with the skull of the God of Death emblazoned on the front, onyx stones set in the eye sockets of the emblem. The three were also holding large bone shields crafted to look like dragon skulls. Not to be outdone by their armor, their weapons were large bone swords, intricately made, that seemed to have Darkness mana pulsing all along the edge of the blade.

Behind those three, the two in the back held bows made out of animal spines, with much more craftsmanship and detail than the normal bone weapons Ryan's mobs wielded. Just like the other three, they were clad in actual armor, though theirs mimicked the archer class gear Matt had been wearing up until he received his dragon scale. Ryan had given these mobs actual gear. And not only that, Blake got a sense the gear wasn't plain old common gear.

Their strange gear aside, Blake could see they had large amounts of mana. If Blake had to judge, he would say these mobs had a similar amount of mana and strength flowing through them as Mini-Steve. Meaning just one of them could likely give a five-man party of gold adventurers trouble. He wasn't terribly worried for his party—after all, they were all Platinum members. In fact, Jack had dueled Mini-Steve, the last time around, all by himself. But something about these five caused a chill to creep through Blake. His senses told him not to underestimate these foes. They were unknown. And unknown things in dungeons were generally dangerous. But there wasn't anything they could do, other than take the plunge and figure out just how dangerous.

"Well, don't keep me waiting," Ryan whispered through Blake's pendant. The dungeon core was watching. The dungeon core was always watching. "They waited so patiently for you to turn back. It's only fair your party face them now." Blake could sense the amusement in Ryan's voice. The core was like a little kid when it came to testing out new mobs. The dungeon had used Blake's party on more than one occasion for that very reason.

"Alright." Blake glanced back at his party members, nodding towards them. They were going to do this right. They were going to be smart about this. No randomly rushing in. On cue, Karan's body began to glow gold as she put up the aura around the party. As the golden light pulsed over Blake, he lifted his shield cautiously in front of him, pulsing Darkness mana into it. At the same time, he sent Celestial mana into his sword, causing it to glow brilliantly with the golden light.

In response, the Skeletal Champions lifted their weapons off the ground and prepared themselves. The way they acted, almost like an actual adventuring party, was eerie. The three in front, serving as tanks, raised their shields exactly like Blake had. At the same time, their shields too were consumed with Darkness mana. Behind them the archers drew back their bows, arrows of Dark mana appearing on the strings. That was new.

The three Skeletal Champions in plate mail moved forward. They walked in step with each other, the sound of their clanging armor reverberating off the stone buildings around them, creating a haunting sound as they moved toward Blake. At the same time, the archers raised their bows in sync, and let fly two darkness arrows. Those flew fast and true towards Blake's party with deadly accuracy. Before they could hit their mark though, they were intercepted by two glowing blue arrows. Matt's skills had grown during his training, and at Platinum he was quite formidable.

As the two sets of arrows collided, the Darkness mana arrows shattered apart, spreading small, jagged shards of Darkness mana all about. The mana sizzled against the aura, covering Blake and his friends, and instantly Blake knew what they were. They were a version of the marksman "arrow rain" skill. These Skeletal Champions were using advanced class skills.

Uh-oh.

Blake didn't have time to worry about those archers though, as the three advancing Skeletal Champions had closed the distance. Without pausing, they leveled their shields towards him, and he watched as the dark onyx gemstones across all three shields lit up. A moment later Darkness mana roiled off the shields, sending wave after wave of Darkness mana blasting into Blake.

His vision waivered, going dark until all he could see were the three Skeletal Champions who had taunted him. Additionally, he could feel the sapping effect of the Darkness mana taunt, the uncomfortable wave of nausea that was an additional effect of taunts done through Darkness mana. Blake didn't like that one bit.

"I'm taunted," he called out. Blake hadn't been under the effect of an actual taunt in a long time. Cane had done it more than a few times to him, and he hated the experience every time. But even if the Skeletal Champions could use taunts, he wasn't overly concerned. It was annoying and unpleasant, but he was stronger than a Platinum 1 adventurer. He was confident he could handle these three. And besides, if they were able to use class skills—up to gold judging by the strength of the taunts, well, Blake still had an advantage. After all, he had extensive firsthand knowledge of all the skills and tricks a Gold Tier death knight could use.

"Just keep em there, Blake," Jack called out, the wolfkin's voice filled with amusement. Jack and Blake liked to spar on occasion, and the wolfkin had been subjected to the Darkness taunts more than once. Blake was certain Jack was more than a little amused by the fact Blake had been taunted. "I'll take care of the —" Jack's sentence was cut off as he let out a low growl. Blake, currently in the process of blocking one of the darkness covered bone swords while attempting to land a strike of his own, couldn't see what had happened to the duelist. But if he had to guess, the third knight, which had left his taunted field of vision, had gone to intercept the Duelist.

"You alright, buddy?" Blake could feel the effects of the taunt wearing off. It seemed the mob's taunt lasted about ten seconds on him, which seemed high for a Gold Tier ability against an individual as strong as Blake was. He had to wonder if that was because of all three of them hit him simultaneously with their taunts, or perhaps it had been empowered by their shields. Blake was pretty sure those shields, along with the rest of their gear, were rare, considering how well they were holding up against his attacks.

He'd landed a Holy Smite on the lead Skeletal Champion's shield, pulsing mana into the attack that would normally shatter an uncommon skeletal fighter's shield and entire arm. To his surprise, while the Darkness mana surrounding the shield had been blasted away and cracks appeared on it, both the shield and the Skeletal Champion's arm had survived.

"Fine. Totally fine." As Jack spoke Blake's vision cleared from his taunt. He saw the wolfkin attacking the third skeletal knight. His swords were moving in a blur, cutting angrily towards the knight. Blake could see the traces of Darkness mana clinging to the silver fur. Jack had been hit by a taunt. *Ha.* So now Jack was dueling one of the Skeletal Champions while Blake took on his two. Matt was doing his best to intercept the rain of arrows being launched at the party, while Cynder was…

A loud roar alerted him to the dragon's presence. Ryan was apparently tired of Cynder dominating the battlefield. The dragon was fighting against three greater clackers at once. The mobs didn't have a chance of beating the dragon, but Ryan had likely sent them to keep Cynder from incinerating all the Skeletal Champions with a fire blast. Tricky dungeon core.

Still, as Blake continued his fight against the two skeletal champions, he couldn't help but find himself smiling. They were tough, impressively so, but it was a welcome fight. They weren't overpowering. There wasn't a sense that a single mistake would result in death, such as when they'd fought against the Nuckalvee or other such powerful creatures for the first time. Instead, it was as if he was dueling against a duo of adventurers not quite as strong as Platinum 5, but definitely stronger and faster than Gold 1. It was exhilarating and fun, and he had to admit, he really liked these new mobs. As he tested them out, the lingering dread of the unknown faded, to be replaced with enjoyment and excitement. These mobs, he would gladly face over and over again.

As much as he was enjoying himself, he knew he needed to end the fight quickly. He was fine taking on two of them. He was fine taking on three or four of them at once, maybe even five if he was being honest. But because they were all close to the strength of a Platinum 5 adventurer, they would prove problematic if the fight prolonged. While Blake had a clear advantage, his party members were only Platinum 4. Plus, they were still somewhat fatigued. After all, they'd faced a lot during this dive, and they were only human—or humanish, in Jack's case. Blake knew it would be better to end a fight like this sooner, rather than later.

With that thought clear in his mind he turned his focus fully onto these two. Now that he had a good sense of their power, and an unfair level of understanding of their skills and tricks, he would end this fight quickly. As his resolve flowed through him, he ordered the bones on his armor to once again detach, sending the swirling fragments rapidly towards one of the two Skeletal Champions.

He used the bones to catch the creature's shield arm and

pulled the appendage back, drawing the arm and shield away from the protective placement it had established. As he did so, he used more of his bones to pull away the sword arm as well, leaving the Skeletal Champion standing there, both its arms pulled behind its back, defenseless. The other skeletal champion tried to come to the mob's aid, but it was too late.

Blake shrouded his sword with Ethereal mana and thrust it forward, penetrating through the creature completely as the ethereal blade passed harmlessly through. Then, with a grin, he released the Ethereal mana and pulsed the blade with Celestial mana, at the same time activating a Holy Smite, even as the now solid blade was violently ejected from the Skeletal Champion's body. Sure, it would cause a bit of damage to the blade, but it wouldn't be enough to end their run...rare swords were durable, after all. The combined effect left a gaping hole in the creature's chest, causing the Skeletal Champion to stumble backwards.

Blasting a hole in a skeleton's chest wasn't fatal, of course. But the Skeletal Champion, arms pinned behind its back, stumbling backwards, had no way to catch itself. It fell to the ground and Blake brought his sword crashing down on its skull. Celestial light blazed as the mob succumbed to Blake's Smite. One down, one to go.

As he turned to face his foe, he noticed Jack had finished his duel against the one Champion in his way, and was now advancing on the two archers. This fight had been fun, but it was about to be over. Then it would be time to see just what kind of loot these mobs dropped.

As he worked against the second of the Skeletal Champions, he couldn't help but admire the weapon it used. If it was a rare sword, he was more than willing to give up the current sword he was wielding in exchange for one of these. While he was hesitant about walking around with the legendary demonic sword out in public, and even hesitant about using the sword in an actual combat situation, he'd moved past his hesitance about using bone related objects. Plus, he couldn't help but think how awesome those darkness-clad bone swords would look with his new bone chest piece. Aesthetics, at times, were just as important to adventurers as the gear itself.

With the thought of new loot in mind he quickly worked to dispatch this final foe, confident Matt and Jack would be able to finish the two ranged foes. He couldn't help but feel exhilarated as he defeated the second Skeletal Champion.

This was what he loved about being an adventurer. The thrill, the challenge against new and unknown mobs, the excitement over new loot and gear, and the feeling of accomplishment and camaraderie when his party defeated a difficult foe or completely cleared out a floor.

It was for these moments Blake would continue coming back to Ryan's dungeon as he and his friends worked to grow ever more powerful. And while they wouldn't be fighting the boss today, it was only a matter of time before he and his party would stand face to face with whatever crazy creature Ryan had cooked up for them. Because that was the life he and his party—his family—had chosen.

But first, it was time for a new sword.

Chapter Forty-Four

RYAN

"Aw, my hero has failed me," Erin bemoaned as she watched Blake and his party teleport out of the dungeon. They'd been doing their best across Ryan's fourth floor and had taken down a second of Ryan's Bone Enforcers, Andre the Giant. The Bone Enforcer had been there to greet them as they got to the cemetery of the town, shortly after they'd taken on one of Ryan's massive skelephants. Between the skelephant and Andre's defensive capabilities the party, worn and weary from their dive, had made the decision to leave the floor.

At that point in time, they'd only managed to find one more of the golden feathers. Technically, there were six golden feathers to be found, and Ryan had set them up to magically appear across the dungeon floor in random locations whenever a party entered the fourth floor. That way, they couldn't simply memorize the location of the feathers and use Erin's aid every single time with ease.

Still, Blake's party had been the only one to make progress through his fourth floor to a respectable degree. Though they wouldn't be the last, as other groups had begun leveling appropriately and were preparing themselves to take on his latest challenge. Still, Erin had really been hoping to be summoned by Blake's group. Blake was not aware of the transformation the fairy had undergone; he was in for a surprise.

"At least you had a chance," Hel muttered bitterly. "I wasn't even allowed out of the room." Hel, normally perfectly composed, was a lot angrier now. She had hated that she was confined to the core room while Blake and his party were diving.

"Hel, you know as well as I do Blake would likely attack you on sight." According to Blake, his father had been possessed by a demon and the Paladin ended up killing himself to keep from being taken over completely. The only true demon Blake had ever seen had been the actual Hel, who had corrupted the Dungeon of Ashes. While the Hel in Ryan's dungeon was merely a clone of that one, and not responsible for anything that had happened to Blake...Ryan wasn't sure the adventurer would be able to see the logic in that. After all, Ryan's hate for the Church had carried over through his resurrection as a dungeon core, even with his memories wiped.

The Succubus looked from Erin to Ryan and let out a heavy sigh. "I know, Darling," she said softly. "I just really want to get out to play and Blake and his party are just so... invigorating." The way she said that made Ryan feel she had more than a small want to go and mess with Blake's party. Ever since Hel had been introduced to the party, via watching them explore Ryan's dungeon, she'd had a strange interest in them, especially in Blake and Jack.

"Well, your safety is more important to me than you having fun with the adventurers," Ryan responded simply. It was his job to keep his two companions safe. And while they were now equivalent in status to Platinum Tier boss mobs, they were still linked to Ryan, and in his eyes, still his precious little fairies. He was going to keep them safe, even if that meant keeping them from something they wanted.

"You're too good to me, Darling," Hel purred. She walked towards his core, her movements exaggerated. If Ryan was still human, she'd definitely be hard to resist. The Succubus reached up a clawed hand, tracing it slowly down his core. "Of all the cores I've memories of guiding, you are truly the most unique."

Erin cleared her throat. Hel shot the Celestial fairy a fanged grin but kept her hand against Ryan's core. "I've not forgotten you either, little one," Hel continued. "Even though you may be brainwashed, I've got a special spot in my heart for you too."

"I'm not brainwashed." Erin sniffed as she narrowed her eyes at Hel. The action caused Hel to break out in a dark chuckle. The Succubus loved picking on the Angel. That had become the norm around Ryan's core room. Of course, as the two began poking fun at each other, Ryan turned his attention away from them, and scanned his dungeon.

From the looks of it there was a new party preparing to head into his first floor, a group of brand-new adventurers led by a Silver 5 knight. They would be fine. Lined up for his third floor was a royal, Silver 1, surrounded by high Gold Tier guards. Ryan let out an audible sigh of his own, regaining the attention of the squabbling fairies.

"It looks like it will be a while before anyone else comes down to the fourth floor." Outside his dungeon, there was a party of Platinum adventurers waiting to dive. But Ryan would have to wait for the royal and his party to go through first. Not only were the parties with royals taking his dungeon slowly now to farm as much experience as they could, safely, they were getting in the way of good adventurers diving into his dungeon. Ryan was tired of them.

"Are you sure I can't tease some of the adventurers on the

second and third floor?" Hel said playfully. "I promise I'll be gentle with them."

"Positive," he replied with a chuckle. Hel really was getting restless. He wondered if he would have to forcefully restrain her soon to keep her from going against his wishes.

"Well then, Darling, I need something else to entertain me." Her voice became deeper, sultrier. "So you better think of something good."

Ryan flashed mentally through his entire dungeon. They'd already checked in on all of his fight club levels. His floors were reset with their mobs. Hel and Erin weren't as fond of item crafting as he was, and they'd already done the crystal renovation on his dungeon floor. What else could they…

A memory rushed into his mind. Something he'd been shown by the God of Death when he'd ascended to Platinum. Something…a lingering promise that had been pushed from his mind almost as quickly as he'd gained the knowledge. The God of Death had given him back his memories of being human immediately after sharing with him the potential of a dungeon that climbed to Diamond Tier.

"Do…either of you know what an Avatar is?" He asked. The dungeon fairies were supposed to have all the knowledge that would be pertinent to dungeon cores and their growth. Hel had the most in-depth knowledge, thanks to her memories from the original Hel, who'd apparently been the dungeon fairy to a lot of dungeons over hundreds of years. Erin, on the other hand, was extremely young in fairy years, and had received…less than thorough training, it seemed. Which was why her reaction, and the smile on her face, surprised both Ryan and Hel.

"I do." Erin's face lit up even more as she realized where Ryan was going with this. He wasn't overly familiar with the concept. The God of Death had given him a glimpse of what an Avatar was… the only way for Ryan to ever have an actual body again. "Are we going to start working on your Avatar?" The excitement from both fairies nearly overwhelmed Ryan.

"I figure, might as well get to work on it, so it's ready when I hit Diamond." That was the teasing portion of it. The God of Death had given him the vision of what an Avatar was, but also the knowledge that it wasn't something a Platinum dungeon could activate. Only those dungeons of Diamond and above could utilize an Avatar. After that glimpse, the knowledge had faded from Ryan's mind...it wasn't knowledge a Platinum dungeon would normally have. But he did, and now was as good a time as any to begin preparing his final form.

The Exalted One

"So he failed in his task?" The Exalted One curled his lip, feeling the fangs underneath as his anger flared for a moment. He'd warned the man. Yet perhaps it had been a task too steep, even for the Death's Breath.

"The target survived...but has been greatly weakened, Exalted One," the cloaked figure said, kneeling before the Throne of Chaos. The man was a Platinum 1 assassin, and had been right-hand man to the Death's Breath. Now that the Assassins' Guildmaster was gone, it was only a matter of time before this man took on that role.

"Weakened how?"

"In the ensuing fight, his right arm was severed, as was his left leg." The cloaked man glanced up. "It is impossible, even for the Duke of Blood, to fight on the same level he used to, with those types of injuries."

The man had a point. The Duke of Blood, one of the most bloodthirsty individuals to ever live, had been a possible threat to the Exalted One's plans. Not because he was worried the Duke would be able to stop him, but because the Duke, who loved nothing more than fighting, would have chosen to stand against the Exalted One's forces just for the fun of it. And ironically, the Exalted One didn't want that level of Chaos to be allowed to interfere with his plans.

Still, the Dreadnaught, the class given to a Chaos knight who reached Diamond, would be less able to use his full might on the battlefield. That didn't mean the fool wouldn't try to be on the battlefield, but a crippled Diamond 3 would be a lot easier to deal with if he did show up. And, while it was never ideal to lose pawn pieces, trading the Death's Breath in exchange for crippling the Dreadnaught, was a fair trade. Besides, he'd fully intended on killing the Death's Breath when the man returned. The Exalted One had never planned to give him freedom. He was not the type to leave loose ends connecting back to himself.

"I suppose there is at least that." The Exalted One let out a sigh and motioned for the man to leave. The assassin bowed once more, then teleported from the room. The Exalted One knew the next time he saw the assassin, he'd be Diamond 3. Now that his Guildmaster was dead, there was no one keeping him from ascending. The Exalted One had always chuckled about the way the Assassins' Guild worked. Members were forbidden from seeking advancement to Diamond 3. Any who tried were killed before they could even beseech the God of their given affinity for the right to ascend.

It was a power play meant to ensure the Death's Breath could keep complete control over his guild of killers. His shadow, his omnipotent might, and the terror, the threat, of dying if anyone attempted to ascend to Diamond had kept the guild members in line for so long. The Exalted One couldn't help but feel a little bit of excitement at the potential chaos that man's death might cause. Chaos in the Assassins' Guild would mean he didn't have to worry about anyone trying to hire assassins to thwart his plans.

"Next," He called out as he calmed himself. There were other matters to attend to. A moment later, a form appeared before him, covered in black robes as well. One of his spies, sent to keep track of the Bone Dungeon. As of now the Bone Dungeon was the only dungeon to escape his grasp. The only dungeon, other than those of the Gods, that had stood against the call of Chaos.

"Over the past month, the residents of Boneville have continued to grow in strength. Multiple parties have climbed to Platinum, and those who were already Platinum have begun to grow in power. The death of the Platinum 5 mage a month ago seems to have been a fluke. The dungeon remains a safe, in dungeon terms, place for adventurers to grow and will likely continue to provide all who seek it the chance to grow stronger."

"Very well." He'd hoped the dungeon had been corrupted enough that it would prove its own undoing. When he'd heard it had killed a Platinum adventurer, he'd been optimistic. If it was deemed dangerous, the Adventurers' Guild and the Church would declare it a threat and take care of it for him. However, the dungeon continued to be an anomaly. He was going to have to push things along. He couldn't very well allow adventurers to continue to grow stronger. That was…counterproductive. After all, he needed less opposition, not more.

"The Bone Dungeon must be destroyed. See that it is taken care of."

"As you wish, Exalted One." The robed man bowed down and disappeared. With him gone, the Exalted One could get back to his other agenda.

"Bring out the prisoner," he said. He could hardly contain his excitement. A glowing portal appeared before him and Marissa stepped forward, dragging their captive along. The figure on the ground looked up defiantly at the Exalted One. She was a tough one indeed. He was right to have been cautious about capturing her.

"Now then, Monica," he said coolly, as he stood up. Power erupted over his right hand, red and black mana crackling dangerously. "Where did we leave off?" He'd accompanied Marissa to capture Monica, the Diamond 3 Death Lord that Alice had dispatched with the last few parties sent to take down the corrupted dungeons. He'd waited until the party was in the final dungeon set to be destroyed before he'd ambushed her. The ambush had resulted in the death of everyone that had accompanied Monica. After all, he didn't need Alice getting word that adventurers were being captured and not killed within these dungeons. That type of information would give away his plans.

The Death Lord had put up a massive fight. She'd also thrown about a few surprises, ranging from her complete willingness to resurrect her fallen allies as undead to fight alongside her, to her ability to summon wraiths and the like from lingering souls around her. Death Lords were formidable, especially when surrounded by death. However, her biggest surprise had been when he'd discovered what she truly was.

The Death Lord glared at him and her eyes flashed, shifting to a glowing red as she fought against the restraints holding her captive. She snarled against the gag in her mouth and as her lips pulled back, they revealed two sharp fangs. He wasn't sure when the change had happened, but the God of Death had turned Monica into a True Vampire.

"Ah, that's right." He continued to step closer to her, his eyes taking in everything about her. Humans were easy to corrupt. This, however, was something he was thoroughly looking forward to. With Marissa's aid he was going to break Monica, and then create the first ever demon-vampire hybrid. That would become a formidable tool for the final portions of his plan. "We were just about to begin playing our little game." His smile intensified as her defiant growls turned quickly into screams.

Chapter Forty-Five

The rest of the week was less interesting than Ryan had hoped, much to his dismay. While there were indeed adventurers strong enough to step foot in his fourth floor and survive an encounter with his Bone Enforcers, only one other group did so all week. They had only taken on a single Bone Enforcer, Badgy the Badgerman, before they headed back to the surface. That being said, there was apparently a good reason for their hesitation. There had been an assassination attempt on a Diamond 3 individual known as the Duke of Blood, whom Ryan recognized as the father of Blaine Dragnov. In other words, Emily and Matt's cold-blooded father.

Ryan was torn on the situation. On one hand, he didn't like Blaine. The Platinum 1 Blade Dancer was Matt and Emily's brother and had made no efforts to hide the fact he wanted Matt dead. From what Ryan had picked up from Blake, the Duke of Blood had tried to have Matt assassinated multiple times. Tried really not being the proper term. Matt had been assassinated in the dungeon town, right in front of Blake. Of course, Blake had brought him back with some secret power available to him due to his Specter of Balance class. Still, the fact was, Duke of Blood and Blaine Dragnov? Bad.

Yet, a part of Ryan respected Blaine, and he owed the man a small amount of gratitude. Blaine had come to his aid, or maybe more appropriately, the town's aid, during the demon attack. The Blade Dancer had taken down a Platinum Tier boss mob known as a Light Ender, turning the tide of the battle and giving Ryan a much-needed reprieve, which arguably helped Ryan defeat the chaos cultists attacking his dungeon from the inside.

Either way, Blaine's actions didn't' change the fact that the Duke of Blood was a bad guy. And honestly he didn't care one way or the other if the man died. But that was Ryan's point of view. From an adventurer's standpoint, an assassination attempt made on arguably one of the strongest humans living in the world, was a big deal. Even bigger, the fact the attempt had been carried out by the head of the Assassins' Guild. A Diamond 3 assassin known as Death's Breath. The Death's Breath had been slain in the attempt and the Duke of Blood was gravely wounded. In one night, two of the strongest humans alive had been nearly erased from the world.

As much as Ryan wanted everyone to keep on diving into his dungeon so he could keep growing stronger, the adventurers had different plans. The political ramifications of such an event were massive, and many of the royals had been called back home to gather more guards and protective forces. Additionally, a lot of the stronger adventurers suddenly found themselves flooded with requests to act as bodyguards. Many of these were extremely lucrative, and a lot safer than diving the dungeon.

Beyond that, the unease that this unheard-of event

caused, meant adventurers were suddenly a lot more on edge. They were waiting for the dust to settle before they took too many risks. Meaning even those parties who could—and should—have been going into Ryan's fourth floor, decided to take it easy that week and just stop after his third floor. In short, it was a week of dismal experience gain from him.

The only silver lining of these events was, Ryan found himself with a lot of time to work on his Avatar. With the chaos going on outside of his dungeon, he figured he should focus his efforts and use the free time he had to prepare for the future. From the combined pool of knowledge from his fairies and the image the God of Death had teased him with, the concept of an Avatar was a simple one. The Avatar would serve as a host body for the dungeon core to take over in order to traverse his dungeon fully.

According to the legends Hel knew, a dungeon core with an Avatar could leave the confines of its own dungeon. Such an action was the talk of legends, and Ryan could only imagine the ramifications an Avatar leaving a dungeon could cause. Plus, he knew he had to wait until he was Diamond to even test out his Avatar.

But just because he couldn't use it, didn't mean he couldn't make it. He and the fairies had got to work. The first task at hand was creating a workspace. That had been easy enough. Ryan carved out a massive empty expanse behind his core room, making the space a hundred by one-hundred-foot square. He wasn't sure how much space his Avatar would need and figured the extra room would be nice once he did get to use his Avatar. Plus, Ryan had been searching for more bone remnants. Erin jokingly claimed he had a bone hoarding problem. He just told her he was an avid collector.

The completion of the Avatar room was bittersweet. On one hand, it was finished, meaning Ryan could continue with his work. On the other, he'd stumbled across some more bone fragments, belonging to some large, reptilian creature. However, he hadn't gained enough to fully identify the blasted skeleton, and with the focus on building an Avatar, he couldn't go hunting for the bones. Which meant that would get added to his to do list, while he moved onto the more pressing matter at hand, Avatar creation.

According to Erin, the Avatar itself was a vessel for the soul within the Core. However, the Avatar alone couldn't sustain the dungeon core. From what the fairy knew, the dungeon core needed to be in contact with the Avatar for it to work properly. From the vision the God of Death had shown Ryan, a staff with the dungeon core resting atop it was the appropriate route to go.

That being said, Ryan's core was already quite large. If it were going to be atop a staff, he reckoned the Avatar would have to be close to forty feet in height. Still, Ryan was merely guessing there; he didn't have any idea on how large his core would actually be once he hit diamond. Furthermore, he figured he could just create his Avatar form now and adjust the size of the bones and its proportions appropriately once he knew the size of his core and the staff he would use.

Size considerations aside, Ryan jumped into Avatar creation with what felt natural: he went with a human sized skeletal form. There may have been a part of him that viewed this as a second chance at an actual life, though as he started creating the form, trying to find the skeleton closest to his own old size, he realized how foolish a thought that was. He couldn't create living flesh. And he didn't want to walk about as a rotting corpse. Meaning his Avatar, the Avatar of the Bone Dungeon would have to be a skeleton.

A few moments of depression later and he'd moved past those thoughts and onto something more exciting—outfitting his Avatar. Obviously, if he was going to be a terrifying god-like being within his dungeon, he needed to be dressed appropriately. Ryan may have spent the better part of a day, or two, on perfecting his armor and clothing, detailing it in golds and silvers, giving himself a draping purple cape, inlaying everything with masterful precision. When he'd finished, his Avatar had been dressed in gear that would have cost an adventurer a fortune.

Only then had Hel reminded him he could give himself magical gear. This meant all the work he'd done on his Avatar, all the care and precision and time he'd taken to make his Avatar look terrifying and regal, had been wasted. Because the logical thing to do was to outfit himself with magical equipment of the highest caliber.

Legendary gear.

The problem was Ryan only knew how to create ultra-rare gear. As of yet, he'd never crafted a unique piece of legendary gear, and even as he tried to do so, he found he couldn't. While he was able to give his Avatar ultra-rare armor and weapons, the vessel was lacking the highest tier of gear to really make it stand out. Save for one thing. He had a single piece of legendary gear he could outfit his Avatar with. Granted, from his understanding of it, the object would be useless to him. But useless or not, by the time he'd finished, his Avatar was wearing the Crown of Sorrows, the legendary crown of bones the necromancer Viktor had used to summon a lich upon the dungeon town so long ago.

From what he knew of the item, it was a necromancer specific piece of gear, which allowed a necromancer to summon a powerful dungeon mob of higher tier than the user. Viktor, a Gold Tier necromancer, had used it to summon a Diamond Tier lich. Ryan was more than a little jealous of that even now, after he'd grown so much. Viktor had been able to summon something Ryan couldn't yet create on his own. In that instance, legendary items almost seemed like cheating. Then again, that power, that massive boost in ability, was partially what made an object legendary.

By the time Ryan finished with his Avatar, the week had come almost to a close; it would soon be time for the adventurers to begin going through his dungeon on their next set of runs. Which meant he would soon get to see Blake and his party again, and hopefully a few other adventuring parties would delve into his deeper depths. He even hoped, weirdly enough, for the return of the royals to the town. As much as he despised them as humans, they did bring with them a fair amount of experience, and a neat item or two.

While Ryan still didn't care for pointless deaths, now that he had his Avatar prepared, and the knowledge of what could happen once he hit Diamond Tier, he found himself itching even more for experience. Because of this, as he watched a group of adventurers leave his dungeon, the last one for the week, he couldn't help but feel...depressed? Ryan wasn't sure, but the waiting, the long hours, weighed more now that he had his human memories. Along with those feelings, the knowledge of what came at Diamond made the waiting feel even longer.

"Alright then, dungeon, guess that's it for the night," Marcus said gruffly, turning his back on Ryan's entrance. The Platinum rogue had taken to talking to Ryan at times, both greeting him and telling him when he was leaving, every day. Ryan wasn't sure why Marcus did what he did, but he appreciated it. It helped feed a part he neglected at times. His human, sociable side. It felt nice, to be able to talk to more people than just Erin, Hel, and Blake.

"Until tomorrow, then," Ryan replied. As he turned his focus back into his dungeon, gazing longingly at his Avatar, a surge of energy, followed by a bright flash and a cry of surprise, ripped his attention back to the entrance. Marcus stood frozen there, surrounded by a glowing prison of golden light. The cause of the burst of energy became evident a moment later. The Zealots of the Goddess of Justice were marching towards Ryan's dungeon. And they had just imprisoned Marcus.

Chapter Forty-Six

"Explain yourself, Paul," Marcus growled. Around him the winds began to swirl as the Platinum 1 rogue prepared to free himself from the glowing prison he had been captured in. Before him, Paul, Platinum 1 bishop, Zealot of the Goddess of Justice, and Ryan's murderer, stood surrounded by about twenty other Zealots. They ranged from Silver to Platinum, all with Celestial mana, and all marked with brands on their palms.

"My dear Marcus." Paul smiled strangely as he stepped forward. "I'm simply doing the Goddess's work." He was definitely crazy, but Ryan already knew that from firsthand experience.

"What's going —" Erin's voice paused as she and Hel peered into Ryan's core. They'd come towards him the moment he saw what was happening, reacting to his sudden change in emotions. He was a swirling mass of rage and confusion. What was going on? Erin's eyes hardened as they locked onto Paul. She was not a fan of the Zealot. Nor the things he did in the Goddess's name.

"The blasphemer," She hissed.

"Oh, I like that reaction, little one." Hel chuckled darkly to herself as she took in the situation. "It seems he and his friends have returned to cause trouble."

"Hush," Ryan silenced the two, just as Marcus spoke again.

"Ha. My pinky finger represents the will of the Goddess of Justice more than you do." Marcus spat on the ground. "You're a crazy fool who fell off her path a long time ago but is protected because the Church is too ashamed to expose you and reveal the sins you have committed in their name. Afterall, I'm sure even rabid dogs have their uses. You've brainwashed yourself and those around you into believing the world is simply light and dark." As Marcus spoke, his winds intensified, pushing against the golden light imprisoning him. The bars of light began to crack. "Don't you know the world is actually —" Paul raised a hand. The group behind him began to glow with golden light. Marcus stopped, eyeing them all coldly.

"You are wrong, Marcus. It is you who has allowed yourself to go down the path of sin. I would never expect a," he paused, spitting on the ground, "despicable *adventurer* to understand. And," Paul's voice went low, "I know full well of your tainted family line. Tell me, how did it feel, knowing your sister was —" Before Paul could finish a blast of wind erupted from Marcus, drawing a thin line of blood across the bishop's cheek. The man smiled as golden light healed the wound, his eyes dancing with amusement.

"Alas, Marcus, I come here not for some pointless discussion. I've received urgent, troubling news about this den of evil behind you. And I've been tasked, by the Church, with investigating these claims fully." He held up a finger towards his cheek, even as he motioned backwards toward his followers, signaling for someone to step forward. "And I'll have you know, before you try any more of your tricks, that if anything befalls me here and now, the Church will come to put the dungeon—and any who stand in their way—down." He smiled sinisterly, and Ryan felt his core go cold. This wasn't good.

As Ryan worked to process that, he stopped the preparations he had been doing. These involved getting ready to collapse the ground under the group if Marcus needed aid. That, was apparently out of the picture now, if what Paul said was true. So, instead, Ryan turned his focus on the individual walking forward from the back of the group, the one Paul had beckoned for. He needed to know what was going on. Alfred, the Gold cleric who'd been a part of Brook's party. Alfred had been in Ryan's dungeon just the day before, with a new group, a group that had descended to his fourth floor. They'd only killed a few mobs before returning to the surface though. What did Alfred have to do with this?

"Your dungeon here is an abomination." Paul continued. "This brave follower of the Goddess has found evidence that this vile Darkness dungeon has trapped within it a creature of the Goddess." *Oh no.* Ryan did not like where this is going.

"What are you talking about?" Marcus stared in disbelief at Paul. "Do you hear yourself? This is just a dungeon. And a good one, at that." The thought of fighting again was written on the rogue's face, but his eyes darted back towards the crowd of followers, all watching him intently. "This dungeon has proved time and time again that he is not a monster."

"He?" Paul raised an eyebrow. "This dungeon is merely a creature of darkness. It is an evil tool of darkness, that brings about only death," Paul said. "As a *true*," he stressed that part, likely in response to Marcus's insult earlier, "follower of the Goddess of Justice, it is my sacred duty to cleanse the world of evil."

He folded his hands calmly before him, looking Marcus up and down. "The decision by Sean to not destroy this dungeon was a foolish one. And now I must put my life and my followers' lives in danger to clean up after his mistake, all to carry out the appropriate justice and to save this Celestial being before who knows what else happens." The band of Zealots all let out a quiet murmur of agreement to Paul's statement. "You've failed, Marcus." Paul stepped away. Marcus stood there, his eyes frantically moving about, trying to process everything. "But don't worry. It will all be over soon."

"You're a fool," Marcus growled again. "You're making a huge mistake." His winds once again intensified. "You're going to get yourself killed over nothing."

Paul, who was now standing with Alfred and the other Zealots, all of whom were linking their hands together, started to chuckle. "As I said, Marcus, my life is for the Goddess. And I've already passed word onto the Church. My divine mission has been blessed. If for some reason this evil creature thwarts me, my death will be the signal to summon the full might of the Church. No matter what happens tonight, no matter what you say or do, this dungeon is going to die."

Alfred's hand went to his pendant, in a motion Ryan had seen hundred, thousands of times before. Suddenly it clicked in Ryan's mind why the Gold cleric had returned to his fourth floor the other day. To link his pendant to the teleportation crystal on his fourth floor. Doing so, would allow him to—

Ryan's focused turned to his teleportation crystal on his fourth floor just as the light enveloped Paul, Alfred, and the other roughly two dozen Zealots. They appeared, instantly, in a flash of light on his fourth floor before he could even think about reabsorbing the teleportation crystal. He'd been too slow, and now couldn't absorb the crystal because of their presence in the area. *Ugh.*

Now standing on his fourth floor, courtesy of his teleportation crystal system, were Paul and an entire force of zealous celestial users intent on his destruction. *This isn't good.*

"Marcus," Ryan called out, splitting his attention between the Zealots and the rogue for a moment. Currently, it seemed the Zealots were taking in their surroundings cautiously. About a quarter of them were Silver—they wouldn't be a problem. Another quarter were mid-to-high Gold; again, not too problematic for Ryan. But what he was worried about were the ten of them who were Platinum, five of whom were above Platinum 3. And then, of course, the Platinum 1 bishop, Paul. Meaning, they had the strength to do some considerable damage to Ryan if he let them run amok. He couldn't help but be worried about what Paul had said. Would killing the man really bring the Church down on him?

"If I kill them, what happens?" He said through the crystal skull by his entrance, the one he used to talk to Marcus.

Marcus looked into the dark pit that was Ryan's entrance, and he could see the answer in the rogue's eyes, even before he spoke. "I don't know what lies they've told the Church. But I know Paul wasn't lying to me just now. If he dies tonight, the Church will mobilize against you. He may be a rabid dog, but he's their rabid dog."

Marcus took out his flask even as his golden cage of light faded away, and took an extremely long swig. "Honestly, the bastard is probably hoping you kill him. He'd want nothing more than to become a Martyr for the Church." Marcus shook his head solemnly. "As if there wasn't enough going on in the world." He sighed and pulled out his flask. "I've a feeling tonight is going to be a long night. I'll stay here and make sure the entrance is secure. It's all I can do; sending anyone in after them would risk bringing conflict between the Adventurers' Guild and the Church. We cannot intervene with a high-ranking official performing their duties, despite how much we might want to." He sighed grimly, "Let me know what happens." And with that he took a drink from his flask and started muttering messages into the crystal around his neck.

"Right, well then." Ryan turned his focus back to his two fairies. So, murdering the Zealots would have to be the last-ditch effort, even if he really, really, really wanted to kill Paul, even more so now. "Do you two have any plans? Any way we can get out of this without just straight up murdering them?" He couldn't help but feel dismayed about the whole situation. They'd plotted and planned a colorful and violent revenge against Paul. And now, Ryan wasn't going to get that justice. All Erin's wonderful, brutal ideas, wasted. This was unjust, unfair. Just like his death had been. That made Ryan's hate for the guy grow even more.

The twinkle in Hel's eyes said she had some ideas. Before she could speak, Erin's hand was already around her own pendant. A moment later, she had teleported from his core room to the entrance of the fourth floor. She appeared above all the Zealots in a flash of golden light making Ryan really, really upset about his blasted teleportation system. It had seemed like such a good idea, yet tonight it was causing him no end of trouble. He made a mental note to devise some safeguards when this was all over with. These crystals were giving adventurers, and Erin apparently, too much freedom.

"In the name of the Goddess of Justice, I demand you leave this dungeon at once." Erin's voice boomed as she spread her wings wide. Golden light radiated from her as she displayed her full glory to them, hovering about twenty feet in the air above them. Erin was going for a diplomatic approach with a touch of theatrical flair. She pulsed Platinum boss levels of mana outwards as she spoke.

Paul, and all the Zealots froze in place, their eyes looking up in awe at Erin. For a moment it seemed as if Erin's plan might work. A second later, golden light rushed all around her, creating a massive golden cage, similar to the one Marcus had been pinned up in.

"Do not worry, oh radiant Angel," Paul said, his eyes so wide they appeared almost completely white. "We have come to free you from this vile dungeon." Paul looked at his followers. They were all looking up towards Erin, extending their palms towards her, showing the balanced scales burned into their hands.

"The dungeon has enslaved this angelic being," he boomed. Ryan would have laughed at the irony if the situation weren't so grave, considering those golden bars had been created by Paul. "We must destroy the dungeon, and quickly, to free her from its vile clutches."

"No," Erin cried out. Her hands grabbed the bars of the cage, and for a moment the cage waivered. A second later though, the other Platinum Zealots standing by Paul glowed golden, reinforcing the cage with their own power. Their eyes were red-rimmed, their faces filled with a strange expression. Something between bliss and sorrow? "Stop this," Erin cried out. Her wings were pressed against her side from how tight the cage was around her. Ryan's anger rose. They were hurting her. "I'm not a prisoner." Erin was crying.

Paul shook his head, a single tear running down his face as he looked at his followers. "Already, the dungeon has gotten its clutches into her. We must hurry, before the dungeon's influence completely overcomes her. In the name of the Goddess, we must put this rabid beast down."

He then pulled out an object Ryan really hated. An item that allowed adventurers to see the location of a dungeon core. Of course such a high member of the Church would have a tool like that. After all, according to what Erin had told him, the Church was regularly involved with working alongside the Adventurers' Guild when it came to destroying dangerous dungeons. For the second time in his life, Ryan found himself wondering, why did it have to be the Zealots of the Goddess of Justice?

Ryan turned towards his Succubus as rage flowed through him. These invaders were hurting his precious Erin. And they were planning on killing him. Part of him wanted to end them right there. Though the fact they had Erin captive stayed his hand on that matter. He couldn't lose his temper just yet, and he wasn't out of options. He had Hel.

"Do as you please. But don't kill anyone. Not yet." He told her.

The succubus grinned wickedly towards him, and a moment later disappeared from his core room, leaving him alone to watch the scene within his fourth floor unfold. Was Paul going to be the cause for his end a second time in a row? That thought fed into Ryan's frustrations, and his bloodlust rose. No matter what happened, Paul would be stopped, if not by Hel's hands, then Ryan's own forces. That was certain.

Tonight, Paul would reap what he sowed.

Chapter Forty-Seven

It took every ounce of Ryan's self-control to resist collapsing the floor all around the Zealots. They were in his dungeon, this was his domain. He could crush them. He could summon his full might against them and squash them like the bugs they were. At least, those were the thoughts raging through his mind. And he was pretty sure they were all true. He highly doubted these fools would be able to survive all his Bone Enforcers at once.

As he looked over the Zealots, he could tell they had come somewhat prepared. They were a varied range of Paladins, the Celestial variant of the elemental knight tank class, battle and war mages, a few Blade Dancers, and—of course—clerics and bishops. And while he'd seen bishops and Paladins before, the other classes were a mystery to him. He'd never even heard of a Celestial mage before, much less a battle mage.

If the circumstances were different, Ryan would have tried to test them out, in order to see what skills they had at their disposal. Given the current situation, and the fact they were definitely on his 'to-murder' list, he didn't care what they could do. In the end, it wasn't even going to matter. Hel had been sent to her work, and he was waiting to see just what she could do. At the same time, he was watching them have to deal with all the traps and random mobs they came across. There was no reason for him to make their trek through his dungeon easy. Either Hel somehow got them to leave his dungeon or they died, once he was certain there was no other way, and that Erin was safe.

"Erin, you need to return to me," Ryan said quietly. The Angel was still hovering midair, trapped in the cage that had been summoned around her. He doubted, judging by how far away the group had moved, that the cage had enough mana to withhold her anymore. Instead, he had a feeling she was in shock over what had just occurred. The people below her were technically followers of her Goddess. They were people she should be protecting. People who should listen to her, given her existence as an Angel. And yet, they'd put her in a cage, ignored her, and hurt her.

"I—" She looked out into the distance at the flash of golden light and darkness as the Zealots marched along. The Paladins were doing a good job at keeping the party protected, and Paul had cast a rather powerful aura onto his party members. The other clerics and bishops were all glowing as well, preparing to heal anyone who got hurt. This group was on a divine dungeon dive to destroy Ryan. The precision and practiced ease they were moving through his dungeon with, meant they knew what they were doing. On second thought, maybe they would be able to handle all five of his Bone Enforcers…

"You heard them. They think you've been corrupted." Ryan could feel her conflicted emotions. No matter how this turned out, it was going to hurt Erin the most. Paul and the Zealots deserved to be punished. Erin agreed with that wholeheartedly, but the fact their demise would bring the Church down upon Ryan was a problem.

"But—" She took a deep breath before she grabbed her pendant. "This is all my fault," she whispered as she teleported back into his core room. "All of this is my fault."

Hel was closing in on the Zealots, though she was keeping to the shadows. She had the ability to make her form invisible and was using her mana to fade into the darkness that was the sky on his fourth floor. Her unique set of skills worked best on those who were unsuspecting of her abilities.

"No, this is Paul's fault," Ryan responded. Hel was nearly there. "He's the crazy one who attacked us."

"Still." Erin watched the scenes unfolding. They'd reached the gallows, where one of his Bone Enforcers was summoned. Those summons were randomized when he wasn't actively controlling them. This time around, his Nuckalvee entered the fray. The appearance of the creature, at least, caused the raid party to pause. But only for a moment, before a rain of magical attacks assaulted the monster. Sure, it was formidable against parties of 5…but against a party of over 20…well, it was destroyed before it could even take a step off the summoning platform.

"Still." Ryan repeated, his frustrations growing. Hel had taken position above the party just as they'd finished decimating the Nuckalvee.

"They thought you'd captured me. If I hadn't begged to be a part of the fourth floor, if we hadn't put in that riddle… Maybe they wouldn't have come."

Ryan, even in the situation, or perhaps because of it, couldn't help but laugh at that. "Really, Erin? You don't think Paul would have found some other reason to attack me?"

"Can you cause a diversion?" Hel's voice flowed into Ryan's mind along with an image of what she wanted. She'd been planning on using the Nuckalvee as the distraction, but he'd died too quickly.

"Certainly." Ryan focused on the entire area the raid group was in and collapsed all the buildings around the area without any warning. At the same time, he commanded a couple groups of mobs to teleport to the area to engage with the Zealots. Not enough to have a chance of killing many of the intruders, but enough for a distraction.

"What hurts the most," Erin continued, watching Hel go to work. "Is, I couldn't even stop them. As a Platinum Tier Celestial being, I should have been able to stop them."

Ryan only partially listened as he watched what Hel did next. The Succubus, completely invisible—and now masked to any of the Platinum members' sensory skills thanks to all the chaos ensuing from the mob attacks—was darting to and fro on the battlefield. As she'd near a group of adventurers, just close enough to not miss, she seemingly blew kisses towards the Zealots. From her lips, Chaotic energy crackled. The mana flew into the humans and sunk into their skin. Those she managed to land her skill on shuddered slightly, before they ceased fighting against Ryan's mobs, their eyes taking on a dreamy appearance.

"Well, that's what you have me and Hel for." Ryan returned his attention back to Erin. "We're a team. A family. And we take care of one another."

They both watched as Hel continued to work. She had managed to land her attack on four Zealots already, though they were all below Platinum. Apparently, just as Viktor the necromancer had limits on what levels of undead he could forcibly control, Hel had limits on the humans she could manipulate with ease. According to the Succubus, at her current strength, Gold Tier adventurers were relatively easy. Platinum Tier adventurers though required multiple bursts of Chaos mana to gain control over, and doing so was risky.

Her plan, therefore, was to gain control of as many of the weaker ones as possible to try and force the raid to turn back. At the very least Hel could compel those she'd ensnared to teleport out of the dungeon. Perhaps if enough left the dungeon and survived, there would be a way to keep the Church from attacking Ryan. Perhaps another visit from Erin, outside of the dungeon, to the survivors, could convince them that Ryan hadn't captured her...and that she, instead, was there at the direction of the Goddess of Justice.

"There is a temptress among us," Paul called out as Hel landed her compulsion on another of the Zealots. "Now is the time to prove ourselves to the Goddess." Paul's form burst with golden light, washing over all his followers as he held his palms upwards. The brands on his hands burst with golden mana as his pristine white robes billowed around him. Ryan had a momentary memory of his death at the man's hands. Seriously, did Paul's robes never get dirty? Sure, Ryan's blood hadn't gotten on the robes when he'd been decapitated by Paul, but surely, during all of the fighting and chaos, something should have stained those blasted robes. Ryan wasn't sure why, but the fact that not a spec of dirt or dust was on Paul's robes, angered him even more.

"This vile dungeon has shown it has not only aligned itself with darkness," Paul bellowed as light radiated from his body. The golden energy pulsed around all his Zealots, instantly cleansing them of Hel's compulsion. To Hel's credit, she had tried to make them teleport out, but Paul cleansed them just as they were reaching for their pendants.

"But as we suspected, has fallen to the call of chaos, as well." The golden light didn't stop at his followers, but instead continued to flow out in a massive sphere. As it passed across Hel, the Succubus let out a startled hiss. Her invisibility instantly faded, leaving her extremely visible in front of the Zealots. Paul looked up at her and smiled evilly.

"See now, my followers, an agent of chaos. Clear evidence that this dungeon is indeed aligned with the God of Chaos." And with that, Ryan knew, there wasn't going to be any way to convince Paul or his followers that Ryan was innocent.

"Behold, dungeon. We shall destroy this vile creature and then know you will be purified as well." All the Zealots began to chant. Ryan felt panic flow through the normally calm Succubus, and her hand shot towards her own crystal pendant with lightning-fast speed. Before her hand even neared the pendant, golden shackles appeared on her wrists and legs. A massive set of golden scales manifested before her, and her form was pinned against them. Hel let out a scream and Ryan could see smoke billowing from her wrists as the scales began to tip.

No. Rage flowed through Ryan as he saw the Celestial mana dancing across Hel. His Succubus was struggling against the bonds, her body twitching as she let out gasps of pain, the scales continuing to tip, slowly pulling her apart.

No.

Ryan's rage turned to fury as his fairies' pain and fear filled the bond. He would not let these people hurt anyone else.

Not this time.

Ryan was done.

He was done giving them chances. He was done trying to think of ways to keep the Zealots from all dying. Nothing mattered to him more than his fairies, his family. The Zealots were going to pay. And they would do so with their lives.

Without another moment of thought or hesitation Ryan ripped open a massive hole in his dungeon. The entire area the Zealots stood on was suddenly torn asunder, dropping them, without any chance to dodge, evade or somehow escape, down, hundreds of feet. They may have been strong, some of them may have been Platinum, but even if they were to survive the fall, they wouldn't survive what was waiting for them. 2,000 mob points worth of skeletal fight club level four, completely focused on the falling humans, with a single order.

To kill.

"You'll pay for this," A voice called out, amongst the screams of falling Zealots. To Ryan's complete and utter surprise, Paul had not fallen. The man was hovering there, his pristine robes flowing out behind him, creating two feathery wings. Ryan knew there had been something magical about those robes. "It is my divine mission to cleanse the world of darkness." The scales attached to Hel tipped even faster now, the pain she was in increasing. Ryan's mind froze for a second, even as the other Zealots met their death. Nothing he tried was going to save Hel in time.

"It is my divine mission to —" Paul suddenly stopped speaking as his robes were pierced by a golden sword. Erin was no longer in Ryan's core room. The moment he'd opened up the floor beneath the Zealots, Erin had teleported out. She'd returned to the fourth floor. She'd returned to Paul.

"You do not speak for the Goddess. You do not walk upon her path." Erin left her golden sword in Paul's back. The Angel had flown towards him and ran him through as Paul had focused on taunting Ryan and trying to kill Hel. His eyes widened as he gazed upon Erin's Angelic form.

"For your sins against the Church," Erin said with a powerful, commanding voice. She held her hand out and a golden halberd appeared. She grasped the massive weapon with both hands and pulled it back.

"I hereby assign your sentence…" The Celestial halberd head grew. "Death."

She swung the weapon with impossible speed and force. It moved so quickly it left in its path a golden stream of mana, showing the trajectory of the weapon. A moment later

Paul's severed head fell from his body, as the rest of him fell hundreds of feet to join the crumpled bodies of his followers below. "No one hurts my family," Erin said with finality, even as tears fell from her eyes. This had been her first kill, and Ryan could feel how conflicted she was.

Still, she'd saved Hel. Erin had saved the Succubus from the bishop. On top of that, she'd eliminated the immediate threat in Ryan's dungeon, and gotten vengeance for his wrongful death. If that wasn't enough, Paul's death had done one last thing. The death of the Platinum 1 bishop, along with the deaths of all the Zealots, had pushed him not only past Platinum 3, but a good way toward Platinum 2. Paul may have gotten his dream and become a martyr, but he'd also become the next stepping stone for Ryan's path to Diamond. Now all he needed was to make sure he hit Diamond before the Church could come for him.

Chapter Forty-Eight

Following the death of the Zealots, Ryan knew he had to act fast. The final moments of Paul's life, while poetic, also meant Ryan had a new problem. He'd gotten stronger but he wasn't foolish enough to assume he could take on the Church by himself. Not yet at least.

"Marcus," he spoke, causing the rogue, who'd been taking a gulp from his flask, to jump slightly. Ryan's voice was urgent. "I need your help."

The rogue steadied himself. Ryan could see worry in Marcus's eyes, something he rarely ever saw. The Platinum 1 rogue had seen more in his life than Ryan could fathom and always seemed so calm and collected. Now though Ryan could see that starting to crack. The rogue was on edge.

"Did you kill them all?" The way Marcus said it told Ryan the man already knew the answer.

"I didn't have a choice." Ryan started. "They wanted to kill me."

"Well then," Marcus took a deep breath. "There's no turning back from here."

"What do we do? What's going to happen?" There was

the whole 'Church is going to kill you' threat hanging over Ryan's head, but he wasn't certain how that would happen. Could a massive force of overpowered Church members show up? Ryan remembered Zacharias and shuddered. The power Diamond level individuals had was on a whole different playing field. Ryan could only imagine what would happen if the Church could marshal a force of Diamond individuals against him.

The rogue looked into Ryan's entrance, his eyes thoughtful for a moment. "First, I'm going to have to contact Alice."

Ryan had heard that name before from Blake. Alice was the Diamond 2 leader of the Adventurers' Guild. On top of that, Blake had informed Ryan that she, like the Specter of Balance, had duel affinities. Meaning she was twice as powerful as Zacharias.

"And then what?" Ryan asked cautiously. He'd killed a good number of Church followers. There was no way this was going to be forgiven. Also, while he'd acted in self-defense, what if killing Paul's force caused the Adventurers' Guild to view him as overly dangerous? No, Ryan figured he didn't have to worry about that. Marcus had been there. He knew what had happened. He knew Paul was the instigator. He would vouch for Ryan with Alice.

"And then," Marcus took another breath. "We will have to prepare ourselves for what comes next." The rogue reached for his teleportation pendant, and then shook his head, muttering to himself something about the walk and clearing his head.

"I'm not evil," Ryan called after him. "I was threatened. You know that." Ryan' grew a little panicked. "I've shown you over and over, Marcus. I'm not a bad dungeon. I never kill without good reason. Those who fall always know the risks." He hated himself for his tone. But everything he was feeling—the panic, the unknown, and the fear—were getting to him.

"I know you're not," Marcus said softly. "I've always known." He kept walking without looking back. "Don't worry, Ryan." Marcus almost always referred to him as "Dungeon." This was the first time the rogue had said his name… the first time he'd referred to Ryan as a person and not just a thing. "I know you're not a monster. Alice knows, as well. But," for a second, he paused. "People are afraid of the unknown. And to many, you are just that, an unknown monster."

"So, what will happen? If you know I'm not a monster, can you convince the Church?"

Marcus chuckled darkly at that. "The Church and the Adventurers' Guild aren't on the best of terms. The alliance is a tense one. The Church has always wanted the dungeons gone. And now, you've given them what they needed to come after you."

"But," Marcus said before Ryan could interject. Ryan knew the dungeons corrupted by the Cult of Chaos had been destroyed. He'd not known the Church wanted all the dungeons destroyed. Why? That didn't make sense. "Adventurers see you in a different light. They know the dangers of diving into a dungeon, but also the riches, the opportunity, you provide them. They know you've kept them safe all these months from outside threats. And we've all noticed you do not kill pointlessly. You are an honorable, fair dungeon. You're like the benevolent dungeons mentioned in legends."

"What's that mean?" Even Hel said Ryan acted differently than most dungeons, yet he'd never figured how different he was. Was the fact he didn't kill with pointless abandon really that big of a deal? Did his humanity, his morals, make him that different from the other dungeons in existence? And if so, was it really him that was different, or did the other dungeons lack proper guidance from their fairies? Ryan wasn't certain about the state of the world. Life had been much simpler as a human…

"It means," Marcus's eyes lit up as a smile crossed his face, "as long as Alice says we can, the residents of Boneville will stand with you, against any threat. It is high time for us to protect you, after all you've done for us."

And with that, Marcus faded away from Ryan's senses as the rogue's winds whipped around him. Ryan figured Marcus was using his rogue skills to hasten his approach to the town, though he couldn't fathom why. Did he have a purpose to approach town in a secretive way, or was he just trying to leave the conversation with Ryan in a mysterious fashion? Either way, it would be a little while before he heard back from Marcus and learned about what the path forward would look like.

"Well, what should we do now?" Ryan asked his fairies as his mind raced with the possible outcomes of his actions. He'd absorbed all the fallen Zealots and cataloged the items they'd had. A few had been fully armed and armored in rare gear, and Paul's robes had been ultra-rare. He'd also gained a few more ultra-rare items from the other Platinum members, though they were less intriguing than the robes that had granted the man the ability to fly.

"Personally, Darling," Hel said, as she leaned against his core, "I would begin making preparations against any further intrusions." As she spoke, Erin nodded.

"Perhaps the teleportation crystals give adventurers too much access?" The Celestial fairy said. Hel smiled towards her in agreement.

"Right, definitely need to rework that a bit." The last thing he needed was to provide a way for a massive force to get into his dungeon this easily. Especially if they were going to abuse the teleportation system the way Alfred and the

Zealots had. Ryan hadn't thought people would utilize the teleportation crystals to bypass floors with large groups who'd never even cleared the previous floors. That was just... cheating. It gave adventurers too much ease of access.

Ryan needed to do a little remodeling. He figured there would be ways he could restrict the immediate freedom of movement adventurers had when they teleported into his dungeon. Ways to ensure people who came in uninvited or with a more hostile purpose than diving the dungeon, could be dispatched swiftly.

He put his focus on that task, drawing both Hel and Erin into it. He'd let his guard down and his fairies had nearly paid the ultimate price as a result. As it was now, they were under the shadow of a threat by the Church of the Goddess of Justice. Now more than ever, Ryan needed to work with his fairies to ensure they were as prepared as possible for any and all attacks that may be thrown their way.

Because, Ryan knew, judging by how close Paul and his party had come to killing Hel, mistakes at this point would result in irreparable damage or death. And Ryan was too close to his goals to allow anything bad to happen.

Chapter Forty-Nine

BLAKE

"What's all the commotion?" Blake grumbled as he opened his eyes. He'd been sleeping peacefully, dreaming of… things…when all of a sudden noise from outside his tent caused him to bolt awake. As he sat up, his ears straining to focus on the commotion, he could tell there was a large gathering of people heading into town. He caught the phrases 'big announcement' and 'Zealots' more than a few times, which prompted his interest enough to chase away the lingering bits of his dreams.

Never knowing what type of activity would happen in Boneville, Blake took the time to equip himself. As much as he wanted to rush out and see what was going on, he knew better. It was important to be ready for anything. His father had taught him that lesson and his time with Cane and Alice had cemented it.

By the time he finished getting dressed and rushed out of the tent, even more people were heading towards the center of town. A commotion of some sorts was occurring, that much was certain. Blake glanced about, checking if any of his party members were nearby. During their downtime from diving the dungeon, they'd all taken to conducting their own training and relaxation activities. Blake usually sparred with Jack, while Emily and Matt would teleport elsewhere to train, returning for the party's evening dinner and shenanigans.

"Blake," A familiar voice called out, followed by a high-pitched, excited cry. He caught a glimpse of Cynder just as the baby dragon landed on his shoulder, nipping playfully at one of the bones on his chest piece, trying her best to steal it away for chewing purposes. Emily was quick to follow with Matt grumbling beside her.

"Any idea what's going on?" He motioned towards the center of town and the siblings shook their heads.

"We'd been out for Cyn's morning hunt, when Jack told us to head back into town." Emily started. They went hunting deep in the forest to find the large elk and other wildlife Cynder enjoyed eating. Even though the dragon could change into her baby and juvenile forms, she had the appetite of an adult dragon now.

"Why'd Jack message you guys and not me?" Blake grumbled.

"He probably didn't want to interrupt your beauty sleep," Matt remarked, drawing a laugh from Emily. "We all know you like to sleep in."

Blake grumbled at that. Sure, he was usually the last of the party members to wake up, but he didn't stay in bed that long. And having a proper amount of rest was important. Especially when you needed to be fully prepared for each dungeon dive.

"That's not —" Blake started to defend himself, but a loud set of roaring erupted from the center of town. The trio looked at each other, and without another word rushed towards the center of town. Given their status as Platinum adventurers, even with Emily being a magic class, they were able to reach town in no time.

"Took y'all long enough," a voice said as a shadow moved away from one of the buildings. Jack was grinning at them as they slowed, though his eyes kept darting towards the center of town. Karan was a few feet further ahead of them, her face an emotionless mask. Whatever was going on wasn't good.

"What's up?" Blake asked as he peered past Blake and Karan. It seemed like everyone in town had turned out, creating a massive crowd circled around the teleportation crystal. On a platform of stone in front of it, stood Marcus. He was trying to calm a group of individuals, but there was some sort of conflict going on. That much was certain.

"Trouble, that's what." Jack motioned for them to follow him as they drew closer, his voice hushed. "Apparently that crazed Zealot, Paul, tried to kill the dungeon last night."

Blake's hand shot to his pendant. Before he could activate it to check on Ryan, Jack stopped his hand, shaking his head in an obvious "not now" way.

"Paul and his party failed. The dungeon killed them all." Blake wasn't sure how he should take that news. On one hand, he was relieved to hear Ryan was okay. On the other… Paul had been a Platinum 1 bishop, and his Zealots had included some high-ranking members of the Church. To have them all die at the same time in Ryan's dungeon could only mean trouble.

"So, what's the commotion about?" Blake suddenly found his throat very dry.

"Marcus is locking down Boneville today. He's going to disable the teleportation crystal at noon until the situation can be handled." Jack motioned towards Marcus. There were a few more yells and cries. Blake saw a rush of flames appear only to be put down by a gust of wind a second later.

"There are a lot of people who aren't fond of that idea," the Duelist stated. "And apparently, the Church is recalling all of their followers from Boneville." Jack looked to Karan.

"Which means, if they leave now, they won't be able to teleport back." That could be a problem. Not only did the Church have a following in Boneville but a majority of the healers in the town were members of it and not the Guild.

If they were to leave Boneville with no chance of an easy return, that could prove problematic for both sides. The town would lose a good chunk of its support staff and the Church members would have to travel to the closest town, which was a couple weeks away, and then have to travel by foot just to return.

Furthermore, there were adventurers in the Guild who were also members of the Church, such as Karan. If they were recalled by the Church and didn't follow those orders… it could create problems. The Church had control over access to the Goddess of Justice's dungeon. All Celestial users who wished to climb in power and needed to access the Goddess's dungeon would be unable to do so if they got on the wrong side of the Church.

Blake looked to Karan, trying to get a read on their healer. Now that she was Platinum Tier, she was a bishop, which gave her a considerable amount of power with regards to the Church. But it also put a lot of pressure on her. If she ignored the recall order in order to stay with Blake and his party, then she could face excommunication by the very Church she'd worked so hard to serve. The Church Blake's father had served as well. But if she heeded the call of the Church, Blake's party wouldn't be able to continue growing, as they would be unable to dive into the dungeon without their healer.

"Did the Church say why it's recalling all of its members?" Blake asked. Deep down he already had a suspicion. He'd already known Paul hated both the Bone Dungeon and Blake for that matter. Now that a large amount of Church members had been killed by the dungeon, there was a single step left. A single reason why the Church would be calling back all its forces. After all, the demon attacks had stopped with all the other dungeons put down. Meaning the Church would only be recalling its people to prepare for a new threat.

"The Church is going to declare a holy war on the dungeon." Karan's voice was soft. As a bishop she would have gotten the full report from the Church. She would have gotten more information than what the recall was about. "Every Church member is being recalled to the Holy City ahead of the public declaration of the holy war, in order to ensure individual members are not attacked in response to the declaration." Karan paused. "And —"

Blake didn't like that. There was an and? "And?"

"The Archbishop has decreed anything that stands in the way of the holy war will be destroyed, as well."

Chapter Fifty

Blake couldn't believe what he'd just heard. Ryan was the last dungeon in existence save for the dungeons of the Gods. He was the final dungeon for adventurers, for everyone, to dive in safely. Blake already knew adventurers wouldn't stand by and let the final thread of their existence be destroyed. But if what Karan was saying was true, any who stood in the Church's way would be killed as well. Would the Church really take on Boneville and all who stood to protect Ryan? Didn't that go counter of what it was supposed to be about? How was any of this just?

"What do you mean?" Blake looked from Karan to Jack. The Duelist didn't have the usual sparkle in his eyes. He looked dead serious. Jack was never far from Karan's side, meaning the Duelist had heard the orders Karan had been given word for word.

"The Church wants the dungeon put down," Jack said, his mouth twisting as if the words had a bad taste to them. "Though if you ask me, it serves that fool Paul and his followers right. The dungeon isn't evil, it isn't malicious. I bet you anything that Zealot planned all of this out. To force the Church to attack the dungeon town." His eyes got wild for a moment. "You know what, I bet you this was all part of the Church's plan to create a reason for the dungeon to be destroyed. After all, the Bone Dungeon is the only dungeon they didn't destroy in the cleansing."

The cleansing was what adventurers had started calling the destruction of all the dungeons. The Cult of Chaos had been efficient in corrupting dungeons, and Blake knew better than most how far-reaching the Cult's influence had been. According to Alice, Ryan was the only dungeon that hadn't been corrupted.

The fact he hadn't been corrupted was a miracle in and of itself; if he had, the whole adventurer lifestyle would have been eliminated out of necessity. The Adventurers' Guild couldn't exist with the knowledge dungeons had been corrupted and turned to Chaos, and were releasing demons upon the world. Still, destroying all of those dungeons had been a difficult task, even it if was the right thing to do. Without dungeons, adventurers' didn't have as much of a purpose. Especially considering the Gods rarely ever let anyone into their dungeons. Meaning without Ryan there would be no more dungeons for anyone.

Granted, he knew the Church had always viewed dungeons in a different light. For as it pained Alice to make the call to put down so many dungeons, the Church had its own special dungeon slaying task force in existence, and they'd been extremely enthused about being able to carry out their tasks.

"Listen to me." Marcus's voice boomed over the massive crowd. Along with it, a powerful gust of wind flew over everyone, stealing the air for a split second from everyone's lungs, causing them to go silent. The display of power caused immediate silence. Marcus was done with trying to calm those who had been causing problems in the front of the crowd.

"Oh, this will be good," Jack whispered. Of course the Duelist had used his winds to counteract Marcus's gust, leaving him with enough air to make a snide remark, even as everyone else found themselves breathless.

"I'm sure you are all worried and confused about what is going on." Marcus looked out over the crowd. Even from his spot towards the back of the crowd, Blake could see how tired Marcus looked. If he had to guess, the rogue hadn't gotten any sleep. "So before any of you do anything you will regret," he said and glared down at a group in the crowd occupying the same location Blake had seen the bursts of fire earlier, "allow me to explain what is going on. The last thing I need is all of you acting off rumors."

There was slight murmuring and Marcus's eyes locked on Jack for a moment. The Duelist had been in the middle of doing just what Marcus warned against…spreading a rumor to Blake. Blake had to wonder where Jack got all his information. The Duelist always knew more than the rest of the party members when it came to what was going on in and around town, and Blake wasn't certain if that was a trait from Jack's days as a thief, his Wind affinity, or his late nights at the tavern.

"First, for those who may not have heard: Last night, a large group of Church members died within the Bone Dungeon." Marcus was solemn as he spoke. "These members belonged to the Zealots of the Light and entered the dungeon upon a wild belief that the Bone Dungeon had somehow captured a follower of the Goddess of Light."

Blake felt himself go cold. Had the Church found out about Erin? Blake knew Erin had been sent to Ryan from the

Goddess of Justice. But he had no doubt believing the Zealots would have twisted that fact if they'd known the truth, and still painted the picture of Ryan being evil because he was a Darkness dungeon. No, simply because he was a dungeon. They wanted all dungeons gone, after all.

"Whatever their reason for entering the dungeon, their intent was clear. They wanted to destroy the dungeon." A large portion of the crowd started yelling and booing at this. Blake could make out more than a few harsh words being said about the Church, and even a few adventurers near Blake's party shot nasty looks towards Karan. There had always been a divide between adventurers and Church members, one that had only widened thanks to the Cleansing. While the Church members were cheering the end of the era of dungeons, adventurers had been lamenting it. Their way of life was being erased, and yet the Church was overjoyed. Without the dungeons, there was a large fear that the Church would be the only organization to grow in power… and everyone had been more than a little worried about that aspect. Especially considering the types of individuals—such as Paul—who existed within the Church.

Marcus held up a hand, silencing everyone with his motion, and the threat of an additional burst of Air. His winds still swirled around him. "As a result, the dungeon did as dungeons do. It defended itself and killed the invaders. The knowledge of the death of these Church members reached the Church of Justice last night. While it hasn't been released officially yet, I know the Archbishop, speaking on behalf of Divine Guardian Solomon, has declared the Bone Dungeon must be destroyed."

Before shouting could start Marcus sent another gust of Air over everyone.

"Alice and I spoke long through the night to discuss our

course of action over this situation. As you all know, I feel the dungeon is not a threat to us. The Bone Dungeon has fought to keep us safe on multiple occasions, and our very existence as adventurers hinges around it. Many of you owe so much of your growth, your livelihood, to the dungeon. Still, there are those among us who likely feel the dungeon may be too dangerous. There are those among us, even, who feel the dungeon needs to be destroyed."

Marcus leveled his eyes at the crowd as he took a deep breath. "Frankly, while I disagree with those of you who think like that, I'm not going to try to change your mind. Nor am I going to call you out. Instead, I'm going to go about with the plan Alice and I have devised to keep the town safe. That is, at noon today, I will be disabling the port crystal to Boneville. The last thing I need is for those who wish the dungeon harm to have the ability to teleport into town on a whim and cause problems."

So far Jack's "rumors" had been spot on. Blake got a feeling a lot of the town members had already heard much of what Marcus was saying, at least to some degree. Still, the rogue wasn't finished.

"The Church has demanded all loyal members of the Church of Justice return to the Holy City at once, to prepare for the task of destroying the Bone Dungeon. I will not stop any Church member from leaving Boneville. I was sworn to protect the dungeon and town, and I will always do all I can to care for those under my watch. If you do not leave, if you do not wish to go to the Church's aid for this task, I will do all I can to protect you."

"If," Marcus's voice deepened, "you leave today, and join the Church and its growing force to try and destroy the Bone Dungeon, know that when I next see you, I will consider you a threat." Marcus's winds swirled even more violently above his head. "For I will not stand idly by while those who wish to harm all those under my protection do so, nor will I take kindly to those who seek to destroy Boneville, nor the Bone Dungeon. I swear on my pride as an adventurer, I will wield my power to its fullest to complete the tasks Alice has given me."

This time, the crowd erupted into cheers, and Marcus allowed it. There were obviously those who did not approve of Marcus's words. Blake could see many Church members shifting uncomfortably, and a few adventurers glancing about. For the most part though they were a combined front. After all, many of them had been diving into the Bone Dungeon for over a year now. This was their home, and they were all family. It only made sense they would fight to protect it.

"Leave or stay, it is your choice," Marcus finished, his winds dying down. "I just ask that today, you do so peacefully."

He turned and walked off the stone platform that he'd erected in front of the teleportation crystal. The moment he left the crowded town center, heading into the Guild Hall, the streets erupted in chaos.

"Blake," Marcus's voice came through the pendant around his neck. "I need to speak with you and your party." Blake glanced at his friends and then at the crowd. It was going to be a long trek to the Guild Hall through the chaos. Brawls and shouting matches were already taking place. Still, Marcus's tone expressed how urgent it was that Blake and his team get there quickly.

"Well, best not to keep the man waiting,' Jack said as he took note of Blake's look. They'd all heard Marcus's voice. "Emily, would you kindly?" The Duelist motioned towards the crowd blocking their path.

Emily grinned as her body glowed vibrantly for a second. Cynder, who had been mindlessly chewing on Blake's chest piece, leapt into the air. A moment later the town center quickly began to clear out as adventurers, Church members, and random individuals all scattered to the sides. Blake couldn't help but chuckle. An adult dragon was a hell of a tool for clearing out a crowd.

Chapter Fifty-One

With the crowd cleared away by Cynder, Blake and his party had no trouble getting into the Guild Hall. From there, they were led to Marcus's office by the rogue's assistant, a Silver Tier thief named Mike. Blake didn't know much about Mike other than that Marcus was training the thief in his downtime and relied heavily on the young man.

"Thank you for coming so quickly." Marcus was sitting behind a desk, drinking heavily from his flask. Blake, having experienced the contents of that flask once before, felt the remembered burn of the drink. He still marveled at the ease with which Marcus could drink the Fireball Whiskey.

"No problem," Blake replied. "What was it you needed to speak with us about?"

The rogue took another swig and lifted up a scroll from his desk. "I've a special mission for you and your party." He held it out towards Blake. Even from here Blake could make out the official seal of the Adventurers' Guild on the parchment. That scroll came directly from Alice.

"Alice thinks you may be able to prevent this war before it starts. Your connection with the Bone Dungeon, your knowledge of it, may be able to save it." Blake stepped forward and grabbled the scroll. It was heavy in his hand. He figured that was more the weight of the task at hand than the parchment itself. Alice was trusting him and his party to stop a war between the Church and Boneville. Alice was trusting him and his party to protect the final hope of all adventurers.

"How?" Blake asked softly.

"It will take time for the Church to amass its forces. With the closing of the port crystal back to Boneville, the Church will be unable to teleport back to the dungeon town, which will give us extra time before they can reach us en masse."

"I need you and your party to take that scroll to the Holy Temple and plead for the survival of the Bone Dungeon. Alice has already set up a meeting between your party and the Archbishop. She has written down what is necessary to pass onto him in that scroll. From there, it is up to your party to convince him that the Bone Dungeon is not a threat."

"Why couldn't Alice just convince him? Why didn't the Archbishop listen to her? Or you? Why us?" It didn't make any sense. If there was anyone the Archbishop should have listened to it was Alice.

"Because as everyone knows, the Church and the Adventurers' Guild do not get along. And while Alice has considerable power and influence, the Church does not respect her. The Archbishop, as a rule of thumb, despises adventurers. As the years have drawn on, he's distanced himself even further from the Adventurers' Guild. Furthermore, in the absence of Solomon, who has remained out of the eyes of the Church for a long time, the Archbishop has further spread his power and influence."

From what Blake knew, the Archbishop was a Platinum 1 member of the Church, and was the second in command to the actual leader of the Church of Justice, a Diamond 1 individual named Solomon. No one had seen Solomon in a long time, the man having suffered a serious injury during a battle long ago. While he retrained his standing as the head of the Church, the Archbishop, his chosen figurehead, had been running the Church ever since.

According to Blake's father, Solomon had denied the Archbishop's request to ascend to Diamond Tier. Apparently, Solomon felt the power of Diamond Tier may have been too much for the Archbishop at the time of his request, and he'd wanted to ensure the man wouldn't be corrupted by the power he would be able to wield. The Archbishop, building upon that idea, had made a new declaration. For fear of the corruption such power could bring with it in the eyes of the Church members, only Paladins could ascend to Diamond within the Church. Because when a Paladin ascended to Diamond Tier within the Church, they were bound, body and soul, to the Goddess of Justice and her dungeon.

As another precaution against corruption, taking Solomon's worry for him further and applying it across the Church and the Paladins, the Archbishop established an additional caveat to that rule. Any Paladin who sought to ascend must swear themselves to him. If they were bound to him, he could ensure their power didn't corrupt them, ensure that they always walked the path of the Goddess, and that they could not attempt to enact a coup over him or Solomon. That had been a big factor in why Blake's father had never ascended to Diamond. As much as his father cared for the Church and his duty to it, he couldn't bring himself to be bound completely to the Archbishop and the Church.

Considering Blake's father had turned down the chance to become Diamond because he refused to be bound to the Archbishop, Blake wasn't sure why Alice would think he could reach out to the man.

"That still doesn't explain why he would listen to us," Blake retorted. He got that the Archbishop and Alice might not have a great relationship, and he already knew the Church and adventurers were on rocky terms. But why would Blake's party have any chance of changing that?

"Because you are Sean's son. Your father did great things for the Church even though he was an adventurer as well. The Archbishop respected him."

"My father refused him —"

"—even if Sean continually turned him down. Not a day went by that the Archbishop wasn't asking for your father to pledge himself to him and the Church and ascend to Diamond. The Archbishop held nothing but high respect for your father." Marcus shook his head sadly. "If Sean were here, I'm sure he would be able to convince him…"

"Do you really think that will be enough? Me being Sean's son?" Blake couldn't fathom how that would be enough. This was the Church they were talking about. "You heard what Paul said about my dual affinities. My Darkness mana makes me the immediate enemy of the Church," Blake said darkly. His father's death still hurt, and he couldn't help but feel the sorrow and rage resurface within him. A part of him actually blamed the Church for his father's death. After all, his father had been on a mission for the Church when he had been captured by the Cult of Chaos. And the Archbishop's decree on the rules for ascending to Diamond had been why his father had never gained that power. If his father had been Diamond, nothing could have ever harmed him.

"You're our only chance," Marcus said heavily. "Plus, Karan is on favorable terms with the Church. She and Jack earned quite a bit of respect during the demon attacks. No, if there is anyone that can change the Archbishop's mind and convince him to call off this holy war, it's your party." Marcus's eyes grew grim as he paused.

"And?" Blake could tell there was something more. Something the Platinum 1 rogue wasn't saying. "What happens if we can't?" Blake had seen how close-minded Paul was. If the Archbishop was anything like the Zealot, Blake's party had no chance in convincing the man to call off the holy war. Especially since he had a feeling Jack was right and this chance to destroy Ryan was exactly what the Church had wanted all along.

"Then, your party is the only one that I trust could get away safely from the Holy City and return here." Marcus offered him a grin, though it came across as half-hearted. The rogue was tired, not just physically but mentally and emotionally.

"What makes you say that?"

"For one, while I'm closing off the port stone into town and have already spoken to the dungeon about removing its interior portal stones for now, I'm sure he will gladly give you and your party a way to return." That part was doable. Blake had no doubt in his mind Ryan would make a special portal stone for him and his party. After all, Blake was bound to Ryan's dungeon.

"And second…even if your party was attacked, I know you've got enough mana to be able to keep your party safe long enough to use your port stone to get to safety." Marcus knew about Ryan's skills as a Specter of Balance. Meaning the rogue already knew of his ability to make not only himself but his allies go Ethereal. Leave it up to Alice and Marcus to cover all the scenarios before sending Blake off into the hornets' nest.

"Let's hope it doesn't come to that," Blake responded solemnly. He didn't want to have to fight against the Church. And if he and his party could save not only Ryan but Boneville—and stop this war from even starting—there was no way he would say no. He already knew his party had the same mindset as he did. They were family, after all.

"One last thing before you leave." Marcus added as Blake

and his party turned to go. Blake had set the scroll on his belt and was in the process of pulling out his crystal pendant to contact Ryan. He would need to link his pendant to a new port crystal before they left.

"What is it?" Blake glanced back.

Marcus's voice was soft as he responded. "I may be out of place saying this, and maybe it's the liquor and my lack of sleep, but...I'm proud of you. You've grown into a fine young man, and I know Sean would be proud, too."

Chapter Fifty-Two

Their trip to Ryan's dungeon was quick…mainly because the dungeon had spread his influence so far that they didn't need to get much past the gates of Boneville to be able to receive what they needed from Ryan. That is, a safe way to return, following their mission to the Holy City of Justice. Ryan had seemed a little more distracted than normal, which made sense all things considered, and the dungeon created for Blake a skull-shaped crystal pendant without much conversation. The dungeon was definitely preoccupied, but at the very least did give them a crystal pendant that, in theory, would return them home, in case anything happened at the Holy City.

From there the party gathered any gear they thought they may need and prepared to leave. By the time they were ready, it was close to noon and the commotion in Boneville was reaching an all-time high. Word had spread quickly that the port crystal was soon going to be disabled. Masses of people were flocking to Boneville, refusing to lose access to the last open dungeon. They knew their time could potentially be short and were anxious to capitalize on as much dungeon time as they could. Blake had a feeling Marcus was going to have a hard time ensuring dungeon dives were orderly from here on out, but it made sense. If the Church got its way, the Bone Dungeon would be destroyed within the month. Meaning there was a chance people only had a single month remaining to ever step foot inside a dungeon again.

At the same time, people were leaving. Shops were closing up, the town church was being vandalized, and fights were breaking out faster than Marcus and his group of officials could quell them. Tensions ran high, understandably so, and all adventurers affiliated with the Church who hadn't already left were finding their safety at risk. Blake could only hope he and his party received a different kind of welcome when they got to the Holy City.

"Remember. Whatever happens, we will make it back here safely," Blake said, looking over his group. Everyone knew what was at stake. And while Karan was beyond uncomfortable with the entire situation, she had agreed to take part in the plan. She may have been a member of the Church, and owed them much, but she was also an adventurer. Her ties to Alice, the Adventurers' Guild, and especially Jack and the rest of the party, were stronger than her allegiance to the Church. In her eyes, it wasn't the Goddess of Justice causing these issues but the people running the Church. This wasn't a betrayal to her beliefs but to the people in power.

"When you say it like that you make it seem like you're worried about something, man." Jack had his thumbs tucked into his sword belt, doing his best to flash a grin at everyone. "We're heading to Libertus. Surely the Holy City of the Church of Justice wouldn't be a dangerous place to innocent, everyday people like ourselves."

Blake offered Jack a knowing smile. The Duelist was doing his best to try and lighten the mood, as he always did, which was sorely needed. A wave of dread washed over Blake as Karan pulled out her pendant. He'd wanted, so badly, to serve the Church, to follow in his father's footsteps. And yet now there was the chance he would have to fight against the institution's servants. It didn't seem right, it didn't seem just.

"Right. We're off to convince the Archbishop to let the Bone Dungeon live and be back in time for dinner." Blake took a deep breath, motioning for Karan to continue. The Platinum bishop nodded and used her pendant to teleport the party to Libertus, the Holy City of the Church of Justice.

As the light faded from around his body, Blake couldn't help but stare in awe. He'd heard of Libertus from his father, but he'd never been to the Holy City. It was nestled in the mountains at the foot of the Goddess of Justice's dungeon and was the headquarters for the Church.

Looking around, Blake could see his father had been underplaying the grandeur of the city. Massive buildings, made from a stone so white it seemed to shine, spread out in all directions. The buildings themselves, already elegant, were adorned with golden decorations and carvings. And then, if the buildings themselves weren't impressive enough, the statues of the Goddess of Justice, rising up in front of them, nearly overwhelmed him.

The town's teleportation crystal had been placed in the center of the city, as was the norm. However, the original designers of the town had built a massive statue of the Goddess of Justice above it. The elegant monument of a beautiful, yet powerful woman clad in armor, holding a set of golden, balanced scales in her hand emitted a powerful aura. It was just a statue, but Blake couldn't help but feel inspired by it.

Unfortunately, they hadn't come to take in all of the architecture and grandeur that was Libertus. Even as he finished getting his bearings, the next thing Blake noticed was a group of powerful individuals moving towards his party. They were clad in shining armor and judging by what he could see with his eyes, they were all high Platinum. What's more, all five of them had Celestial mana. If Blake had to guess, they were being welcomed to the city by a contingent of Paladins.

For a moment Blake tensed up as he watched them approach. It was clear they were making their way towards his party. While they didn't appear hostile, they didn't seem too friendly, either. Not only that, Blake was suddenly feeling extremely self-conscious. Given the chaos of everything that had been going on, he had completely forgotten the fact that maybe…just maybe, he should have tried to somewhat hide his affiliation with the Bone Dungeon and the God of Death. Standing there, in a bone-covered chest plate, with a bone sword hanging at his side, definitely wasn't going to gain him any points with the Church. How could he have been so stupid?

"Karan," the lead Paladin said as the group reached Blake's party. The man, appearing middle-aged, nodded briefly towards her. He then shot a scowl at Jack, which the Duelist returned with a grin. Apparently, they shared history of some kind. Blake wasn't sure if that was going to be good or bad for him and the party.

"Mikael," Karan responded, returning the slight nod. "I'm assuming the Archbishop sent you?"

"Indeed," The man, Mikael, responded. "We've already been briefed on the situation and were informed we were to bring you to the Archbishop the moment you arrived." The Paladin looked over the party, his eyes pausing for a second on Cynder, but then moving to Blake. His eyes were cold and hard. "Though, if we'd had our way, you would have never been allowed into the city, not with this abomination."

Off to a great start. Blake thought, doing his best to fight his rising anger. Paul had treated him like something that needed to be destroyed and he'd brushed it off as the mindset of a fanatic. Besides, the Zealot had proven his fanatical idiocy when he'd gone into Ryan's dungeon and set off this whole situation. But Blake hadn't expected such open hostility from someone that wasn't a Zealot.

While the Church would never let him join their ranks due to his Darkness affinity, he'd always had at least neutral relations with its members. Back in Boneville, he'd even been on friendly terms with some of the clerics. But apparently, that wasn't the way of things in the Holy City. It would seem amongst the pure white streets, underneath the golden statue of the Goddess, even a single mark of darkness was treated with immense disdain.

On second thought, Blake was happy he hadn't hidden his gear. He wasn't ashamed of who he was. Not anymore. Especially as his mind replayed Marcus's final message to him. He knew in his heart his father, the great Paladin Sean, would be proud of him. That was enough.

"His name is Blake," Karan said in response to Mikael's insult. While her tone was level, Blake could see her eyes burning, matching the indignation he felt. "And he walks the Goddess's path truer than you. I've forgotten how blinded by the light those who never leave the City have become. You've become blinded by prejudice." Karan's tone dripped with venom at the end, and the already tense situation grew even more intense. While Blake appreciated Karan's defense of him, he'd not expected her to be the one to escalate the situation.

Mikael's eyes narrowed but he didn't say another word. Instead, he spun sharply around and began walking away. In his haste, he shoved past an old lady, knocking her roughly to the ground. Mikael didn't even look down at her as he kept moving, even as Blake saw the woman's head, which had hit the ground, begin to blossom with red. Blake's anger flared, but a hand on his shoulder, Jack's hand, stopped him. The wolfkin shook his head, even as Karan's hands lit up with golden light as the bishop healed the poor lady.

"Not now," Jack whispered quietly. "Trust me. Not a good time." The Duelist nodded towards the remainder of the Paladins, all who were waiting for Blake's group to follow after Mikael. Their eyes were hard, all of them looking away from the incident as if it hadn't occurred. All of them except for one. One Paladin, out of the whole group, offered a single nod towards Karan, acknowledging what she had done, and a slight bow towards the old lady, who moved as quickly as she could away from everything that had happened.

"They're all looking for a fight," Jack commented as they began walking. "Except for Alec, that is. Alec's good people." The Duelist motioned towards the one Paladin who'd acknowledge what had happened and flashed him a smile. The briefest of smiles appeared in the Paladin's eyes in response, but that was all.

"If you say so," Blake responded quietly. His group had been surrounded by the Paladins the moment they'd followed after Mikael. The way they were flanked felt more like they were captives and less like they were guests. Blake really didn't like that feeling.

"Quiet back there," Mikael called out, silencing Jack before he could respond. They walked the rest of the way through the massive city in silence, heading towards what Blake assumed was the Holy Temple of Justice, and the Archbishop. He really hoped the Archbishop was not like Mikael. He also prayed to the Goddess of Justice that, by some miracle, they would accomplish their task. Because from the look of it, the only thing Blake could guess the Church members disliked more than dungeons and adventurers, was an adventurer with a Darkness affinity.

Chapter Fifty-Three

"Greetings, my children." A man clothed in golden robes, radiating with the Celestial mana of a Platinum 1 individual, said to the party as they entered a massive room. As Blake had expected they'd made their way through the city and to the massive temple that was the Holy Temple of Justice. Once inside the grandiose temple, adorned all over with statues of Angels and other Celestial creatures, every doorway inlaid with the Scales of Justice, they'd been led to what he had to guess was the main meeting chamber.

There, past rows and rows of lavish seating, enough to fit at least a thousand—likely more—a massive chair rose within the room. Behind it, another effigy of the Goddess of Justice rested, and atop the chair, this man. The man, Blake assumed, was the Archbishop of the Church of Justice. The man who held Ryan's fate in his hands. The man who now had the final word in what would happen to the era of adventurers.

Karan bowed to the man. While her status as a Platinum 4 Celestial mana user granted her the position of bishop in the Church, there was an additional hierarchy. She may have had an honorary position, but she was below the Archbishop. And as such, she was giving him the respect he had earned, or deserved. Blake wasn't quite certain which.

"Father," Karan started, looking up towards the man. Blake noticed the five Paladins who'd been their escorts had all shifted toward the sides of the room, taking up assigned positions alongside another handful of Paladins. With over a dozen of them in the room, all Platinum Tier, as well as the Archbishop, Blake was a lot less confident in his ability to keep the party safe. If things went badly now, he needed to prepare to instantly teleport his party away. Otherwise, they would be done for.

His thoughts were pulled away from his escape plans as Karan continued. "Thank you for allowing us to meet with you on such a short notice."

"I wish we were meeting under better circumstances, my daughter," the Archbishop stated. "I'd never dreamed a meeting such as this would be the first time I got to meet my dear friend Sean's son." The Archbishop turned his eyes towards Blake as he spoke. The first thing Blake noticed was how old he appeared. As a Platinum 1 mana user, he should have aged incredibly slowly. Meaning he'd either taken a long time to reach Platinum, or he had been alive for a very, very long time.

"Blake, is it?" The man's grey eyes seemed to take in everything about Blake as he spoke. For the first time since he had entered into the Holy City, a Church member's eyes didn't linger on Blake's armor. "I've been informed you have something for me?" He held out a hand. Blake walked slowly towards him and handed the man the scroll Marcus had entrusted him with.

The Archbishop unfurled it, his eyes looking over the contents. Blake and his party were left in silence as the Archbishop read. Even Jack, who would normally have grown bored of the silence and said or done something, stood there quietly, eyes watching the old man. They were all aware of how dire this situation was.

After what felt like an eternity the old man rolled the scroll back up, placing it down on a table beside his chair. Then he leaned back in his seat, his eyes seeming lost in thought as he began to speak.

"We are at a turning point in the world," he started. "The age of dungeons is nearly over, and with it I feel—and Solomon feels—we can truly enter into a grand era of peace." He looked down at Blake. "Do you know why that is?"

Blake looked up at him, his mind a complete and utter blank. He wasn't certain what he had been expecting for this meeting, but it wasn't this.

"Uh…"

"Because, my dear son, without dungeons in this world, power will not be so easily obtainable." His eyes shifted to each member of Blake's party. "When I look down at the five of you, I see five individuals with immense power. However," his tone shifted slightly, "I also see five individuals who haven't truly experienced enough life to wield their power appropriately." He leaned back before he continued.

"Dungeons have offered people the chance to grow in strength and wealth at a dangerous speed. Dungeons allow those of wealth—or those who may be corrupt, or impure— to grow and thrive in the world. Dungeons breed powerful individuals. And power, without life experience or morals, is an extremely dangerous thing. And it isn't even just the morally corrupt that dungeons pray on." The Archbishop shook his head. "No, power is a siren's call. And the quicker one obtains it, the more tempting that call. Even the most righteous, the sincerest, the purest, can be tempted by power."

"But —" Even before Karan could interject the Archbishop's hand rose, his eyes narrowing dangerously.

"For who knows how long, the age of dungeon divers, the age of the Adventurers' Guild, has created opportunities for corruption to grow." He turned towards Blake. "Dungeons have allowed the rich in this world to seize and hold onto their power. Humans have gained the power to long outlive their allotted time, to hold onto their power for far too long. Dungeons have created a world that favors the strong and tosses the weak aside. Dungeons have tainted this world for far too long. And dungeons have been the cause of too much sorrow to ever be forgiven."

The Archbishop's eyes once again sought Blake's, and his voice was soft, solemn, as he continued. "You know, Blake, if not for the existence of these dungeons, the Cult of Chaos never would never have become a threat. And, without the Cult of Chaos," The Archbishop leaned forward, his voice a whisper, filled with sorrow and certainty, "Sean would still be alive."

Blake flinched at that. His mind flashed back to his father's final moments, the final defiant moment his father ended his own life before the demonic force within him could completely take control.

"While the Church doesn't condone wanton destruction," the man continued, "Personally, I feel it is a blessing the dungeons revealed their true nature, and became corrupted by the Cult of Chaos. It showcased just what a danger dungeons were. It showcased to the world, for all to see, that dungeons were merely creatures of Chaos; wild, vile creatures that only cause suffering and death. And with that revelation, the Church has finally been allowed to begin cleansing the world of those dens of sorrow. The Church has finally been given the chance to bring the world into a new era of happiness and peace. The Church will finally be able to eradicate the world of dungeons once and for all."

"Obviously," the Archbishop's looked over the whole party, "some will argue that dungeons are not malicious, that dungeons are not a threat. They will point to the dungeons in which the Gods reside, as proof. These dungeons are not the same. The dungeons of the gods are their very homes. Their seats of power, where they can interact with those they've deemed worthy, and for them to give the world guidance, and shape its future as they see fit. Those dungeons are sacred. The dungeons we've destroyed, this Bone Dungeon of yours, whose innocence you've come to plead for today, are nothing like the dungeons of the Gods."

He paused, his hands drumming on the arms of his chair for a moment. "This Bone Dungeon of yours." The Archbishop said the words as if they left a bad taste in his mouth. "According to what Alice says, it has not only resisted the corruption of the Cult of Chaos but has actively sought to protect the lives of those living in...Boneville?" His voice went flat as he said the town's name. Hearing the Archbishop say the name out loud caused Jack to break and, for a second, the Duelist's chuckle could be heard. Immediately after, there was a soft thud and the sharp intake of Jack's breath, as Karan elbowed him in the gut.

"That—that is correct," Blake answered. "Ryan, er, the Bone Dungeon, has aided the town multiple times. We were there to witness the dungeon's efforts in defeating the necromancer Viktor, who wished to harness its power for dark reasons. And the dungeon was instrumental in defeating the demonic forces that tried to destroy Boneville. The—"

"—And," the Archbishop interrupted, "Alice would have me believe that this dungeon has an affinity of sorts with the Goddess of Justice. Could you elaborate, Blake?"

Blake went cold. Part of him wanted to call upon Ryan, to

have the dungeon speak for himself. But for some reason, that idea didn't seem like the proper path. The Archbishop had his mind set on dungeons. If a God didn't live in it, then it should be destroyed. Meaning he probably wouldn't care to hear Ryan speak.

Additionally, given the way the Zealots had twisted Erin's existence within the dungeon…Blake doubted having Ryan—or Erin, for that matter—speak before the Archbishop would accomplish much. The man had his mind set on the destruction of the Bone Dungeon. The man before him was someone whose life's work was finally coming to a close. Blake could tell that much.

"I—" He paused, what should he say? What should he do?" "While I cannot fully understand what relationship the dungeon has with the Goddess of Justice, I do know that the dungeon has granted me the powers of a Paladin. Powers that are only meant for those sworn to the Goddess of Justice, to the light."

The Archbishop looked Blake up and down once more, a small smile creeping upon his face. "Yes, I've heard of some of your powers. Though it is odd you come here professing to wield the powers of the Goddess while clad in bones. And," he pointed at Blake's breast plate, "some would consider that design, the combination of the Goddess of Justice and the God of Death's symbols, to be extremely blasphemous." By the way he stressed that portion, Blake had no doubt he was one such person. Ryan's artistic nature was going to be the death of him.

Blake started to protest, but the Archbishop stopped him. "Still, I had hoped you could provide me with more details about your precious dungeon. A solid reason to spare it. But I can see that you cannot."

Before Blake could open his mouth, the Archbishop continued. "However, I can see it on your face, and the faces of your party…you believe in your dungeon. You've come here, knowing what is at stake, to prove that it is not evil. And while it may be purely sentimental, there is a part of me that wants to believe you. After all, I've always wanted to have faith in the world and believe that anything—and every-thing—has good within."

Blake's mind went blank. *What?* "Then, you'll spare Ryan?" Blake asked hopefully.

"Do not misinterpret my words. Those are the sentiments of an old, wishful man. As the Archbishop, as the representative of Solomon, as the head of the Church, I cannot turn a blind eye to the recent death of so many followers of the Goddess at the hands of the Bone Dungeon. But what I can do is extend to you and your party a simple token. A token that has been earned through the hard work of all of you in helping deal with the Cult of Chaos. A token in honor of my memory of Sean. An opportunity to prove that the Goddess does indeed have something planned for this dungeon of yours. As a humble servant of the Goddess, IF she does have plans for the Bone Dungeon, I will ensure it is not destroyed."

Suddenly things were going a lot better than Blake had planned.

"I'm going to give you and your party a chance to ensure nobody questions the justice in the actions of the Church." The Archbishop smiled down at them and Blake felt his hope flee. Those eyes, for just a moment, held something else in them. Those were eyes that said the Archbishop already had his mind made up. This was all a farce. Whatever was going to come next, Blake knew the Archbishop already had the outcome planned.

"How?" Blake asked. "How can we convince you to spare the dungeon?" Even if the Archbishop had his mind made up, Blake knew he would be held to whatever he decreed next. If Blake's party accomplished the task at hand, they would be able to save Ryan. Blake knew better than anyone that his party could—no, would—accomplish the impossible.

"A week from now," the old man began, "I will allow your party to teleport into the heart of the Goddess of Justice's dungeon. There, you will have the chance to confer with the Goddess herself. If you can convince her of your pleas and have her gift unto you the legendary Sword of Justice, then it will prove the Goddess has decided to spare your dungeon. However, if you cannot return with this artifact of power, then the Church will take it as a sign, and we will begin our march on the Bone Dungeon. For if the Goddess does not deem to step in on behalf of your dungeon in this way, then it will be certain, unquestionable justice that the Church will issue onto the land. The Church will be confident in the knowledge that it is the divine mission of the Church of Justice to bring about the end of the era of dungeons."

"Consider yourself lucky, my son," the Archbishop continued. "The ritual to open the path to the Goddess can only be conducted once a week. I am offering up to your party this sacred moment, to try and accomplish your goal. Remember my kindness, no matter what the outcome."

The man waved a hand, motioning towards Mikael. "Mikael shall see to your accommodations for the next week. I hope you understand for your own safety, I cannot allow you outside of the Holy Temple. While I trust you would not cause problems, it is best to prevent any potential misunderstandings that might occur until it is time for you to speak to the Goddess. If you've need of anything during your stay, please let one of my Templars of Light know, and they will see to it you are taken care of." The look on Mikael's face said otherwise. Blake had a feeling it was going to be a very, very long week.

"Thank you, Father." Karan said with a slight bow

towards the Archbishop, though her voice was strained. Blake bowed as well. He had a strong feeling the task they'd been given was one the Archbishop didn't expect they could accomplish. In fact, Blake had a feeling the Archbishop was just using this as an opportunity to strengthen his cause and silence any nay-sayers. For as he said, if the Goddess didn't give them this legendary sword, and therefore refused to aid the Bone Dungeon, that would mean the Archbishop was right in his call. And that type of confirmation, directly from the Goddess, would go a long way in garnering support for the Church and silencing those who stood against them.

In a sense, the Archbishop was using them to try and prevent as much resistance as he could. Which, while Blake disagreed with the whole situation, he couldn't fault the man for that. The less resistance, the less innocent lives lost. But Blake knew there was only one way to ensure no lives were lost. He looked up, forcing all his confidence into his gaze as he locked eyes with the Archbishop.

"We will complete your task," he said boldly.

The Archbishop smiled towards him. "I pray to the Goddess you do. If not for your dungeon's sake, for the sake of all those who will otherwise die if you fail." Then, as Blake's party turned to leave, Blake heard the Archbishop faintly whisper, "It truly would be a miracle if she granted you the very sword she denied your father."

Chapter Fifty-Four

RYAN

Ryan couldn't help but be proud as he looked out over the expansive area that was under his command. For the past week, ever since Blake and his party had left for the Holy City to try and call off the impeding attack, Ryan had been busy. His normal energy, spent creating new mobs and items or messing around with mob evolution, traps, and of course, skeletal fight club, had been put to a much more purposeful task.

That is, he'd spent the entire week preparing every ounce of land under his control for attack. If the Church wanted to bring him down, so be it. If the Church was going to be his enemy, he was going to make sure the cost to bring him down would be steep. Because while he was certain the Church had the means to destroy a dungeon his size, especially given the fact that part of their job was cleansing the world of evil dungeons, he'd done quite a bit to make himself as dangerous as possible.

"Are you sure you don't need to construct additional pylons?" Erin's comment pulled him from his moment of metaphorical back-patting. He quickly...er, as quickly as he could, scanned the miles and miles under his control. The pylons she was referencing, Pylons of Influence, were tower-like structures which allowed his influence to spread in a hundred-foot spherical radius around the pylon. Previously he'd built them in fifty-foot intervals to ensure that, if anything happened to one, the influence sphere wouldn't be eliminated. After all, without a sphere of influence his mobs would simply crumble.

"I'm pretty sure I have enough pylons," Ryan returned. He'd increased the frequency of these, putting them roughly every forty-feet of each other in square-like clusters. It created a massive grid across his bone zone, ensuring there were no gaps of what his influence covered.

"And the traps? Are those all set up?" Erin had been going over a mental checklist on preparations for the attack, doing all she could to ensure they were as prepared as possible. Ryan knew the thought of fighting the Church of Justice tore deeply at the Celestial fairy. She felt responsible for the whole situation and saw her inability to talk sense into Paul as the reason for the current threat. She'd also been the one to kill him...but that was neither here nor there. Regardless, she was doing all she could to help.

"Honestly, Darling, you've got the ultimate tool to take them down at your disposal." The Chaos fairy stepped up alongside her Celestial counterpart, peering into Ryan's core. "You're hurting yourself by not following my plan."

Hel's plan, if you could call it that, was to create an undead army of actual undead. Not the undead mobs Ryan normally made, but resurrected adventurers. As a Darkness dungeon Ryan knew that was one of his greatest strengths. This was the power, the ability, that made him the most dangerous type of dungeon in the eyes of the Church. The fact he could raise up any adventurer, any living thing, which died within his dungeon, turn it into an undead creature, and set it upon the world. In doing so, the undead not only didn't count against his mob points, but could leave his dungeon, leave his sphere of influence, and survive. On top of all of that, anything those creatures killed, would still give him experience.

"Only as a last resort," Ryan responded firmly. "As long as there's still a chance Blake can convince the Church not to attack, I will not begin creating undead mobs like those."

"Your morals are so...peculiar at times, Darling." Hel shook her head but stepped away. "Will you at least let me out to play, then? Since you won't take my advice seriously?"

While Ryan had been hard at work preparing his Bone Zone for the invasion, the adventurers had been hard at work as well. It seemed word of Boneville closing itself off to the outside world, as well as the looming threat of the Church against Ryan's dungeon, had caused quite the stir. More people had flocked to Boneville hours before its tele-portation crystal was deactivated than Ryan had ever imag-ined. The town had expanded by over a thousand individuals in a couple hours. On top of that, Ryan had over-heard multiple groups mentioning there were many more planning to make their way to Boneville via more pedestrian means.

The population bump also increased the number of people who wanted to dive into Ryan's dungeon. Because there was now a possible limit on how long they had to adventure within the dungeon, people were throwing caution and reservation to the wind. The runs were getting faster, the party sizes larger, as more and more individuals took on the dungeon.

On top of that, it seemed Marcus had lifted some of his previous restrictions with regards to parties running into Ryan's dungeon. It was first come, first serve. Any and everyone who could, tried to give Ryan's dungeon a shot. It was chaotic outside his dungeon now, as people fought and struggled for the right to dive.

The chaos outside led to even more chaos inside. There were many, many more deaths within Ryan's dungeon as people rushed into him. Even as some groups saw their experience and wealth shoot up as they figured cut efficient ways to clear out Ryan's easier floors in a free-for-all farming session, others bit off more than they could chew and died.

In the span of a week, Ryan had jumped to Platinum 2. If not for the threat of the Church, a part of Ryan would have felt remorseful about the increased deaths within his dungeon. Now though, he was just watching his experience, wondering if he'd be able to hit Diamond before the Church arrived. If that happened, his chances of survival would greatly increase.

As it were, the extra mob points gave him even more mobs to throw at adventurers and to fuel his undead skeletal army when the Church arrived. During this time, Hel had been begging Ryan to let her out into the dungeon. Given her past, and the countless dungeons she'd been a part of, as well as the fact they'd all been destroyed, Ryan had sensed a bit of panic in her. She tried to hide it, but he could tell she was getting restless.

Hel, the Chaos fairy, his Platinum Succubus who had centuries worth of memories, was nervous. She was worried. She was afraid. And, as such, she wanted to get as much out of the remaining time she likely felt they had as possible. Which was why Ryan's continued assertions that she couldn't go to any floor other than the fourth, continued to rub her the wrong way. But Ryan couldn't blame her. He was losing himself to his tasks, keeping his mind from the impending doom, if Blake failed. Hel, on the other hand, was forced to sit, wait, and likely think about the past.

"It looks like a group of ten is on their way to the third

floor," Ryan responded to her question about heading into the dungeon. The stronger groups had begun joining forces to increase their survivability. While it cut the amount of experience they gained from killing mobs—since the experience was now split between ten people instead of five—surviving was rather important. You couldn't gain experience if you were dead.

The influx of adventurers and royals and newcomers to Ryan's dungeon, and the threat of destruction, had led to these tactics. It was more a means of survival, a final way to grasp experience and wealth, than what they were used to. Furthermore, Ryan had noticed these groups had more seasoned adventurers in them, and surprisingly, nobles as well. They were pairing up, creating unlikely teams where before there was animosity, in order to get more bodies into the dungeon at one time.

"Is that a yes, Darling?" Hel said with a low growl of anticipation. Ryan sent her a mental nod and the Chaos fairy rushed out of his core room. She was going in search of a good hiding spot to stalk the ten-man party. She'd been improving her tactics over the course of the week while Ryan and Erin had been improving the Bone Zone. Ryan also knew, while he was preoccupied with improving the Bone Zone, Hel had been a little more proactive than he normally would have allowed her to be.

The survival rate of parties heading into his fourth floor had plummeted the moment Hel was unleashed upon them. However, he was turning a blind eye to the Chaos fairy, at least for now. He wasn't going to complain about the spike in experience. too much. After all, it would be irresponsible of him to not chase after the power to survive.

And, in his mind, Ryan had already made the difficult decision Hel asked of him. If Blake contacted him and told him the Church wouldn't listen to reason, was still going to seek out Ryan's destruction, then he would ensure they were met with any and every defensive capability Ryan had at his disposal. That included the Church's worst nightmare. If push came to shove, Ryan had already decided he would begin reanimating those who fell in his dungeon to fight against the Church.

His survival, and the survival of his fairies, mattered more to him than his moral code. Because, at the end of the day, moral codes were pointless if you were dead.

Chapter Fifty-Five

"Tomorrow is the day," Ryan commented to his two fairies. It was nearing the middle of the night and the last group of adventurers had left his dungeon probably an hour ago. With the imminent possibility of Ryan's destruction, Marcus had allowed people to dive into the dungeon a lot later than normal. In fact, Marcus had been letting people have a freer rein within Ryan's dungeon. As it stood now, the rogue was spending more time ensuring the town's safety than regulating who was heading into Ryan's dungeon. Part of that, of course, was due to the fact the rogue was confident Ryan could take care of himself.

Ryan had spoken with the rogue on that very matter and come to that conclusion. Short of anything too dangerous, say an extremely high-level party equipped with legendary artifacts or items from the era of dungeon-killing, or perhaps Diamond level individuals, Ryan was pretty confident he could keep himself safe. Which allowed Marcus to spend more of his time ensuring Boneville was safe and secure.

"I'm sure the Goddess will see fit to give Blake the sword,"

Erin responded. Apparently, Erin no longer had a direct connection to the Goddess, just as Hel couldn't contact the God of Chaos. They could pray to their deities and hope their prayers were heard. However, outside of their respective dungeons, it was very rare apparently, for the Gods and Goddesses to make an appearance. Erin had mentioned that earlier in the week when Ryan asked her to make sure the Goddess would clear everything up. After all, the Goddess was the one who'd brought Ryan back and tasked Erin with taking care of him and helping him grow stronger. In a sense, the Goddess was the reason they were in this situation to begin with.

Needless to say, Erin's admission that she couldn't actually contact the Goddess directly had come as quite the surprise. Especially considering Ryan had seen her be possessed by the Goddess once before, to save Blake's life. Ryan had also gotten used to the idea of contact with the deities considering he'd had run-ins with the God of Death on multiple occasions. But his fairies had assured him those were unique instances. In other words, miracles.

"Your Goddess's followers are the reason we are in this mess," Hel said, scoffing, though her comment had a little less venom than normal. She had been rather active during the day, with Ryan giving her a lot more freedom on the fourth floor considering what the next day was supposed to bring. As such, Hel had caused more than a handful of deaths and gotten to spend a lot of her energy out in the dungeon, enjoying her time as a Platinum Succubus.

"And your God's followers are the reason Blake's father is dead and all the other dungeons were destroyed," Erin retorted quickly. Hel opened her mouth to speak but closed it for a moment. Ryan could feel the flash of anger going through her at the reminder of all the Cult of Chaos had done. Especially because it reminded Hel that she wasn't an original dungeon fairy, but a clone of one. A fact she despised the Cult of Chaos for.

"You're right, little one," Hel responded coolly. "Perhaps we shouldn't blame our chosen deities, but instead their followers?" The Succubus looked at Erin, a wry smile on her face. "Is it fair to say the followers are often far too different from the Gods?"

Before Erin could respond to Hel's statement, and luckily before their conversation could devolve into even more theology and the like, something outside of Ryan's dungeon caught his attention. A group of five moving incredibly quickly from Boneville towards his dungeon.

"It seems we have some late-night visitors," Ryan interrupted the two fairies. "And..." He looked them over, recognition instantly flowing through him. After all, this party was well known to him. "It seems our night has gotten much more interesting than religious talk."

Ryan focused the massive center of his diamond core to portray, crystal clear, the approaching party as they advanced. His viewpoint shifted from pylon to pylon, watching the party from overhead as they covered the miles that separated Boneville from Ryan's entrance.

The group was moving faster than normal humans could. But then again, Boneville didn't really have "normal" humans. Gold and Platinum level adventurers could close the distance from Boneville to the Bone Dungeon in just a few minutes. Quicker, too, if the group left their magic classes behind, since the physical classes had a lot more mana enhancing their physical traits than the magical classes did. Of those, the archers and rogues, the classes that dealt with speed and agility, could even outpace the tanks and classes which focused on endurance and strength.

It came as little surprise when the party arrived that none of them showed any signs of exertion, despite the haste with which they had covered the distance. In fact, they all looked as relaxed as if they were out for a leisurely midnight stroll.

"Greetings, Dungeon," a voice called out. Strong, confident, and somewhat arrogant. Ryan focused on the speaker. The man was the same as he had been the last time Ryan saw him. A powerful figure, dressed in leather the color of blood, inlaid with rubies cut to look like flames. He still had the air of bloodlust around him, even though, from what Ryan knew, the man had been keeping busy killing demons.

"Blaine Dragnov," Ryan said, keeping his voice level, godly. He'd been doing his best to keep up this façade, of sorts, of being an all-powerful demigod dungeon. Only his fairies, and the Gods, got to know who he truly was. The soul of a young man who'd been murdered in cold blood for crossing the Zealots of the Goddess of Justice. All-powerful Bone Dungeon was a much better persona to portray. "What brings you to my dungeon this late at night?"

The Platinum 1 Fire affinity Blade Dancer looked at the crystal skull from which Ryan spoke and smiled coldly. The man's blue eyes burned with an icy fire and Ryan could feel something other than bloodlust flowing from him. Something about him had changed.

"I've suddenly found myself in a unique position," Blaine started. "My father has been gravely injured. While he is still extremely powerful, he no longer has the ability to truly lead the armies." Blaine placed his hands on the hilts of the two swords he kept on his person. Ryan knew those swords were cursed weapons, blades which would use Blaine's own life force, to grant him immense power for a short amount of time. They were, quite literally, the definition of a double-edged weapon. And yet Blaine wielded them with no fear or regard for his own sake.

"Oh?" Ryan started. He'd heard about the assassination attempt on the Duke of Blood's life. Apparently the Duke, a

Diamond 3 Dreadnaught, the highest form of Elemental Knight with a Chaos affinity, had lost an arm and a leg on top of other injuries both external and internal. While the leader of the Assassins' Guild had failed to kill the man, his weapons, his methods, his abilities, had ensured the man was a lot less powerful than he'd been prior to the assassination attempt. Even with magic, even with a Celestial feather, the Duke was crippled. Even at Diamond 3, you weren't immortal.

"Indeed." Blaine drew his swords, looking at his party. "As such, I've gotten…permission," He said the word as if it disgusted him, "to ascend to Diamond once I've gained enough experience. Finally, I can utilize the allotted Diamond slot given to my family." The blade dancer's form glowed red for a moment, and two fiery swords appeared behind him as he drew his cursed swords. "As such, I've run here all the way from Valta with my party to take on your dungeon and conquer your fourth floor."

He brandished his blades. "And of course, if I accomplish my task tonight, and reach my goals…" He smiled wickedly at Ryan's crystal skull. "I figure the best place to test my new powers at Diamond will be on the battlefield, fighting those who come for you." Blaine chuckled. "After all, I've just now started to find dungeon diving fun."

Ryan realized what that other emotion, that other vibe, he was getting off the Blade Dancer was. It was pure excitement. The man not only was looking forward to slaying Ryan's mobs, but he had a goal he wanted to reach. A goal Ryan could help him reach.

"Very well," Ryan said. He did his best to keep his voice controlled even as excitement flowed through him, as well. All this time, there hadn't been a single party who'd made it to his boss room. Not a single group had reached his final creature, his greatest creation. But now a party had appeared which Ryan felt could reach the depths of his dungeon and defeat his final boss. Especially because, as he looked over the rest, he realized something. Before, Blaine had been Platinum 1, while his companions had only been Platinum 5.

Now, through all their fighting, all their efforts against the demonic armies which had threatened the land before the dungeons had been eliminated, the rest of Blaine's party had grown. Now, all five were Platinum 1. They would be the strongest group to ever dive into Ryan's dungeon. Stronger even than Blake's party. And, if they succeeded…the thought of having Blaine at Diamond 3, fighting for his dungeon against the Church, sent chills of excitement through his core. The man was a monster. Ryan could only imagine how powerful an ally he would be in the fight for Ryan's survival.

Beside him, Ryan could feel Hel and Erin brimming with excitement as well. They had both come to the same conclusion as Ryan. Before the night was done, they would get to see the grandest fight in Ryan's dungeon to date. A fitting way to pass the time while they waited for the new day. The day they would find out Ryan's fate with the Church, to be decided by Blake's hands. Blaine and his party were about to help Ryan and his fairies pass the time in the most brilliant of ways.

"Enter if you dare."

Chapter Fifty-Six

Ryan hadn't had many experiences with Blaine. The few he did have in the past showed to Ryan that the man was cold, calculated, and ambitious. He was confident, but he had a right to be. To say Blaine was powerful was an understatement. Ryan already knew that, he'd seen Blaine in action before, watched him take down a Light Ender by himself.

But now, as Ryan watched Blaine make his way through his fourth floor, there was something else Ryan began to notice about the man. His power, his strength, didn't just come from himself. The Blade Dancer could fight like he did because of the party members behind him, supporting him. The more Ryan watched Blaine, the more it seemed the man purposefully threw himself full force into every fight, to ensure those behind him were safe. At first, Ryan had thought Blaine was just using his members, but the more he watched, the more he was certain Blaine actually cared about his team.

Blaine Dragnov cared.

For the first few levels of Ryan's dungeon, as Blaine and

his party had decided to start on the first floor, it was a complete massacre. Ryan's mobs instinctively tried to run away from the terrifying humans, and yet Blaine took them all down without a moment of hesitation. Nothing but ash and charred bones remained as Blaine walked through the dungeon, guiding his party through the first and second floor with ease.

When he reached the third floor, Blaine gave pause. After a moment, he'd motioned towards one of his allies, the Earth bishop Isaac. As Ryan had seen before, the bishop covered Blaine's swords in stone, which melded with Blaine's own Fire mana to create a molten covering. From what Ryan had observed, this greatly increased the destructive capabilities of Blaine's swords, and he used these enhanced weapons to continue his slaughter of Ryan's mobs.

Blaine made it all look easy. His trek through Ryan's third floor seemed little more than a warmup for the fierce warrior. However, Ryan began to notice, ever so slightly, there were a few things about Blaine he'd missed in previous encounters. First, Blaine was always extremely quick to strike. The Blade Dancer, a class known for its extremely high agility, flowed effortlessly around the battlefield, engaged in a dance of death to the tune of his burning blades. It was elegant, beautiful, and deadly. But the longer Ryan watched the dance, he'd noticed, in those blurring moments, as Blaine moved around, that there was a pattern to his dance.

Blaine, upon entering a room, would first move to strike the enemies who posed the greatest threat to his party. He would purposefully move past melee mobs to take down the ranged mobs before they could attack anything. And if he couldn't instantly kill those threats, he made them his number one priority. He moved as quickly as he could, cutting a path of death, to attack those that posed the largest threat not to him, but his party members. All the while, as he conducted his blade dance, no matter how destructive he was, the finesse with which he wielded both his physical blades and the two swirling fire blades which floated around him was perfection. Not a single attack made its way past his defenses.

His flawless defense slightly confused Ryan. Blaine had two legionnaires in his party. The man, could exert less effort if he utilized them to provide cover for the Bishops and focused purely on the offensive. It was something Ryan pondered as the party finished his third floor. He couldn't tell if Blaine was being overly confident, cautious, or something else, with regards to his style. The more Ryan analyzed it, the more it left him wondering. To say the least, he'd never seen a party act as Blaine's did. And that was saying something, because Ryan had seen a lot of parties.

Ryan's evaluation of Blaine evolved as the party of five began their assault on Ryan's fourth floor. "Assault" was very much appropriate, with the ferocity with which Blaine and his team took on this new challenge. The mobs, much stronger than the third-floor mobs, still melted before Blaine's mighty swords. And as the fighting intensified, as the creatures grew stronger, realization finally hit Ryan.

The reason Blaine was attacking the largest threats first and foremost was because Blaine wanted to keep his party safe. In his own way he was doing everything he could to support and protect those four who stood behind him, empowering him and letting him go all out.

On top of that, Blaine's efforts seemed to allow his legionnaires to do something a little more...unorthodox. That is, while Ryan was used to legionnaires creating walls of swirling shields or massive barriers to keep themselves and their party members safe from powerful attacks, Blaine's did something completely different. Instead of creating defenses for themselves, they used their skills to encase an area of the battlefield, creating small arenas wherever they went for Blaine to dispatch the mobs uninterrupted, without fear of being ambushed.

It was insane. It didn't make any sense. The swift-moving melee class, armed with swords covered in molten rock and armor covered in protective icy mana, which clashed constantly with Blaine's own Fire mana, was doing the job of not only damage dealer, but tank. Meanwhile, the tanks of the party were using their abilities to trap in mobs and force them into close-range combat with Blaine. All the while, the bishops were empowering Blaine, enhancing his combat ability tenfold.

This strategy left Ryan speechless as he watched the ballet of death unfold across his fourth floor. The Bone Enforcers, at the very least, gave Blaine pause, but not as much as Ryan would have preferred. Often times, the larger Bone Enforcers actually found themselves at a disadvantage compared to the rapidly moving Blade Dancer who seemed to be everywhere around them at once. And, he hadn't even activated his cursed weapons yet. The boost in support he was receiving from his allies now that they were Platinum 1, just like he was, had greatly increased Blaine's combat efficiency since Ryan last saw him. His strikes were stronger, his defenses more powerful, and his confidence in his allies even greater.

As they made their way towards Ryan's boss room, the massive cave-like structure at the far side of his fourth floor, a thought crossed Ryan's mind. The more he watched Blaine's party, the more he realized Blaine and his group were more like a team of adventurers than many groups from the Adventurers' Guild. Blaine's party, who had fought together against who knew what types of foes, had become so close that no words needed be spoken. They simply knew how each of them would react, knew the roles they played, and they executed them flawlessly. Their dungeon dive so far, had been filled only with the sounds of dying mobs as they conducted everything wordlessly. Something only the tightest knit teams could do.

In that way they showcased the true potential of a group of Platinum 1 members, in the most absurd ways possible. This affirmed another thought in Ryan's mind. Where there was a will, there was a way. Neither a person's class mattered, nor their affinity. What did matter was how they used their skills and strengths to cover any weaknesses in the party, and to get the job done. As Blaine's party finally made it to the entrance to the boss's chamber, it was crystal clear his party was extremely good at getting the job done.

However, everything they'd fought now, from his Bone Enforcers, to his Skeletal Champions, and even the Tiger Queen he'd added to the floor, since he had the mob points, wouldn't prepare Blaine's team for what was next. For as the blade dancer entered the room, showing the slightest bit of fatigue after decimating the fourth floor so far, Ryan could feel his boss coming to life. His creature, finally waking from its long slumber, preparing for its first ever challenger.

"You've one chance," Ryan said from a crystal skull which he'd placed just inside the entrance to the cavern. It was a massive expanse, a great sprawling void which Ryan had filled with various crumbled ruins, destroyed statues, and the like. "For once you pass this point, only victory will allow you to leave." Ryan's boss was that deadly. He knew that when he'd created it. If they didn't defeat the boss, Ryan doubted any adventurers would be able to flee. Once they engaged this creature, the only way to survive was to win.

"Very well," Blaine paused for a moment, closing his eyes. As he opened them, they burned with an even greater passion. He didn't even look back at his party members. He didn't need to. The four party members were all watching

Blaine, with grim determination. They would follow him to any battlefield. They would support him against any foe. Their lives were his and his life was in their hands. "It's a good thing I never lose." And with that, his party entered the boss's chamber.

____

Chapter Fifty-Seven

Blaine and his party advanced slowly into the massive expanse of Ryan's boss room. Unlike on his first two floors where the boss was evident as soon as adventurers stepped inside the room, there was absolutely no sign of Ryan's fourth floor boss. Something he'd learned following some trial and error with regards to dungeon building. Early on, Ryan's first floor didn't even have a door leading into Steve's room, and adventurers had abused that, attacking the poor skeletal mob from outside his room, killing him without even stepping foot into the boss room. Ryan had come a long, long way in his dungeon creation.

Already, Blaine's party was searching for the platform from which this boss would rise. That mechanic, which he'd implemented on his third floor, had been carried over to his fourth floor with his Bone Enforcers. The mechanic not only let Ryan summon the mobs in the proximity of adventurers, it also added a bit to the theatrics of a boss fight. The intimidating boss slowly rising from beneath the floor to meet the challengers was pretty epic, in Ryan's eyes. While he did use it for the Bone Enforcers, his boss mob got something a little different. Because his fourth-floor boss was a little more…permanent.

Just like his first and second floor, the boss was always in the boss room. Unlike those floors though, even if you entered all the way into the room, you wouldn't be able to find the boss. Part of this was because Ryan had built his boss room quite deep into the rock bed, meaning Blaine and his party were in a massive cavern that had to be half a mile or more in diameter. The expanse was filled with broken statues and columns. Ryan had tried to create the feeling of a fallen civilization within the boss room.

The ruins and debris spread all about also served another purpose. Cover. Not only for the adventurers but also for Ryan's boss. While the boss existed deeper in the room, Ryan had given him countless ways to traverse its home. The massive room was lit by strangely flickering lights. Everything that the light touched belonged to the boss. And even though Blaine was confident now, Ryan had a feeling that before the end of this fight, the Blade Dancer was going to learn just how powerful the fourth-floor boss was.

"It is time," Ryan whispered excitedly to his fairies. He of course had the entire boss room shown within his diamond core while he kept track of Blaine and the boss. The five-man party was moving cautiously, scanning the area for any sign of a threat. Blaine's body was still covered in his ice armor, his swords still glowing with magma. They were on edge and prepared. At least they thought they were. Nothing on his fourth floor could truly prepare anyone for what they would face in this boss fight.

As Ryan watched his boss move about, its massive form snaking through the tunnels and paths Ryan had created as it prepared itself to attack, he could tell this fight was going to be the most interesting one he'd ever seen. In part because his fourth-floor boss was the most expensive mob he'd ever created. His first-floor boss, Steve, cost him 25 mob points. Buttercup, on the second floor, cost a total of 50 points. Meanwhile, the skeletal mage bosses from his third floor were 250 points apiece. His fourth-floor boss dwarfed all of those in cost, at a whopping 775 points.

Not only that, there was another difference in his fourth floor boss. Up until now, Ryan's bosses had all been created from common mob variants. While he had unlocked uncommon mobs on his third floor, he'd only used those for regular mobs. The fourth-floor boss gained a lot of its cost from the fact it was based upon a rare mob. The rarity of the mob, of course, caused its cost to be rather high before the multiplier was added point-wise to turn it into a boss mob. Additionally, by turning a rare mob into a boss, Ryan found the special abilities and traits of the rare creature amplified by quite a bit.

Honestly, Ryan didn't have a way of judging just how strong this boss would be. He'd seen what a rarity boost did to mobs, and how they became tougher. He'd also come to learn over time that a creature's mob points didn't dictate its strength. There were a lot of factors that went into determining how strong a mob was, and how effective it would be against adventurers. These factors ranged from not only the base type of the mob but its cost, its abilities, its environment, its rarity, and also important, the type of party the mob was facing.

Such factors were hard to pinpoint in order to create the perfect type of encounter for adventurers. Ryan's "testing" phase for his floors had caused some deaths that likely could have been avoided. The Andre the Giant fight, of course, being one of the most recent points in that regard. That Bone Enforcer had a lower cost than Ryan's third floor boss, but had killed a Platinum adventurer and nearly caused a party wipe.

So, as he watched Blaine's all Platinum 1 party prepare themselves, the Blade Dancer standing cautiously yet confidently within the room, his eyes searching for his target, Ryan couldn't help but feel his excitement building even more. How would this unique party, a party whose entire style focused on buffing a single member of the party, do against his boss? Would the composition help or hinder the party? And how would they adapt, change, and take care of the creature that was rising up?

Even as these thoughts crossed Ryan's mind, he saw the shadows move, saw the light in the room flicker as his boss made himself known. Ryan watched in pure anticipation as he saw the slightest hint of surprise cross Blaine's face as nine massive serpentine heads erupted from hidden passages all around the room. It was finally time for Ryan's fourth floor boss, his rare nine-headed snake monstrosity, to take the stage.

"Behold," Ryan said, his voice echoing down into the room, breaking the momentary silence as the humans and the boss took note of each other. "Shydra, King of Sneks."

He did his best to make that sound ominous. His nine-headed snek boss reminded him of the stories of the hydra he'd heard as a child and read about through various absorbed books. A monstrous serpentine creature said to appear in swamplands and in marshes. It was fabled to have countless snake-like heads which would regrow once severed. Of course, his first thought had been to simply add an S to the name, for skeletal, which gave it the name Shydra. Which, sounded less terrifying than Ryan wanted, but fit his normal naming convention. So, he added the additional bit at the end to make his boss sound regal. Ryan had really wanted to break his trend of having bad boss names with his fourth floor, and he felt, with the Shydra, he'd accomplished that.

He also did his best to ignore Erin and Hel's snickering at

the name. Maybe it wasn't as impressive as he'd thought. He also told himself Blaine hadn't smirked when he announced the name. The latter, that smirk from Blaine he'd been trying to ignore, at least disappeared the moment the battle started. Because it was hard for the Blade Dancer to smirk when nine massive skeletal snek heads opened up to launch fangs the size of a human, shrouded in Darkness mana, towards Blaine. Eighteen human sized projectiles were a pressing enough problem to make anyone's smile disappear. Blaine was about to learn Ryan's boss had much more bite than the name implied.

And despite what its name might suggest, his boss was neither shy, nor meek.

Chapter Fifty-Eight

"That was unexpected." From how Blaine's party had worked the entire trek through Ryan's dungeon, he'd honestly expected Blaine to intercept...somehow, all eighteen fangs coming towards him. Honestly, Ryan had been quite curious to see if the Blade Dancer could pull that off. Instead, as the projectiles all launched towards him a wall of shields appeared all around him, cocooning him in a floating protective fortress. For the first time since Ryan had been introduced to Blaine and his party, the legionnaires had used their skills to protect Blaine rather than simply shut out other mobs.

"It seems their teamwork goes deeper than we thought," Hel said, her eyes watching Blaine intently. There was a hunger there as she focused on him. The Succubus had a hunger for adventurers in general, but Ryan knew she favored the man more than others, save for Blake and Jack. The Succubus was drawn to powerful and unique individuals. Blaine was both of these.

"Still, I'm interested to see how they go about defeating Shydra. Considering Blaine is their only offensive member."

That fact was something Ryan had been thinking about as the Blade Dancer had neared his boss room. The Shydra had nine skeletal snake heads, all covered in dense Darkness mana. These converged into a single massive body, which the Shydra kept hidden further back underneath the boss room. Its nine heads, interacting separately, wove about underneath the floor and could strike from any and every angle possible in the room.

Because of this, Blaine essentially had nine different targets he would have to focus on trying to bring down, while also watching out for attacks from all the different heads. Ryan had expected Blaine to try to handle it all by himself. Because that's how he always operated. Meaning he'd been taken by surprise to see the legionnaires react on his behalf, wordlessly. From the way they had reacted to the opening attack, Ryan guessed they had preconceived rules about when the legionnaires were to protect Blaine, and when they weren't. If Ryan had to guess, they knew Blaine's capabilities quite well and had been instructed to only protect him if the incoming attack was something he wouldn't be able to fully handle himself. In this manner, both Blaine and the legionnaires, would better manage the amount of mana they were using for their various skills and abilities.

"Well, he does have those cursed blades," Erin mentioned, motioning as she spoke towards the two swords Blaine wielded. Both of the blades were cursed weapons. Weapons which would drain the life force from the user in order to give them a drastic boost of power in the short term. They were extremely dangerous to use. If the person using them wasn't careful, their very essence could be sucked into the blade. Ryan actually had access to creating cursed objects himself, but he very rarely dropped them as loot. He was actually slightly curious as to where Blaine had gotten his blades.

"I doubt he could defeat the boss before they consumed him." The other incredible fact about Blaine was that when he did activate the cursed objects, he did it concurrently in battle. A single cursed object would drain a human quickly, though the timeframe differed from person to person from what Ryan understood. Using two at once would create an even more dangerous situation for the user, though the increase in power would also be amplified by a large amount. So far, Ryan had only seen Blaine activate those cursed objects once, against the Light Ender. They were his final trump card in battle.

"Whatever happens," Hel licked her lips, "I'm sure Blaine is going to put on a great show for us." Ryan couldn't agree more, and he went silent, watching the fight unfold.

The eighteen fangs had smashed into the massive shield wall, driving into the mana-created shields with enough force to penetrate partway through. However, the legionnaires had done their job well, and not a single fang reached Blaine. Instead, the Blade Dancer remained standing there calmly as his eyes took in everything around him, searching out his foe and observing all of the different heads that had attacked him.

A moment later, the shields faded away and the fangs were pulled back towards each of the Shydra's heads, drawn towards them by tendrils of Dark mana. It was the most basic form of ranged attack that existed in Ryan's dungeon, yet it was constantly improving. As the mana of the creature grew stronger, the projectiles were launched with greater speed and force, and the size of the projectile could increase as well. Meaning, even as adventurers armored themselves with more powerful defensive skills and items, the penetrating and destructive power of Ryan's ranged mob attacks increased as well.

Blaine took one last moment as the nine heads prepared

to launch another set of attacks. Then, he finally acted. With blinding speed, he rushed towards the closest head, about fifty feet to his left. When it had emerged from the ground, it had twisted up from the floor and wrapped itself around a stone column. As Blaine rushed towards the creature, the two flaming blades hovering over his back began to spin rapidly, creating a fiery wheel of flames. Meanwhile Blaine's two lava-encased swords began a dance of their own, moving so fast they left an afterimage. To the naked eye, it appeared as if Blaine were wielding a dozen swords at once.

The head he was approaching seemed transfixed for a moment on the glowing blades. The eye sockets fixated on the mesmerizing light display that was his glowing swords and flaming wheel, and for a brief moment, Ryan watched in disbelief as that singular head began to sway lazily back and forth, seemingly on beat to the dance Blaine was performing.

Had Blaine expected this reaction? Surely there was no way he could have expected the snek to be charmed by his dazzling display. Still, the Blade Dancer acted as if he'd planned it and took advantage of the head's momentary trance. With athletic ability fueled by a massive amount of passive mana, Blaine leapt towards the giant snake head, rotating his body rapidly as he did, twisting into a spiral. His two lava-encased blades jutted out from either side of him, and with the massive rotation of his form, created a tornado-like blade storm. Just ahead of his body, attacking at an angle perpendicular to his own rotation, his fiery wheel of blades crashed into the snek's head.

The flames cut deep into the Darkness mana, causing it to part, though the two fiery blades dissipated as they smashed into the thick snek skull. The purpose of that advanced flame wheel was clear. It wasn't to kill, it was to open up the path to the skull, clearing away all of the Darkness mana that had reinforced and protected the head. This opening was exploited by the twirling dervish that was Blaine. His two physical blades rapidly sliced into the skull, again and again and again, his momentum forcing the blades to cut dozens, perhaps hundreds, of times into the skull before his rotation finally slowed and he dropped back towards the ground.

Even as he landed on the ground, his two fiery blades reappeared, and he prepared for a counterattack. However, the head he had attacked had been effectively destroyed, the skull crumbling to pieces, raining down bone shards atop him. And while his focus was fixated directly on the head he'd just destroyed, his legionnaires were doing a grand job keeping him—and their party—protected. Swirling shields of mana covered Blaine's back and side, stopping the ranged fang attacks that had been launched towards him. Additionally, the legionnaires had formed a circular wall of floating shields around themselves and the two bishops, protecting them from an additional barrage of fangs.

In theory, this kind of fighting could work. Blaine could take down each head, one at a time, while his legionnaires used their skills to provide protection from any ranged attacks, and the bishops used abilities to keep Blaine's attack and defense enhanced.

Unfortunately for Blaine and his party, such a tactic wouldn't work on the Shydra. It was, after all, a Platinum Tier rare boss. Meaning it had many more skills and abilities than just ranged fang attacks and multiple heads.

Even as Blaine hit the ground, his eyes admiring the destruction his swords had caused, dark tendrils of mana shot out from the stump that was all that was left of the ninth head. The mana pulled the falling pieces of skull together and began to, ever so slowly, reform the head that Blaine had destroyed. At the same time, even as the Shydra's mana worked to regenerate its crippled head, the other eight heads changed up their tactics.

Before, the Shydra had been testing Blaine's party, getting a feel for the skills and abilities of those who had entered its lair. The party had thwarted its probing attack and had hurt it. Meaning the Shydra was done playing games. Now, the boss fight could truly begin. Ryan hoped, for Blaine's sake, that the Blade Dancer and his party had more tricks of their own. Otherwise, this fight was going to be over before it could truly get started.

Chapter Fifty-Nine

Blaine was good. Like, really, really, really good. Ryan watched awestruck as the Blade Dancer moved fluidly about the field, engaging the various heads, dodging their strikes, their lunges, their ranged fang attacks, and doing his best to trade blows with them. Even with the Shydra ramping up its offensive skills, sending off Darkness taunts at regular intervals towards Blaine, as well as its deadly breath attack, Blaine hadn't faltered.

The man moved faster than the roiling taunts could reach him, and he used his fiery mana to burn them away before similar taunts could reach his allies. As for the breath attack, which consisted of a life-sapping stream of Darkness mana filled with thousands of tiny bone shards, his legionnaires were always quick to summon a shield in the way to absorb the attack. And it wasn't the fact the shields were summoned to stop the breath attack that was impressive. Instead, it was the precision with which they used the skills.

The moment the Shydra tried to begin one of its breath attacks, a head arching backwards as an immense ball of darkness began to grow within its skeletal maw, a massive shield made of mana would appear just in front of the creature's mouth. The mana stopped the attack dead in its tracks and caused the massive amount of Darkness mana to erupt to the side harmlessly.

With the legionnaires keeping these more powerful area of effect skills at bay, Blaine and his swords were doing the job of three damage dealers at once. Still, it became clear as the fight dragged on, that Blaine's team would not be able to overcome the boss as they were. Because of the "Blaine-centric" fighting style of the party, they just couldn't burn down enough of the boss heads to really cause an impact before the regenerative features of the boss handled the damage dealt to it. And while the regeneration took a considerable amount of mana from the boss…this was a Platinum Tier mob and it had plenty of mana to burn.

Meanwhile, the five party members, no matter how strong, were human. Even if they were able to counter or negate most of the boss's skills, they were still being worn down. Another nasty effect of the Shydra Ryan had noticed, was that even being close to it, within the presence of its Dark mana, sapped the strength of those fighting it. Blaine's flesh, even now, had started to turn grey wherever bits of Dark mana had made their way through all of his defensive barriers to meet his flesh before they could be burned away. It was minor, but it was enough over time to begin causing him to slow.

"It seems we've finally met a worthy foe," Blaine called back to his team as he finished a devastating barrage of attacks on one of the Shydra heads. Two currently lay in ruins, Dark mana repairing them, as this third one crumbled to the ground. Ryan had been keeping track, the record so far was four heads down at once. Impressive, but not even halfway to keeping the boss down. His Shydra could keep fighting until it either ran out of mana or all nine heads were destroyed at the same time. So even if Blaine destroyed eight of them, if he couldn't take down the ninth before the regeneration finished on the damaged ones, the boss would just get back up and keep fighting.

At Blaine's words—the first he'd spoken since this fight began—he rushed towards his party, skittering to a halt just in front of them. With impressive reflexes, with a speed that should have been impossible at this stage of the fight, he spun rapidly to deflect a massive incoming fang before it hit him. As he hit the ground though, having completed his impressive display, Ryan saw him take a heavy breath. He was definitely feeling fatigued.

His party members were showing some strain too, their efforts at keeping him covered in their protective mana—as well as the attempts to keep the shields up— had slowly been eating away at their mana reserves. They'd been at it for almost ten minutes now and still hadn't managed to gain any significant ground.

"I may be able to bring him down with my swords," Blaine said to his party, his eyes scanning the room, watching for an attack. So far, he still hadn't activated his cursed swords. If Ryan had to guess, he'd been trying to get as good a read on the Shydra as he could without having to resort to his cursed objects. Ryan figured Blaine wanted to make sure he'd seen all the boss's tricks before he utilized his trump card.

"But," he continued, "I'd rather be sure we will destroy it completely." He glanced back for the quickest moment, to his party. "We're going to have to go all in." For the first time, Blaine's voice held something other than mere confidence. It had gone soft for a moment. As if his statement, his declaration, was also an apology.

His party members didn't say a word, yet they all nodded in response to him, their eyes hardening. The party's silence this entire time was slightly unnerving, and Ryan wasn't sure why Blaine seemed the only one to speak. Still, even without words, he could tell the party had a perfect understanding of each other, and of what must be done. And, while Blaine's party hadn't spoken, Ryan could tell they weren't there simply out of duty or because they were being paid to do so, like he'd seen with most royals.

What he sensed between Blaine and these four was the type of familial trust and bond that only the closest of parties could have. It was wholesome, in a way, and left a better impression of Blaine than that of the cold, calculated killer Ryan had assumed him to be.

"Let's kill this creature, then, and cement my path to Diamond." As Blaine spoke, his eyes seemed to blaze with a newfound fire, and red mana engulfed his body. At the same time, each bishop of the party reached around their necks, pulling out strange emblems. The Earth bishop pulled out what appeared to be a wolf-head with a large, cracked emerald in the middle. Beside him, the Water bishop's emblem was a large trident, with a similarly cracked sapphire in its center. Ryan could make out the volatile swirling energy within each gem which denoted the objects as cursed. Apparently, Blaine wasn't the only one to use cursed objects in his party.

As one, both bishops activated their cursed pendants and a massive amount of energy erupted around them as they did, seeming to charge the very air around with visible power. As the lifeforce-turned-mana flowed from them, Ryan watched as Earth and Water mana flowed over Blaine, whose body was pulsing with Fire, though he'd yet to activate his own cursed objects.

This massive display of mana was not lost on the Shydra. The boss, feeling something was amiss, launched a full-out attack on the party. Fangs flew towards the party, breath attacks were launched, taunts were launched. Essentially, every skill at the boss's disposal was launched. Three of the snake heads actually rushed towards the party, trying to come down and strike from different angles. The Shydra definitely felt threatened by what was happening. However, before the attacks could hit, a burst of mana from the legionnaires lit up the entire room. As the light faded, it revealed massive shields circling around the party, shields of mana ten times thicker than the ones they'd summoned thus far.

These massive shields perfectly intercepted every single attack coming the party's way. A quick look at the two legionnaires showed their shields glowing brightly, the gauntleted hands holding them having cracked gems within. Every member of Blaine's party, save for the Blade Dancer himself, had activated cursed objects now. Their lives were now, even more literally, on the line. Everything was riding on what Blaine did next.

The legionnaires, with their abilities bolstered by the sudden rush of power from their cursed objects, were able to do more than block the Shydra's assault. As the attacks rained down on the party, the glowing shields pulsed, reflecting the attacks back towards the Shydra. The three heads that had tried close-range attacks on the party, upon crashing against the summoned shields, were knocked backwards with enough force to actually crack their skeletal structure. Of course, Darkness mana was already flowing into those cracks and patching them up, but still, Ryan was impressed. It wasn't often a defense was so strong it could serve in an offensive capability.

Still, the true focus of all of this was still Blaine. The mana flowing from the bishops was rushing over the Blade Dancer, and his swords were completely encased in green mana. Massive amounts of stone were growing along the metal. As Ryan watched, the stone encrusted sword seemed to grow in length, thanks to the new rocky material being added to it. While the blades grew in length, Blaine angled their tips towards the ground, giving them even more space to grow.

Growing Earth swords aside, the Water mana flowing about Blaine was encasing his entire form in a protective coating that was instantly turned into mist as his Fire mana raged around his body. However, as Ryan watched, the Fiery mana around Blaine began to pulse from around his body and into his swords, running from his arms into the hilts, only to disappear within the layers of expanding stone. As that happened, the Water mana around his body condensed and formed a shining layer of ice armor.

With the armor formed, Ryan figured the Water mana was done. Instead, he watched as it began to snake around the stone blades, each of which now had to be at least fifteen feet in length, if not more. These tendrils swirled around in a vortex, creating an almost cyclonic rippling effect over the solid rock. And all the while, Blaine just stood there, his eyes burning with impatience as he watched the mana around his body carefully. Whatever he was waiting for came a moment later, when the Water mana reached the very tip of the stone blades. Blaine's eyes widened in excitement and without warning the two broken rubies on his swords' hilts burst to life as he activated his cursed blades.

"Behold my true powers, Dungeon," Blaine said coolly as his Fiery mana pulsed into the two massive stone blades. Even as the Fire mana flowed into his blades, his flaming mana swords which hung about behind him soared high above his head, linked directly to his body through a visible string of Fiery mana. As the stone blades started to glow red, the rock beginning to slowly melt, the two swirling blades of flame above Blaine began to grow. No longer were they normal, elegant weapons. Instead, the blades grew, their mana condensing, until each was roughly the size of three men, and the mana solid. These two massive weapons began to spin ever so slowly above Blaine, picking up speed as the crazed Blade Dancer's smile continued to widen.

"Behold my final dance before Diamond Three." The stone the bishop had created had melted away now and Blaine was no longer holding two swords. Instead, in his hands were two roiling, whip-like weapons that seemed formed of molten rock. Around them the lava was contained by the spiraling Water mana which was elongating the material and forming it to create the massive whips.

Without warning, even as the Shydra doubled down on its attacks against Blaine, the Blade Dancer began his dance. It started out slowly as he rotated his wrists, working the lengthy lava whips about in a simple manner. In response to his actions the two flaming swords above him continued to pick up their pace, heat roiling off of them in all directions as they did, the flames causing the room to illuminate as if by a sun.

The Shydra turned all of its focus to Blaine, the boss identifying this man as the main threat to its very existence. The heads launched attacks at him as Blaine continued working up the speed of his weapons. As expected, Blaine's legionnaires intercepted the attacks. This time though, the attacks, while nullified, shattered the summoned shields. Ryan looked away from Blaine just in time to see one of the legionnaires take a knee, his face strained and pale. He was at his limit, and his friend was not far behind. Their massive mana expenditure had drained them, and so had the use of their cursed objects.

"Leave the rest to me," Blaine said without looking back at his companions. The legionnaires nodded, and their gauntlets stopped glowing. They were out of mana, and they were out of the fight. Everything now rested on the Blade Dancer.

Emboldened by its success against the party's defenses, the Shydra launched another barrage of devastating attacks towards Blaine. Obviously, the fact the annoying shields that had been blocking the boss's attacks had dissipated had emboldened the boss. It could tell the Blade Dancer was vulnerable. The legionnaires could not come to his aid anymore. To the boss, and Ryan, it seemed as if two members of the party were down.

What happened next was a spectacle Ryan wouldn't have believed, had he not seen it. Without a moment of pause or hesitation, Blaine increased the speed of his lava whips. In a blur his two cursed weapons encircled his entire body as he spun in an elegant, brilliant manner. The weapons whirled about with impossible speed, leaving an afterimage of mana and lava.

Without missing a beat, the whips intercepted and effectively blocked every single attack against Blaine. Even if that wasn't impressive, Ryan could tell, from the trails of after image, that Blaine was masterfully controlling the whips in such a way they were just barely avoiding his teammates. Given the fact these weapons were over fifteen-feet each, and the dire situation they were in, and the exhaustion he must have been feeling, Ryan was more than a little impressed. This man…was something else. And, with the attacks blocked, Blaine's eyes sparkled as a smile crossed his face. He was dancing between life and death now, and he was loving it.

The Blade Dancer quickly rotated his wrists and suddenly pirouetted into a different direction, changing the course of the weapons, bringing them along on his brilliant, deadly dance. A moment later he snapped his wrists again, and gracefully shifted about on the battlefield in a manner only someone of inhuman skill could. In doing so the twirling, spinning whips rocked outwards like two angry waves, forming a large arc, building up energy until each tip cracked against a separate Shydra head. For a moment, the weapons seemed to freeze in time.

That moment was shattered as a shockwave erupted across the room, the force of the weapon, combined with the sudden crack as Blaine masterfully manipulated the weapons at just the right point, caused a concussive wave of power and energy to blast apart the two Shydra heads.

And, even as the bones shattered apart, even as the Darkness mana was blown aside by the explosive power of the two flame whips, the massive blades above Blaine moved downwards, twirling counter to his dance. These two powerful swords of mana above him were the partner to his wild attack, and they followed up their whip counterparts to cut into a couple of Shydra heads which had been working to attack Blaine from his blind spot. As the massive wheel of death severed the heads, the condensed mass of mana cutting cleanly through them as well as a few of the stone columns in the room, Blaine was again moving. Or, more appropriately, he'd never stopped.

Ryan couldn't fathom how much control Blaine had at this stage in the fight. His weapons, his mana swords, his awareness of his allies and the boss. The man seemed to be in a perfect state of flow. That pure, adrenaline-fueled moment where perfection was demanded, where death waited for the slightest mistake. The dance Blaine was showcasing for all who watched, was one that left Ryan, his fairies —and, likely, his party—captivated and breathless. When it ended, one side would be victorious.

Four heads were down in the span of a few seconds. And not only were they down...they were obliterated. Meaning the boss was going to need to spend even more mana to repair these heads. Which gave Blaine a larger window of time to destroy all nine and claim victory. The remaining heads of the Shydra were not pleased.

All five of them let out a massive roar and arched back, angling themselves to surround Blaine in a pentagram-esque pattern. Their mouths opened, first launching their massive teeth towards Blaine, immediately after beginning their breath attacks. Meanwhile, the dark auras around their necks intensified, extending the range of their life draining aura. Sadly for the boss, Blaine's own massive aura, his Fiery mana, and his icy armor kept that deadly aura at bay.

In response to the attacks, Blaine reacted in kind. If they were going to launch their final coordinated attack against him, he was going to meet them, head on, as he always did. Blaine never ran from danger. He cracked each whip, lightning fast, out to either side of him, aiming towards two heads, intercepting the oncoming fangs as he did. The speed and power behind his whips caused those bone fangs to disintegrate as the whips cracked into the snek heads. The two heads snapped shut instantly and exploded in an eruption of Darkness mana and bone shards, the breath attack cutting off before it could even begin.

Simultaneously, his spinning blades each shot out in different directions, rotating as they did to become a massive, vertical wheel of death. The immense heat and light from the burning blades incinerated the Darkness mana propelling the bone fangs forward, causing the man-sized bones to fall harmlessly from the sky. At the same time, the wheels of fire parted the Dark breath attack like a knife through butter before they split the heads vertically.

The final head, the one directly in front of Blaine, changed its tactic the moment Blaine sent his weapons out to his side and his two swirling mana swords away from him. The head rushed towards him, moving lightning fast as it struck at

Blaine. The strike of the Shydra was its fastest attack—after all, a snake could launch a strike faster than the blink of an eye. For a second, Ryan thought Blaine was done for. It took another moment for his mind to process what it had just seen.

The Blade Dancer saw the attack coming and summersaulted backwards. No, more appropriately, Blaine seemed to take flight with the amount of force he put into his jump. As he flew through the air, his unnatural, inhuman, impossible skill was further exhibited.

Mid-summersault, just as the Shydra striking at him hit the spot he had been a mere moment before, Blaine brought his hands together, clapping the two sword hilts together with the lightning-fast movement. His whips responded to both the speed and force with which he'd brought their hilts together, causing the two flaming tongues to follow. At the same time, his swirling fiery blades rushed past him, mere inches from his leaping frame, and came down like a spinning wheel of destruction atop the Shydra's final head, cutting completely through it as the whips crushed both sides of it.

The spinning wheel of flames raced down the neck, following the bone and Darkness mana back into the boss's lair, seeking out not only its whole length, but driving through all the stone and rubble to destroy the boss's body.

If, for a minute, Ryan had thought the Shydra could regenerate a head before Blaine had finished them all off, that devastating wheel of fire removed any hope for that. The Shydra had been obliterated.

However, it seemed that move had been an all or nothing attack. Just as the final head was destroyed, Ryan watched both bishops collapse, their mana instantly disappearing from Blaine's weapons, causing his fiery, molten whips to immediately return to just being swords. Both bishops' faces were bone white, their eyes sunken into their skulls, covered by dark rings. By the appearance of the reaper beside each of them, they'd been mere seconds from death, yet they'd held out until Blaine finished his attack.

That they'd managed to unleash so much mana and empower Blaine in such a way was awe-inspiring. Ryan had thought they were going to fall to his boss, yet they had managed to not only overcome it, but annihilate it. And somehow, Blaine, using two cursed weapons, had lasted longer than any of his party members, and was still—

Ryan stopped that train of thought as he watched Blaine land from his summersault. It was not a graceful landing. The moment his feet touched the ground his legs shook, and it seemed he mustered all the strength he could to try and right himself. However, in that moment something in him seemed to break and his face went from elation to frustration as his swords fell from his fingers. He barely managed to catch himself from falling face-first into the ground.

There he stayed, on hands and knees, breathing heavily. The man was bleeding from his eyes, ears, and nose. And Ryan watched him cough up blood as he looked, white-eyed, angrily, at the ground.

In the end, Blaine's group had overcome the Shydra. They had reached their goal. But in doing so they'd pushed themselves to the brink of death. Ryan had a feeling this was the furthest Blaine had ever been pushed, considering the state the man was in. Ryan couldn't feel there was any better way to truly earn what you were searching for in the dungeon, than in a life-or-death battle such as this. And for that, Ryan figured he would reward the party for their spectacular battle. After all, they were the first and only party to defeat the Shydra, so their rewards should show.

"Congratulations, Blaine." Ryan's voice echoed from a

crystal skull he spawned in front of the exhausted man. "Allow me to reward you for —"

Blaine rose a shaky hand and wiped the blood from his mouth. He looked like he was moments away from death, yet his eyes were hard as he looked at the crystal skull. "I got what I came for, Dungeon," he said, the struggle to speak evident. "With this, I can finally climb to Diamond Three. I need nothing else." He stood shakily to his feet, stumbling for just a moment. His eyes went to his party members, all of whom were still on the ground, all in similar shape to Blaine.

"However…" he looked back at Ryan's crystal skull. "If you wish to reward us," Blaine pointed towards his party. "They are deserving of whatever treasures you wish to bestow."

The statement meant Ryan was only partially upset with the Blade Dancer. as he mentally stopped crafting the ultra-rare swords he'd been making for the man. They would have been so much better than those cursed swords, he was certain of it. Still, if Blaine didn't want new weapons, he would at least make sure the party got rewards suited for what they'd done. And as Ryan thought about it, perhaps it was for the best he didn't give Blaine ultra-rare blades. After all, he could only fathom what the Blade Dancer would be capable of at Diamond 3. Considering the amount of power he already wielded; Ryan was slightly terrified by what the man would become.

At least for now he took comfort in knowing Blaine was on his side.

Chapter Sixty

BLAKE

"It is time." A Gold 2 priest stated simply. Blake and his party had been gathered, impatiently, in a rather large waiting area. For the past week they'd been confined to the Holy Temple, unable to leave, unable to even move about without an escort at all times. Blake had hated it. It felt like he was under arrest. And even though he was getting stir crazy, he knew Jack was taking it the hardest.

"Finally." The Duelist stood up excitedly, winds whipping about him for a moment. "I swear I was going to die of boredom in here." The wolfkin looked at his party. "Let's get this over with and get back to Boneville. At least they know how to have a good time there." One of the Church's tenets was the absence of vices such as liquor and gambling.

Of course, those rules were predominately for the strict members of the Church. Adventurers affiliated with the Church usually broke some of them. Which was why Karan often enjoyed wine with them in the evenings after dungeon runs. But a week without gambling for Jack was tough. Especially because their games of dungeon mobs, even without bets, were viewed as gambling by the Church. Granted, Blake had a feeling it was more that the cards and game had originated from the Bone Dungeon that was the basis for the ban on them.

While Blake could understand Jack's frustration, it hadn't been the lack of drinking or gambling that had caused him to become stir crazy. It was more the waiting in general. For how important this was, for everything that was on the line, sitting around doing absolutely nothing for an entire week had been excruciating.

"If you would please follow me." The priest didn't even respond to Jack's comments. The white robed man simply sniffed, turned, and began heading down the massive hallway he'd come from. As Blake and his party moved out of the room they were flanked by their normal set of guards. They might be "guests" of the Church but there wasn't a moment they weren't reminded of the precarious position they were in. If things didn't go well within the Goddess of Justice's dungeon, Blake would have to be quick to get his party to safety.

"How is it? Outside the walls?" Karan asked the man leading them. As a bishop, she was still an important member of the Church, even if she was an adventurer first and foremost. Based on the hierarchy of the Church, she outranked the Gold cleric leading them. Meaning the man would likely answer her questions, at least to some degree. Karan's relationship with Blake and Jack soured how willing they were to actually offer information to her, regardless of her station.

"The city is packed. It's all the guards can do to keep order. Everyone knows why they've been summoned, and the people are eager to begin the crusade. Only a miracle will stop this conflict now." The priest directed them down a separate hallway, one that Blake hadn't gone down before. In fact, he realized he had no idea where the priest was leading him and his party.

"Well, good thing we're going to pull off a miracle," Jack responded. The "miracle" of course, was them returning with the legendary Sword of Justice. That was what everything hinged upon. The Goddess of Justice granting them the same legendary sword she hadn't even given Blake's father. That whole week, while he'd waited for this moment, Blake had begun to realize what that meant. The Goddess had gifted his father with extremely powerful gear. His father's armor, shield, and sword had all been gifts of her design. She'd favored him. And at Platinum 1, he'd been one of the most powerful members of the Church. And yet, she had not given him the legendary Sword of Justice.

"The only miracle is you haven't gotten yourself killed yet." The man in front of them lowered his voice, to barely a whisper, as he finished, "Mutt." Of course, it wasn't quite soft enough to not be heard. Even if Jack's senses weren't increased because of his wolfkin blood, all of the party members were Platinum 4...they had enough mana to give them superhuman hearing.

"Don't." Matt was quicker to act than Blake. The archer's hand shot up to Jack's shoulder. The wolfkin, to the surprise of everyone, didn't even seem phased by the insult. He simply grinned towards the man's back. Granted, the Duelist's teeth had sharpened, revealing fangs, and his eyes were glowing golden. With his growth to Platinum, Jack had gotten more control over his wolfkin traits and could trigger them to smaller degrees, without having to do a full transformation.

"What can I say, maybe I've already got your Goddess's blessing." Jack let out an amused laugh as he wrapped his arm around Karan's waist, pulling her closer to him. Of the two, Karan's face was the mask of anger. She was extremely defensive of Jack, Blake knew that. He also realized, with the bond the two shared, Jack had likely felt her anger flash and was ensuring she kept it in check. Everyone was on edge with what they were about to face. The last thing they needed was additional conflict before they were even granted their audience with the Goddess.

"Your kind is an —" Before the man could continue, a calm, cool voice interrupted. Through the distraction of the cleric's provocation, they had reached their destination.

"That will be enough." The voice, sweet, almost musical, came from someone Blake didn't know. They'd been led deep within the Church, to a set of doors he'd not seen before. They were emblazoned with the scales of the Goddess and had massive opals embedded into each door atop the scales. It was almost exactly like the symbol on his shield, though his had an opal and an onyx, to represent not only the Goddess and Celestial mana, but the God of Death and Darkness mana.

"Bridget." Karan's voice held a hint of surprise, and the party's bishop smiled brightly towards the woman. She looked to be around the same age as Karan, and judging by the way she looked at Karan, Blake guessed they must've had a fairly good relationship.

"It is good to see you well, Karan." Bridget returned Karan's smile. She radiated an almost motherly kindness about her. Her soft, brown eyes shifted over the whole group, never once changing from her happy, welcoming look. Combined with her straw-like brown hair, Blake had a feeling many in the Church must have fallen for her. "You've definitely surrounded yourself once more with quite the group. It feels like only yesterday we were both new Silver clerics heading off to a dungeon town together."

Karan nodded back, though her hand tightened on Jack's arm, for just a moment. Karan's past was bittersweet. And if

Bridgett was referring to Karan's first dungeon experience at Silver, Blake knew it meant she was referring to the Dungeon of Ashes. The first dungeon tainted by the Cult of Chaos, the dungeon that killed Karan's original party and her fiancée… who also happened to have been Alice's son.

"Pity we had to come together again under these circumstances," Karan responded. Bridget gave her a slight nod and a sad smile. Her eyes hardened, and the soft features were replaced as she took on a more serious, dutiful attitude.

"The Archbishop has informed me of the mission you are on. He has instructed me, as the Gatekeeper, to allow you to visit the Goddess of Justice." She motioned towards the doors behind her. "These doors will take your party deep within the heart of the Goddess's dungeon. She personally designed them, to ensure the Church would always have a way to seek her guidance and gain her aid. Though of course, she put in place requirements to ensure such access was not abused."

As she started speaking, Celestial mana flowed from her into the door. At the same time, dual bracelets on her wrists came to life with golden light. Furthermore, golden symbols seemed to burn themselves into existence across her skin. As Blake focused on them, he realized they were small, faint tattoos, sparkling with golden light.

"I am the Gatekeeper." As Bridget spoke, Celestial mana flowed from her body into the two opals, filling them with light. They began to shine, and with that light, the scales on the door came to life. So captivated was he by the process, he barely noticed his party's guards stepping back slightly.

"I am the Key Master." Bridget glowed even brighter as she continued, and even more runes began to glow around her. Ever so slowly, the two doors began to open. He peered past them, wondering what he would see, but was blinded by the golden light flowing outwards from the doorway. This door didn't open into a room. Instead, it was a portal of mana that would take them to the Goddess. A portal, which he could tell, was being fueled completely by Bridget. Considering the amount of mana such a portal likely consumed, Blake could understand why the Church utilized this portal once a week, at most.

"I have deemed you to have an honorable purpose to enter the heart of the dungeon. I have deemed you worthy of passing through these doors." The two doors crept even further open. Considering how Ryan's crystal system had backfired, allowing enemies to get closer to him within his own dungeon, Blake had to admit this was smart. This process, the restrictions the Goddess had set for opening this doorway, seemed like a surefire way to ensure only those who should, could make it deep within the Goddess of Justice's dungeon. At least, without having to try and fight their way through the Goddess's dungeon from its entrance. Which Blake knew the Church also kept well-guarded.

"Shall we do this?" Blake looked at his party for a moment, just to confirm everyone was ready. They'd been over this, they all knew what needed to happen. And they knew the moment they entered the Goddess's dungeon, there was no turning back. This was a task they could not afford to fail, no matter what.

"After you, buddy." Jack motioned for Blake to take the lead, and he did just that...Blake could tell, while everyone was nervous, there was an air of excitement flowing through the party. After all, it wasn't every day adventurers...well, any living being for that matter, got to meet a deity. At least, that would apply to normal people. Apparently, Emily was on rather good terms with the God of Fire, and both she and Matt had met him. Furthermore, Blake himself had been personally saved by the Goddess of Justice. He'd even spoken with the God of Death. But, other than those instances, which were normally completely unheard of, meeting Gods in person was exceedingly rare.

Which of course meant Jack was really excited for this moment. Because the wolfkin Duelist loved being able to say he'd seen and done things no one else had. And everyone in the party knew he hated when Matt brought up that he'd been in the presence of a God and Jack hadn't.

"Alright. Let's do this." With that, Blake stepped through the glowing, swirling energy, closing his eyes against the sickening myriad of brightly flashing lights. He felt the sudden shift in air temperature, the immediate change in scents and sounds, as he passed through the portal. One moment, he was in the temple, full of the smell of incense, his feet on solid stone. The next, he was standing atop grass, the fragrant aroma of flowers filling the air and the sound of gently trickling water ringing in his ears.

"Welcome, Blake," said a voice, gentle yet strong, as he slowly opened his eyes. "I've been expecting you."

Chapter Sixty-One

The first word Blake thought of, the first description he had for the Goddess of Justice as he opened his eyes and looked at her for the first time in the heart of her dungeon, was, "powerful." That was evident by the blinding amount of mana roiling off her, so much so that his eyes had to blink multiple times to try to see through her aura. Massive mana aside, her form in and of itself spoke of power. She was clad in armor fitting a warrior; brilliant, golden armor inlaid with countless opals, adding even more of a shimmer to her appearance, as if she were wearing pure light. With every movement, the armor splashed a constant array of dazzling colors.

Next to her, leaning against the throne atop which she sat, which was located in the back of the grassy clearing they were standing in, was a halberd. The weapon itself looked to be masterfully made, and while it appeared very artistic, Blake had no doubt in its lethality.

The head of the halberd, instead of being the normal, axe-like style Blake had seen used, was replaced instead with the visage of a set of scales. One side of the scales was much larger and lined with a deadly-looking edge, while a spike protruded from the smaller portion of the scale. Just by looking at it, and at the Goddess of Justice, he figured that weapon had seen a lot of use.

Across from her weapon was a giant golden tower shield. To Blake's surprise, instead of the Scales of Justice on the center of the shield, a brilliant golden sun blazed. And it literally blazed, for there was a massive, pure diamond sitting in the middle of the shield, radiating its own boundless amount of energy.

As Blake tried to focus on it, a brief thought crossed his mind. The only time he'd ever seen something similar, the only thing he could compare it to, was the core of a dungeon. Though unlike the perfect sphere of the dungeon core Blake had seen Alice destroy, this gemstone appeared to only be a half of a sphere, its flat end set within the center of the golden sun.

As if all these things weren't enough, Blake also noticed a massive tiger curled up behind her throne, its head angled ever so slightly. The creature seemed to be resting, though Blake was pretty sure he'd seen its eye crack open, ever so slightly, at their arrival. Regardless of if the creature was awake or asleep, it, too, glowed with brilliant power. In fact, everything about the Goddess of Justice, her armor, her shield, her halberd, and her pet, it all screamed power.

However, even though the Goddess of Justice radiated power, looking at her face, looking into her deep grey eyes, Blake couldn't help but notice something else. She was exhausted. It was as if she was worn to the very bone. He got the feeling he was looking at someone who had been fighting an endless battle and was now on the brink of exhaustion.

Those tired, powerful eyes looked at Blake and his party with a strained expression as a slight smile crept onto her face. She lifted a hand as she spoke, motioning towards them. "Come, we've much to talk about."

In that instant, five chairs appeared magically before her. Blake looked at his party members, all of whom were looking over the Goddess, their faces revealing a wide range of emotions. Of course, the sudden elbow from Karan into Jack's stomach showed the Duelist was perhaps engaging in his usual train of thought. Blake couldn't help but grin as he felt a little bit of the stress leave his body. It was good to see not even a Goddess could phase Jack for long.

As they approached the chairs, the Goddess had summoned for them, Blake got a better look at the tiger. The beast—a perfect, beautiful, deadly creature—opened its icy blue eyes and looked at the party with little interest as they sat. Those eyes paused for a moment on Cynder, then on Jack, and finally focused on Blake. Under that gaze, Blake could sense a level of power and intelligence which signaled the tiger was more than a pet. Still, after a moment, the tiger let out a slight chuffing sound and closed its eyes again.

"From what I've been able to gather, you are here on behalf of the," she paused for a moment, before letting out a heavy sigh, "Bone Dungeon."

Blake looked at his friends, uncertain if they should respond to the Goddess or allow her to continue. Furthermore, he was suddenly uncertain of how he should act in front of her. She was a Goddess, after all. How was he supposed to act before a Goddess? Blake pushed the question out of his mind as quickly as it came up. Alice had trusted Blake and his party on this mission. Ryan, Erin, and all of Boneville were counting on them. Now was not the time to let himself be tongue tied or worry about etiquette.

"We are," Blake started. "We need your blessing to prove to your followers that the dungeon is not evil. And that it can be allowed to remain."

The Goddess took a deep breath before she leaned forward, causing her armor to again dance with a thousand colors. She folded her hands in front of her, looking keenly into Blake's eyes.

For a moment, Blake felt the entire world disappeared. He was caught under that powerful gaze. It overpowered him. He'd been under a similar gaze before, with Alice's strange, swirling, colorful eyes, which seemed to allow the Guildmaster to see the future of a person.

This gaze from the Goddess was something different. It felt as if she were looking over every single ounce of him, consuming every aspect of him, and peering deep into his very soul. To say it felt like he was completely laid bare before her would have been an understatement. In that instant, Blake was more vulnerable than he had ever been in his entire life. It was terrifying.

After what felt like an eternity under her gaze, the Goddess leaned back again, unfolding her hands as her shoulders slumped against the throne.

"I've seen what you have seen." She said simply. "I know what you know." She paused for a long moment, her eyes filled with sorrow. "And just as I feared, there is so much more at stake here than a single dungeon."

____

Chapter Sixty-Two

"What do you mean?" Blake managed after a moment. Had he heard the Goddess correctly? What did she mean there was much more at stake? The fate of the dungeon was huge. A battle between the Church and the Adventurers' Guild was huge as well. This was potentially the end of the era of adventurers. What else could be at stake?

"I fear we are at a turning point in the world," the Goddess began. "And whatever happens next, will change the very dynamic of the world as we know it."

"How?" Blake said shakily. The Goddess was being cryptic, and he wanted to understand.

"For that, I will need to explain a little more about the world to all of you," She said simply. As she spoke golden goblets appeared at the feet of each member of his party, as well as a variety of foods ranging from steaming hot bread to glistening fresh cooked meat. "Please make yourselves comfortable while I begin."

Before Blake or any of his party members could process what had just happened, a very excited cry from Cynder caused Blake to jump. A moment later the dragon, in its tiny cat-sized form, rushed from Emily's shoulder onto the ground to gobble up a massive piece of meat. Mere seconds later the little dragon let out a sigh of contentment as it began to work happily on the rest of its new meal. With that, Blake and the others grabbed the goblets the Goddess had summoned for them, as well as a piece of food. The appearance of it all definitely made his mouth water a little. He could tell without even tasting it that the food would be better than any he'd ever had in his life. The moment he bit into the soft, buttered roll, his suspicion was confirmed. It was all he could do not to stuff the entire thing into his mouth as the Goddess began.

"It all began when the World Smith, the father of all the deities, decided to leave this world in our hands." As she spoke, it seemed as if her mind drifted to the past, to the very moments she was describing.

"The World Smith, who created the groundworks for this world from nothing, split his powers, the forces which governed the world, into six different orbs. These orbs were Life, Death, Fire, Wind, Water, and Earth, and they were linked to the six types of mana which existed within the world."

"Six types of mana?" Blake questioned silently. That didn't make sense. There were seven basic mana types… Celestial, Chaos, Darkness, Fire, Wind, Water, and Earth…

The Goddess looked at him and nodded. "In the beginning, Celestial mana and Chaos mana did not exist. Furthermore, Darkness mana as you know it, was known as Death mana." Blake felt a chill run down his spine. And it seemed the Goddess noticed that.

"Over time, people began to refer to Death mana as Darkness mana, purely because of the negative connotation applied to the thought of wielding the power of death." She shrugged.

"So, what happened?"

"These six orbs of power were divided amongst the World Smith's seven children. To his eldest, the World Smith gave the Orb of Death. And, to his youngest, a pair of twins, he gave the Orb of Life." She smiled fondly. "That is, to my twin brother and I, he granted the power over all life."

"For a long while," she continued, "everything ran smoothly. There was a balance in the world, and as we worked with the powers our father left us, we slowly began to give a new shape to the world. Faust—my twin brother—and I worked together to use the Orb of Life to create the first living creatures on the world. The humans." She smiled towards Blake and his party.

"From there the other Gods tapped into our powers, melding their powers with the power of life to create additional races. Earth and Life created the elves; Fire and Life, the dwarves; Water and Life, the merfolk, and so on." She glanced towards Jack. "There were even instances of further collaborations, such as the creation of the wolfkin, which came from a combination of Death, Life, and Earth."

"With the creation of our own races, each God began to build their own followings. My siblings split across the world, claiming massive expanses of land for themselves and creating grand dungeons within which they could experiment with all the powers they had at their disposal. Even more so, these dungeons served as ways for them to help their followers grow and gain powers, as well as to create vast riches and items."

That seemed very similar to how dungeons still operated today, Blake thought.

"After some time, cities began to spring up outside of these dungeons, and the races continued to grow more powerful and more numerous." The Goddess of Justice paused, her face taking on a more serious expression. "Which was when everything began to change."

"It all started when the Fire nation attacked. The followers of the God of Flames—my brother Phyre—had always had a more...fiery nature. They struck out against their neighboring inhabitants, the giants, followers of the Air God, and chaos spread across the land."

"The destruction caused by these conflicts forced the Gods to reconsider what they were doing with their powers. We devised new ways to try and occupy our followers and to reward them. Our joint solution was the creation of dungeon cores. These cores gave us the ability to place the souls of our most devout, or those we deemed as worthy, into magical diamonds upon their death. Through this process, these individuals would be given a second life, as dungeon cores. And these new reborn individuals, through their newfound powers as dungeons, would be able to create for the world new challenges, new places to explore, to conquer, and to occupy their time with. Essentially, we created dungeons to give our creations a way to push themselves and keep themselves occupied and sated, without having to senselessly kill each other.

She paused for a moment and the room went eerily silent. Blake and his party hung on every word of hers. This was fascinating and yet, it hadn't explained what exactly was going on, or what it had to do with the pressing matter at hand.

"I will get to it soon, Blake," she whispered. The comment caused him to jerk in surprise. Could she read his mind? "It's clear on your face." She laughed lightly, a sad, tired laugh. That response...didn't confirm or deny if she could read his thoughts.

"With the creation of these dungeons the world once again entered a time of peace. However, the dungeons soon led to an unregulated amount of growth amongst the races. Too many were climbing in power too quickly. Even as Gods, we were not omniscient. We were learning as we went along. We used the Orbs of Power to place further rules upon the land, creating the Tier system. We established for all races, and living things, the leveling system that is still in place today. And we implemented the hard limit of three Diamond Tier members of each race and affinity, to ensure balance could be maintained."

Blake was aware of that hard limit. He'd learned about it during his time with Alice. A lesser-known restriction, which was why the Church and Guilds all kept such strict records of their members They needed to keep tabs not only on their most powerful members, but also know when there was an opening for a new member to climb to Diamond.

Because of the limited amount of Diamond Tier slots available, these positions were strictly regulated. Guilds, the Church, and some families, such as the Dragnovs, earned the rights to a Diamond Tier slot through deed, trade, or some other means. By doing so, they could work to keep their ranks bolstered by those they felt would best serve them with that power. Or, in the Church's instance, hoard all the slots of Celestial mana positions.

"All the things we created and implemented were meant to ensure balance. And for a long while, balance was created and maintained," the Goddess continued. "While there was peace, Faust and I began to take turns governing over our people whilst the other walked the lands in secret, interacting with all the living creatures of the world." Another sad smile. "It was truly blissful, seeing all the good, all the life our power had created. And yet the sins, the horrors I saw people commit as I traversed the world scarred me. It drove within me the resolve to not only create balance, but justice in the world. I wanted to use the power I'd been given to ensure no wrong went unpunished. To ensure the world was a just place to live."

She paused. "During my quest for justice, I failed to see Faust had set upon a different path. My brother wanted something more than justice for our world. He wanted to create a perfect form of life. A perfect existence. An immortal, perfect race." Her eyes went dark. "And in his quest to do so, he left our righteous path. That was when everything began to really change."

She was silent for a long time. So long that Blake almost felt the urge to break the silence and ask her to continue. Just as he opened his mouth, she began anew.

"My brother began experimenting on the humans and other races. Abusing the power of the Orb of Life to twist and change living things. He inflicted excruciating pain on the very creatures we had created, the ones we were supposed to protect. And from these experiments, from these poor souls, he created new monstrosities…all in the name of creating a perfect lifeform. In his mind the suffering of the few for the good of the many was a just cause." Her eyes hardened. "I disagreed."

She lifted a hand and the shield beside her throne disappeared, reappearing against her arm, giving Blake and his party a closer look.

"We fought for control of the Orb of Life, and in our conflict… the orb was split in two."

Chapter Sixty-Three

After this revelation, that the Orb of Life had been torn asunder in a battle between the very Gods themselves, the Goddess motioned down at the shield she held and to the stone set in the center. The half-stone Blake had observed earlier, the one that reminded him of a dungeon core. The stone that blazed with godly amounts of power.

"The piece I took control of, began Celestial mana. It maintained the healing aspect of life mana that is so coveted by the people of the world. Celestial mana is still linked to the core aspects of life, and as such has the greatest effect and ability to heal the living." The shield disappeared from her hand, returning to its position against the throne. A moment later the Goddess shifted her hand and suddenly the sword Blake kept on his back disappeared. It reappeared in her hand before he even realized it had gone missing. The Goddess uncovered it, showing the twisted demonic blade Blake had recovered from his father's body.

"Faust's half of the orb became Chaos mana. It was the volatile, twisted portion of life. It had the ability to enhance the physical aspects of creatures and to manipulate and change things based on intent and emotion." As she spoke, dark red and black mana crackled across the blade. "With Chaos mana, Faust was finally able to create what he wanted. A nearly indestructible species, possessing immense power and strength. Chaos mana was the gateway to creating creatures whose vices, their deepest-rooted passions and feelings, gave them immense power. Chaos mana allowed Faust to create demons."

She closed her hand around the sword and it disappeared. This time, it materialized in front of Blake, lying gently on the grass at his feet. Looking down at it he noticed a set of scales had been emblazoned upon the hilt. "Chaotic power—or, more appropriately, the power of emotions and feelings—is not inherently evil." She said, looking at Blake. "If your emotions, your passions, drive you to a just cause, they should be embraced. Such emotions have always been a source of power for the living. Just remember, unbridled emotions such as rage, lust, envy, greed, and so forth, can corrupt even the purest of hearts." Blake couldn't help but realize that was very similar to what the Archbishop had said. Perhaps the old man really did try and lead the Church according to the Goddess's wishes?

That thought fled his mind and he nodded slightly towards her in response. Blake still remembered all too well how he'd felt when he'd absorbed the Chaos mana from his father. How he'd felt as he channeled that mana through his body, allowing the rage to flow through his veins. He'd gained immense power during that time but had lost a part of himself to the moment.

"How does all of this tie into the current situation of the world, Goddess?" Karan interjected. The bishop had been silent the entire time, watching her Goddess closely. Yet now, as she spoke, she bowed her head deeply towards her deity, her voice full of reverence. This was her deity. The Goddess she'd lived her life in servitude of, the one whose teachings she tried to always follow and emulate. Much better, in Blake's opinion, than a lot of those who claimed to be in service of the Church.

"Ever since that day," the Goddess started, "my brother and I have been in conflict. The splitting of the Orb of Life also split the mana within the races. Suddenly those who had originally had a life affinity before, found themselves with either Celestial or Chaos mana. The Church of Life split into the Church of Justice and the Church of Salvation." She chuckled darkly. "Because, of course, Faust claimed his power, his Chaos mana, could save the races by turning them into demons. In that, he was offering them salvation from their mortal bonds."

The Goddess's eyes shifted, the perceived weight upon her increasing as she continued. It was as if speaking of the past weighed greatly upon her, even now. "From that moment on, our two sides warred against each other. Over time our sibling rivalry led to an all-out war. The Church of Salvation declared a war on all living creatures and tried to take the world by force. Their goal: to grant everyone in the world salvation by twisting them into demons. And while the Church of Salvation was snuffed out in defeat, the battle itself ended in a stalemate. Our oldest brother, Death, stepped in, with his own forces, to keep myself and the other Gods from destroying Faust within his very stronghold."

"Why would Death stop you?"

"Because Death cares the most about the balance of the world," she said, though it seemed the statement caused her a bit of irritation. "In my eldest brother's eyes, the world needs to maintain a perfect balance. While he stepped in to keep Faust from being destroyed, he only intervened enough to ensure the battle ended in a stalemate. In other words, he did just enough to keep the balance."

"After the destruction this conflict caused, the Gods agreed to pull back much of their influence from the world. We agreed to keep ourselves confined to our dungeons, decreasing our direct reach over the world. It was evident that, whenever we got too involved with the world, we caused greater conflict and harm came to the land we'd been entrusted. In short, we came to realize, our attempts to improve the world had been destroying it."

Her voice was bitter as she finished. It was evident she blamed herself for a lot of what had happened. A weight Blake wasn't sure she should be carrying all on her own. Especially considering what he'd been learning about Faust. And, humans, people in general…had to own up to some of the blame as well, right?

"I'm sure it comes as no surprise that my brother has not been following those rules." The Goddess chuckled darkly. "No. Instead, Faust has been working behind the scenes to make his vision a reality. While the rest of our siblings have been abiding by the rules we put in place for ourselves, Faust has been working to figure out ways around those rules. And while I've been unable to confirm what he has been doing, and what he has planned, I know he has been hard at work to implement his plan.

"Given the current situation of the world, I can tell his plans are about to be completed. Whatever it is he has been preparing, it is about to come into fruition, unless we stop it. Of course, that's a lot easier said than done, considering the rules and regulations I have to follow. My powers outside the dungeon have greatly diminished over the centuries."

She held up a finger. "Which is where your Bone Dungeon comes into play. That dungeon, that soul within the dungeon core, is my last effort. He is the final dungeon cores I was allotted to create. The last dungeon to be created in the land actually."

"Another stipulation we'd decided upon as we tried to guide the world and fix the damage we'd caused. But that is a tale for another time. Just know that Ryan is my one remaining tool to try and thwart Faust. I've waited and bided my time, watching for the perfect soul to become my last-ditch effort, my final hope. The Bone Dungeon is that, the soul within is a pure one I felt I could trust to rise up and save the world."

"Then...why is he a Darkness—er, Death dungeon?" Blake asked. If Ryan was supposed to uphold all the values of the Goddess of Justice, it definitely didn't make sense for him to have a Darkness affinity. Though, the connection to the Goddess of Justice had already been clear, considering Erin's presence within the dungeon. Blake just didn't know the Goddess was actually responsible for placing Ryan's soul inside of the dungeon core.

"Because unfortunately," the Goddess's voice was bitter, "Ryan was killed by members of the Church. And while I tried to erase those memories from him to ensure he would walk a righteous path, his anger at the Church and his unjust murder led him to choose Death as his affinity."

At this revelation, Jack, who up to this point had been happily eating the food provided to him by the Goddess of Justice, choked on his food with laughter. Tears in his eyes, fighting for breath even as he coughed up his partially chewed meal, he looked at the Goddess.

"Seriously," he shook his head, "your Church really cannot do anything right, can it?" He continued laughing for another second before he suddenly went quiet, his flesh draining of all its color. The white tiger, who'd been feigning sleep the entire time, was directly in front of Jack, its eyes fixated on the wolfkin's, bloodlust roiling off of it.

"That's enough, Rapha," the Goddess said calmly. The white tiger opened its mouth wide, revealing its massive, deadly teeth in a yawn. The statement was clear: Had Rapha wanted to, she could fit Jack's entire head within her giant maw. The tiger turned and walked back towards the Goddess, before taking a seat next to her, leaning towards the Goddess. On cue, the Goddess reached out and gently began petting the beast's fur.

"You've made a very good point, Jack. As much as I hate to admit it, the Church has strayed for far too long from what it once was. Due to my limited capacity, it has sadly become a shadow of its former self. Unfortunately, there have been those who have taken advantage of the Church and its influence to spread their own ideals of justice. And, as much as it pains me, when my followers do visit me, they often misinterpret or twist my teachings to suit their own ideals." She shook her head sadly. "That is why we are here. In this moment, with the Bone Dungeon's—with Ryan's—life on the line, I am certain Faust is pulling the strings behind everything. My brother has put his final plans in motion. His end goal is near."

She looked at Blake. "Yet even with all of this, I am hesitant to make my next move." She stopped scratching Rapha. She seemed to be preparing herself, choosing the next words carefully.

"Because honestly, Blake, I'm not sure what action I should take next. Do I grant you the Sword of Justice and thus declare my support for the Bone Dungeon? Doing so would spare it, but what if that is what Faust wants? Or do I allow my followers to destroy Ryan? I'm not sure which path leads to Faust's goal. Or, even if either action can stop him."

Her voice dropped to a whisper, and it seemed the immense weight drained the strength from her. "This could very well be the last action I ever do to affect the world I was tasked with protecting. And I know that my actions, my feelings and convictions in the past, are what have led to this moment. In my quest for justice, chaos has taken over the world. I'm afraid of what my final decision may bring. Will I thwart my brother's plans and return the world to how it once was? Or will I doom the world to chaos? Because if he accomplishes his goals, he will turn the world into one of demons and chaos."

She slumped into her throne, eyes looking across his party. The very weight of her words suffocated the room. And Blake suddenly realized why this matter was so important. This was potentially the Goddess's final action. This was the Goddess's final moment to try and right the wrongs of the world. If she failed, he got the feeling she—and perhaps the world as they knew it—wouldn't be around for long. Whatever the God of Chaos was planning, it seemed if he got his way, he would have the upper hand on the other Gods. He would have control of the world. Suddenly, her exhaustion made a lot more sense. The Goddess was at her limit.

"I don't know much about this chaos and justice thing," Jack, back to being Jack, said offhandedly, "but obviously your followers are the ones who messed this whole thing up." The Goddess turned her gaze to Jack as he continued, "So, maybe you should do the just thing here and right the wrongs they caused?" He shrugged. "Because it's not right we adventurers should have to lose the only dungeon remaining for us to dive because one of your followers decided to go all high and mighty and got himself killed."

The Goddess looked at Jack, her gaze unreadable. Karan's look, on the other hand, was extremely readable: pure shock. The Duelist simply resumed eating a large turkey leg, though Blake could tell Jack was purposefully avoiding Karan's gaze. The wolfkin had never had a good opinion of the Church, so it made sense he would be emboldened in this situation. And to be fair, he did make a good point.

"Please," Blake started, taking Jack's comments as an

opening. While he was certain he couldn't fully grasp all that was at stake, even after hearing the Goddess's story, one thing was certain. There were hundreds—no, thousands of people depending on him and his party to clear Ryan's name and protect Boneville. Even more lives if he counted the loss of life which would occur if the Church and Adventurers' Guild clashed over the Bone Dungeon. He didn't know about the conflict of the Gods, but in this moment he felt in his heart the right thing to do was to keep the peace.

"We may not have all the answers. We may not know what will happen or what your brother has planned. But as it stands now, we are here to ensure justice is carried out. Ryan is innocent. If you do not give us your blessing now, if we do not return with the Sword of Justice, the Church and the Adventurers' Guild will come to blows. Not only will the Bone Dungeon likely die, but think of how many people will die on both sides."

The Goddess looked at Blake for a heartbeat and nodded ever so slightly towards him. As she did, a gleaming sword appeared in front of him. The weapon was made of opal, radiating Celestial light. The guard was a set of balanced scales; the pommel a radiant sun. All along the blade, golden runes were etched, glowing with unbridled power.

"When I was younger, I acted rashly, believing my path the right one. That led to conflict, it led to death. Then, I held my tongue, doubt creeping over me, and I let the Church go its own way, fearful that if I tried to guide them, I would once again fail. Now, I know that through both means, I've let the world down. I'm not perfect, I know that, and I believe now, perhaps, I shall take one last risk, one last gamble, and do what I've never done before. I'll stop carrying the burden all on my own. I'll put my faith in those who have proven their devotion. This sword should have gone to your father, a follower who I held in the highest regard. If I'd given it to him, perhaps he would not have met the fate he did. I will right that sin, and entrust you with the Sword of Justice."

"Thank you," Blake said, standing as he did to grasp the sword. The moment his hand wrapped around the hilt, a surge of Celestial mana flowed through him. The sword nearly engulfed him with the raw power in its blade. Never had he held such power. "We will make sure the world doesn't fall to chaos."

"I pray that you do," she said. "The fate of the world is now in your hands."

And with that, she was gone. Blake and his party suddenly found themselves alone in the dungeon chamber, no sign of the Goddess, her throne, or the white tiger.

"Whelp." Jack stood up, looking wistfully at the ground where the pile of food had been a moment ago. With the disappearance of the Goddess, all the food and drink had disappeared as well, as if it were a subtle hint that their time in the dungeon was now at a close. "I guess it's time we head back and make that Archbishop guy declare the Bone Dungeon's innocence." Jack grinned at Blake, though the Duelist's eyes were admiring the blade in the party leader's hand. "I cannot wait to see the look on his face when you show up with that."

Blake laughed, taking a moment to rewrap the demonic blade and place it across his back. With that task done, he looked at his party and nodded towards Karan. The agreement had been they would return to the center of town when they'd completed their visit with the Goddess of Justice. The Archbishop had mentioned the teleportation crystal there was the only way to enter the city, for safety reasons. Meaning it was the only way they could return. According to the old man, he'd be waiting for them along with his closest followers to spread the word of the Goddess's decision.

"Let's go save the Bone Dungeon." With those words

Karan grasped the crystal around her neck, activating it to teleport the party away from the Goddess of Justice's dungeon and back to the Holy City. Blake couldn't help but smile as they teleported away. They'd done it. They had done the impossible, they were completing a miracle. And now, they would not only save Ryan, but stop whatever the God of Chaos had planned. With this, everything would go back to normal. Together with his party, his family, they could save the world.

Chapter Sixty-Four

The Holy City was on fire.

Saving the world was suddenly more urgent than they'd thought.

They'd teleported from the calm of the Goddess's dungeon to chaos. All around them the architecture burned as cries of agony filled the streets. While the Holy City was full of capable Celestial mana users, it was also filled with thousands of devout followers of the Church of Justice, many of whom were ordinary people. Often, people chose not to undergo the process of awakening themselves to mana. Instead, they decided to live ordinary lives, letting others put themselves in danger to keep the rest of them safe. Meaning, under the current assault, they were powerless.

"Just perfect," Jack said as he looked around. They'd teleported back to the port crystal, as had been the original plan. According to the Archbishop, he was to meet them there.

However, there was no sign of the Archbishop. In fact, save for a slew of corpses on the ground, ones Blake recognized as city guards, there weren't any living beings in their immediate vicinity. Whatever had happened here, the fighting had quickly moved into the city. As was evidenced by all the cries of fear, pain, and sorrow erupting in the distance.

Blake scanned around the area, pumping mana into his eyes as he did to increase their power. He was searching for the Archbishop's mana. The man was Platinum 1, meaning he would have one of the more powerful souls in the area.

What Blake saw, confused him. Here and there, he could see smaller souls. Many of these made up the followers of the Church. Their affiliation was obvious by the large quantities of celestial mana users grouped together. Sure, the Church wasn't solely made up of Celestial followers, but the vast majority of their members—especially those who climbed in power—were Celestial users. It was an unwritten rule that if you had a Celestial affinity, you were supposed to become a member of the Church. The only exception to that rule was Blake, because of his Darkness mana affiliation. The Church refused to accept any Darkness or Chaos mana users.

His confusion as he looked at all these souls though, was the anomaly he kept seeing on these souls. The non-Celestially aligned souls had strange flickers of red and black flashing through them. Chaos mana. The only reason he didn't chalk this up as impossible was because he had seen this exact same thing happen once before, when his father had been possessed.

"The Cult of Chaos is here," Blake said, his blood beginning to boil. They were supposed to have been eliminated, but he'd known in his heart that wasn't the case. Besides, he remembered all too well that Marissa and that Succubus had escaped from the dungeon and were unaccounted for. Even though all the corrupted dungeons had been destroyed to try and prevent the Cult of Chaos from summoning any more demons, Blake had known they were still out there.

Jack sniffed the air as his eyes shifted to their wolfkin state. At the same time, the winds around the Duelist picked up. "I'm not smelling or sensing any demons, Blake. Are you sure?" The Duelist and Karan had the most experience fighting demons. They'd been assigned as a defense force by the Church to protect a small town against the raids when the demon attacks first started.

"I can see the Chaos mana," Blake said. He had explained his powers to the party. They knew exactly what his eyes were capable of. With that statement, the argument was over.

"Alright, so what do we do?" Matt asked. "We can't just stand here and do nothing." The arcane archer had a very good point. The sounds of fighting continued all around them, as did the screams of terror. A sudden explosion rocked the city and Blake turned his eyes in its direction. In the distance, just on the edge of his vision, he could make out two glowing sources. One, a bright golden light, surrounded by an additional amount of golden souls. The other, larger than the largest golden soul, a soul black as night. And for a second within that darker soul, Blake saw a flash of crackling blood red.

"Follow me," Blake said, taking off down the streets and towards the source. Whatever was happening, he had no doubt it was the massive amount of Darkness mana that was leading the attack. If they could get there and help the Celestial users—whom he assumed included the Archbishop and his Paladins—they could help the city. That was the top priority. People were dying, reapers were all around, and he needed to stop it.

They ran through the streets, the sounds of intense fighting escalating as explosions continued to rock the city. Bodies were piling up. Alleyways were littered with them, many already harvested by the reapers, who left behind the grey death orbs Blake had grown accustomed to seeing. Whenever they came upon a survivor, they paused just long enough for Karan to bathe the injured person in golden light, stabilizing their wounds enough to stave off the reapers. They didn't have the time nor the mana to spare to heal everyone, but they could at least keep them alive for when the fighting died down.

"You guys notice something strange?" Jack asked as they continued rushing through the streets.

"What?" Blake asked. Jack's tone sent chills down his spine.

"Some of the dead bodies are adventurers," Jack whispered, just loud enough for the party to hear as they turned a corner. It was a good thing he did, because around the corner was a large opening where a group of three city guards stood defensively, their eyes white with fear.

"Don't come any closer," the lead one, a Gold Celestial mana user, said. The man leveled his pike towards Blake and his party even though the man's hands were shaking something fierce.

"We are here to help," Blake said forcefully. "Whoever is fighting beyond here needs our help." He had already seen two of the orbs snuff out and turn grey. The Celestial side was losing the battle. Whoever that mass of Dark and Chaos mana was, they were lethal.

"Don't try to lie to us," The second guard said. "You adventurers just wanted us to let our guard down, so you could betray us." The man looked at Blake's party as he spat on the ground. "Your kind is killing innocent people. And why? To keep your precious Darkness dungeon alive?" He took a step forward, his words seeming to embolden him. "You all deserve to die."

Blake let out a heavy sigh. "We don't have time for this," he said, exasperated. "Jack." Without another word Blake sent a wave of Darkness mana roiling towards the three guards, taunting them. The moment the Darkness mana connected, Jack disappeared from Blake's side, reappearing behind the guards. With Blake's taunt on them, they had no idea where Jack was, nor any way to defend themselves. In a split second, Jack had knocked all three out, and Blake and his party were in the clear to keep going.

"We need to get to the bottom of this," Blake said. Another explosion rocked the earth, and he saw one of the buildings on the side of the street crumble. The fighting was taking its toll on this part of the city. "We need to—"

He paused as they finally reached the area of the battle. There, in what used to be a marketplace, the Archbishop bled profusely from countless wounds, three Paladins standing by his side. On the ground rested the remains of three other Paladins, their bodies ripped open. The Archbishop and his guards radiated with golden light, a massive shield of mana surrounding them, as their eyes seemed to scan the open expanse.

For what, Blake already knew. He could see the Dark mana shifting across the ground, moving through the shadows with impossible speed. Even with all his mana, Blake could barely keep up. The form, a Diamond 3 Darkness mana user with Chaos mana flowing through them, as well. A form, or, more appropriately, a creature Blake had hoped to never see again.

Because while it definitely didn't look like the last one he'd fought, there was no mistaking that flash of fangs, nor the incorporeal movement, nor the gaunt, pale skin. What was attacking the Archbishop, what was leading the attack on the Holy City, was a Vampire. And even worse…as Blake watched the Vampire smash into the golden barrier the Archbishop had erected, sending a shockwave all around the marketplace, Blake realized something else. He recognized the Vampire. Though, when he'd known her, he was pretty sure she had been human.

"It can't be," Blake whispered.

"Did Ryan do this?" Jack asked, his eyes glowing golden. The Duelist was using his wolfkin traits to follow the flow of the battle. "Is this another A-a-ron moment?"

Blake shook his head, hands tightening on his weapons. He knew this wasn't Ryan's work. Ryan had never come in contact with her...The woman had gone missing, last Blake had heard.

Suddenly, the Goddess of Justice's words made more sense. He could see now there was more going on than just the fight to keep Ryan alive. Because somehow, someway, he was watching Monica, the Diamond 3 Death Lord adventurer and mother of Cane, fight against the Archbishop of the Church of Justice as a Vampire.

He didn't get a chance to think about what was happening. In the span of a second, he was no longer watching Monica from afar. Instead, the Diamond 3 Vampire was mere feet away from his face, her eyes blazing red, her fangs glistening as she smiled. Chills rushed down his spine as his mind replayed the encounter with his father in the Dungeon of Ashes. He'd thought he'd gotten over that moment of his past, but in this instance, at this very second, it all rushed back to him. The memories, the tragedy, the pain all left him frozen. It was happening again. Someone else he knew had been corrupted by a demon. Was he going to have to kill her? Would she kill herself? What was going—

"Good job, Blake." Monica—and it was Monica's voice—said sweetly. She smiled even as pillars of bone erupted from the ground around her, blocking Jack and Matt's attacks instantly. Her body went incorporeal as flames washed over her. Even as Blake stared in disbelief. He couldn't' move. He couldn't speak. His mind was trapped in that terrible moment. The fear, the trauma, causing him to freeze even though he knew he needed to act.

"I always knew you would achieve greatness." She let out

a laugh and her hand shot out, impossibly fast, and grabbed the sword he held. His mind screamed at him; he needed to do something. He tried to respond, he did. He called for his mana, but it moved too slowly. His muscles, his grip on the sword, failed him. He couldn't react in time, not in this state. Before he even knew what had happened, both the sword and Monica were gone. He saw her soul sinking back underground, her incorporeal Vampiric skills allowing her to easily float beneath the ground.

As she moved away from Blake, startled cries of agony caught his attention. Bones exploded from the fallen bodies of the Paladins, dark tendrils of mana wrapping around them, forcing them from their fleshy confines with explosive force. The target of this attack was obvious, and Blake gave the Paladin's credit, as they moved around the Archbishop, protecting him from the Diamond-strength corpse explosion. The explosion of bones, empowered with Diamond 3 levels of mana, punctured arteries, completely tearing apart the poor men.

They died instantly, but they died fulfilling their duty. The Archbishop was alive.

He saw the Dark soul of Monica fade from existence after that, leaving the Archbishop as the sole survivor in front of him. At the same time Blake noticed various souls wink out of existence, the ones tainted by Chaos. In that split second, for a reason he couldn't fathom, Monica and the forces that had been laying siege to the Holy City, disappeared.

He didn't have time to think about everything that was happening. As his very confused party turned towards him, and as he turned towards the Archbishop, he was met with something just as terrifying. The Archbishop was glowing brilliantly as golden light erupted in the sky above Blake and his party.

"Traitors," the Archbishop spat. "I trusted you." He

continued, his eyes wide. Blake could only imagine the nightmare the Archbishop had just witnessed. "I thought you were your father's son." As he spoke the golden light above Blake and his party solidified. Blake was well-aware of what was about to come down upon him and his party. "But I saw you hand over the blade. You…you've betrayed the Goddess and your family. You and your kind," he spat, "you adventurers have all been corrupted by the darkness of that dungeon. You all only seek power, no matter the cost."

His eyes flashed with pure, unadulterated rage. "Atone for the sins of your traitorous kind. May your death bring solace to all those you've damned." And without giving Blake and his party a chance to speak, the Archbishop called down the most powerful skill a Platinum 1 Celestial mana user had access to.

There was only one thing Blake could do.

Chapter Sixty-Five

"I guess it's down to war." Marcus's voice was heavy as the Platinum 1 rogue leaned back against his chair. Blake's party stood before him, their clothes and gear still covered in ash and blood from the Holy City. Just before the Archbishop's Divine Judgement would have ripped into Blake's party, he had grasped the pendant at his neck and teleported them away from the Holy City and back to Boneville. Or, more appropriately, just outside of Ryan's dungeon. The dungeon had hidden the teleportation crystal inside one of the bone teeth that made up its entrance and linked it to the pendant he'd given Blake.

Once they'd arrived, they rushed towards Boneville, knowing Marcus needed to be updated on the situation as quickly as possible. They still weren't certain about what was going on, but it was clear something had been set in motion, something they didn't have any control over. It was just as the Goddess of Justice had said—what followed might decide the fate of the world.

"But we had the sword," Blake said weakly. "The Archbishop said that sword would be proof the Goddess wanted the Bone Dungeon to survive."

Marcus let out a sigh and shook his head. "And then the Archbishop watched you hand that sword over to the monster that had been attacking their Holy City." Marcus had a point, and Blake was still fighting with himself over his inaction in that instance. He couldn't let himself fail like that again. That could have been the death of him and his team.

"So, what do we do?" Jack asked. "Just wait here? Just sit around and wait for the Church to destroy us?"

"I'm not —" Marcus started, but was cut off.

"I'm tired of the Church dictating everything that happens in this world," Jack growled. Blake could see his fangs grow—the Duelist was fuming. "Why do we even have to listen to them? Why are we scared of them? We're obviously stronger than they are."

"I'm afraid you haven't seen the true might of the Church," Marcus whispered softly. "The strength of the Church isn't in its individuals, even if it boasts the strongest living human in existence." He shook his head. "The true strength of the Church comes in the legendary items they bring to battle."

"We've got Alice, all of the Adventurers' Guild, and a freaking dungeon on our side." Jack chuckled, the sound a little bestial. "I doubt the Church can pose much of a threat to us."

"Jack." Karan grabbed the wolfkin's arm softly, calming him instantly with her touch. He looked down at her, his eyes and fangs shifting back to human. Everyone, not just Jack, was worked up. And how couldn't they be?

"If it were the Church on its own, perhaps we would stand a chance." Marcus stood up from his chair. "However, as the Goddess of Justice told you, the God of Chaos is up to something. All this feels orchestrated. Not only that," he walked to the front of his desk, continuing to face the party, as he leaned back against it slightly. "But whoever is behind this, they've now got Monica on their side."

"Do you think they've corrupted another dungeon?" Blake asked hesitantly. "Monica was a Vampire. We know Ryan is able to make Vampires… so couldn't other Darkness dungeons do that, as well?" Even as he said those words out loud, he realized what implications that could have.

"The only other Darkness dungeon still in existence is the God of Death's." Silence filled the room. If the God of Death had turned Monica into a Vampire, there was no telling how powerful she was. From the size of her mana, Blake had guessed Diamond, but it had been a larger mana pool than what a Diamond 3 should have. Similar to what had happened with A-a-ron…When Ryan had reanimated the foolish noble, the Vampire had been much more powerful in undeath than in life. It wasn't that part that scared him, however.

"You don't think the God of Death has sided with Chaos again?" The Goddess of Justice had mentioned the God of Death had before taken the side of Chaos in order to ensure the world remained in balance. What if the God of Death was once again choosing sides? Was he helping bring the Church down? Or did the God of Death have a plan of his own to stabilize the world? And what did the Bone Dungeon have to do with it? How involved was Ryan? Was the dungeon telling him everything?

"If we're getting caught up in a battle between Gods," Marcus pulled out his flask and took a drink, "Then I don't think anything we do matters." He sighed as he took another long swig from his flask. "But I wouldn't be an adventurer if I rolled over and let whatever happens happen."

"So, what's the plan?" Jack asked. "Do we take the fight to the Church?"

Marcus shook his head, a small sad smile on his face. "We already tried to send more spies. Port crystal has been deactivated. And they are vetting ever person in the city now. The spies we had in place had to flee."

"Then, what?"

"We prepare for war. The Church has mobilized, and they are finalizing their preparations. They will begin marching in the next day or so, and it will take an army of their size about a month to reach our doorsteps. When they do arrive, we will show them a unified front." Marcus grabbed his Guild pendant. "Now I suggest you guys spend this month preparing as best you can. Get as strong as possible, and do so safely."

"What are you going to do?" Blake asked.

"I've got to go discuss the war effort with Alice. If we are under siege, I'm going to see who the Guildmaster thinks we can call to our aid." And with that, the rogue was gone, leaving Blake's party standing alone in the Boneville Guildhall.

"Well, you heard the man," Jack broke the long silence. "It's time for us to train like never before." The wolfkin flashed the party a smile, doing his best—as always—to break the tension. It did little; everyone was still on edge. This was huge. This was so much more than they'd ever planned on facing. It was one thing to fight dungeon mobs. It was another to go to war against living beings.

"How about we all rest today?" Karan asked before Blake could say anything. The bishop looked over the party, her eyes tired. This had to be hitting her the hardest. It was now confirmed she was going to have to fight against the very Church she followed. "And safely, Jack," Karan continued, offering the Duelist a wry smile, "means you don't get to try and duel any Bone Enforcers." Jack had mentioned on a few occasions he would like to try and duel the Bone Enforcers, specifically the Badgerman, in Ryan's dungeon once he climbed to Platinum 3. Something the party had been adamant against him not trying out.

With that statement, followed by Jack's groan, Blake could feel at least a little of the stress leave him. They had a month to get stronger, a month to get everyone in the party as close to Platinum 1 as possible before the Church arrived. A month left together, diving the dungeon as a family, before the final battle for the Bone Dungeon would take place. Blake resolved to treasure every moment they had left.

The Exalted One

The Exalted One looked down at the weapon in his gauntleted hand. The golden runes upon it shone, the blade's Celestial mana pulsing. Because Chaos and Celestial mana were cut from the same cloth—both derivatives of life mana—it felt natural to him.

"You did well," He said slowly, looking down at his latest pawn. Monica, the Diamond 3 Death Lord, Monica the Vampire. A creature of immense power, the only one of her kind outside of a dungeon. The first human in over a century to willingly be turned into a creature of Darkness. She must have been Death's favorite follower, for him to grant her that honor. And now, she was quickly becoming one of the Exalted One's favorite tools.

"It wasn't enough," She said. Her fangs glistened as she spoke, eyes glowing an intense red. The thing about Vampires was, they had the ability to feed on living things. Normally they drained a small amount of life from a creature in the form of blood and could sustain on that for a long while. From what he'd learned of Monica, she'd sustained herself on wildlife. In doing so, she could avoid the overpowering urges Vampires suffered when they'd consumed the blood of one of the sentient races, such as humans or elves.

That Vampiric trait had been part of what helped him corrupt her. Normal torture had proved ineffective, albeit entertaining. What he'd eventually learned though, was with the right amount of Chaos mana pushed into the Death Lord, forcing her past her inhibitions, he could force her to feed on humans. And once she'd started, still under the influence of the Chaos mana, she couldn't stop. With Marissa's help they'd corrupted Monica and made her thirst, uncontrollably, for the blood of humans. Meaning when she'd finally been allowed out to complete this task, she'd excelled at it.

"Your reward, as promised." He said, waving a hand towards her. Part of his agreement with her was that she was to leave the Archbishop alive, and that she was to return the moment she got the sword. He'd been certain the Goddess would give that interesting young man, Blake, the Sword of Justice. After all, the Goddess was out of options, and with her great Paladin, Sean, disposed of, Blake was the only one she would have deemed worthy to wield the weapon.

Marissa stepped through one of the doors, leading a dozen prisoners behind her. The Vampire's eyes flashed with excitement. and he chuckled darkly as she set about her feast. "You'll get even more when we begin the final attack." With the Sword of Justice out of reach for his enemies, there was nothing else that could stop him. This was the final weapon in existence he could think of that would have proved a problem to him. And now, he could destroy it.

He wasn't worried about the Church. They were pawns to him, even if they didn't know it. The dungeon was a nuisance, but the Church was going to deal with it for him. And now, not even the adventurers were a threat to him. Without the Sword of Justice, there was nothing they could use that would threaten him. After all, there was no one living who could challenge him.

Now then, he just had to wait. He would send the Sword of Justice to the God of Chaos, so the God's dungeon would dispose of that troublesome weapon. And then, all he had to do was wait for the Church and the Adventurers' Guild to clash. With both sides gathered on the same battlefield, he would eradicate every remaining annoyance at once. The moment those forces clashed, his time would finally come. For during that battle, he intended to finish off the final hope for mankind. Because surely, Alice would step foot on the battlefield. And he had been looking forward to killing the dual affinity plasma user for far too long.

He could hardly wait.

Chapter Sixty-Six

War was at his doorstep. Once more he was threatened, once more he was challenged. Only this time, for the very first time, Ryan was prepared. Or at least, as prepared as he could be.

For a month, he'd done all he could to ensure victory. Some of his preparations and tactics might seem underhanded, but when it came to his survival, and the survival of Erin and Hel, he didn't care about fighting fair. Especially if the Cult of Chaos was involved in all of this, because he highly doubted they would fight fair either.

"Tomorrow's the last chance for peace," Erin commented atop his core as they once more scanned through everything. According to Blake, the Church of Justice's forces were about two days away. The massive unit, thousands strong, had stationed itself far enough away to avoid stepping foot into Ryan's influence. Which was of course probably a smart thing to do. It also spoke to the fact that the Church was good at dealing with dungeons.

From what Blake had told him, Alice, Diamond 2 leader of the Adventurers' Guild, was going to arrive in Boneville that night, along with the rest of her forces. Over the past month it seemed the Adventurers' Guild had been hard at work gathering resources and preparing for this war as well. However, while the Church of Justice seemed almost militaristic, the Adventurers' Guild was not. It was made up of adventurous individuals who enjoyed grouping up, diving into dungeons, and challenging themselves to grow stronger and chase riches. There wasn't a greater cause they fought for; everyone had their own drives. Meaning, it was a little more difficult to rally them, even to protect Boneville and the last dungeon that defined their role in society.

Alice was to meet with the leader of the Church's forces in the morning, trying once more to establish peace and stop this war before it started. Judging from everything Blake had told Ryan, the core had a hard time believing peace could be achieved. Still, if this amount of loss of life could be prevented, Ryan would be okay with that. He hadn't managed to gain enough experience to reach Diamond, which meant he wasn't as strong as he'd have liked to be.

"Honestly, Darling…" Hel could sense his emotions as he ran through everything. His dungeon was empty, devoid of both adventurers and mobs for the first time since his existence. Every mob of his had been reabsorbed, from the smallest skrat to his fourth-floor boss, the Shydra. For once, all 9,600 of his mob points were available to him. All the resources he had, as a Platinum 1 dungeon, were now at his disposal. And yet, all he could do was sit here and wait. That was the worst part of it all.

The Succubus was apt to read his emotions, and she could sense his growing anxiety. "You've done all you can." She flew atop his core, sitting beside Erin. The two had grown even closer over this last month. They seemed much more like sisters from an estranged family than rivals. Which made sense, considering Celestial and Chaos mana originated from the same source, Life mana. "Nothing they bring forth can stand before you. When this war is done, you will reign supreme."

"Besides," she cooed "with all the fighting, you will gain the experience you need to reach Diamond Tier in no time."

She had a very good point there. As much as he was against the massive amount of death that would take place if this war began, he couldn't deny he would gain from it; the fighting was going to happen over lands under his influence, after all. The Adventurers were aware Ryan was fighting alongside them. They trusted him to help keep them safe, and they knew fighting on his land would give them an advantage against the Church.

"It all hinges on tomorrow," Ryan said quietly. "Whatever happens," Ryan paused, composing himself as he did. "I want you both to know just how much you mean to me." As he spoke, he pushed as much emotion as he could through the bond he shared with the two. "Really, you two are my family. I wouldn't have made it this far without either of you." He stopped, his emotions getting the best of him. From the two fairies came an overwhelming amount of love.

They really had come far together. As he thought about it, he couldn't help but wonder at the path that had brought him to this point. His first memories as a dungeon core, his bumbling about as Erin tried to teach him the ways of the dungeon. His first encounter with Death, his defeat of the necromancer Viktor. Then Hel joined the family, and while initially she'd caused tension, now he couldn't imagine life without her. Without her, he wouldn't have survived. After all, she was the sole reason Marissa and the Cult of Chaos members within his dungeon had lost their protection, allowing the adventurers to defeat them.

"Everything will work out," Erin said softly. Her voice was cracking, her eyes full of tears. "The Goddess of Justice believes in you. And I believe in you." She paused as she started to shake slightly.

"You truly are the greatest dungeon I've ever encountered, Darling." Hel said. The Succubus offered him a soft, genuine smile. Something he rarely saw come from the chaotic creature. It was full of emotion; love rather than lust; admiration rather than hunger. It was a powerful, tender, vulnerable smile. "You really are special, Ryan."

With that Hel went quiet. The three of them sat in silence within his massive core chamber. His two fairies, their feelings for him, the faith everyone had put into him, it would all be for naught if they lost the war. And Ryan couldn't allow that. As they sat there silently, he felt empowered. He'd made the right choice in his preparations. Even if he'd been uncertain about it, he'd done all he could. Whatever happened next, he was as prepared as he ever would be.

Of course, while his fairies' words had helped calm him, there was another factor that helped give him a little more confidence. Because while as a dungeon he'd done everything he could with regards to mobs, traps, and tools only a dungeon could have at his disposal, he'd done one other thing. He'd freely helped boost certain Adventurers as high as he could in preparation for the war. If he was going to potentially die, then he was certainly going to break a few dungeon etiquette rules to stay alive.

This meant that, while he wasn't sure what the Church had at its disposal, he was well aware the Adventurers' Guild had suddenly seen an influx in Platinum-level members, all outfitted with ultra-rare gear. And then of course, there was Blake's group, all five of whom he'd boosted to Platinum 1. Thinking of them, he couldn't help but smile. Oh yes, he'd done everything he could to prepare.

Chapter Sixty-Seven

"I wish we could have met on better terms, Ryan." As promised, the leader of the Adventurers' Guild, a Diamond 2 Archmage named Alice, had arrived. He wasn't sure when she'd done so, as he still had no way of seeing inside of Boneville. However, the moment she'd stepped foot onto the land he'd made his own, he'd become instantly aware of her presence. How could he not? The woman had terrifying power at her command. What's more, she'd started to talk to him instantly, as if she could feel his attention on her.

"You could have visited sooner," Ryan responded shortly. Probably not the best response, but he was a bit nervous about everything going on. Alice was a dual mana user, like Blake. The difference in her power to that of Zacharias, the Diamond 2 Archmage and leader of the Mage's Guild, was staggering. At Diamond 2, humans had access to 24,000 points of mana, but she had 48,000 points at her disposal. Which put her rather close to God Tier in power.

What's more, Ryan could feel the power fluctuating off her from a combination of her equipment and the pure mana within her. He'd never felt something so powerful, save for when he'd been in the presence of Death. With her on the field, he couldn't help but feel emboldened.

"You're correct." She let out a laugh. While the situation was dire, she seemed completely relaxed and composed. On one side of her was the newly leveled-up Platinum 1 Blake. Because today's mission was simply a meeting with the Archbishop of the Church, in order to try and stop the war from starting. Blake had informed Ryan, Alice wanted to make sure she didn't come off as...too intimidating. Additionally, the Guildmaster had wanted to leave Marcus, who had advanced to Diamond 3, behind, in case anything happened.

Given the strength of Alice, Ryan couldn't fathom anything happening. In fact, he couldn't believe the Church would willingly stand against her, considering the amount of power she wielded. Her power dwarfed Blakes, even though the Platinum 1 Specter of Balance was nothing to laugh at with his 19,200 points of mana.

"Perhaps I should have visited, however, you'd be surprised how troublesome running a guild can be." Alice continued, speaking to Ryan even as she made her way at a rapid jog towards the far edge of his influence, where she was set to meet with the Archbishop. The meeting spot was an area just at the edge of his influence, so that the Archbishop could be outside Ryan's influence while Alice and Blake could safely stand within it. In this way, it was agreed neither side would act on the other during the parlay. Additionally, it gave Ryan the ability to listen to everything discussed, which worked fine for him. It was his survival at the heart of it all, after all.

"I am grateful, though." She was moving fast, faster than anyone should have been able to. Even though she had 48,000 points of mana, Ryan knew as a mage most of that mana went to her spells and abilities, not her physical aspects. Still, she was moving with ease, while Blake, whose body should have been stronger and faster than Alice's, was struggling to keep up. "For what you've done for the Guild. You really are a special dungeon."

Ryan scoffed, though he couldn't help but feel a small amount of warmth flow through him. Was Alice the protective mother sort? Hearing such praise from her brought back memories of his own mother from a time long ago. ...before he'd been turned into a dungeon core.

"Perhaps you'll explore my dungeon when all of this is done?" He was trying to change the subject quickly. He didn't need memories of his past floating up now. They were nearing the meeting place; Ryan needed to focus for all of this.

For a split-second Alice seemed to almost stumble. Seemed, being the main descriptor, because her foot blurred for a moment, instantly righting her and keeping her moving forward. In that moment, for a mere instant, the calm, collected smile on her face faded and her swirling, mysterious eyes, seemed to go sad.

"Perhaps." She spoke softly, but her eyes betrayed that statement. Whatever it was, Ryan had no doubt she had no intention of ever exploring his dungeon. And while a part of him couldn't help but wonder what had come over her, why she wouldn't, he'd be lying if he wasn't relieved. He had no doubt Alice could single-handedly walk all over his dungeon as he were now. Everything about her radiated that type of power.

The duo continued on in silence, leaving Ryan to poke about the area under his control as they made their way towards the meeting ground. Everything was in place. He had enough pylons, he was certain of that. His crystals were set, his traps in place, and his bone siege engines created. And, as he looked around, he confirmed there were no unwelcome visitors moving about on his lands.

At least, none that he could sense. Following the intrusions in the past, he'd learned he could set up a type of magical tripwire system around his influence. If anything physical touched his tripwires, even if they were magically hidden from his sight, he would know. Currently, the only ones (other than the animals of the forest) tripping his mana wires, were Alice and Blake.

"No matter what happens, Blake…" Alice's voice pulled his attention back to the pair. They slowed, perhaps five hundred yards away from the designated meeting place. In the distance, Ryan could make out a handful of figures moving towards Ryan's influence. The Archbishop of the Church of Justice, and the man's guards. The way Alice focused on them, the Guildmaster must've sensed something off about them, enough to put even her on edge. "Promise me you'll survive."

Blake looked at Alice, his face full of questions. Ryan couldn't help but share the adventurer's need for answers. He hadn't known Alice long, but he didn't need to, not to tell that those words were out of character for the Guildmaster. What was it about that advancing party that had shifted her attitude so quickly? Why was she worried about Blake?

The Specter of Balance looked at her, but she simply shook her head. It was clear she wasn't going to elaborate, and Ryan got the feeling Blake knew better than to press for questions. So instead, he simply nodded. "I promise."

Alice smiled and turned back towards the group approaching them. "Good." She started walking towards the edge of Ryan's influence. Towards the meeting area. As she did, the opposing party neared as well. They were outside of his influence, so Ryan couldn't gather any information on them.

The Church's party was comprised of six members. Five of them were heavily armed and armored in gleaming golden plate mail, emblazoned with the Scales of Justice. They surrounded the sixth, an older man wearing long golden robes, carrying a staff atop which the Scales of Justice sat perfectly balanced.

"Is that really your play?" Alice called out as she stopped on the edge of the influence. Her eyes flashed, swirling with a variety of color, as her voice echoed powerfully towards the opposing party. From the direction of her gaze, she seemed to be looking directly at the man in the middle, and more appropriately, her eyes were appraising the staff the Archbishop carried. The members of the Church had stopped perhaps fifty yards away from Ryan's influence, as had been agreed upon. "You won't even come to talk on an even basis?"

The man in the center of the group smiled towards Alice, bowing his head slightly. "It is the only choice I have, Alice. This matter is outside of my hands. The Adventurers' Guild was given a chance, yet you betrayed our trust. The Holy City was set ablaze. Hundreds of innocent civilians were killed by the hands of adventurers." The Archbishop, turned and pointed his hand towards Blake. "And that man committed the gravest sin of all. He relinquished our most holy weapon to a creature of darkness."

"You know Blake would never do such a thing," Alice called back. "You know in your heart Sean's son would never betray the Church, even if it turned its back on him."

The Archbishop shook his head. "Perhaps I was wrong in trusting Sean's bloodline. Even if he is descended from some of the greatest members of the Church of Justice to walk the land. That man there," his voice deepened, "has been corrupted by darkness."

Blake started to speak, but Alice raised a hand, stopping him.

"And what of me? You do not trust my word; you ignore the fact the Goddess did indeed give Blake the Sword of Justice. The signs are all there, yet you turn a blind eye to them. And now," she motioned towards the staff he carried, "this is your answer? You're going to bring *him* here, from his sacred duty, for this? Just listen to me. Call this war off, and let us be done with this whole thing."

"You should be happy I'm choosing this option. My word alone is enough to bring about the end of that dungeon. But against my better judgement, I will acknowledge the Goddess did present the Sword of Justice to the traitor beside you. In acknowledgement of that miracle, I deem this matter one for only the highest authority of the Church to decide upon. This matter is no longer in my hands. It can only be decided by Solomon."

Alice smiled darkly. "You mean you want to end this conflict with a display of force before the war begins. You're a coward. But let us see what the old man has to say." As she spoke, the Archbishop slammed his staff into the ground. Golden light erupted around him and the armor of his five guards burst into brilliant light. Runes appeared on their shields and Ryan watched from a distance as the scales that emblazoned their shields and armor all tipped to one side.

"I've already conferred with him. He has agreed to this meeting. He has agreed with me, that I am making the best decision for the Church. You should be honored, Alice. For the first time in over a century, Solomon shall leave his sacred duty." A golden portal appeared before the Archbishop and from it a figure appeared. "For the first time in over a century, the Hero of Justice once again walks this land."

Chapter Sixty-Eight

"Alice." Blake's voice was panicked as the man stepped through the portal. Against the gleaming light of the strange golden gateway, Ryan was having a hard time making out the figure. He was tall, that much was certain. He was covered, from head to toe, in shining armor. As he stepped from the portal, Blake's voice got more urgent. "Alice."

"I can tell," she whispered back to Blake. "Something is wrong."

"No—" Before Blake could say another word, the man spoke, his voice powerful.

"It has been a long time Alice." He removed his helm as he finished speaking, and Ryan couldn't help but gasp in surprise as the man's face was revealed. He looked ancient. More than that though, an entire half of his face was burned away, disfiguring him.

His one good eye glanced from Alice to Blake. Blake's hands were twitching, and the adventurer's glowing eyes were staring hard at the man. Ryan could tell Blake was on edge. The adventurer knew something. However, neither side was giving him an opening to speak.

"It seems the Gates of Chaos have been treating you well, Solomon," Alice said. "I'm quite surprised you actually left your sacred duty to come speak with me today. Consider me honored." She sounded completely unimpressed.

"Gates of Chaos?" Ryan asked Hel immediately. That was the first time he'd ever heard that term.

"The God of Chaos's dungeon can only be entered through the Gates of Chaos. That man," Hel hissed as she pointed towards him, "has been responsible for keeping them shut, ensuring no one can come, or go, from the God of Chaos's dungeon."

"He's been keeping a God at bay?" Suddenly, Ryan was a lot more worried for Alice, Blake, and himself. What was this man capable of?

"No," Hel whispered quickly. "The God of Chaos cannot leave his dungeon. That man has simply been fighting any demons that try to escape, or anyone foolish enough to try and make their way into the Dungeon of Chaos."

"How—" Ryan started, but Erin interrupted.

"Because he's Diamond 1." The angel was in pure awe. Of course the Celestial fairy knew about him. Even though, judging by how old the man was, Erin was too young to actually know much about him. Ryan figured she'd overheard information about him when she was still learning to be a dungeon fairy.

"I'm certain no one will attempt to breach the Gates during this short meeting," he said calmly. "And if they do," he shrugged, "I'll deal with them later." He held out a golden gauntlet, and a massive Celestial axe appeared. "After all, you should already know, being the only Diamond 1 human in existence has its perks." From his confidence, Ryan wondered if the man knew that Alice had dual affinities. If he didn't, then he was in for a big surprise.

"Now, the quicker we finish this fight, the quicker I can

return to my sacred duty." He smiled. Or at least, half his face twitched a smile towards Alice. The other half, the damaged part, was unmoving.

Alice smiled back, though her eyes were hard. "Must we? I really do wish we could settle this without bloodshed." She pointed behind Solomon, towards the Archbishop and his men. "Isn't your Church supposed to uphold the value of life? Isn't your Church supposed to uphold justice? What about this is just?"

Solomon took a few steps forward, past the guards who all stared awestruck at the man. Only the Archbishop was unphased by his presence. Rather, the old man seemed to be rejoicing in the presence of Solomon. If Ryan had to guess, the Archbishop hoped Solomon would defeat Alice here and now, to settle this whole matter.

"From my understanding, this is justice." He swung his golden axe once, and Ryan watched in horror as an entire swathe of his forest was blasted away with golden light. That single axe stroke had sent a blade of Celestial mana nearly five hundred yards into his forest, decimating all in its path. And that seemed like it had been a practice swing. "The dungeons of this world have been corrupted by Chaos. This *Bone Dungeon* has ruthlessly killed my dear Church members. And when given the chance to repent..." His eyes leveled on Blake. "The Adventurers' Guild betrayed the trust of the Church, launched a surprise attack, and forfeited the Sword of Justice to the forces of darkness." He swung his axe again, blasting away another swathe of forest, destroying one of Ryan's pylons. *I must construct additional Pylons,* Ryan muttered in his head as he instantly replaced that one.

"I find it hard to believe one as worldly as yourself wouldn't see that there's something more vile at work here," Alice called back. Around her, mana began to crackle. "You, above everyone else, should understand what is at stake. All of this stinks of the God of Chaos. How can you act as if you only see the world in black and white? You're but a shell of what you used to be, Solomon. You're not fit to lead the Church anymore."

"Alice." Blake's voice was an even sharper hiss now. As he spoke, the Specter of Balance reached out and grabbed Alice's wrist.

"Me, unfit?" The man laughed, and as he did, Ryan watched him hold out his other hand. A crackling black and red energy raced along his hand. The armor around his left side changed, twisting and contorting, into a demonic visage as a jagged spear of Chaos mana appeared. 'No, I've actually never been better. And trust me, I know exactly what is going on in the world." Without warning the spear of Chaos mana was thrown, impossibly fast, towards Blake and the stunned Alice. At the same time, Chaos mana erupted from Solomon, blasting back the Archbishop, and his guards.

Ethereal mana shrouded Blake and Alice just before the spear reached them, turning them ethereal. The Chaos mana weapon flew passed them, soaring another hundred feet to impact against a tree. Judging by the crater left in the weapon's wake, it was a good thing Blake had reacted as quickly as he had.

"You?" Alice chuckled. "Even you have been corrupted by Chaos?" Purple mana crackled around her as Blake's mana faded, returning them to the solid plane. "Oh, how the mighty have fallen, Solomon."

Solomon, seeming now part demon, part holy warrior, looked at Alice. This time the smile fully crossed his face, his burned side now that of a demon. "Corrupted? Don't make me laugh." He chuckled darkly. "I've always been this way." Another spear appeared in his clawed hand, but he held it lazily as he watched Alice.

"Would you like for me to tell you a little secret, before

you perish?" Even as he spoke a ball of purple light appeared over Alice. "Is that a no?" He asked, smiling coldly at her, his eyes shifting hungrily before her and Blake.

Alice didn't respond. Instead, a white-hot beam of pure plasma ripped from her, heading towards Solomon's chest. As it neared him the beam condensed until it was no larger than a hand, yet completely solid.

Solomon's smile widened, revealing the fangs on his demonic side, as the attack raced towards him. That crooked, twisted smile, was the last thing Ryan saw as the man's entire form was engulfed in the blast of plasma. Alice's attack hit him with impossible force. On impact, the entire world erupted into blinding purple light.

The light lingered for a few moments, and as it dissipated into a mushroom-shaped purple cloud, Ryan saw something that he couldn't believe. Solomon remained. That massive attack, that had enough force to obliterate everything around the man, hadn't even touched him. All the bodies of his followers had been incinerated, the ground now a massive crater, the land behind him practically turned to glass from the attack. And yet he was standing, calmly, on a piece of land, completely untouched by Alice's attack.

The only change to the man was to his armor. Or more appropriately, his entire form had been covered by armor made from a pure white mana. A type of mana Ryan had never seen before. This could only mean one thing. The man standing before Alice, the Diamond 1 Solomon, had dual affinities. And that meant...

Alice was completely outmatched.

Chapter Sixty-Nine

BLAKE

He couldn't believe what was happening. This...this shouldn't be happening. He'd been taught legends of an ancient hero of the Church, a man by the name of Solomon. He was said to have led the Church against the forces of darkness and Chaos, and singlehandedly taken down the leaders of those who opposed him. He'd put himself in the line of fire to protect the world, and in doing so, had suffered grave injuries. That man, the Diamond 1 Champion of the Church, Solomon, was said to have been so grievously wounded, he could no longer be seen in public.

And yet, not only was Solomon most definitely well enough to go out in public, he was powerful. Beyond powerful. From the moment he had arrived, Blake had been nearly blinded by the power flowing from the man. And it got worse.

The man's soul had revealed to Blake a dark truth. He had not only Celestial mana, but Chaos mana as well. The two swirled about differently though. Those who were corrupted by Chaos mana had the black and red mana dancing around their original mana, fighting to overcome it. This man's mana swirled in harmony with itself. That meant only one thing. This man wasn't corrupted; he had an affinity for both mana types.

This had been confirmed the moment he threw a Chaos spear towards Blake and Alice. Whatever was going on, Solomon was a Diamond 1 dual affinity, meaning Blake and Alice were no longer the strongest individuals on the battle-field. Alice had come to the same conclusion and reacted accordingly. She had sent a blast in his direction more powerful than any attack Blake had ever seen. From the amount of mana Alice pulsed into it, that blast had to have consumed most of her mana pool. She was trying to ensure the man died in that single attack.

Yet he remained completely unscathed, as the dust settled.

"How—" Alice started, only to be drowned out by Solomon's laughter.

"How?" He chuckled even more as his entire body began undergoing a demonic transformation. "How, you ask?" Black wings sprouted from his back, wings mimicking those of the demon Blake had seen in the Dungeon of Ashes. The wings of the demon who had accompanied Marissa, the leader of the Cult of Chaos. As if on cue, a dark portal appeared behind Solomon. From it, Marissa, the leader of the Cult of Chaos, emerged. Though, Blake could immediately tell she had grown much stronger. Previously a Platinum 1 Chaos user, she was now Diamond 3. Though, just like Monica, her mana was stronger than a normal Diamond 3 should've been. If he had to guess, it had to do with the fact that she no longer appeared human. In fact, Marissa seemed to be a demon now.

Blake didn't have a chance to think on this though, because Solomon began to speak once more. "Because, Alice, I am the oldest follower of the Gods of Justice and Chaos."

An axe and spear appeared in his hands. This time, the weapons were formed from pure white mana instead of Celestial or Chaos. "I am the only being alive capable of wielding Life mana." The weapons blazed with blinding light as power flowed off him. A new level of fear crept into Blake. This was not good. They needed to leave. Now.

"Why are you doing this?" Alice called back. She was looking at the man, trying to figure out how best to handle this situation. Blake wanted to run. Like right now. But the Guildmaster was still trying to figure out if this situation was salvageable.

"Because for my entire life, ever since the Goddess of Justice asked me to turn against the God of Chaos, I've been plotting and planning for the day to right that wrong." He took a step forward and the ground shook with the power of the step. "Asking a follower to turn against the God he worshipped, simply to aid in a fight that had been caused by the twin deities' personal squabbling. How pathetic."

He shook his head. "From that moment, I resolved myself. I would play along, until someday, I could right all the wrongs in the world." He smiled, his eyes completely sane, though what he was saying sounded mad. "And how might I do that? Why, by becoming a God, myself, of course. Because on that day, I realized the Goddess was no longer fit to lead the people." Another step and another tremor. "You've no idea how long I've worked. How much I've planned." He pulled back his arm, the spear leveled towards Alice's chest. "And with you out of my way, I can finally complete my life's work."

"Solomon—" Alice shook her head before her eyes hardened. Her wrists rotated, and Blake watched two bracelets appear on her wrists, one of sapphires, the other of rubies. All the gemstones on the bracelets were cracked and cloudy. Those were cursed objects. Still, the Guildmaster activated them, and Blake's very body began to burn from the amount of mana that crackled around her. She was going to fight. She fully intended to bring him down, here and now.

"You're the spitting image of what the Church preaches about. You've let yourself be corrupted by power." Blake's Celestial mana worked to heal his burning flesh as the ground around Alice began to disintegrate. Her entire form was bathed in crackling plasma, with stray bits arching out, setting fires and leaving craters all around the two of them. "Your mistake though, was assuming you had defeated me."

"It's the Exalted One," he said, the name sending chills down Blake's spine. "And you've already failed." Solomon's arm moved in a blur. The spear, which a second ago was in his hand, disappeared.

"No." Blake reacted as he spoke. He couldn't see what was happening, but every part of him told him they were in danger. His Ethereal mana rushed from him. He needed to protect Alice, he needed to keep them safe from the-

His mana stopped flowing. He completely released his Ethereal mana, as his mind registered what had happened. The mana had been unable to reach her. His mana had been stopped by Alice's own overwhelming power as she launched an attack on Solomon. However, as the sky opened up above the Exalted One, runes swirling underneath him—a spell that very well may have ended the man—the Plasma mana stopped.

The reason immediately obvious. A glowing white spear protruded from Alice's stomach. White Life mana pulsed from it, sending shocks through Alice as she dropped, stunned, to the ground. Her mouth opened for a moment, the Archmage trying to process what had just happened. Everything had happened in the blink of an eye. Somehow, someway... Solomon's attack had moved faster than either of their mana.

"Alice." Blake dropped to his knees, his hands glowing golden as he reached out to her. She turned her head towards him, her hands clutching at the weapon protruding from her. A small bit of blood was already flowing from her lips. Blake could tell the wound was fatal. "Alice," Blake tried to grab the spear, but the moment his hands touched it agonizing pain rushed through his body as enormous amounts of life mana assaulted him. He tried to fight through the pain, tried to pull the weapon from her, but instinctively his hands let go as his vision waivered and he hovered between consciousness.

"It's no use," the Exalted One taunted as Blake tried again. Alice had recovered enough from her shock that she'd reached around her neck, pulling out her Celestial feather. If they could remove the spear, that feather would be able to instantly heal her. There was still hope. "As long as I stand here, that spear will be impossible for you to remove, and—" The Exalted one smiled, holding up a hand He snapped his fingers and instantly Alice let out a gasp of pain. The spear let out a massive pulse of mana, forcing Blake away from her as pain rushed through his body. "As long as I'm still here, that spear can act as a conduit for my mana. Try again, and you'll feel more than just a shock, Blake."

Solomon, the Exalted One, let out a chilling laugh as he looked at the scene before him. Behind him, Marissa hovered, her eyes watching the whole scene with a look of pure enjoyment. The demon was loving this as much as Solomon.

"I'll kill you," Blake growled, rising slowly to his feet. He started to take a step forward, but before he could, a voice whispered behind him.

"No—" Alice's voice, soft, pained. "You promised." Blake looked back towards her, his heart demanding he rush at the Exalted One. All he needed to do was remove the Exalted One from this whole situation, and it would be over. If he could free Alice of that spear, he could save her. He wasn't going to let someone else die on his watch. He…he couldn't.

"I know all about you, Blake," the Exalted One called out to him. "I know of your powers; I know what skills your strange class has." He held out a hand. "I would be lying if I said you didn't intrigue me a little. While I can't spare your dear Guildmaster there, if you join me, I can promise that I won't kill your party members." He smiled wickedly. "I know you've lost far too many of your loved ones to my plans already."

Blake's anger rushed over him, and he took another step forward, his hand going to his sword. "Blake," Ryan's voice called to him this time, stopping him. "You're running out of time." Blake saw the reaper standing beside Alice, waiting patiently to collect her soul. *"You cannot save her."* A voice said in his mind, coming from the reaper. *"You cannot pay her toll."* Blake knew the reaper was right. While he could resurrect those who had died, he needed to be able to provide the same amount of mana as they could wield for payment. And at Platinum 1, Blake didn't have the mana needed to resurrect Alice when she died.

"I'm going to assume that's a no," the Exalted One called back. "Pity. I would have gifted you your father's old gear, had you joined me." The man shrugged and looked back towards Alice. "I know you can hear me, Dungeon," he shouted. "Know that tomorrow you will be destroyed." He began to leave. "While you won't join me, I've at least got a task for you. A simple one at that, Blake. Tell all those in your precious town that any who stand before the Church's forces in defense of the dungeon will die. Tell them that if they value their lives, they will stand down, and abandon the dungeon town—and their lives as adventurers. Tell them that, if they wish to continue walking this world, they would be wise not to stand against me or my forces."

He stepped away. "Or don't." He chuckled as he raised his fingers once more, his back turned to Blake now as he began to depart. "Those who remain tomorrow…their blood will be on your hands." And with that, he snapped his fingers once again. Alice screamed out in immense pain.

"Alice." Blake ran back to her. There was nothing he could do against the Exalted One. That much was certain. But maybe they could still save her. Maybe there was some way to do something for her?

"Blake." She lifted a trembling hand up towards him, tears streaming down her face as she placed a hand against his cheek. Her flesh was cold and on fire all at once, the life mana burning away her very essence. It seemed to him that her body was actually beginning to fade away into strange flecks of golden light.

"Alice. Please. How can I help you? How can I save you?" He needed something. Anything. There had to be a way.

"You…can't." She fought to smile up at him, her eyes sad. They no longer swirled with power. Instead, for the first time ever, they appeared a normal hazel. "I was careless, arrogant. I underestimated him. Too used to being the most powerful person in every battle I guess…" She sighed. "I should have been more careful. I should have done a better job." She coughed, and more of her body began to fade away.

"No. This isn't your fault." Blake grabbed hold of her hand, trying to pulse Celestial mana into her, trying to heal her. The moment his mana struck against that of the spear, it was pushed away. "It's my fault. I should have protected you."

"Just like your father, always wanting to keep people safe." She closed her eyes. "I suppose that is what my sister saw in him." She let out a pained sigh.

"I'm so proud of you, Blake." Alice's voice was weak. More and more of her body was fading away. "I know your parents would have been proud of the man you've become." Blake could feel the tears filling his eyes. How could she say these things? What did she know? He'd failed to protect everyone. He'd failed, time and time again, to keep the people he cared for safe. He was a nobody.

"Never give up on yourself, Blake." Her hand was light, the weight of her flesh gone from it. "I believe you and your friends, along with the Guild and Ryan, can win." Her breathing was even slower now, only audible because of his enhanced hearing. "Remember, you are never alone."

"Alice, please, no." He was crying. His chest hurt. This time, there wasn't rage to grab hold of. There wasn't Chaos mana lose himself to, to dull the pain of the moment. All he could do was watch as Alice faded away before him. "We can't do this without you."

A small, very Alice smile appeared on her face. "I'll always be with you, in your heart and memories." And with that, her form completely disappeared into white light. For a moment, the spear remained, before it too evaporated, leaving Blake alone and broken.

He turned his head upwards towards the robbed figure of the reaper, extending his hand towards the servant of Death. "Please," he begged, "just give me a little more time with her." He drew upon his mana, "I'll pay a toll, I'll do whatever you want. Just, please…a few more moments."

The reaper's dark hood turned downwards towards him and it extended the lantern. The lantern, which Blake realized, held nothing in it. In fact, there wasn't even a grey orb remaining where Alice had been. There was no soul, nor a soul fragment.

That man is playing a dangerous game. A gravelly voice said within Blake's mind. It wasn't the reaper that spoke now, but the God of Death himself. *A dangerous game, indeed.* And with that, the reaper faded away, leaving Blake alone, sobbing in the forest. He didn't have the strength in that moment to stand. In that moment, all he could do was cry. To let out all the emotion, everything he'd been holding in.

This wasn't just about Alice's death. This was everything. The Guildmaster's death had been the final straw. Everything within Blake burst open, overwhelming him. Pent-up sorrow rushed over him as his body felt cold. Even though Alice had told him he wasn't alone…he was.

"We will get through this, Blake," Ryan whispered softly through his pendant as Blake's body was wracked with sobbing. "We will avenge Alice," the dungeon core said.

"Remember," a female voice said quietly behind Blake. It was soft and gentle, yet filled with pain as well. The pain of someone who was hurting, just as Blake was. He felt a warmth spread over him, as a set of arms wrapped around him from behind, a figure engulfing him in an embrace, holding him as he grieved.

"We are always with you." Blake sat there, in Erin's embrace, crying his eyes out for how long, he didn't know. As Erin comforted him and held him as he battled his despair, he could feel resolve building up. The Exalted One was going to pay. But even more powerful than the thought of revenge was the promise he made to himself. Blake would not allow the Exalted One to hurt anyone else close to him.

He would do whatever it took to make sure the Exalted One was stopped tomorrow.

Chapter Seventy

"I can't believe she's dead." Marcus sat at his desk, completely white. The newly ascended Whisperer, which was the Diamond class for an Air affinity rogue, seemed to age instantly at the news. He'd met Blake—along with the rest of the Specter of Balance's party—at the edge of town. Alice's absence was immediately noticed. Still, Blake had refused to speak to them until they were within Marcus's chambers in the Guild Hall. The tale Blake had to tell needed to be told in secret. Plus, Blake was certain he wouldn't be able to compose himself as he told it.

"It happened in an instant," Blake said solemnly. Tears had filled his eyes once more as he looked down at his hands. The emotions were still as raw as before. Ryan and Erin had helped him regain his composure and strengthen his resolve, but he still hurt. "There was nothing I could do."

Marcus nodded and started to pull out his flask. His hand stopped as he lifted it towards his lips. He shook his head and set the flask back onto the desk. "Not now," he whispered faintly, before he turned to look over Blake's party. Marcus's eyes refocused and seemed to harden. The sorrow was there but it had been pushed aside in place of something else: Determination.

"No one is immortal," Marcus began. His voice cracked. "As adventurers, we know that better than most." He rose from the chair, scratching his chin. "I know this news is not welcome. The loss of Alice couldn't have come at a worse time. Even worse, not only have we lost our Guildmaster, but it turns out Solomon has been pulling the strings this whole time." He shook his head. "A dual affinity Diamond One. It's hard to imagine." He went silent for a long moment, his eyes searching.

"Still, Alice would not want us to waste this day of preparation. She would not want us to wallow in self-pity and sorrow. She would not want us to be afraid. Instead," he turned to look at Emily and Matt, "she would want us to take advantage of this situation to tip the scales of the battlefield in our favor." Marcus was looking the two siblings up and down, his eyes working up a plan.

"How?" Jack asked. The wolfkin looked ragged. Alice had been close with a lot of adventurers. She'd had a part in every one of Blake's party members' lives. Her loss hit them all hard. However, Alice's loss hit Karan the hardest. Because Alice was like a mother to her. And so Jack, who was linked with Karan, was having to juggle both his grief and hers at the same time. "How do we turn the loss of our Diamond Three leader into an advantage?"

"Alice's death means there are open Diamond Three slots for both Fire and Water mana users." The Whisperer scratched his chin some more. "And, because we are the only ones to know of her death," Marcus offered them a sad smile, "we can…skip ahead in line, so to speak, and have two capable, ready Platinum One members ascend to Diamond right away."

"Oh, that's going to piss some people off." Jack managed

a chuckle, "and it's totally unfair." The wolfkin grinned at the siblings. "But, given the circumstances, I can't be too upset that the two of you will reach Diamond before me."

Marcus nodded and waved a hand at Jack's comments. Even as he did, he walked towards the two siblings. Their faces showed they were still trying to register everything going on.

"If we survive tomorrow, I'll deal with the ire of the other Guilds." Marcus commented. Technically, there was a waiting list of Platinum 1 members who had earned the opportunity to ascend to Diamond if a spot in the three allotted human slots for that mana type opened up. And Blake had a feeling the Guild wasn't slotted for the next ascension, considering Marcus had just climbed to Diamond Tier. If he had to guess, the Mages' Guild or Assassins' Guild would technically be next. Neither of which they would want as enemies, but given the situation, this was a gamble they needed to take.

"Good point," Jack said. "After all, if we all die tomorrow, no one will know you broke with all the rules and traditions. I like your way of thinking."

Marcus offered the Duelist a grin and turned back to Emily and Matt. "Will you two do it?" Marcus looked at them, his eyes firm yet pleading. "Only you can make this choice." Climbing to Diamond wasn't like climbing to any other rank. Not only were there strict restrictions in place on who even got the chance to ascend to Diamond, but it was apparently an extremely...unique and painful process. Those who reached Diamond Tier were nearing the point of becoming gods. The amount of mana such an individual had access to—and the skills unlocked from their class—changed them in irreversible ways.

"We don't have much of a choice," Matt responded, looking at the party as he spoke. "And it's not like we have a reason to pass up this opportunity."

"Yes," Emily said firmly. Her eyes blazed with a certainty Blake had only seen a few times. She wanted this. She wanted the power to finally stand equal to her father, the Duke of Blood. This ascension would put her brother and her on equal terms with him, and ensure they never had to fear the man again.

"Perfect." Marcus scratched his beard again. "I'm going to need to get the proper materials to allow for the ascension." He looked at the party. "But that shouldn't be much of a problem now. After all," he let out a quick laugh, "I suppose I'm technically the man in charge of the Adventurers' Guild now." His voice was filled with bitter sorrow.

"What about the rest of us?" Blake asked as Marcus made his way back to his desk. The Whisperer was already rummaging through his desk, pulling a variety of weapons and items from different compartments. Blake had no idea Marcus kept so many knives in his desk.

"The rest of you need to make sure you're ready for tomorrow," Marcus said, grabbing what he needed before he motioned for Matt and Emily. "You two come with me."

Once they stood beside him, Marcus nodded to the rest of Blake's party. "We will overcome this. We will survive tomorrow." And with that, he and the siblings disappeared, leaving Karan, Jack, and Blake standing alone in the Guildhall.

"Right." Jack looked around for a moment, taking in the absence of Marcus and the two siblings. "I...really can't believe all this is happening." The Duelist let out a long sigh, shaking his head. Beside him, Karan simply stood. She was still processing everything. Not only had her mother figure died, but her entire religion, the hero of the Church itself, had turned out to be evil.

"Whatever happens, we will get through this." Blake said firmly. "We will avenge Alice, and make Solomon pay." Saying it aloud was a way for Blake to try and solidify those feelings within himself. Still, his mind was trying to figure out what else could be done to prepare. There had to be a way for him to help more, had to be a way for him to get stronger. He needed to be stronger.

"I'm sure we will." Jack grinned, though the wolfkin's eyes betrayed his feelings. The Duelist could try and put on a strong façade, but Karan's emotions were too much even for his normally carefree attitude. "I'm going to—" He paused as he looked from Blake to Karan. "We're going to go for a walk. To uh, clear our heads, and sort some things out." Jack, who suddenly seemed a bit jumpy, motioned towards Blake. "You going to be okay by yourself, buddy?"

Blake nodded towards his friend. The wolfkin paused as he passed Blake, Karan at his side. "You did everything you could," Jack whispered. "Make sure you don't beat yourself up over this, man. You've always done all you could."

And with that, Jack reopened the wounds Blake had tried to staunch. Though he was resolved to win tomorrow, he was still, very much so, beating himself up. If he'd been Diamond, would he have been able to protect her? Was there anything he would have been able to do, to keep her alive? Alice had been the strongest person in his life, and she had been killed by the Exalted One with ease. How many people would Solomon kill tomorrow?

"Thanks," Blake croaked, but the words fell on an empty room. Jack and Karan had already made their departure. Blake let out a sigh and looked around. He needed to compose himself. He needed to make sure he was calm and collected before he left. He could only imagine what questions he would be faced with outside. The news of Alice's death needed to be kept secret for now.

Blake let out a sigh and walked over to Marcus's desk and let himself slump down into the chair. On the desk sat

Marcus's flask. Difficult to believe the Whisperer had left it there. Blake grabbed it and took the top off, taking a long swig of the Fireball whiskey. This time, he was ready for the burn as the liquor rushed through him. As the blaze within faded, he went back to the time he'd spent with Alice. As he played through his memories of her, his hand reached into the item pouch he kept on him. From it, he pulled the gem she'd given him when she defeated the corrupted dungeon core. She'd promised to tell him what he could use it for when he reached Diamond. Now though...she was gone. And he still had no idea what he could do with the stone.

"You don't seem the kind to use something like that," said a familiar voice. Blake had been so engrossed in looking over the stone, he'd forgotten where he was. As he glanced up at the voice, his eyes widened. Blaine Dragnov, now Diamond 3, was standing in the doorway.

"You know what this is?" Blake asked hesitantly. Ryan had mentioned Blaine to him, and said the newly ascended blade dancer had promised to help in the fight against the Church. Blake didn't like the guy, especially considering his relationship with Matt and Emily. But if the man knew something about the stone, Blake figured it couldn't hurt to ask.

"What it is, isn't that interesting." He stepped closer to Blake, a dangerous smile on his face. "What it does, is much more intriguing...At Diamond Tier, it can unlock a single, God Tier trait, at random, for you permanently." He licked his lips. "But if you were to use it before then, you would instantly advance to Diamond Tier for your class, and gain Diamond 3 mana levels."

"Why didn't—"

"But it's also said you'll die shortly after." Those words fell on deaf ears, as Blake's mind raced. If what Blaine said was true...

"Thank you," Blake said, standing instantly as he pocketed the stone. His mind was made up, his resolve set.

Tomorrow, no matter what, no one else he cared about would die.

Chapter Seventy-One

Ryan prepared himself mentally for what he needed to do. It was hard. Preparing himself in that state. Trying to keep himself calm and collected. Every ounce of him was in full-on panic mode. What he had witnessed earlier in the day had truly shaken him. Beforehand, he'd been confident they would survive. With Alice joining the fray, he'd been certain everything would work out.

Then, the Exalted One had appeared. That man had slain Alice, a Diamond 2 dual affinity user, with ease. Even worse, his Life mana had killed Alice in a way that left behind neither body, nor soul. Meaning it completely negated Ryan's ability to bring back the dead, which really put a damper on his contingency plans.

Worse yet, he was certain the man had planned everything that had happened up until now. Viktor, the Cult of Chaos...even Paul. Ryan felt that man had been behind it all. Which also meant, he was likely extremely confident he would be able to handle the adventurers and Ryan the following day. That was the part that scared Ryan the most. It didn't seem to be a misplaced bravado or arrogance. It was a cold, calculated confidence, born from centuries of planning, preparation, and power. It was the confidence of a god.

"Are you certain about this?" Erin hovered anxiously beside him, her Angelic form keeping itself aloft with her large, feathered wings. While she no longer flitted about or showed her emotion as plainly as she once did, Alice's death had shaken her. She was more like the vulnerable, worried Celestial fairy he'd met so long ago.

"We don't have a choice," Ryan responded. This was the only way. Honestly, he'd wanted to do this anyways, but not on the cusp of the battle. Especially because, from what he could tell, his ascension was a shaky situation in general.

"Besides," he continued, "if this doesn't work, we will be killed tomorrow." That was the situation they were in. He could sit and wait for the battle tomorrow. And watch as the Exalted One carried out his plans to completion. Or he could attempt to ascend, using the experience he'd gained from Alice's death to climb to the next Tier, and utilize that new power to overcome the Exalted One. If, for some reason, the ascension went wrong, well...it just meant he would die a day sooner. But if it succeeded, they would have a fighting chance. Nothing ventured, nothing gained.

"He has a point, little one." Hel was doing her best to remain calm, but Ryan could feel a trickle of her emotions. She was worried. Not just for him, but for everyone. On top of that, the Chaos fairy was furious. This Exalted One was the one who'd cloned her. He was the one who'd been pulling the strings all this time, the one who, according to her, was twisting what the God of Chaos wanted. She wanted this man stopped, but she was also scared of him. All three of them were. "As we are now, that man, would destroy us all."

Erin furled her wings and lowered herself gently, putting a hand against Ryan's crystal core as she did. "Whatever happens, Ryan," she whispered, "know that I thank the

Goddess every day for sending me to you." She pushed her forehead against his core, trying to hide the tears in her eyes. Ryan was touched, and he did his best to keep his emotions at bay. He needed to steady himself and be prepared for whatever happened next. After all, he was certain in a few moments he would once again be in the presence of a God.

With that thought, he summoned his level triangle and experience triangle as he had so many times in the past. Then he began the ascension process.

First, he pushed the two objects together, willing the golden shapes to draw closer to each other, marveling as they lit up with a brilliant light. Though this wasn't the first time he'd done this, he still enjoyed the process. The two triangles combined, creating a six-sided star, and began to spin rapidly in front of him, Dark mana being pulled from him into it. Ryan had made sure he was full of mana this time, and all of his mobs had been absorbed before he began the process. He needed to be as prepared as possible for what came next.

The star spun faster and faster, pulling in more mana, creating a dark void before him. All the light in the room, even the glow of his crystal, was sucked into that dark void, until he could see nothing. He waited a long time, his focus pulled into that void, waiting for the light to appear. It had always appeared before. But the black just kept swirling and consuming.

He didn't know how long he stared into the void, waiting for some sign it was staring back. In that emptiness, all time faded away. All he knew was darkness, nothingness. As time stretched on, his mind, which had been razor-sharp, wandered for a moment. He didn't have time for this. When was the God of Death going to arrive? He waited for the light to appear, waited for a sign, yet nothing came. All there was, was Ryan and the darkness.

Enough of this. He raged as his patience fled. He did not

have time for silly games. Not now, not with death literally at his doorstep. He sent his mind, full force, into the darkness. If the light wouldn't appear, if the familiar rush of power wouldn't begin, then he would seek it out. He would search for the power he needed and grasp it with his own might. He was tired of playing the God's games anyways.

"I was wondering when you would come." Death's skeletal face appeared, his eyes glowing darker than even the void around them. The god's visage was that of an ever-shifting skeleton, switching from a small, childlike form, to an older, brittle one, going through the cycle of life and death time and again. As Ryan watched that ever-shifting shape, the God's consciousness brushed against his. Knowledge flooded into Ryan's mind faster than he could process it. "I was beginning to grow worried you wouldn't make it." The God of Death chuckled.

"You know what I'm up against," Ryan began. "You knew I would come for the power to face this foe."

The God nodded even as his form shifted to that of a child, beginning its aging process once more. It was... extremely difficult to watch. "I know a lot of things." The child skeleton folded his hands over each other as the bones slowly grew. "But I cannot predict the future. And I most certainly did not predict this."

"Regardless," he continued, "I do know that even if I were to allow you to ascend to Diamond—"

"If?" Ryan blurted out. He wasn't here for an if. He needed this ascension.

"If," The God nodded, "you likely won't be able to defeat Solomon on your own."

Ryan didn't like that. What did the God know? What type of game was he playing?

"What do you mean?" He needed answers. He needed power. And he needed both quickly.

"Solomon is not a normal human."

You don't say, Ryan thought sarcastically. The God's eyes narrowed, and Ryan silenced himself. He realized the God of Death may be able to hear his thoughts, given their current connection. And while Solomon seemed like a god…well, the God of Death was an actual one.

"Solomon is from a time long ago. A time before the Orb of Life was split. A man who wielded life mana in its purest form, and who gained the use of Celestial and Chaos mana when the Orb of Life split. He is one of the original followers of the Church of Life."

Ryan's mind raced. Just how old was this man? According to Hel, the split had happened long, long ago. It had been ancient information even according to her memories from centuries ago. There was so much that had gone on since then, including the war between the Church of Justice and the Church of Chaos. The war in which Death had sided with Chaos.

"He's old. But then again, when you reach that level of power, age is meaningless. And while Death will eventually come for all, it can be held off for a long, long time, given the right circumstances." The God of Death chuckled again.

"When the Orb of life Split, that man, a Silver member of the Church at the time, became a leader in the Church of Salvation. That is, the church of Chaos users. His ability to continue wielding Life mana gave him an extremely large advantage against other members of the Church, and he used his power to quickly gain influence and grow in strength. He was the one who headed the Church of Salvation when it finally clashed against the Church of Justice."

"But—" Ryan paused. "I thought he was keeping the dungeon of the God of Chaos sealed. I thought he was a hero of the Church."

Death, now a teenage skeleton, grinned. "Oh, he was. He

changed sides as the battle clashed, throwing away his allegiance to Chaos and condemning himself to keep the Dungeon of Chaos sealed for all eternity. In doing so, he "cleansed" himself. His Chaotic mana was drained from him by one of my reapers, leaving him scarred and removing—or so it was thought—his ability to use Chaos mana. Through it, Life mana should've been beyond his reach. That was his penance, to restore balance to the world."

"Apparently," Death growled, "Solomon and my crafty younger brother deceived not only my sister, but myself as well. Because it seems he has regained his use of Chaos mana and his ability to utilize Life mana as well."

"So, are you going to stop him?" Ryan had to ask. If this man was so powerful and such a threat, it would be helpful for Death to take care of him. It would definitely save a lot of lives...And it seemed Solomon wasn't on Death's good side.

"Sadly," Death began, "Per our arrangements following that catastrophic clash, my siblings and I are not allowed to directly interfere in the world of the mortals unless certain circumstances are met." Death's form shifted to that of an adult skeleton as his focus intensified on Ryan.

"While I would like to fix this situation myself, to restore balance to the world, as has always been my task from Father...my hands are currently tied."

"Then allow me to ascend and I'll handle it for you." Ryan hoped he sounded a lot more confident than he felt. It would be a tough fight.

"How about we make a deal?" Death chuckled again. "A single, simple deal, which may or may not even come to pass?"

Ryan's mind immediately screamed that this was a trap. But he wasn't in a position to bargain.

"I'm listening."

"I'll allow you to ascend. Hopefully, you and your allies

will be able to overcome Solomon. As long as he is stopped, I've no preference as to how it occurs. Though, he did take from me my dear Monica." Death cleared his throat for a moment, and then continued. "But—"

Here it is.

"If at some point you believe you are going to fail, activate this artifact." An image flashed into Ryan's mind of The Crown of Sorrows, the legendary artifact he'd received long ago. The artifact he'd put on his Avatar already...which made him suspicious. Had Death been guiding him to this path all along? "By utilizing the Crown of Sorrows, you, a Diamond Tier Dungeon, will be able to summon to the battlefield a God Tier entity. In other words, me."

Ryan stared at Death. Well, that would be simple. Why wouldn't he just—

"If I can just summon you...why not start off with that?" Ryan asked. Seriously, why hadn't Death started with that?

"Ah. The moment you use the Crown of Sorrows...your life becomes forfeit to me. After all, a being such as myself being summoned demands a high price. My form will inhabit your Avatar. I will need a vessel, and all of your powers will be at my disposal. And once I leave, once the battle is over, your core, your vessel, will be destroyed. At Diamond, you aren't capable of safely serving as a vessel to a God."

Ryan went cold. Death was giving him the ability to win the fight. The ability to summon a God to the battlefield. But doing so would mean the end of Ryan. As much as Ryan was prepared to sacrifice everything to save the things he loved... He didn't want to make that sacrifice, not if he could avoid it, not if there was any other way. Still, he needed to make this deal if he were going to ascend.

"Deal," Ryan replied firmly. As the God said, he may not need to summon him to the battlefield. A Diamond 3 dungeon was nothing to laugh at. Surely, between his own powers and the combined strength of all the adventurers, they could bring down Solomon. There had to be a way to win this that didn't end in Ryan's death. He would make it so.

"Good." Death's visage began to fade, leaving behind only a grinning skull, as more power than Ryan had ever imagined rushed into him. With it, the vast amount of knowledge regarding his new skills, mobs, and abilities that came with being a Diamond Tier dungeon. Images rushed through his mind of the things he could now create, gigantic 5,000-point mobs called Colossus', massive-sized mobs, and empowered armored humanoid mobs.

Additionally, he got a hint of the God Tier skills, of the power that would be his if he survived long enough to the point he could make constructs known as phantasmal mobs, humanoid skeletons that had Ethereal powers. In a sense, Death had given him yet another reason to survive.

And as the darkness around him began to fade, his mind slowing from the onslaught of knowledge, something else floated across his mind, for just an instant. Another image, a last, parting gift from the God of Death.

"Ryan?" Erin's voice pulled him away from the final image in his mind, excitement flowing through him. The God of Death had given him a brilliant idea. And with the power he now had at his disposal, he couldn't help but feel certain he would be victorious tomorrow.

"It worked," Ryan responded, his vision focusing on the core room, which suddenly seemed, much, much smaller. His core had grown with his ascension. Not only that, Erin and Hel had grown as well, their forms radiating power. Oh yes, a Diamond dungeon was nothing to scoff at.

"Obviously it worked, Darling," Hel drawled, her eyes showing a mixture of excitement and worry. "But it also took longer than anticipated."

Ryan's calm fled. "What do you mean?"

Hel motioned towards his core. He was the only one who could pull up the images of the world outside the core room. "By our best guess…it's nearly morning. The battle will begin soon."

Ryan scanned the forest, confirming the Adventurers were massing outside of Boneville, preparing themselves. In the distance, past his influence, he could make out what appeared to be the approaching enemy army.

Nothing like cutting it close.

"Well then," Ryan quickly began sorting through his mental catalog of bones. "There's no time to waste."

Chapter Seventy-Two

"This is just cruel." Ryan grumbled as he looked at the catalog. He was Diamond Tier. There were lots of new things he could make, including a lich, which he was totally going to. However, his dragon skeleton, which he'd been holding onto, was still out of his reach. Apparently, it counted as a special creature all on its own, and was not something he could summon until he was God Tier.

"What is, Darling?" Hel and Erin were both at his side, preparing themselves for the battle to come. They were watching carefully as the enemy forces approached. The army was slowly appearing on the horizon, a force like an encroaching wave of shimmering armor. It was massive. Ryan didn't have much time. They would need to begin attacking before long. The benefit of him having spread his influence so far was that he would be able to attack the enemy forces for a long time before they even got close to his dungeon.

"The God of Death gave me an image of my Avatar riding atop an undead dragon, and yet," he sighed, "dragons are a God Tier monster."

He grumbled as he started doing mental math regarding

what he should prepare for the approaching army. At Diamond 3, he had a whopping 19,200 mob points to play with. Which was a lot of firepower at his disposal. He hadn't really fathomed just how much power he would be able to wield when he ascended. Honestly, he felt a bit like a god right now…other than the whole not being able to summon a dragon bit. Freaking dungeon rules.

"Can you make a different dragon mob?" Erin asked innocently. Ryan focused his attention on her, trying his best not to comment. Before he could say anything, Hel began.

"She's got a point, Darling." Hel smiled, revealing fangs. "Couldn't you fuse some of your mobs together and create a dragon of your own?"

"Er…" Ryan couldn't believe he hadn't thought about that. After all the creative construction he'd done throughout his fourth floor, how had he not thought about that? Surely, the God of Death had only given him the image to spark his imagination. A way to encourage Ryan to reach for greater heights, to give him a better chance in the fight. The God of Death wasn't cruel enough to taunt him with something out of his reach, was he?

"We can certainly try," Ryan responded excitedly. He turned his focus to the massive, empty expanse that was the skeletal fight club battlefield below his fourth floor. If he were going to do this, he needed a lot of room. At the same time, he began populating the forest with the opening forces he would utilize for this battle. Ten-thousand mob points worth of Skeletal Archmages suddenly sprang into existence in the trees, looking out into the plains from which the enemy forces advanced. They'd been given a simple command: Begin attacking the moment the enemy forces came within range.

"So, what are you thinking of combining?" Erin asked, her voice filled with excitement. The enemy was at their doorstep. Masses of reapers were already appearing all throughout, preparing for the harvest. And yet, the thrill of creating an undead dragon mob was still one of overwhelming excitement. Ryan's excitement was momentarily replaced with concern, as a wave of exhaustion rolled over him.

"One second," he said, waiting for the feeling to pass. Sure, he had a massive amount of mana now. Sure, his ability to replenish his mana had exceeded how much he could spend when he was Platinum. But mass summoning that many sets of mobs, even at Diamond, had drained more than half of his mob points. And even with his massive expanse of influence, his mana return was slower than expected. Meaning he felt that sudden emptiness deeply. *Ouch.*

"Careful, Darling." Hel offered him a knowing smile. "Don't get overzealous, otherwise you might wear yourself out before the fun truly starts." She shot him a wink.

"Noted," he responded, taking another moment to track how much mana was flowing back into him. A big part of growing in strength was tracking how much of his mana reserves would be used for his stronger mobs, as well as how quickly his mana reserves would be refilled. The stronger he was, and the more mana he had at his disposal, the more he had to keep track of. Being a dungeon core was no easy task.

After a few more moments, the slight dizziness passed as his mana reserves adjusted. It was a good thing he hadn't tried to mass summon all 19,200 points worth of mobs. While he had that many mob points, creating the skeletons and animating them all instantaneously would have been a devastating draw on his powers. Which he would have more than just felt.

With his mind cleared and part of his focus turned towards the battlefield, waiting for the enemy to draw within range, he turned the rest of his attention back to the important matter at hand. Creating a dragon for his Avatar to ride atop into battle; truly, the concept was exciting and daunting at once. It couldn't be as simple as combining a clacker with one of the massive lizard-like skeletons he'd found deep underground...could it?

Knowing he didn't have the time to think on such things, he summoned one of the massive creatures. It was large, even larger than his elephant skeletons, close to forty-feet in length. Height-wise, it stood at roughly twenty-feet. The creature was bipedal, with a set of powerful legs, a really big head, and little arms. From his bone bank, he knew it was called a Tyrannosaurus Rex. The creature was a massive skeleton, and cost him 50 mob points to summon. A paltry amount now, but he knew it would quickly multiply. Especially with what he had planned.

Next, Ryan summoned one of his giant clackers. Compared to the Tyrannosaurus Rex, the giant clacker was... not so giant. Still, combining the two would hopefully create what he truly wanted. Without another moment to waste, he pumped Darkness mana into the two, urging them to combine.

The Dark mana enveloped both mobs, creating two enormous eggs, then drew them together. As many times as Ryan had combined mobs, he still loved this fusion process. It was epic, and the anticipation, the excitement, to see what would be created, was so—

The Darkness egg shattered, sending bone fragments flying all over the place. Turned out, those two mobs were not compatible. *Figures.*

Erin let out a moan of complaint. They really didn't have the time to fail multiple times with this process.

"Any other ideas?" Ryan didn't have many flying mobs. And it was going to be hard to figure out what could combine with a Tyrannosaurus Rex to create a dragon. Maybe he needed to change what he was fusing on the body side? Maybe the Tyrannosaurus Rex wasn't the correct type of skeleton to fuse to try to create his own dragon? Or perhaps that was too close to a proper dragon, and so dungeon magic was telling him no? It wasn't clear what allowed his fusions to succeed or led them to fail.

"Hmmm, Darling." Hel looked at him, eyes gleaming. She was onto something. "What did the dragon look like, the one the God of Death showed you?"

Ryan pulled the mental image up in his mind and pushed it towards his two fairies. It was a lot easier to show them than to try to explain. After all, how could you explain the image? A massive, reptilian creature with two clawed feet, giant wings, and a serpentine body—simple enough, but it didn't capture the

"Well, there's your mistake." Hel clicked her tongue, Something Ryan remembered his own mother doing when he was a young child and he'd made a mistake. It irritated him and made him homesick at once. "That's not a dragon."

"What do you mean, that's not a dragon?" He looked at the image again. "Other than the fact it doesn't have front legs, that looks pretty darned close to Cynder—"

"Close, but not quite." Hel patted him. "It's okay, Darling. This is what your fairies are for." She flashed him a smile. "That's a wyvern. A cousin of the dragon, weaker and smaller than those massive, mythical beasts. One of the Air dungeons I've memories from had one...And I've got some good news for you."

"What's that?" Ryan asked. How had he not known what a wyvern was? He'd absorbed so many books, yet none of them mentioned wyverns. Were they a creature from before the dungeon wars? They had to be. It amazed him how much knowledge was lost through time. What would he do without Hel...?

"I'm pretty sure if you created a boss version of your giant clacker and combined it with your Shydra, you could create your very own wyvern."

If Ryan could have, he would have kissed Hel right there. It was crazy, yet brilliant. And if there was one thing he had learned during his time as a dungeon core, it was that crazy was the way to go. The crazier things were, the less predictable, meaning they had a greater chance of succeeding.

Without a moment to spare, Ryan did as Hel suggested. He took his giant clacker, which only cost 15 mob points, and turned it into a boss mob. The moment its transformation was complete, turning it into a 75-point mob, he reabsorbed it to lock in its pattern, just in case this didn't work. A look out at the approaching army, told him he didn't have time to waste. The force had paused just outside his archmages' range. And though they'd drawn closer to his influence, meaning he could see even further past their front ranks, he couldn't see the end of the army...Ryan he didn't have time to waste. There was a lot of work to be done against that force.

He summoned his Shydra, which cost over ten times what the Clacker boss did, at 775 points. After, he summoned his clacker boss again and merged the two. He watched as his pride and joy, his Shydra, curled up tightly as the Darkness mana surrounded its powerful form and all nine of its heads before completely obscuring it. Then the two Darkness mana eggs began their fusion process, pulsing with Darkness mana as they came together.

Something in his mind told him more was needed. This combination would work but it needed a catalyst. It needed something to force it into being. The answer came immediately, as if granted to him by the increased knowledge that had unlocked when he reached Diamond. To create this mob, he needed to pump even more Darkness mana into it.

Because this creation would transcend his normal dungeon guidelines for boss mob creation and in doing so, it needed to meet the appropriate mob cost to justify its powers. For the first time ever, he pushed more mana into the dark egg than the combination had any right to cost.

Essentially this mob would be the equivalent of a rare massive skeletal beast turned boss mob. Meaning it needed the correct amount of mana to bring it into being. And luckily, even with his 10,000 mob points worth of archmages lined up for battle, Ryan still had enough mana to feed the demands of this creation. Without a moment of hesitation, he pushed more mana into the egg, demanding the creature come to live. This would work. This had to work.

More and more mana flowed through him, feeding into the egg as the two slowly merged to create one, massive, pulsating egg of Darkness mana. He kept track of the mana, marveling as it passed the 1,000 mark. The egg crackled dangerously, fighting to stay together. Even as it struggled, he pushed more mana into it.

It passed the 2,000 mark, and began to stabilize. At 3,000, it solidified more. Once it passed over 4,000—sitting at 4,080 —it stopped shaking entirely, and turned a solid black. The egg had grown in size, and Ryan could feel the strain of that much mana passing through him at once had cost him. This one creature cost him nearly one-fifth of his mob points. Yet, he had no doubt in his mind this would be worth it.

"It's alive." He cackled madly as the fusion completed. Maybe he was a bit lightheaded from all that mana expenditure.

Ryan watched expectantly as, ever so slowly, the egg began to hatch, cracks of light racing across it as the creature revealed itself. The first thing Ryan noticed, as the mana surrounding the mob splashed away, was that it had two massive, skeletal wings, covered in nearly completely solid

Darkness mana. The wings alone had a wingspan of a hundred-feet.

The next thing he noticed, was his creature had gained all the Shydra's many heads, plus an extra one, putting it now at an even ten. All of the heads had shortened as the body became more proportionate to match the wings, and it had developed two massive, taloned back feet. It wasn't perfect and had nine more heads than what the God of Death had shown him, but there was no doubt this was a creature his Avatar could ride into battle.

Because of everything that was happening and what had led to the creation of this massive creature, Ryan had part of a name in mind. A quick mental flip through all his knowledge of dragons from ancient lore and stories he'd heard as a human, gave him the other part of the name as well. He didn't even consult his fairies as he applied the name. The creature, his wyvern, would be known as **Trogdor—Death's Visage**. After all, this creature would be death to every enemy who laid eyes on it. As the name was applied, Ryan immediately noticed one last thing about his mob. Something that explained why this creature cost him so much to create.

"You've done it," Hel whispered. "I... I never expected I'd ever see one."

"That's because Ryan is special," Erin said breathlessly, pride evident on her voice.

The Shydra's name had been a blue, indicating it was a rare boss mob. Death's Visage was a different color. Somehow, someway, Trogdor - Death's Visage, his 4,080-point Boss mob, was Ultra-Rare. As if it were aware of the attention on it, all ten heads lifted to the sky and let out a mighty roar. The sound shook the entire chamber, and tendrils of Dark mana floated all around. Riding Trogdor, his Avatar would turn the tide of the battle. His enemies would be like peasants before Trogdor's might. He was certain of it.

And it was just in the nick of time, because as the roar died down, light from the battlefield drew his attention. The army, which stretched perhaps a mile in width, was erecting massive, golden tubes. These cylinders, looking like strange metallic cannons, pointed towards Ryan's forest. From the looks of it, the floating, gleaming weapons were hovering above dozens upon dozens of Church members.

As he watched, one of the tubes began to glow as mana was fueled into it. Golden light condensed at the front of the tube, and a moment later a massive beam of Celestial energy erupted from it. The explosion ripped into his forest, and destroyed a tenth of his archmages and a handful of pylons with a single shot. Ryan cursed and instantly began rebuilding his pylons as more of the tubes began to glow, preparing to fire.

"Looks like the battle has started," Ryan said grimly, his excitement over summoning Trogdor suddenly dampened. He now had bigger issues. He needed to deal with the enemy's siege weapons. And he had no doubt these weapons were just one of many the Exalted One had prepared for this day. Looking over the army, he could see various objects further back within the army. Objects he had no knowledge or recollection of—but they looked powerful. Objects he was certain would cause him no small amount of headache in this fight. Ryan had a feeling this battle was going to be a long one.

Chapter Seventy-Three

"That's not even fair," Ryan groaned, watching another batch of his mobs get disintegrated and disappear into nothingness. He'd started this battle with 10,000 mob points worth of skeletal archmages. That made for forty skeletal archmages all positioned in the cover of the woods, just waiting to unleash Platinum Tier magical attacks on the Church's forces. Considering the only Diamond individual in the Church was Solomon, his mobs would have had devastating effects on some of the normal Church members.

Unfortunately, the Church had come prepared for dungeon warfare. And they were methodical in their approach—blasting any and all signs of his mobs they could see with long-range magical weapons. According to Hel, those cannons had been made by the Church, long ago, specifically for hunting down dungeons. Because of course the Church would have specialized long range weaponry to deploy against a dungeon. Why wouldn't they? *Freaking Church of Justice...*

"I warned you," Hel said simply. "I've told you, Darling, the Church was always a threat. That organization's hands are stained with the deaths of more dungeon cores and fairies than any other group." She shook her head. "They know what they're doing." She'd told him they had weapons that could attack him from range, but this far away?

Ryan groaned and looked over the battlefield. The adventurers were on the move, albeit slowly. They'd amassed outside of Boneville and had since dispersed in small groups to move into a variety of positions. The adventurers had already decided not to fight the Church head-on. To do so would mean a slaughter. Instead, the adventures were going to do as they had always done, fight in groups to take on their foes, forming small units and teams to fight alongside each other. Their teamwork and guerilla style tactics would likely serve them well against the Church. After all, while the Church may have a history of destroying dungeons, Ryan and the adventurers figured many of those making up the Church's army didn't have a history of fighting humans and other living creatures.

"It's still annoying," Ryan grumbled.

"We knew this wouldn't be easy," Erin responded. "The Church is one of the world's most powerful organizations, and the Goddess has gifted her followers with many tools to carry out the Church's missions through the years. Many were commissioned and used by Solomon himself to defend the Gates of...oh..." Erin trailed off. They all knew now that the Goddess, whether knowingly or not, had been aiding the enemy. Solomon had been using the Church and the Goddess, all for his plans of reaching this point. Reaching this day. The day he would try and become a god. If he wasn't stopped now, there would be no one around with enough power to stop him.

"I'm glad the Goddess was so generous," Ryan responded dryly. He could only imagine what other tools the Church had at its disposal. How many gifts had the Goddess granted her followers, and how many had been created at their hands? Still, if they were going to use siege weapons against Ryan, he figured he could return the favor. The Church wasn't the only side capable of using such tactics.

"So…" Ryan surveyed his forces. He only had a handful of archmages still up. Seriously, that had been such a waste. Without a second thought he reabsorbed those remaining mobs. No reason providing extra target practice for the Church. Then he pumped a decent chunk of mana into the outer perimeter of his influence, building up a stone wall about ten feet in height and width. He doubted it would last long against the Church's cannons, but it would buy him some time to prepare countermeasures. Ryan had a vast array of knowledge and plans all his own, and the ability to make them at will. If this were to be a war of attrition, Ryan would win.

Yet unease flowed through him as he worked to make his own siege engines. The Church had firepower. They were using it to blast large swathes of his influence and mobs and forest, but he was certain that wasn't all they had. If it were, he found it hard to believe they would have slain as many dungeons as everyone claims they had. No, this was but a teaser of what was to come, and when it did, every moment would count.

He needed to strike back and cause damage to their side before they got serious. He needed to hurt their forces at least to some degree. From what he could tell, the Church outnumbered the adventurers at least ten to one, but he had a feeling it was a much higher ratio, considering he still couldn't make out the end of their forces.

Ryan started by erecting a simple line of bone trebuchets, then summoned a group of skeletal minions to man the massive siege weapons. He cursed as a golden beam of light blasted through his wall and decimated one of his engines. It was a lucky shot but frustrating, nonetheless. In response, Ryan split his focus, patching up his crumbling bone wall and reinforcing it with Darkness mana, strengthening it against attacks. The downside of all of this was, the Church's Celestial mana weapons were going to be twice as effective against his mobs and defenses, just as his attacks would be against them, all because the two mana types were polar opposites.

With his trebuchets (minus one) manned and ready, he summoned his ammunition. While he'd used such siege weapons before to attack demon forces in his bone zone by slinging massive bone balls and other things, this time he had a new tool to utilize. Sure, launching exploding masses of Darkness mana and bones to erupt in shrapnel was effective and all, but Ryan could do that and more, with his latest and greatest projectile. He'd not been idle during this past month.

Ryan summoned his new weapons, large grotesque balls of rotted flesh, onto each of the trebuchets. The masses of flesh, appearing near the point of rupture, were a new trap Ryan had devised. Not only was the stench, according to his fairies, completely unbearable. On top of that, he'd filled these rotting flesh balls with his psychedelic mushrooms. These mushrooms, in a state such as this, could create fume clouds that were as potent as if they were ingested or injected. It was brilliant. And of course, for good measure, there was still plenty of bone shrapnel within. It would not only cause additional damage, but could help inject the toxins within anyone in the blast radius. A win-win situation for Ryan.

"Fire the puffballs." His fairies winced as he gave his mobs the command. Of course, his mobs didn't need to hear him say it, since he mentally commanded them. Still, it was fun to say, and Ryan had named them after the very type of mushroom he'd gotten part of the idea for this bioweapon from. Who would have thought absorbing a book on fungi would be so helpful? The puffball was a mushroom that could explode to forcibly expel its spores into the wind in order to spread itself even further across the land. Ryan had simply modified that concept for maximum effectiveness

He watched with satisfaction as the weapons massive arms swung, flinging the puffballs far into the air. Ryan had removed the trees in this section to ensure his trebuchets would have no issue launching their munitions... A lesson learned from his previous demon army experiences...siege weapons in a forest were rather problematic.

The masses of rotting flesh flew true, clearing Ryan's wall even as another blast of Celestial mana ripped into it, shaking the earth as fragments flew everywhere. It didn't matter to Ryan. He didn't care about that wall. What he cared about was hitting the Church's forces and taking down as many of them as he could. With the puffballs and the psychedelic properties of those spores, he would spread a special type of chaos among their forces. Had he been in a different situation, he may have considered that quite ironic.

As the puffballs neared the enemy forces, two things happened. First, he watched as small lines of Celestial mana shot from smaller, raised objects that looked almost like boxes. From what he could see, teams of Church members were manning those boxes, filling them with Celestial mana, which was launched high into the sky to intercept the puff-balls. The Celestial mana tore into every one of them, causing them to burst mid-air. As they exploded—spreading their noxious fumes, sending rotten flesh, bone shards, and mushroom pieces about—a golden light shimmered around the forces to reveal, for a moment, a barrier of massive proportions.

As he took a longer look at the army, he could see, spaced periodically through the front lines, individuals holding massive glowing shields, three times the size of a normal one. These shields glowed brilliantly, and it was clear they powered the barrier. Judging by how many of them the Church had, that particular object must've been another of the gifts from the Goddess to her followers from a long time ago. Perhaps even the war versus the forces of Chaos.

"It would be so much easier if they came closer," Ryan grumbled, arming another set of puffballs. Summoning them wasn't a problem. He was certain he could launch enough that eventually they would run out of mana. The problem was, he couldn't help but feel he was running out of time. He needed to do something to them before whatever happened, happened. Because he felt when the Church made their next move, he wasn't going to like it.

And, as he launched the next set of puffballs, summoning even more trebuchets as he did, preparing to send an endless onslaught of attacks towards the enemy, something shifted on their side. A large portion of the army shifted like a sea parting, to allow a massive figure clad in shining armor to walk causally forward.

Ryan instantly knew who this man was. Solomon was taking to the battlefield, walking calmly past his forces and out of the protective barrier of his army, straight towards Ryan. With each step the Exalted One took, Ryan's anxiety rose. This wasn't going to be good.

"I'm going to need more puffballs."

Chapter Seventy-Four

The closer the Exalted One got to Ryan, the more frustrated Ryan became. Mainly because the Diamond 1 Life mana user was impervious to everything Ryan was throwing at him. And Ryan had been throwing a lot at him. Well, Ryan had been throwing a lot at both the army, and Solomon… but mainly Solomon. However, every attack, every puffball, every magical spell from the archmages he'd summoned, simply faded away when they got within five-feet of him.

"Honestly, Dungeon." the Exalted One was grinning as he stopped just outside of Ryan's direct influence. The spot The Exalted One had chosen to approach was just shy of where the man had slain Alice the day prior. "Did you truly think I would approach you without proper precautions?"

The man chuckled and reached to his chest, pulling from it a pendant. The pendant appeared to be a blazing sun made out of opal, the gemstone of Celestial mana. Within the center of the sun another gemstone flashed, one Ryan had seen once before, a subjugation crystal. Granted, the one in the pendant was much smaller than the one that had been placed in his dungeon, but it was still alarming. The blasted artifact that he'd seen in his dungeon could create a sphere sixty-feet in radius that would negate anything that didn't utilize the same mana as the one who had activated it.

"A subjugation crystal?" Ryan said aloud. He'd summoned an ominous crystal skull before Solomon, even as he continued to launch attacks at the man. A dungeon could always hope.

"Of a sort." The Exalted One laughed, putting the pendant away. "Subjugation crystals were created by mortal hands to quell the powers of dungeons. These objects allowed for the destruction of dungeons, which were once thought to wield the power of demigods. Doing so enabled those who conquered dungeons to claim the very core of the dungeon, a material that could be utilized to unlock amazing powers." His eyes flashed. "What I wear is something much more potent. A legendary artifact, created by the Goddess of Justice to aid me in my quest against the God of Chaos." He chuckled darkly. "A pendant which, while active, will negate any attack—physical or magical—that comes at me from a source other than Celestial."

Solomon looked around himself, smiling cruelly as he did. "And I can assure you, there isn't a Celestial being capable of taking me on. After all, not only am I Diamond One, but I have dual affinities." He gave another chuckle. "So even if there had been another Diamond Celestial mana user around, they couldn't best me."

He looked into Ryan's crystal skull. "I suppose the Archbishop did me a favor by creating that hairbrained rule of his. Had Sean ascended to Diamond…he likely would have evaded my clutches, and perhaps become a champion worthy of saving the humans." He shrugged. "He was the Goddess's favorite, after all…which made twisting him into a demon all the more enjoyable." The Exalted One's eyes flashed with amusement.

"You're not going to win this," Ryan replied grimly. He launched another massive set of attacks aga nst Solomon. If the man had to keep funneling mana into his amulet to make it work, then, in theory, Ryan could wear him down by attacking en masse. The man may be Diamond 1, but he had a limit to his mana just like Ryan did.

"I'm not going to win? In that you're wrong dungeon. I've spent far too much time planning for this moment to allow myself to lose." He chuckled and rose a hand in the air. A massive golden set of scales appeared in the sky above him, level on both sides. "No hard feelings, but your existence doesn't fit within my plans." His hand came down, and the scales tipped to one side.

Celestial mana erupted forth from the man, blasting away all of Ryan's trebuchets, his wall, and his pylons, for a good quarter mile swathe. More startling though, was that as the golden light pulsed into his forest, incinerating everything of his it touched, flashes of light erupted from the army behind him. Crystals roughly the size of a human flew from the army, rushing towards Ryan's forest. A dozen of them smashed into the ground in the now cleared swathe of land.

The Exalted One grinned and stepped forward. With that single step, he caused the very earth to crack and golden mana rushed from him to every one of the crystals. The moment the golden mana touched them, they came to life, floating into the air to hover roughly six feet off the ground, light bursting from them in all directions. The light extended into a two-hundred-foot radius, instantly destroying Ryan's hold on the land as the massive subjugation crystals—no, orbs, blocked out his Darkness mana.

"You see, Dungeon." Solomon walked calmly into the protective area, calling out loudly, as Ryan's influence had now been pushed back, in an instant, a quarter mile. "While the side of Chaos has always been strong, the

Goddess of Justice's followers have always been quick to… judge. Which made it so easy to mold them into the military power they are today." He chuckled. "Ironic, no?" Ryan could feel panic welling within him. He needed to destroy those spheres. "The world is going to be thrown into chaos all thanks to the Church of Justice." Solomon continued laughing.

"I hate him," Erin said. In the distance, the Church's forces marched towards their newfound area of influence. It was slow and methodical, but if this were their tactic, Ryan had no doubt they would be able to overwhelm him sooner or later. After all, his massive powers were useless if things he created with Darkness mana couldn't enter those spheres.

Then again… when in doubt, stalactite out.

Ryan's newly summoned siege engines launched large opals towards the subjugation spheres. Ryan had brainstormed with his fairies how to deal with such weapons if they were to appear. From what Hel knew of the tools, long as they were active, they would prevent anyone or anything not of the associated alignment from entering. They would also keep out attacks that weren't associated with the appropriate mana as well. As such, his normal physical attacks would be a no-go, considering they were made with Darkness mana.

However, because opals were the gemstones of Celestial mana…they theorized opals might be able to penetrate the barrier. Technically, it wasn't aligned with Darkness mana. The rules of magic got a bit fuzzy at times, so they figured, at the very least, it was worth a try.

Their hypothesis paid off. As the massive opals flew towards the subjugation zone, the stones glowed golden and passed through the barriers as if they weren't even there.

"Huzzah," Ryan cheered, watching them fly with deadly accuracy towards the orbs. Before they could reach though, a golden light shimmered in front of each orb as Solomon enacted protective barriers against the attack.

"Nice try, Dungeon." He chuckled as Ryan's attack failed. "But honestly, did you believe you were the first dungeon to think of something like that?" He turned back, checking on the status of his forces. Ryan checked as well. He could finally see the end to their forces, but that didn't give him any hope. This army was massive, more than ten-thousand people strong.

"Who do you think it was that cloned Hel? I know exactly what resources you have available, and I know what knowledge you could have gained from that failed tool of mine. Fight as hard as you'd like, but you won't be able to stop me. This method of fighting was specifically designed to ensure it drained a dungeon of its mana faster than any army could. And that wasn't even accounting for one such as myself."

An intense wave of anger washed over Ryan, and he couldn't tell if it originated from himself, Erin, or Hel. All three of them were currently flush with anger at Solomon's words. This man was toying with them, flaunting his power. It was bad enough he was here. But the level of confidence he paraded, the way he treated Ryan as if he were a bug that needed squashing, was infuriating. It was too much. This man needed to be stopped.

"How about this, then," Ryan said smugly. He summoned even more trebuchets, launching larger opals at the spheres of subjugation. As he did, he prepared a new weapon, one he'd discussed with his fairies. Something he could only risk using here and now, before the Adventurers got too close to the battlefield.

Not even Ryan knew how much destruction this weapon would cause. Frankly, right now, it didn't matter. He wanted to hurt Solomon...he needed to hurt Solomon and take down those subjugation spheres. If he wanted to survive this battle, he had to use this attack now. And Ryan was certain Solomon wouldn't be expecting it because it was something he knew Hel had never seen before either.

Without warning Ryan pulsed mana into the massive teleportation crystal he'd erected, two-hundred-feet underneath Solomon, just at the cusp of the subjugation orbs. The teleportation crystal was larger than the one he'd gotten from Archmage Zacharias, and larger still than the one in Boneville. He'd found the giant crystal deep within the ground, and it was the largest one he had in his collection. A special crystal he'd prepared for an instance like this. One he had been planning to use as a last-ditch effort, because he had no idea how much damage it would cause.

Given the situation, this seemed to be the appropriate response. If he didn't remove those orbs, his mana regeneration would continue to dwindle. If he didn't remove those orbs, Solomon would win.

The runes glowed to life along the massive crystal, causing it to pulse with power. Because of how large it was, it took a sizeable chunk of mana for Ryan to activate. Of course, he had mentally checked to ensure it wouldn't leave him exhausted. As the crystal hummed to life, he prepared his trebuchets and readied himself, knowing he would need to launch an all-out assault the moment he saw any opening.

Then, everything froze as the last of the glowing runes sprang to life, the flawed one. It lit up with a bright flash, and for a moment, Ryan's entire focus was drawn towards that light. Then, it happened. The massive crystal erupted, spreading out the mana pushed into it, amplified by the error in the runes. The catastrophic explosion ripped apart the earth, shaking the ground for miles.

The subjugation orbs flared, the power of the blast pushing against their own. The magic barrier of the subjugation orbs reflected the explosive force outwards, blasting in all directions along the orbs' perimeter. As an added bonus to the destruction, the explosion was diverted toward the lead columns of the advancing army, causing some damage. Though, considering they were Celestial users, he doubted any of the injures would be permanent.

"Truly, that was—" Was all Solomon said, his voice loud and confident even against the roar of the explosion. Just as the destructive power of the rupturing teleportation crystal subsided, the second, more terrifying aspect of the explosion occurred. For a split second, everything in the radius of the explosion was affected by the vast, sucking void of an anti-mana field as the crystal's blowback occurred. All the subjugation orbs deactivated, falling to the ground and cracking from the sudden loss of power. For a split second, from Ryan's safe distance far outside of that mana-less zone, he saw a frown cross the Exalted One's face. This attack was something he hadn't been expecting.

"—Impressive." Solomon finished, even as he turned to face the barrage Ryan had launched at him. The mana void, as he called it, only lasted for a second. It created a mana-less zone, where magical items couldn't work, and mana couldn't be regained. Of course, it didn't have any effect on the internal mana of a living being…unfortunately. Otherwise, this fight would have been over. As it was, this gave him a window of opportunity to destroy the subjugation orbs while they were unpowered. It also allowed him to get in some attacks on the indominable man standing before him. A moment to wipe that smug smile off his face. Ryan wasn't going to miss out on that.

Solomon's arms spread wide as he closed his eyes, flying rocks, opals, puffballs, and various magical attacks and bone attacks all flying in his direction. Just before they all connected, Ryan saw the man smile, and it sent chills through his core.

Chapter Seventy-Five

BLAKE

"Change of plans," Ryan's voice came through Blake's pendant moments after the world finished shaking. Whatever was going on, it was intense. "I need help. Right now."

Blake looked at the group he was with. The original plan had been for the adventurers to split up into the woods and attack the army once they got within a mile of Boneville. Till then, Ryan was supposed to be handling everything. After all, Ryan was a Diamond 3 dungeon now, and he had claimed he would be able to greatly weaken the enemy forces before they got too close.

"What's the problem?" The battle hadn't been going on that long. Ryan shouldn't need their help already. There was no way he'd done enough damage yet. And Blake could only wonder what the Exalted One had up his sleeves.

"The problem," Ryan's voice was strained, "is that I can barely stop this blasted monster from moving. I can't focus on him and the army at the same time." Another explosion rocked the ground as Ryan spoke, though it was much weaker than the first one. "I'll hold him off. But you guys need to start acting. We need his army gone if we are going to defeat him."

Blake nodded towards Marcus, who had been sitting next to him. The Diamond 3 Whisperer pulled a pendant from around his neck and began issuing orders. With Alice's demise, Marcus was the most senior member of the Adventurers' Guild and had taken charge of the situation. Everyone who'd remained behind to fight against the Exalted One had linked their pendants with his in order to ensure they could receive messages in a timely manner. The pendants, as always, proved an amazing tool for ensuring cohesion even in a danger-filled, chaotic environment.

"We are going to begin attacking the army. Be smart, be swift, and make sure you all come back alive," Marcus said, his gruff voice issuing the orders quickly, his eyes firm. "And whatever you do, do not engage with the Exalted One."

The night prior, when Marcus had returned via Ryan's secret portal crystal with the newly promoted Emily and Matt in tow, he'd gathered all the adventurers within Boneville together. There, he and Blake had told of all that had happened that day. They'd told of Alice's passing, they'd told of Solomon's true visage. And they'd told of his chilling words. To their dismay, a quarter of those in the city had decided to flee. They weren't going to openly turn against the Adventurers' Guild, but they'd decided their lives were too important to risk against a power as terrible as Solomon's. The death of Alice had been a deep blow to morale.

"I was growing tired of waiting," an arrogant voice said. "Come, siblings." As the speaker, Blaine, continued, he drew both his swords. He glanced calmly from his entourage, towards Matt and Emily, "Shall we show the world the true power of the Dragnov family?"

Matt's eyes went hard at Blaine's words. Blake couldn't blame him. Even if Blaine hadn't been the one to send the

Assassins' Guild after Matt, he had been the one to report Matt and Emily's continued existence to their father, The Duke of Blood. Meaning he was at least partially to blame for Matt's assassination. Even if he was here to help, it was on neutral terms, at best.

"We are not your siblings," Matt responded darkly. Now Diamond 3, Matt held a new title. The pinnacle of his class, the Water affinity variant for Diamond arcane archers: The Glacial Archer. "You and that man have made it clear. And we do not wish to carry that name." Matt's tone matched the icy nature of his skills.

"Besides," Emily's eyes seemed to dance with fire as she spoke—a stark contrast to her frosty brother. She, like Blaine, had a Fire affinity. "We no longer have anything to fear from you. After all," she grinned at Cynder, the baby dragon sitting peacefully atop her shoulder, "Matt and I can easily match you in strength."

Blake half expected their brother to lash out at that instant. He may have offered Blake a bit of advice the day before, but he still had the air of bloodlust around him that said he favored fighting above all. His calling was purely for war, for death. Instead, the Diamond 3 Blade Dancer, known now as a Dragon Dancer, simply smiled at them.

Blake couldn't help but wonder who of the three was the strongest now, since they were all Diamond 3. The other thought crossing his mind, if just for a second, was the fact that the Dragnov family now had a total of four Diamond-level individuals. Considering humans were only allotted a total of 21 Diamond slots...the Dragnov family had nearly a fifth of all the Diamond slots allowed for their race. And if you compared them to the actual amount of human Diamonds in existence, the family was even more powerful.

"Interesting." Blaine's eyes flashed with something. Was it excitement? Approval? Blake hadn't seen much of Blaine, but it seemed the man was no longer the cold-hearted killer he'd been when Blake had first met him. Perhaps he was a little more human? Maybe, just maybe, Blaine was here because he wanted to help and not only because he owed Ryan for allowing him to complete the dive that gave him the experience needed to climb to Diamond. Then again, judging by the swirling tempest of soul fragments that circled around the man from all those he'd killed, maybe he was just here so he could kill Church members. "How about a friendly family wager then?" Blaine asked.

"We're not—" Matt started, but Blaine held up one of his cursed blades.

"Whichever of us slays the most enemies, will claim the title of strongest in the Dragnov family." Blaine's eyes shifted from Matt to Emily. Matt may have wanted nothing to do with the family name, but Emily's eyes responded with excitement to Blaine's challenge. Blake remembered all too well what Emily had told him about her quest for power. She wanted to force her father, her brother, and all those who'd looked down on her for being a girl, to admit that she was powerful. Blaine's wager, was a surefire way for her to prove that.

"Deal." Emily smiled even as Matt shook his head. Matt would go along with it, because his purpose for gaining power was to keep his younger sister safe.

"Well then, try not to fall too far behind." Without another word Blaine began moving towards the sound of battle, his sets of bishops and legionnaires following after him. While Blake generally wasn't a fan of Blaine, he had to admit, he was happy to have the man on his side for this battle. Adventurers may have excelled at killing monsters in dungeons, but Blaine and his party had an extensive amount of experience fighting humans. Their father may have been the Duke of Blood, but he'd heard whispers of Blaine's nickname on the battlefield: The Crimson Executioner. A title earned by killing thousands. This battle against the Church was another normal day for him and his party.

"Right." Marcus rubbed his chin for a moment, looking over Blake's party. "Remember. Do not engage the Exalted One." His eyes locked onto Blake as he spoke. "Revenge will come later. The best way to honor those who have died is to live." Marcus's eyes went soft for a single moment as he spoke. "Trust me, Blake. They wouldn't want you to kill yourself trying to avenge them."

Blake tried his best to hold Marcus's gaze but turned away at the last moment. The sorrow that filled Marcus's eyes ate away at Blake. Did he know? Did any of them know? There was no way anyone could know what Blake was planning. There was no way Blaine would have told them what he had in his possession. What it meant for him, for this battle.

"Don't worry about us," Blake responded, trying to keep his voice calm. "We'll make it out of this alive." He shifted his gaze across his party, then back to Marcus. "All of us."

Marcus nodded, offering them a small smile as he did. "I'll expect you to keep that promise." As he finished speaking, his body began to fade. Marcus's job during this battle was to utilize his skills as a Whisperer to spread countless traps across the battlefield for the enemy forces, as well as to bolster any struggling groups, while keeping communication open. His class was more suited for support and surprise tactics rather than direct conflict.

With Marcus gone, it was just Blake and his party sitting in the clearing.

"Well, guys." Jack's voice broke the silence, the Duelist shifting to his massive wolfkin form. "Shall we get to it?" Jack's eyes blazed with excitement, while Karan stood by his side. Her eyes were firm. She'd found her resolve. If Solomon had secretly been working for Chaos, he'd corrupted the very

Church she'd grown up in. It was her job, as a follower of the Goddess of Justice, to right those wrongs and end this conflict.

Blake took a deep breath, drawing his bone sword from his sheath, hefting his shield up as he did. He looked over at his party. They were not only his friends, but they were also his family. They'd grown so much, come so far since their first dive, so long ago. And Blake was going to do everything in his power to keep them all safe. No matter what, his family would survive this day, even if he didn't. "Let's do this."

Chapter Seventy-Six

The forest was awash with souls. All around, Blake could pick up those of the adventurers rushing towards the enemy forces, those of the Church's army preparing to face the oncoming attackers, and then, surrounded by a massive crater, surrounded by swirling bones and darkness obscuring normal sight, Blake could see a soul that burned with immense power. The soul of the Exalted One.

Ryan hadn't been kidding when he said he couldn't handle them both. The dungeon core seemed hard at work, judging by the massive explosions, eruptions, and flashes of magic going on within that swirling area. The dungeon core and the Exalted One were having an all-out battle, a clash to see who was more powerful, who could last longer against the other.

Blake had no doubt the Exalted One would be the stronger. After all, he was a dual affinity Diamond 1 individual, and had a mana level equal to a God Tier individual. Something Blake couldn't even fathom.

Still, Ryan was powerful and capable, and Blake trusted the dungeon core to handle the situation. At the very least, with the Exalted One kept busy by Ryan, the adventurers had the freedom to engage with the Church of Justice's army without worrying about the Diamond 1 life user getting in the way.

Still, as Blake and his friends reached the end of the forest —which showed the scars of the explosions and fighting that had been going on before Ryan had called for aid—Blake could tell they were going to have trouble during this fight.

First and foremost, something was amiss. Every one of the souls he could see in the army, in the mass sea of souls extending backwards for at least a mile, was tainted by Chaos mana. Every single one. Solomon had corrupted them all.

The other worrying aspect was that on top of that Chaotic mana flowing through them, Blake, could make out a few dangerously large mana sources in the army. They weren't at the forefront of the forces, but waited patiently further back, keeping themselves hidden from Ryan and the adventurers. Blake's eyes could make them out because the power of their souls dwarfed those in the army. It also helped that he had seen these souls before. The souls of the Diamond Vampire Monica and the demon Marissa.

"Looks like the battle's already begun," Jack commented as they paused to look out at the scene. The adventurers, in their small parties, had begun to strike at the army by the time Blake and his party arrived. Almost all the attacks, ranging from arrows and ranged weapons, to magical bursts of force, smashed into a golden barrier or were shot down by Celestial mana. The army had come prepared for a long, massive battle, and they had prepared well

Luckily, with the Exalted One battling against Ryan in the forest, the Church was no longer using the massive cannons that Blake figured had caused all the damage to the woods. Such weapons the massive golden tubes he could see in the army, were likely meant for large-scale damage, not precision attacks. With the adventurers striking in small, agile groups, the massive cannons were ineffective, unable to adjust quickly enough to target the fast-moving clusters of enemies.

And the small box-like weapons the soldiers were using to intercept the adventurers ranged attacks, as well as the shields they used to create their barrier—those had weaknesses. Eventually, they would fall. It was a matter of doing enough damage to break through. If they could manage that, the real fight could begin. But, doing so was going to be no small—

"And there he goes." A trio of magical bursts blasted against the golden barrier from one of the army's flanks. Adventurers were doing their best to fight as spread out as possible, but Jack's comment drew Blake's attention to a specific group—to a figure burning with high-level mana. Not only had Blaine arrived before any of the other adventurers, but the man had been planning or preparing a nasty trick all his own.

Whatever he was doing, it was ready now. Because Blake watched as a large, fiery soul rushed with inhuman speed towards the army. Blaine was covered in icy armor, and he had sent three massive blades of flame, each at least thirty feet high, into the barrier. As those projectiles blasted against it, Blaine made use of the weapons he was holding, two whips made of molten rock.

They slammed into the shimmering barrier, causing a shockwave to blast across the ground, sending debris and smoke into the air. The increased length of Blaine's weapons, combined with their weight and the force Blaine had put into the strike, caused the barrier to crack. Blaine, taking that moment as an opening, directed his three fiery swords downwards into the protective dome, focusing on the cracked portions of the barrier.

Emboldened by the bloodthirsty Diamond 3, more and

more adventurers burst from the forest. No longer were they just chucking long distance attacks at the Church from the safety of the forest. Now, they saw a chance to fully break the barrier. Now, they were charging in, increasing their attacks while the Church forces tried their best to launch a counter-attack of their own.

Blake and his party watched as cracks began spiderwebbing across the Celestial barrier. Within, the souls of the Church members holding the large, glowing shields began to waiver. One by one, those souls began to snuff out, the humans falling to the ground dead, their shields dropping beside them. Drained by the concerted attacks all over the barrier, they died in agony from mana overuse.

The weakening barrier caused an urgent buzz of activity within the Church. Their previous apprehension to utilize the massive cannons seemed to have been lifted as the golden barrels began to glow. Most of the adventurers the cannons were aimed at, moved aside the moment they realized what was being leveled at them. However, Blake couldn't help but wince as he watched one group of adventures disappear as the golden weapon blasted into them, leaving only a smoldering crater where they had stood. Some groups were not as agile as he'd hoped. On top of these siege cannons, he saw something even more alarming. Above Blaine, who continued to smash against the crumbling barrier, a swirling, telltale attack began to prepare itself. Divine Judgement was about to be unleashed upon him.

"Are you ready, Matt?" Emily grinned at her brother as Cynder let out an excited cry. The night before, when they'd been discussing their battle plan, Emily had made it clear she and Matt had already figured out how they could best interact in the battle. Because she was now Diamond, Cynder could reach her most powerful form—short of well, God Tier. That is, Cynder could assume the form of an Elder dragon.

On top of that, Emily and Matt had both practiced riding atop Cynder, even before now, and were confident they could best aid in the battle from high above. After all, there was no safer position on the battlefield than atop an Elder dragon.

"Let's do this." Matt nodded to his sister as they stepped away from the party. "I'll show that smug bastard," Matt grumbled as he drew his bow. Clad in his dragon armor, armed with his bow with its pulsating mana string, Matt was the image of a deadly dragon rider from the tales of old. And as Cynder took on her true form, that of an Elder dragon, Blake paused in awe. Dragons were mythical beings of old, the most powerful creatures of the God of Fire. Their mere presence was said to be capable of leveling battlefields. And now, before him, an Elder dragon appeared.

Cynder's body glowed a deep crimson as she climbed higher into the air. With each flap of her wings, flames erupted around her and her size grew. Even though she was traveling with immense speed upwards, her form continued to grow, her size becoming more and more impressive. The fire around her blazed in the sky like a second sun, drawing attention towards the rising dragon as she continued to climb.

Once adorable, she transformed, her body hardened and muscled, growing to monstrous proportions. The Elder dragon, over a hundred feet in length, radiated power. Her wings, spreading outwards, casting dark shadows on the battlefield, shimmered like a burning flame. With her trans-formation complete, she let out a roar that shook the very land around them. It was a roar that awoke some primal fear within Blake. His instincts told him to step back, to flee before the might above him. To say an Elder dragon was powerful was an understatement.

With her transformation complete, Cynder quickly flew back towards the party, sending out a gust of wind as she slowed her descent, touching down just long enough for the siblings to rush towards her, moving with practiced ease up her muscled leg. They climbed onto her back, where spacing between the flame-shaped spikes created perfect seats for them.

"Ugh, they're so cool," Jack groaned, bringing Blake back to reality as the siblings climbed atop Cynder. The dragon let out another roar before she beat her mighty wings. The power from those wings ripped the trees behind her apart, sending them crashing through the forest, and causing Jack to let out another sigh. "It's so not fair."

The siblings offered the party a simple wave, as Cynder continued to ascend, before the Elder dragon turned its attention on the army. From Cynder's maw came a massive blast of fire which rocked the entire barrier and caused even more cracks to appear. More than a dozen souls within the barrier turned grey, the massive drain of keeping that fiery blast at bay was more than the humans could handle.

As Cynder launched another attack, Blake pulled his gaze from the dragon in time to see the Divine Judgement release on Blaine. Just before the attack could hit the man, still hard at work destroying the barrier, shield after shield appeared above him. The legionnaires who followed him had created a veritable stack of mana shields, each one larger than the previous, to stop the attack. The Divine Judgement ripped into the magical forms of protection but failed to penetrate all the way to Blaine. Their teamwork, their bond, had improved, Blake could recognize that much.

"Whelp… I feel like our approach is going to be underwhelming, now," Jack grumbled, his fur bristling. He wanted to join the fray, but a lot was going on right now. "So, what should we do?"

Blake took in the battle, watching as Cynder continued working against the barrier. The army had switched part of its focus from the approaching adventurers to trying to take down the Elder dragon. Unfortunately for them, the dragon wasn't alone. Flashes of blue intercepted attack after attack from the Church, keeping Cynder safe from anything she couldn't dodge. And, on top of that, when an attack did manage to somehow make its way past Matt's attacks, Cynder's body would simply pulse with fire, and the attack would disappear. Emily's powers, her Diamond 3 pool of mana, was focused on enhancing her dragon's speed, power, and defense to even greater levels. As long as Emily had the mana, nothing would be able to penetrate her dragon's hide. Those two were doing all they could to make up for the loss of Alice. They were going to ensure her death hadn't been in vain.

Blake looked around the battlefield, trying to take everything in. His party had hung back purposefully, to ensure they would be able to take in the battlefield and decide best how to take part. Obviously, Matt and Emily had decided how they could help between those two and Cynder, they were more powerful than a small army. Adding Blaine into the mix, the Dragnov family alone was showcasing the might of a full-blown army against the Church. Of course, they were all still human, meaning their mana reserves would run out. And when that happened, the tide of the battle might shift.

As such, it was imperative Blake understood, that they take in the battlefield, and make sure their actions would best serve the fight. His goal had been to wait until the Church's barrier was broken, to move in. After all, they didn't all need to waste mana on that glimmering barrier, not when Cynder and Blaine were doing so much damage.

However, even as the barrier shattered, giving them the opportunity to move in, another explosion ripped through the world. This time, the explosion wasn't over the Church.

This explosion wasn't the adventurers doing. As Blake glanced for the source, he felt his heart sink.

Just as the adventurers were about to cause real damage to the Church, now that its followers couldn't hide behind their barrier, the Exalted One had broken free of his battle with Ryan.

"Truly, this is an exciting battle," the man's voice boomed through the forest. He was amplifying his voice with his mana. "But my people, my forces, need their hero." His body shone brightly, bathing the land in white light, washing away the attacks Ryan launched towards him. A moment later, he was gone, and Blake saw his soul reappear within the middle of the army.

"Behold the power of life." Solomon chuckled. His white glow continued to pulse around him. "Behold, the power of a god."

Chapter Seventy-Seven

The moment the Exalted One returned to the army, the tide of the battle, which had been shifting to favor the adventurers, changed. White light pulsed from his body, making him a shining beacon so bright it was blinding. Power flowed from him in droves, pulsing through the army, washing over everyone. As Blake watched, barely able to keep his eyes open but refusing to pull away, he saw what was happening. It was terrifying.

Somehow, the Exalted One was bolstering the power of each and every member of his army. Suddenly an army that was comprised of Silver and Gold individuals was filled with those capable of rivaling Platinum levels of mana. The empowered souls burning brightly and fiercely throughout the battlefield.

"Go forth and crush the opposition," Solomon's voice echoed out. The army, which had previously been fighting in uniform ranks, changed tactics. The members, all enhanced by Solomon, flooded out in all directions, flinging attacks and abilities at anything standing in their way. As Blake watched from a distance, he could see they all had a slight, white glow pulsing all along their forms.

His mind drifted back to Alice's final moments, the white glow around her. Just what was this life mana? What could it do? How could it be stopped?

"Ryan," Blake called into his pendant. He couldn't tear his eyes away from the battlefield. The sudden change in momentum was obvious. The adventurers tried to return to the safety of the forest and Ryan's influence, but it was too late. They'd gotten too close to the army. Almost as if they'd been baited in. "We need your help."

"You don't say," Ryan responded harshly. "I'm working on it." With that the Dungeon Core went silent. What was with that response? What would Ryan do next? Whatever it was, could Ryan keep the adventurers from being wiped out here and now? If Ryan couldn't stop the Exalted One head-to-head, there was no way he would survive if the adventurers were annihilated.

"We need to do something," Blake said, looking at Jack and Karan. There was no more time to stand around and wait for good openings. They needed to join the battlefield. They needed to join the fray and hope and pray to the Goddess of Justice, the God of Death, or whoever would listen, that Ryan and the adventurers could somehow overcome this battle.

"Finally," Jack growled in excitement, he turned towards the battlefield, his eyes searching. "Where are we going?"

Blake motioned towards Blaine. "We will need his help. We're going to try and take down the strongest members of the army."

"Solomon?" Jack's voice faltered.

"No," Blake shook his head. They still needed to stay away from him. There was no way they could stop him. At least, not permanently. "The Vampire and demon are in the back. I have been watching them for a while now, I'm not sure why they haven't joined the fight, but I'm guessing they may be guarding something. With the shield users down and the canons less useful at close range, we have the upper hand. But if the Church has any other artifacts to turn the tide of the battle…we need to eliminate them before they can use them. Perhaps then, even with their increased power, we can do enough damage to force the army to retreat."

It was the only explanation Blake had for why those two souls hadn't joined the fight yet. Those two Diamond 3 monsters were up to something. And he didn't want to let them get away with whatever they were planning. The sooner they were removed, the better.

"Oh, good." Jack let out a sigh of relief. "Do we really need to have him help, though?" Jack groaned as they moved towards Blaine. The man was fighting a dozen or so Church members as they rushed towards him, his massive molten whips incinerating those they impacted with. Having broken through the mana barrier, Blaine had been carving out a swathe of death and destruction in his way towards the massive golden cannons.

The man knew taking out siege engines was important when fighting an army. However, the arrival of the Exalted One, and the fiercer, more powerful Church members changing their battle tactics from defense to offense, had slowed him down. Even so, Blaine was smiling as he continued to cut his foes down, despite the seemingly endless stream of forces rushing towards him. Blake was pretty sure he could hear Blaine calling out a number each time he got a new kill…He'd been serious about keeping count.

"Can you think of anyone else we can rely on to help?" Blake asked. Above, Cynder let out a mighty roar and sent a wave of fire down on the army. A swathe of Church members disappeared, leaving behind no souls, no bodies, nothing.

Whatever it was, that white glow Solomon had given his followers was having the same effect on the Goddess's followers as it had on Alice. Meaning, when these people died, nothing remained. And no bodies meant no bones... Blake was really glad he had his bone chest piece for his skills.

"Someone else? As a matter of fact..." Jack grinned his wolfish grin, and paused for a moment. He rocked his head back and let out a long, powerful howl. The sound reverberated through the battlefield. A moment later, a chorus of additional howls echoed back, coming from deep in the forest. "I can think of more than one."

"The pack?" Blake watched the wolfkin twins and their pack appear from the woods. Marcus had mentioned they had taken to calling the woods around Ryan's dungeon home, but they had been undecided about aiding in the battle. Fighting an army out in the open was contrary to their normal fighting style. After all, Rasha and Sasha were both assassins.

"Are you sure?" Blake asked his friend. While they had earned their freedom from Sasha during their duel, Blake wasn't quite sure he felt entirely comfortable with them. And he was even more surprised that Jack was on good enough terms with them to call for aid.

The wolfkin royalty and their pack came from the woods, all in their wolfkin forms, the twins' still larger than Jack's half-breed transformation.

"We've come as requested." Sasha looked down at Jack, her eyes serious. "Does this mean you will uphold your end of what was discussed?" The words came as a surprise to Blake. Had Jack made some sort of arrangement with the twins? Blake had to wonder if speaking with Sasha was why Jack had disappeared so quickly yesterday.

"I've thought about it," Jack responded, nodding from Sasha, to Rasha, "but there were a few things that, the more I thought about, the more I decided need to be discussed." He offered a half-hearted chuckled towards them. "Fighting alongside all of you will put me in a more favorable mood for these negotiations than fighting alongside that guy." Jack motioned towards Blaine, who was continuing to decimate everything that came near him.

Interestingly, Blake noticed Solomon hadn't moved from his spot. Instead, he simply continued to radiate his white light. What was the man doing?

"Jack," Karan said, exasperation evident. "We talked about this." Karan definitely knew whatever was going on, meaning Blake was the only one in the dark. Still, he figured Jack either really, really disliked Blaine, or whatever it was being discussed with Sasha and Rasha wasn't as grave as their previous terms. Whatever it was, Blake was going to trust in Jack and Karan.

"Sorry, Karan." Jack looked at her sheepishly. "I just really don't like him."

Sasha grinned at the two. "Very well. We shall discuss these things after the battle." She glanced at Solomon, her eyes narrowing. "Though if you expect us to stand against that man, you must know, it's impossible."

Jack nodded, motioning towards Blake and then the rear of the army. "We're going to fight a Vampire and a demon, not that monster. Blake says they're hiding in the back of the army, likely protecting something important."

Sasha looked over Blake, her mouth turning into a small smile. "Well then, Blake, it would be my pleasure to fight alongside you. Lead us to our prey." Her lip curled up slightly, showing the back of her fangs. "I look forward to seeing how you've grown."

Blake definitely felt uncomfortable under her gaze. It reminded him all too well of her strange fascination with him. Still, she was capable, as was her pack. And with Jack,

Karan, and the wolfkin, they had surely bolstered their numbers in preparation for what they would face. Still, Blake wasn't happy with the forces they had at hand.

"We're still going to need a Diamond level adventurer." Blake commented. Sasha and Rasha were both Platinum 1, but the rest of their pact was mostly Gold Tier. The demon and the Vampire were both of greater strength than a Diamond 3 adventurer, perhaps equivalent to a Diamond-level dungeon monster.

Jack motioned towards Emily and Matt, high in the sky. "Hello. Those two?"

Blake shook his head. "They're busy." The dragon and the two adventurers on top of it were hard at work deflecting ranged attacks and conducting diving sweeps at the golden canons. They were likely the only thing keeping the Life mana-infused Church members from overrunning the adventurers. Their presence was needed at the front, where they could occupy the attention of the enemy, allowing the other adventurers more freedom to attack.

"I swear...all of this, and I still have to work with that guy." Jack let out a low growl. "You're going to owe me after this."

"It's only for one battle," Blake responded. "Besides, who else would willingly join us as we take on a demon and a Vampire?" As he spoke, the air around him seemed to intensify and Marcus appeared.

"If you're taking down Marissa," the Diamond 3 Whisperer said grimly, "then I'm coming along."

Jack, smiled triumphantly, motioning towards Marcus. "There."

Marcus chuckled at Jack. "And I've someone who can aid us against the Vampire, as well." As he finished speaking, Blake noticed a large dark mass of mana rushing towards them from the forest. It moved with impossible speed, a shadowy form, stopping just as it neared the party. "It's going to be like a family reunion."

"Cane?" Blake said. He looked over the man who materialized before him. Sure enough, it was the death knight who'd trained him when he'd first become Gold. Judging by the size of his soul, he was stronger now. No longer was Cane Platinum; he was definitely a Diamond Tier.

The man's eyes flashed red as he grinned at Blake, revealing two long fangs. It was definitely Cane, but he was no longer human. "Rumor is, my mother joined the other side." He held out his hand, and his massive legendary weapon appeared, a giant dragon bone club. "The God of Death tasked me with returning her soul to him."

If Cane was torn up about that aspect, his eyes didn't show it. In fact...it seemed as if the concept of fighting his mom excited him. They had always been a strange family. Considering they lived on the fringe of the God of Death's lands, surrounded by undead, reapers, souls, and the like, their callous nature towards death made sense. Everything, in the end, belonged to their God.

Looking at the forces around him, Blake's confidence surged. With the wolfkin, with Marcus, with Cane, and with Jack and Karan, they could take down those two massive enemies. And with them out of the way, surely they could devise a way to help bring down Solomon. Maybe—just maybe—Blake wouldn't have to use the gem in his pouch.

Maybe just maybe, he could survive this battle after all.

Chapter Seventy-Eight

RYAN

"Are we sure this is going to work?" Erin was a worried mess as Ryan finished the final preparations. He didn't blame her. So far, nothing was turning out as planned. The Exalted One was impossibly strong and they'd had to resort to bringing in Blake's adventurers much sooner than planned. Even then, it wasn't enough. Ryan couldn't pin down the blasted Life mana user. Everything he did to the man simply amused Solomon. It was as if the Exalted One was toying with him. And Ryan did not like that feeling at all.

"I've done everything I can think of." The God of Death had given Ryan the image of an Avatar when he first ascended to Platinum. With his ascension to Diamond, he'd gained the full knowledge about what an Avatar was and how he could use it. The Avatar would serve as his vessel, his physical form. With it he could literally move his influence with him. As long as he was in his Avatar, he could spread his influence in a massive two-mile radius from wherever his Avatar, and thus his core, was.

While using the Avatar though, he would make himself more vulnerable. While the Avatar itself would house his consciousness, he would have to physically carry his core around. From the vision Death shared with him of an Avatar, the most obvious and easy way to do this was to affix his core to a staff. Ryan was no longer fond of that idea. It made his core too…obvious, too vulnerable.

As such, while he knew there was a rush for him to reenter the battle, he'd taken the time needed to adjust his Avatar accordingly. Now, as he finalized everything, he closed up his Avatar's chest cavity and reapplied the armor and gear to the massive skeletal creature. Ryan had decided to put his core in the Avatar's very center, playing up the concept of him being the core even more than previously.

"Whatever happens," Ryan said as he prepared to activate his Avatar. "Stay as close to me as you can." His fairies had refused to be left alone in the dungeon while he went off to fight. Given that they were now fairies to a Diamond 3 dungeon, they held considerable power. They would be useful on the battlefield. Ryan was just worried for them, because he was certain they hadn't seen all of Solomon's tricks. And the Exalted One terrified him. At least all those blasted Subjugation Orbs had been destroyed. Otherwise, Ryan wouldn't have dreamt of taking his core to the battlefield.

"But of course, Darling." Hel was covered, for once, in armor…albeit extremely formfitting armor. Ryan had crafted it for her and ensured it was as powerful as he could, lining all of it with Darkness mana and even inlaying it with blood-stones to boost her Chaotic powers. Erin, on the other hand, was clad in full gleaming plate mail, appearing much more a formidable Angelic warrior than the frail, innocent Celestial fairy he knew.

"We will always be by your side," Erin confirmed.

"Then, lets rejoin the battle." Ryan knew he couldn't dilly dally any longer. Checking on the battlefield showed the adventurers were now being pushed back by the forces of the Church. All the members of the Church were covered in a glowing white light that seemed to be strengthening them to some degree. Many of the adventuring parties were struggling to make their way back towards Ryan's influence. The Church members were keen to ensure no one got too close to Ryan's influence. At least the Goddess's followers recognized his power, even if Solomon viewed Ryan as a pest.

And while the battlefield was shifting in favor of the Church, there were still pockets of resistance from the adventurer side. Blaine was obvious. That man was a monster unto himself. Then there was Cynder. Ryan would be lying if the appearance of Cynder as an Elder dragon hadn't made him even more eager to join the battlefield. After all, if one dragon was not enough to turn the tide, perhaps two could.

"Again with the jealousy, Darling?" He chuckled as Ryan's focus had drifted back to Cynder and her riders. He'd focused on them just in time to watch Cynder blast a good swathe of the Church's army apart with obvious ease. If it weren't for the Exalted One, Cynder alone could have kept the Church's forces at bay for the adventurers.

"She's so powerful," Ryan grumbled.

"And you're even more so," Hel said. She placed a hand gently on the shoulder of his Avatar, leaning in as she spoke. "Now, activate your Avatar, summon your steed, and be the first dungeon core to have walked this land in centuries."

With those words Ryan did exactly that. He pulsed mana into his Avatar, willing his conscience into the massive skeletal form, calling forth the magic granted him as a Diamond-level dungeon core. It was time to bring his Avatar to life. For a moment there was a terrifying rush, as if something were pulling him away from himself. For a second, he felt disjointed, and then suddenly he was no longer within his core. Instead, his power rushed through his skeletal body, and for the first time since he'd become a dungeon core, he was looking through actual eyes. Well…eye sockets, but he really wasn't going to be technical right now.

"Right, then." As he spoke, he felt his jaw bones moving. He tested out his body, marveling at it, and ignoring the fact that he didn't have flesh or muscles, as best he could. Sure, he was just a massive amount of bones animated by Darkness mana, but it didn't matter. He had a body. He was finally more than a floating magical core.

"It is time we rejoin the battle." His voice was dark and powerful.

With a simple mental command, he began pushing the stone above him aside. As it shifted apart, he commanded the ground beneath him to rise. While he was now in his Avatar, he still wielded all the power he normally did over all that he held influence on. With simple, easy thoughts, he could control everything around him.

Ryan couldn't help but feel exhilarated as they rushed upwards, ascending through all the floors of his dungeon to burst out of the ground, his massive Avatar's form towering powerfully in the forest. Once he'd arrived above ground, he pointed, instantly creating a clearing as he absorbed all the trees in the area. There he summoned what would be his steed, his mount, for this battle. Erin and Matt had Cynder, the Elder dragon. Ryan had Trogdor—Death's Visage, the 4080-point ultra-rare boss mob.

The creature formed before him in mere seconds, and Ryan walked calmly over to the massive ten headed bone wyvern. The heads all turned to look at him, as it flexed its massive skeletal wings, the Darkness mana that created their webbing, sending dust flying in all directions. The lengthy bone tail behind it swished about with anticipation, leaving a trail of pale, lifeless ground underneath.

Trogdor, just like the Shydra, had its life-draining aura.

Anything living that wasn't specifically connected to Ryan, in other words, everything but his fairies, would be drained by that aura if they came too close. it. He held a hand out as he neared its side, and reins made of Darkness mana appeared in his hands, linking to all ten of the heads at once. He leapt onto the creature, marveling at the pure strength that flowed through his Avatar. As he landed atop the back of the mighty beast, the bones on its back shifted to form a perfect saddle for him. Beside him, his fairies hovered easily with their wings.

With another mental command and a tug on the reins, Trogdor flapped its massive wings, lifting its terrifying form into the air. Up in the sky, exhilaration filled Ryan as he looked out onto the world with his own eyes. For a moment, his worries and his fears were forgotten. For a moment, all he felt was the thrill of being alive…so to speak.

However, that thrill was short-lived as a massive blast of energy slammed into Cynder in the distance. From up high, Ryan could make out the Elder dragon, even if the rest of the battlefield seemed minute. While he couldn't see everything, he saw enough to know Cynder was in trouble. While he doubted the Church had expected a dragon… they appeared to have contingencies for massive flying creatures. It may have taken a while, but those countermeasures were now in full swing. As more explosions erupted around Cynder, Ryan knew he needed to hurry.

"Let's go."

Chapter Seventy-Nine

It took mere minutes for Ryan's presence to be spotted as they flew rapidly to join the fray. Given his size and the size of Trogdor, that made perfect sense. As they approached, Ryan could feel his influence spreading in all directions, keeping up with his Avatar, a perfect radius in all directions. He also couldn't help but notice, he still retained his link back to his Dungeon, and everything he'd ever spread his influence too, meaning his rate of mana regain, wasn't being affected. He'd been a little worried that as an Avatar, he could potentially lose his control over everything else he'd touched...which would have greatly hurt his mana regeneration rate. Something that would have been detrimental for this fight.

But that wasn't the case, and so, as he rushed towards the battlefield, he prepared an army of his own. While he may not be able to summon mobs directly around the adventurers or the army, per the annoying rules of dungeon magic, he could prepare forces as he flew there.

Below him, he summoned everything he could fathom. His Bone Enforcers were called forth, his Tiger Queen, hordes of clackers, and more importantly, his skeletal champions. On top of those, he summoned a veritable army of skeletal fighters and archers, as well as liches and skeletal riders.

He even threw in some of the massive reptilian creatures he had, specifically the one he'd previously tried to combine with a clacker to make a dragon. They were weaker than some of the other mobs he was summoning…but he figured their size and look would cause the enemy to foolishly think they were more of a threat. They definitely demanded attention.

As he neared the battlefield, he couldn't help but smile. Not only was the sky now filled with his skeletal monsters, but the ground was a veritable mass of bones and Darkness mana, his creatures all heading towards the battlefield. And he wasn't done. He kept summoning mobs as he flew, populating the sky with an even greater variety, including his griffons and their skeletal mages, until every last drop of his mob points had been spent. It was all or nothing now.

"Are you alright?" Erin asked beside him, noting he'd slumped slightly in his bone saddle. It was risky, summoning that many mobs all at once. But he didn't have time to think about the risks. He needed to turn the tide of this battle. He needed to take control of it and put the Exalted One on the defensive. He couldn't afford to let that man do as he pleased.

"I'm fine," Ryan grunted. His head was swimming but he wasn't worried. The world was aflush with energy and as they flew towards the battlefield, he could feel his mana filling back up. By the time they reached the battle, he would have enough mana to do whatever was needed. And by the time anything too threatening targeted him, he would be powerful enough to protect himself. Part of the reason for the mass summoning was to ensure there was too much chaos, too many new targets, to allow the enemy to react in an organized manner. Besides, Ryan was confident Trogdor would be more than capable of handling the battle as Ryan regained his mana.

"Remember, you two," Ryan said as they neared. Cries of terror and surprise could be heard from the battlefield, and he watched as a golden beam of light blasted towards one of his griffon riders. The skeletal creature dodged easily, and the archmage atop it launched a fireball in return. Ryan chuckled in satisfaction as the fiery attack erupted over a group of Church members. "Stay by me at all times."

"But of course, Darling," Hel responded. She was eyeing the battlefield hungrily, and Ryan could tell she wanted nothing more than to be cut loose so she could release her powers upon the foes below them. Still, there were too many unknowns for him to risk letting the two out of his sight. At least for now.

"Now, while we—" Ryan was interrupted by a loud roar as a large spear of light blasted through Cynder's wing. The dragon growled in fury and launched another blast of fire towards the enemy army as it struggled to stay upright. Judging by the fluctuating red mana around the dragon, Emily's mana was running out. Apparently, the Diamond 3 adventurer had misjudged how much mana she could channel into her Elder dragon. Ryan figured not only did the transformation and empowering of Cynder take a lot of mana, the summoner and dragon had been taking on plenty of attacks from the Church of Justice.

Which made sense. Prior to Ryan's arrival, the dragon and its riders were the largest target for the army to attack. Devastating fire power alone didn't make something invincible. Plus, they were fighting the full might of the Church of Justice, which was no small feat, considering it was the most powerful army in all the land. Still, as they made their way towards Cynder, he could tell they'd done a mammoth amount of damage to the enemy.

Craters scarred the ground from countless fire blasts, and Ryan could see huddled groups of injured Church members working frantically to heal the damage they'd taken at the hands of the dragon. While it was evident they'd been killing countless Church members, just as before with Alice, Ryan saw no sign of bodies or souls. An additional bit of knowledge the God of Death had granted him, as he ascended, was that Life mana, the Exalted One's power, allowed him to return anyone he'd affected directly to the world as mana.

This transference bypassed death's role, and left behind neither soul nor body. Just as Life mana had created the original life in the land, to Life mana they would return. Ryan figured that aspect of it rubbed the God of Death the wrong way. After all, everything that died was supposed to belong to him.

And Ryan had realized something about the Exalted One's power as the fight had been going on. Ryan had been keeping a close eye on his opponent's use of mana, which seemed nearly infinite. Eventually, Ryan had realized why. While it was obvious the Exalted One was enhancing his followers with Life mana, every time someone he'd touched with Life mana died, Ryan sensed the man's mana spike, as if he'd gained back not only his own mana but that of the dead. It was almost like the Diamond 1 Life user had the powers of a dungeon—the ability to absorb the power of his fallen followers and use it for himself or redistribute it to his remaining forces. Essentially, he had a never-ending supply of mana, and he was using it to constantly improve his forces.

Additionally, as long as he was capable of doing this, it deprived Ryan of souls and bodies for his own skills. Sure, he could use the adventurers' souls and bodies but there were far fewer of them than Church members. And Ryan had really been hoping to take advantage of his enemy's dead, not his allies'.

"Let's give Cynder some aid," Ryan called to his fairies, directing his ten-headed wyvern towards the dragon. As they made their way towards Cynder, Erin flew ahead, at Ryan's behest, to begin healing it. As she did, Ryan kept his focus on the battlefield below, watching the chaos unfold.

His Tiger Queen had sent her skeletal tigers on a hunt, chasing down Church members left and right. His Bone Enforcers had spread out and were decimating groups of Church members. The adventurers, after overcoming their initial terror over the sudden presence of so many skeletal monsters, were rallying behind Ryan's mobs, using the appearance of his army to heal themselves and get to safety. Those still capable of fighting, were using the skeletal army as a sort of meat shield. They were letting his skeletal mobs take the brunt force of the Church's attacks, while they launched attacks safely from behind.

"What's going on?" Emily called out as they neared. Only Blake knew of Erin's existence, and none of the adventurers he interacted with knew of Hel's existence. Plus, the fact he could summon an Avatar was a secret until now.

"I figured you might have needed my aid on the battle-field," Ryan called out from his Avatar. As he spoke, Erin's form lit up with golden light, her feathery wings shining brilliantly as she began healing Cynder's wing. Emily's eyes widened as she looked at Ryan, and he saw her mouth his name questioningly.

"Yes, I'm Ryan," he responded. A moment later they were rudely interrupted by a blast of golden light. Looking down he saw the followers of the Church had mounted versions of their golden cannons pointed skywards. They were aiming it towards him and his mount, its runes glowing as it powered up. Seriously, he hated all of their siege weapons.

"Take a moment to get your mana back before you rejoin the fight," Ryan said, turning Trogdor towards the cannon. With a mental command, all ten of the heads arched back. A moment later, ten beams of Dark mana, filled with swirling bones, flew down towards the battlefield. The breath attacks converged on the cannon, then erupted outwards in an explosive death. The members who'd been preparing to fire the cannon were all slain. To his annoyance though, the cannon remained.

Even more annoying, was that just as he disabled that cannon, another began glowing in the distance. It was no wonder Cynder had been struggling. The Church had brought all of its resources to bear for this fight, and he had to wonder, if Ryan's side won this battle, would it be at the cost of the entire Church of Justice?

"I see you've come out to play." Solomon's voice echoed across the battlefield, drawing Ryan's attention to the man. He'd seen him already—it was impossible not to. The Life mana user's entire body was covered in glowing white light, which continually pulsed outwards across his followers.

No one had yet tried to attack Solomon. The adventurers were scared of him, choosing to attack the weaker Church members instead. He couldn't blame them for that, even if he wished someone would at least try to hurt the man.

"I've never been a fan of the Church," Ryan called out, directing his ultra-rare wyvern's attention towards the man. He wasn't certain of all the attacks his boss mob had at its disposal, but he was excited to find out. He gave the creature the go-ahead to launch everything it had towards the Exalted One, encouraging its outer heads to lay waste to any Church members they saw as well.

"Neither have I." Solomon chuckled darkly, simply standing there, not attacking. Whatever he was doing, Ryan figured he couldn't attack in his current state. That, or he once again was working on something else. Something Ryan doubted he would like. "But every god needs his followers to die for him. And I must thank you for your part in this. Everything is truly going to plan."

More mana pulsed from Solomon, even as a roiling wave of darkness flowed towards him from Trogdor. At the same time the wyvern flapped its massive wings, sending a rain of bone shards down onto the battlefield. As the shards hit the ground, they erupted, spreading what Ryan instantly recognized as the poisonous gas from his dungeon's mushrooms. *Neat.*

He'd stopped launching his puffballs earlier, out of fear of hitting the adventurers with them. But Trogdor's attacks were in the center of the army, all around Solomon, meaning there was no chance of hitting any of his allies with the toxic fumes.

"I'll make you pay for everything you've ever done," Ryan called down towards Solomon. "I'll make you pay for Alice." As he spoke, he summoned a spear in his hands, arming it with an opal spearhead. "I'll make you pay for what you did to Hel." He threw the spear, summoning another as he did. "I'll make you pay for Sean." Another spear, thrown in quick succession. "And I'll make you pay for everyone the Church has ever wrongly hurt."

The spears flew true towards the Exalted One with impossible force. The physical strength of his Avatar was not to be ignored. Unfortunately, before the spears reached Solomon, they were blasted out of the sky. Ryan hadn't expected that to work, but he figured he would give it a try.

Besides, he needed to keep the Exalted One occupied while his skeletal army and the adventurers worked against the forces of the Church. They needed to hold out long enough to deprive him of his army. While Solomon may have been ridiculously powerful, Ryan was certain that, with his might, combined with the adventurers' own, they could take the monster down. There was no way he could survive against all of them on his own.

"I told you, dungeon. Nothing you do can harm me." Solomon laughed even louder. "No matter what you do, the outcome will be the same. I've planned this all out. I know how it ends." He pulsed again, even more Life mana flowing from him. Ryan could sense the Church members growing even stronger as he did that.

He was transferring the power of those that had been slain back into the remaining army. For each death, the mana pool with which he enhanced the army, increased. If Ryan's understanding of Solomon's power was correct, all the Church deaths on the battlefield were actually helping increase Solomon's power. Ryan really didn't like that thought.

"At the end of the day, you will die, and I will win. You cannot stop what I've set in motion. Nothing can."

"We will see about that," Ryan said smugly. He gave his wyvern a new order. If the Exalted One's forces were going to get stronger as the battle went on, Ryan's side needed to kill them all even quicker.

After all, if Solomon had no one left to empower, the current skill he was using would be useless, and surely he would lose all the excess mana he'd been collecting. So, even though Ryan really wanted to keep launching attacks at him, he switched tactics. It was time he lived up to his calling. He would use his powers, his Darkness mana, to spread death.

Chapter Eighty

Ryan was no stranger to death. He was a dungeon after all. And on top of that, his specialty was dead things. So, when it came to taking charge of the battlefield and causing as much devastation as he could, as quickly as he could...he excelled at that. Especially when he wasn't torn up over the loss of life happening in his presence. The Church of Justice, the Exalted One, they had come for his life and for all he held dear. They had forfeited their right to live.

With his focus pulled away from the Exalted One, knowing he couldn't take the man down—at least not yet— he turned his vast senses to the battlefield. His summoned mobs were doing as they were meant to, destroying Church members left and right. His more powerful creatures, the Bone Enforcers and skeletal champions, were targeting more difficult groups of foes, and were using their enhanced skills —or sheer size—to overwhelm them.

Meanwhile, Ryan could see the adventurers had begun to rally around his added forces. Sadly, their rallying hadn't been as effective as he'd have liked, considering the remaining

Church members grew stronger with every death—while the remaining adventurers were getting lower and lower on mana. While it seemed, at least from what Ryan could tell, the members weren't gaining access to higher-level skills and abilities, their physical aspects and the amount of mana they could wield were increasing as they received the transferred mana from the Exalted One. Solomon obviously viewed his Church members as disposable, recyclable even…whereas Ryan didn't have the liberty, or want, to throw away adventurer lives.

However, if Solomon was going to view his people as expendable, Ryan was going to take advantage of that. He figured massive, area of effect style attacks and abilities would likely be the most useful in this situation. Meaning Trogdor—Death's Visage, went on a rampage. The wyvern flew all around the army, spraying death, destruction, and toxic fumes left and right.

Meanwhile Ryan willed puffballs into existence as they flew around, dropping the bioweapons on top of the army below him. With their defenses down, and many of their siege weapons now unmanned and impossible to get close to, the puffballs were successful in crashing down onto the ground, spreading more death and chaos.

As all this devastation rained down around him, Ryan turned his focus to one other task. While he couldn't do anything with the fallen members of the Church, he wasn't so restricted when it came to adventurers. Those who had already died before his arrival were easily animated into mobs with a thought and a little bit of Darkness mana. He gave them a simple command— destroy the Church—leaving the how at their disposal.

Those who were freshly slain Ryan focused on a little more, creating enhanced versions of the individuals. He pumped enough mana in them to keep their souls within their bodies, creating high-level Vampires to run amok on the battlefield. He didn't try to subjugate them, feeling it was best to leave their emotions and thoughts intact for this fight. After all, he was certain their rage would turn all of their focus, bloodlust, and newfound abilities onto the enemy that killed them.

And of course, for those who were near death, Ryan sent Erin down, gracing them with the true healing blessing of the Goddess of Justice. Erin went to and fro, spreading light and sparing the lives of those who fought valiantly to keep him safe. Ryan was a benevolent dungeon, and would reward and aid those who fought on his behalf.

Hel, on the other hand, took action any chance she could. As they flew low, spreading death in the form of Darkness and bone shards, Hel would send out pulses of Chaos mana, working to twist the minds of those members of the Church she could. To her dismay, her abilities were less than effective. The more she tried, the more frustrated she grew. After a while, she simply huffed and resorted to snapping necks with the bladed whip Ryan had made for her.

Apparently, the Church members were already under the effects of a different Succubus. What really frustrated her was that this other one was the stronger than her, which was why she couldn't take control of the Church members. So, Hel resorted to killing them instead. There was a lot of spite in her actions, and Ryan didn't blame her. They both knew who that other Succubus was.

He pulled up on the reins of his mount, directing it to fly higher as a beam of golden light shot towards him. The blast narrowly avoided his mount and he willed a wall of bones into existence within the sky just in time to block a swarm of arrows launched in their direction.

Ryan was greatly enjoying the amount of creative freedom

he had with his Avatar. Because of the large spread of his influence, he was able to create nearly any inanimate object he wanted to, from thin air. It was like being within his dungeon, but out in the open. Which, Ryan could appreciate, was part of what made an Avatar so deadly.

When you were diving a dungeon, you knew there was safety outside its reach, once you left its domain. But an Avatar could continue to chase you down. Unfortunately, the massive amount of Church members and adventurers kept him from ripping open the ground and dropping the army to its death. The only reason he could use that tactic in the dungeon, was because he'd prepped every ounce of his dungeon for such a task. It was a time- and mana-intensive skill. Same with summoning large-scale solid objects to drop on the Church. The larger the object, the greater its mass, the more mana it took. And Ryan was trying to be selective with his mana.

The final benefit of this conflict which Ryan was quickly realizing, was the massive amount of experience gain he was receiving. While he didn't get the full amount of experience from each kill because of the quantity of people involved and the fact the humans were gaining experience from killing each other as well, Ryan was still passively gaining a lot. He could already tell the vast expanse of experience needed to go from Diamond 3 to Diamond 2 was quickly being filled. How powerful would he be if he survived to the end?

Regardless, he was eager to reach that next level. The boost from Diamond 3 to Diamond 2 would greatly increase his capabilities. It would give him an additional 4800 mob points to utilize for this battle. And Ryan couldn't help but imagine what type of chaos he could spread with that many more mob points. He was thinking a second Trogdor would be in order.

"You're fighting a losing battle," the Exalted One called to

Ryan. Since his arrival on the battlefield, Ryan couldn't even count how many of that man's followers he'd slain. Yet still the battle raged on, and Ryan could tell that the amount of living individuals on the battlefield was much lower on his side than on the Exalted One's. Sure, there had been less adventurers to begin with, but Ryan sensed they were dying at a faster rate now. They may have initially been stronger and more experienced, but the constant boost in power the Exalted One was providing to his followers, combined with their vast amount of healing capabilities, meant his forces had a higher survivability.

Ryan was still losing this war of attrition. Worse, he could tell his attacks, the attacks of his forces, were becoming less and less effective. Sure, Trogdor was still destroying large groups with ease, but his Bone Enforcers were suffering. He'd already had to resummon his Nuckalvee once and the Tiger Queen had been respawned quite a few times.

From what Ryan could tell, he was starting to have less free mana with which to attack, and was using more of it to keep the stream of his mobs up on the battlefield. That was the biggest worry and the largest frustration. He'd been on the battlefield for less than an hour, and the momentum was already balanced again and starting to shift away from his side. They needed something—some way—to hurt the Exalted One. But only Celestial attacks could even penetrate his legendary defenses.

"Blake." Ryan sent the message to the only Celestial user he could fathom would be capable of helping in this situation. When he'd entered the battlefield, he'd seen the Adventurer heading to the rear of the army to deal with some rather powerful foes. However, he needed Blake now.

Sure, the Platinum 1 Specter of Balance wasn't anywhere near the same strength as the Exalted One. But Blake didn't need to be. Not with Ryan there to support him. If they worked together, as they'd always done in the past, maybe, they could bring this monster down. "I need your help to take down the Exalted One."

Chapter Eighty-One

BLAKE

They'd found the demon and Vampire hanging back at the very rear of the army. And while he'd already felt nervous about engaging them, the long dash past the Church's army, which spread on and on and on, had done little to help ease those nerves. It had simply made Blake realize just how large a force they were up against. And that had only fueled the dread he already felt.

Upon reaching Marissa and Monica, his suspicions had been confirmed. The two massively powerful Diamond 3 monsters stood casually in front of a massive sphere larger than anything he'd ever seen; even larger than the Platinum diamond core he'd watched Alice destroy. The orb the two were guarding appeared to be made from diamond, and was larger than a building. Even stranger—if this situation could get any stranger—was that the sphere wasn't resting on anything. It simply hovered between the two, pulsing with a strange, faint light.

Sadly, Blake didn't have much time to look over the orb. As they neared the two, their presence was immediately noticed. After all, their force wasn't exactly meant to be stealthy, and it was nearly impossible to sneak up on Diamond Tier individuals anyways.

Marissa took note of them first, smiling a hungry, devious smile towards Blake before her eyes hardened on Marcus. Meanwhile, Monica's eyes flashed red at the arrival of their forces, an almost crazed, hungry look across her face. She didn't even seem to register that her son was amongst the group. In fact, the way she looked at them all, it was as if she simply saw them as her next meal.

"Is it finally time to do this, brother?" Marissa drawled, her eyes looking Marcus up and down. She smiled sweetly at him. "Even with your increased power, you're no match for me now." She laughed and spread her arms wide before Marcus could respond. Behind her, a crackling portal of Chaos mana opened, and from it waves upon waves of demons began rushing forth, swarming toward Blake and his party. Monica took this swarm of chaos as an opportunity to drift amongst the flow, making a beeline towards the adventures with superhuman speed. Blake barely managed to make her target, one of the younger wolfkin, go ethereal before she struck at his now incorporeal form.

That gained Blake the ire of the Vampire. Luckily, Cane stepped in to take on his mother's next attack. It was a clash between two Diamond 3 Death Lords, both turned into Vampires by the God of Death. A battle that Blake was more than a little intrigued to watch, though for obvious reasons, he had to tear his eyes from it. For even as the two Vampires flashed about the battlefield, Marissa's demonic forces launched attacks of their own. Blake's forces found themselves instantly in a fight for their lives.

A fight that they had to win.

The only time Blake turned back to watch Cane again on the battlefield, and just for a moment, was because the man activated his legendary club. The massive form of the shadowy dragon, formed of Darkness mana, appeared around his former mentor, completely cloaking him. As he swung the weapon it was as if the dragon was swinging its mighty tail, destroying the ground as it cracked the earth apart. Cane's weapon was not a subtle one. Then again, Cane wasn't subtle, either. Luckily, he'd drawn his mother away from the group before their battle fully began. Otherwise, Blake's side would have lost members to the explosive, destructive nature of the two's battle.

Blake turned back to the fight at hand just in time to block an incoming demonic claw, his shield easily catching the impact. From the force of it, the demon wasn't strong, only high Silver or low Gold. And, as his forces continued to dispatch them, the flow of demons slowed from the portal. Blake felt the only reason Marissa had summoned them, was as a distraction. After all, the longer the fight went on, the more it was evident she was doing her best to take full advantage of the chaos as hand.

Initially, Blake had thought Marcus was going to take her on. However, the demon had a different idea of how the battle would go. With the demonic forces taking on the wolfkin, and threatening anyone they neared, Marissa had flapped her leathery black wings, lifting herself higher into the sky above the battle. Then, she faded partially from view, her form going almost completely invisible. Most worrying, was that her weapon, a dangerous whip he knew could put anyone it hit under her control, went invisible as well. It was then that she began launching attacks of her own.

To Marcus's credit, the Whisperer—his body fading into wind as the battle raged on—was doing his best to stop her. If Blake had to guess, Marcus was using his abilities and his wind mana to sense when and where Marissa would strike. This belief was confirmed as time and time again the whip was intercepted by wind just before it could hit one of their allies. The few times the whip made it past Marcus's efforts though, the effects were instant.

Chaotic mana would crackle from her whip, making it visible for a moment, flowing directly into her target. The targets were almost always Gold Tier wolfkin, and on impact the poor creatures became instantly possessed in a sense. Blake could see the Chaos mana flow into them, wrapping tightly around their souls. The moment that happened, they instantly began attacking their former clan mates and allies. Marissa's whip, her powers, were those of corruption, seduction, and control. Even though she was armed with dangerous claws and impressive speed and strength, what they really needed to worry about were her abilities.

Which, would have been fine one on one. In fact, as they finished off the demons she had summoned, the battle was starting to get easier. With the mobs out of the way, and the prolonged time on the battlefield allowing Marcus to begin setting invisible traps of his, it was becoming easier to pin down the demon and avoid her invisible whip. Unfortunately, she wasn't out of tricks.

Just as the last demon fell, she reappeared for a mere instant to show them a wicked smile. "I hope you enjoyed the foreplay." She chuckled darkly and twisted about both her wrists, as if stretching or cracking them. A set of chains appeared in her hands. With a smile, she tugged at the chains. From behind her, just in front of the glowing crystal, a crackling door appeared. The chains were connected to the front of the door, and with her tug, they began to open.

From behind the door came something even more terrifying than her fallen demon forces. From it came adventurers —or at least, what had once been adventurers. That much was obvious from their gear, and Blake recognized a few from his time at the Adventurers' Guild. They were those who'd gone missing during the quest to destroy the corrupted dungeons. While they'd been assumed killed, apparently something much worse had happened. They'd been captured by Marissa.

Not only that but the Succubus must have had her way with them during that time. Nearly all of their souls were covered with chaotic mana, only a hint of their previous affinities remaining. As they stepped through the door, their eyes black and unseeing, the true terror began. Chaos mana crackled all around them and they shifted, unnaturally, twisting and changing, becoming demonic creatures.

While they were definitely no longer their former selves as they transformed, Blake could see their souls flare. With their transformations, the Chaotic power within them grew. As they took on their demonic forms, they assumed an even greater power than before, putting them easily on par with Platinum adventurers. The battle was again an uphill one.

"Blake," a voice came from around his neck as he fought, grabbing at his attention. Ryan was calling to him. "I need your help to take down the Exalted One." Blake managed to keep his composure enough to block the attack that had been launched at him by one of the adventurer demons. That didn't seem to be his only worry. For at the sound of Ryan's voice, Marissa's full attention turned to him.

"I don't think so," she said, chuckling again, reappearing for a moment to look at him. Her eyes blazed hungrily, and she stayed visible as her whip lashed out towards him. It moved with unnatural speed, Chaos mana crackling along it as it flew towards him. He went incorporeal, allowing the weapon to phase through him even as he positioned himself to avoid an oncoming sword blade as well. When he let his Ethereal mana fade, swinging his bone sword into the demon before him and cutting deeply into the creature, he couldn't help but feel a pang of regret.

This was another life he'd been too weak to save. And he

could only imagine how many had already been lost on the battlefield. He had no idea how long they'd even been fighting, but it felt like a lifetime. Everyone around him was starting to waver. They were all nearing their limits. While they had vast powers, prolonged fights such as this where they were required to utilize all of their focus, their skills, and abilities, were draining. And while the Diamonds were still going strong, having a larger supply of mana to pull from —and a quicker refresh rate—the Platinum's were starting to slow. Even worse, he could tell more and more of the Golds were falling, too. Sasha and Rasha's pack numbers were quickly diminishing.

"Thanks, Darling," Marissa said sweetly, her eyes looking past Blake. His mind paused for a moment at the statement before he turned around. What he saw sent a chill down his spine.

Rasha's massive soul was moving rapidly away from Blake, the Dark mana of the Platinum 1 wolfkin's soul showing the telltale signs of Chaos mana. In his effort to dodge Marissa's whip, he'd allowed her to strike the wolfkin fighting alongside him. Blake had reacted instantly and saved himself...and put Rasha in danger.

He tried to respond, but the wolfkin was already near its target. Even as Blake sent out a wave of Ethereal mana, he knew it was going to be too late. His reaction time, his mana, both were fatigued from the fighting they'd already been doing. All he could do was cry out, "Karan."

The bishop looked at him just in time to see the massive form of Rasha rise out of her shadow, his eyes blazing with bloodlust as he thrust both of his Darkness blades at her. There was no way Blake could protect her. Nothing he could do to save—

Karan's form was thrown to the side as Jack barreled into her. The Duelist shoved her aside, using his Wind mana to catch her as she fell, even as he turned his blades to block Rasha's. Unfortunately, in his rush to get there, the Duelist was unable to fully block the attack. Because Rasha hadn't just been attacking with his blades. Instead, Darkness mana had rushed all around his feet, sending countless shadow spikes upwards to where Karan had been moments before. Blake watched, powerless, as Jack was impaled by dozens of massive, shadowy spears.

"No!" Karan's scream ripped through the battlefield. It was full of anguish and rage. But it wasn't the only sound that filled the battlefield. For, even as Jack slumped, his blood falling to the ground, another form rushed to where he had been. Sasha barreled past Jack's bloodied form and tackled her corrupted twin to the ground.

With her brother pinned, Sasha let out a massive roar, and Blake saw her moon shaped crown flash with brilliance. Mana flowed off her, and the Chaos mana tainting Rasha dissipated, Sasha somehow overcoming the compulsion placed on him by Marissa's legendary whip.

At the same time, Karan rushed towards Jack, her form glowing brilliantly. Jack had suffered extensive damage, and Karan was going to use a large amount of her remaining mana to heal him. In his momentary lapse of judgement, with him going ethereal to avoid Marissa's attack, he'd caused all of this. Because of him, his party was extending more mana and resources than they could afford to. His moment of failure was going to cost them this fight.

"Blake." Ryan's voice echoed through the pendant again. The dungeon core was adamant. But Blake couldn't leave this situation as it was. He couldn't abandon his party. They needed him. Now, more than ever, he couldn't abandon them. If he left now, their fate would be sealed.

Even if he stayed, he wasn't sure they were going to win this. Not now, not after the damage he'd just caused. If something didn't change, this fight was over. He looked over the battlefield and his mind was made up. Ryan needed him. His party needed him.

At least…that was what he'd always told himself. But he realized that had been a lie. They didn't need him. He wasn't strong enough. They needed something better, something more powerful than he was. They didn't need a Platinum 1 Specter of Balance. They didn't need Blake anymore. If he couldn't save them then he was just dead weight.

"I'll be there soon," he said into the pendant. Without hesitation, he pulled the gemstone from his pocket. Then, he did as Blaine had told him. He channeled his mana into the gemstone, opening himself up to it. The gem responded, glowing brilliantly, before it erupted in his hand. For a second, the world, everything around him, seemed to freeze.

From the corner of his eye, he saw a reaper appear holding in its hand an hourglass. The reaper tipped the hourglass, and from it, mana rushed into him. His body came to life with visible golden and black mana crackling about him as he forcibly ascended. He knew doing so would mean his death, but he didn't care. His party, Ryan, the adventurers… everyone needed this of him.

They needed the power of a Judicator.

Chapter Eighty-Two

As the power finished rushing into him, the world seemed to unfreeze. Or at least partially. With the influx of mana flowing into him, his senses heightened once again, and he felt as if the world were moving slower. He now wielded over 38,000 points of mana, meaning his physical traits, enhanced by eighty percent of that mana, had skyrocketed. His body, previously empowered by 15,360 points of mana, was now enhanced by 30,720 points of mana. In other words, his power had instantly doubled.

With the vast amount of power flowing into him, his mind was filled with all the skills and abilities at his disposal. That had been another aspect of the item. Using it unlocked the full potential of the next Tier and class. To tempt those to use such a taboo item, the Gods had given it the ability to make sure they were at their peak for the short amount of time they had. And the skills and abilities of the next Tier for a class were often what truly caused the spike in power.

According to Blaine, the crystalized remains of the Dungeon of Ashes served as a legendary item. It wasn't certain where it came from, only that it could be obtained by slaying dungeons of Platinum or higher. However, the item normally only dropped if it was slain by a Diamond Tier individual. This was because the item itself was meant to serve as a tempting tool for Diamond Tier individuals, similar to cursed items. Using the item could grant a god-like ability, but at a cost.

According to Blaine, it was rumored Alice had lost her ability to have children when she'd used one herself, after her son had been killed by the Dungeon of Ashes. In her grief, she had been chasing god-like power that would allow her to bring him back. Instead, she got her mysterious eyes, rumored to let her see flashes of various futures a person could experience. A power she fought constantly against, a power that could have driven her mad.

Because Blake wasn't yet Diamond Tier, the crystalized core amplified his powers, forcibly ascending him to Diamond, allowing him to bypass the normal process. Which was important, because there was no way would he have been able to ascend to Diamond otherwise. After all, the tools needed to ascend, as a Celestial user, were hoarded by the Church. It was obvious he wasn't going to be able to use those, even if he could get the artifacts needed for his Dark affinity. However, as Blaine had informed him, the item was said to cause death after a short amount of time. And the appearance of the reaper at Blake's side, confirmed that fact.

Still, Blake had carried it into battle. Because while it may kill him, he knew he couldn't pass up the chance to save those he cared about. If it came down to himself or those he loved, he would gladly trade his life for theirs. And so, with Ryan calling for his help, with his team outnumbered, Blake had done the logical thing. The only thing he could.

His eyes locked on Marissa, the Demon's eyes uncertain for the first time. Even as one of her twisted demonic adventurers swung its weapon at him, he made himself go incorporeal. In doing so, the weapon passed through him harmlessly. At least, that's what would normally happen. This time, as the creature passed through his incorporeal form, the Ethereal mana drained the very essence of the creature. He forcibly ripped the poor creature's mana from its body, a penance it had to pay for touching his ethereal form. As a Judicator, he didn't need to utilize his Spectral Grasp. Anything that touched his Ethereal mana could be drained.

Without looking away from Marissa, Blake spread his mana outwards. He used the increase in his mana to make all his allies, save for Cane and Marcus, go ethereal. As every one of them now became impossible to hit, Blake drew in all the mana from the creatures attacking them, stockpiling even more Chaotic mana within his reserves as his vast quantity of Ethereal mana faded.

Normally, he'd have been worried about that, but here, now, he couldn't be bothered. On this battlefield, surrounded by the death of countless adventurers, he had access to even more mana in the form of the grey, drained souls left behind by the reapers. As his Ethereal mana began to deplete, it refilled, nearly instantly, from the very souls of the slain, twisted members Marissa had summoned to fight against them.

"No." Marissa's eyes widened as she watched Blake take a step towards her. He willed Darkness mana from around him into his armor and his sword. He willingly shattered his bone sword to send the shards flying towards Marissa, wrapping around her, pinning her to the ground with strong strands of darkness. At the same time, he sent his mana to those of the wolfkin who'd fallen. They couldn't be saved, yet they could still be used. With a lack of emotion brought about by necessity, he pulled the bones from them, using these to finish off the demonic forces who'd already had much of their mana drained.

"You can't kill me." Marissa said defiantly as Blake approached. "You don't have the mana." She cackled even as the Darkness mana around her tightened. "Even with your powers. A true demon like me cannot be killed by something like you." Her eyes flashed with Chaotic mana, and the binding Darkness mana around her began to fade away. Blake pushed more of it into the bonds, forcing the power into her, cutting deep into her flesh. Still, it sizzled and crackled, her mana fighting against the bonds. "You cannot kill me. I've been blessed by the God of Chaos. I've been chosen by the Exalted One. I am protected from all but the God of Chaos's weapons."

She was growing frenzied now, struggling against her bondage, screaming gleefully as he drew ever closer towards her.

"Then what if I killed you with one of his weapons?" Blake pulled the legendary sword from his back. The twisted, Chaotic blade he'd gotten from his father, the weapon they'd armed Sean with when they'd twisted him to the sides of Chaos. Blake had never understood the weapon and had been unable to draw its power out. But now, with the Chaos mana he'd drained from those demonic creatures around him, he figured he would be able to draw out its power.

The Succubus looked at the sword, laughing as Blake's hand lit up with Chaotic mana. The black and red energy raced along the sword. Dark, twisted runes lit up across the blade, carved in a jagged, chaotic script.

"You're a fool." She chuckled. "You cannot wield that blade." Blake felt the Chaotic mana flowing from him into it, rushing rapidly into the weapon, which was trying to draw more and more from him. It was as if the blade thirsted for it. If it was so hungry, Blake figured he would oblige. After all, if anything could kill a true demon, it had to be a legendary weapon.

"Only demons can wield those weapons. You've killed your—" She stopped talking as the last drops of Chaos mana Blake had were sucked into the blade. Instead of stopping its hunger, Blake felt it reach further within him, drawing into it his Celestial mana as well. The runes on the hilt, the Scales of Justice the Goddess had inscribed upon it, began to glow.

"Impossible." Marissa's bravado was gone. In its place, true fear. Blake felt his Celestial mana continue to rush into the sword, golden light tracing along with the Chaotic mana, twisting, merging. The demonic runes flickered as golden Celestial runes appeared, as if transposed over it. The crackling, twisted sword shimmered, shifting from demonic to a blade Blake had seen once before. A blade that looked extremely similar to the Sword of Justice.

It shifted and twisted, Chaotic and Celestial mana pulsing into it, changing its form over and over again, until it finally solidified. The hilt was pure gold, formed in the shape of a set of scales, the scales of Justice. On one side of the scales was an opal, on the other, a bloodstone. In the middle was a larger gem, a brilliant diamond glowing with a pure, white light.

The blade itself had become a weapon of pure mana. No more was there twisted steel or metal. Instead, it was pure, condensed, mana. White mana, the mana of Life. Somehow, the swords had taken his Celestial and Chaos mana and fused the two together. Somehow, the two legendary swords had merged into something even greater.

"Behold." As he looked at it, a name appeared in glowing, golden light. "The Sword of Creation." He leveled the sword towards her. "It is time you face justice." And with that, he swung the blade down at Marissa. The weapon passed through her form, as if she wasn't even there. It left no cut, no wound, but her body glowed white. A moment later, her Chaos mana began to fade away, and her demonic form dissipated. In its place, a much younger Marissa was revealed. A kinder, gentler woman.

This new Marissa was shocked, a tumult of emotions flickering across her face. Then her eyes sought out her brother.

"I'm sorry, Marcus," she said. Her eyes were no longer crazed. They were kind, caring eyes. "I'm sorry for everything." A single tear flowed from her eye, as her form began to fade. Marcus was there in an instant, his hands holding hers, his eyes pained. This Marissa was a simpler, purer form. She wasn't the Cult of Chaos' leader. This was Marissa as she had been, before her corruption.

"No." Marcus shook his head, tears filling his eyes. "I'm the one who let you down." His voice cracked. "Forgive me."

She smiled and lifted a hand up to his face. Then, Marissa faded away to nothingness as her faint voice was lost to the winds around the Whisperer. Blake wasn't sure what he'd just witnessed, but he had no doubt it had to do with the power of his blade.

"Blake." Ryan's voice was desperate now, and Blake turned his attention back to the battlefield. With Marissa's death, the demonic side of the forces were slain. All that remained was the Vampire, and Blake was certain Cane, Marcus, and the others would have no trouble dealing with her. A quick glance at the reaper by his side told him he needed to hurry.

"I'm on my way," He responded to Ryan.

"I'm sure you know," Blake said in response to Marcus's gaze. The Whisperer gave him a sad nod. From the look in his eyes, the poor man was nearing his own limit, emotionally, at least. Hopefully, Blake and Ryan could finish this fight soon, so Marcus wouldn't have to deal with too much more death.

He turned his gaze towards Karan and Jack. The wolfkin

was healed, and Karan and the Duelist were both looking questioningly towards Blake. He simply offered them a smile, trying his best not to let his voice crack. "Everything will be okay now, I promise." And with that, before he could break, he turned and ran. With his powers, he stepped from the physical plane to the ethereal one, allowing him to move even quicker across the battlefield. His powers were already waning, he was running out of time. They needed to finish Solomon off, and quickly.

Before Blake died.

Chapter Eighty-Three

RYAN

Ryan wasn't sure what Blake had done to anger the Exalted One. But he was certain it had been the adventurer, considering the timing. One second Ryan was hard at work trying to break down the Exalted One's barrier to no avail, while letting Trogdor freely slaughter all the Church members near them, the next second the Exalted One's face flashed with anger. The mana flowing from him amplified once again, creating a physical burst of energy that Ryan could feel, At least…as well as a skeletal body *could* feel.

"I must admit," the Exalted One, a hint of anger on his voice as he looked down at Ryan. The mana roiling off him was so intense now it was washing away any strands of Darkness mana that flowed near him. That, combined with the fact the Church members were now nearing Diamond levels of strength, had put Ryan on edge. It had also increased his sense of urgency. Whatever the Exalted One had been planning, he was certain they were nearing the finale.

"You and your Adventurers have destroyed quite a few of my pawns." He glanced back towards the rear of the camp. A large battle had been taking place at the very back of the camp earlier, and Ryan had been able to tell that Blake and his friends had been fighting back there. A quick check in the area showed Marissa and the demonic forces she'd had at her side were all gone. Additionally, Blake's force was making short work of the Vampire they were fighting. *Good job, Blake.*

"Maybe you should take better care of your things," Ryan retorted. He summoned a set of bone walls just in time to intercept a few attacks that had been heading towards a group of adventurers. They nodded towards him in thanks before continuing on with the fighting.

"Tools are tools," Solomon said simply. His anger was gone, replaced again with his calm, collected tone. "Mine all served their purpose. The time I've been waiting for is nearly here." The white light around him flashed once again, bolstering his followers further. Ryan glanced around, panicked. Where was Blake? How long before the man got here? They needed to stop whatever it was that was about to happen. He could tell that much, in the pit of his core. "Perhaps you should have chosen better pawns for yourself," the Exalted one said, chuckling as he smiled darkly towards Ryan.

"The adventurers aren't pawns," Ryan responded. "They are valued companions." As he spoke a figure materialized behind Solomon. A split second later, Solomon let out a pained gasp, and Ryan couldn't help but let out a chuckle. Blake had arrived, his Ethereal mana flowing powerfully around him. His hand touching the Exalted One's back as the hilt of a strange, brilliant sword passed through Solomon's skin. A solidified blade of white light protruded from his chest.

"Impossible," Solomon grunted, looking down at the weapon. For a single moment the light around him faded. Blake's stab had not only pierced the man but had also passed through the pendant he wore. *Go, Blake.*

"Adventurers do the impossible daily," Blake responded, puling the blade free as he stepped away from the Exalted One. The white light stopped pulsing from him, and the glow around the members of the Church started to fade. Their movements began to slow, and Ryan could tell they were losing the power boost Solomon had given them.

The Exalted One placed his hand on his chest once more as a white light started to surround him. To Ryan's surprise, there wasn't a single mark on the man from where Blake's sword had pierced him. Yet, it had done damage. His pendant had been destroyed.

"Adventurers should know their place." Solomon's gaze turned dark. His face twisted into a mask of anger, and the man's eyes blazed with crackling, chaotic energy. In an instant his visage changed into that of a demon as a golden axe appeared in his hands. A split second later, the axe was swinging directly towards Blake. Ryan summoned a bone wall to slow the attack, even as Blake's form went ethereal. The golden axe blasted through the bone wall, sending fragments flying out in all directions, but passed harmlessly through Blake. Solomon grunted in surprise yet again.

"Perhaps you should know your place," Ryan's favorite adventurer said before his form returned to the physical world. He pointed his hand towards Solomon and a spear of white light appeared. The weapon blasted into Solomon's chest, reminiscent of what had happened to Alice.

Again, Solomon let out a grunt of pain, his hand pulling the weapon from his chest. His body flashed with white light, but it quickly faded away. "That's not enough Life mana to defeat me." He grinned, flexing his hands. Ryan watched as the man's muscles bulged, demonic flesh crawling over him. He was undergoing a demonic transformation, which would greatly enhance his physical traits.

"My turn," Ryan said smugly. Now that Solomon's barrier

was down, Ryan could join the fray properly. As Solomon prepared to attack Blake, Ryan rushed in, summoning a spikey bone shield onto his Avatar's arm as he did. The shield had bone shards reinforced with Darkness mana, which he slammed into the Exalted One. The shield pierced armor, but stopped against the flesh, even though each spike had to be as large as the Exalted One's limbs, and insanely sharp. He had put all of the force of his Avatar, his Diamond Tier manifestation, into that attack. How tough was this man?

"You're going to need either a *lot* more of that inferior mana—" Solomon pushed against Ryan's shield. The bones began to crack. "—Or some actual Life mana, to hurt me." With inhuman strength Ryan's Avatar was sent flying backwards as if he were no more than a sack of flour. Even as he was sent away though, Blake rushed in, taking advantage of the opening Ryan had made.

At least, the perceived opening. As the adventurer stepped forward, he was forced to suddenly go ethereal as a deadly-looking tail, which had grown from Solomon's lower back, lashed out at him. It was a long, twisting appendage, much like Hel's, though this one appeared to drip some sort of venom from the end. Even as Blake faded from the physical realm, the tail stopped before it touched the adventurer. Solomon was hesitant to let it get too near to Blake.

Blake, seeing the chance, swung his gleaming sword downwards, solidifying his arm and the weapon in time to slice into the tail. Again, the weapon passed through, but left no wound behind. Instead, a white light flashed on the tail, showing the path of the blade, before the light faded away.

"You've no idea what you're doing with that sword." Solomon chuckled. "You're wielding the most powerful sword in existence, and you've no idea how to use it." His tail lashed out at Blake once more, forcing the adventurer to go ethereal again. Solomon's hands glowed brightly, and he created two gleaming swords of white light. Unlike Blake's, they were solely made of mana and not legendary artifacts.

"We need to do something," Hel said from behind Ryan. Ryan got to his feet and gauged the battle, looking for openings as Solomon and Blake clashed. The Exalted One was still radiating too much Life mana for him to get any of his mobs closer. And his attacks didn't have enough power to penetrate the man's defenses fully. But Blake's sword, formed of Life mana, was cutting easily into the Exalted One. Was Life mana the key? If so, how was Ryan supposed to get his hands on that?

What he really needed was a weapon with Life mana. He was seriously envious of Blake's sword.

"I grow tired of you." Solomon said as Blake shifted out of existence once more. Blake was using a lot of mana, and Ryan had noticed that the soul fragments around them had been quickly dispersing. Blake must have been using them to fuel his power. It was a neat trick, but one that had limits. It also stole soul fragments Ryan had been planning to use to create mobs. Sharing a limited resource, in a fight such as this, was not ideal. But considering Blake was actually hurting Solomon, he figured this was a better use of the souls.

"That makes two of us," Blake said as he lunged at the Exalted One. Ethereal mana erupted from Blake, washing over the battlefield immediately surrounding him and Solomon. As it did, the tendrils of mana that touched Solomon stole some of the color from him, creating a pallid plane of existence. "How about we finish this?"

Blake's eyes closed and he swung the sword downward at Solomon. As he did, sets of scythes appeared from the grey Ethereal mana surrounding them, also swinging towards Solomon. The weapons clashed against his side, digging in deep, though again, without cutting into flesh.

Instead, Ryan could see them seem to shift within the man, crossing to connect against his mana, his core... his soul. In response, a flash of Life energy pulsed from within Solomon. The scythes shattered and the ground was instantly cleared of the Ethereal mana. Blake was sent flying backwards. As he landed Ryan watched him intentionally release his sword, the blade flying a good hundred feet away from him and landing on the ground. *Crafty Blake.*

"Trading your life may have granted you temporary power," Solomon said, raising a clawed hand as his white spear appeared in his hands again. "But I wield powers greater than you could ever fathom." The spear was sent forward, flying towards Blake's chest.

The adventurer, instead of looking scared, smiled at Solomon. That smile was the only warning the man got.

"Thanks for the sword," Ryan said happily as he swung his newly summoned Sword of Creation towards Solomon. Ryan had summoned it for himself mere seconds after he consumed the one Blake had thrown away, right onto the ground that was now part of his influence. Because of the size of Ryan's Avatar, his Sword of Creation was as large as Solomon.

Ryan swung the sword downwards with impossible force, amazed at how much mana it drew from him. He understood why Blake had been consuming so many soul fragments—the sword demanded a high cost to stay empowered.

Still, he was glad to pay that cost if it meant Solomon could be defeated. The blade passed through the man, cutting easily through his form. Just as when Blake had used it, the weapon didn't sever the man. Instead, it left a trail of white light, to show how Ryan's blade had cut through him. A normal weapon would have cleaved Solomon in two. On second thought, a normal weapon wouldn't have cut into the man at all.

Solomon's spear disappeared as he stepped backwards, his eyes looking up in surprise at Ryan's Avatar. He stumbled for a moment, his body pulsing white, as he took a knee. His eyes flashed with light and his demonic form faded for a moment. White Life mana pulsed across him, and Ryan could tell that mana wasn't Solomon's own. This was the Sword of Creation's doing.

"No," the Hero of Justice said quietly as the strength seemed to begin to fade from him. "No," he said again. His face shifted, and he was once again the man Ryan had seen yesterday. The scarred leader of the Church, half his face human, the other half burned and ruined.

Ryan stood triumphantly, his Avatar towering over Solomon, noticing that Blake was slowly getting to his feet and heading towards Solomon's side. Ryan swung the sword again, knowing better than to give Solomon an opening. Ryan had watched plenty of boss fights to know your foe was always strongest when you thought him defeated.

"No." Solomon's eyes flashed with power as his voice echoed across the battlefield. More white light surrounded him.

"You've lost." Ryan's sword passed once again through Solomon, this time horizontally, the blade slicing through the man's chest. Once again it left behind no visible wound. Solomon's body flashed with white light, the energy pulsing through him. He began to glow a pure white, the light completely enveloping him. This was just what Ryan had seen happen to Alice before she started to fade away.

And this is when he disappears. Ryan thought. And then a gleaming spear crashed into his chest as Solomon's form, instead of disappearing, completely solidified. *Wha—*

Chapter Eighty-Four

The tip of the spear was pressed against Ryan's diamond core. The weapon, one formed of Chaos mana, twisted violently as Solomon tried to drive it deeper into him. Ryan's hands clutched at it, his eyes focusing on the man. He should be dead. He'd cut the man so many times with that legendary sword. Not to mention all the attacks Blake had done. *Blake.*

He glanced downwards and to his right to see Blake skewered by a multitude of glowing weapons. Celestial spears, Chaos spears, and in Solomon's other hand, a glowing spear of white life mana, pierced deep into Blake's chest. Had Solomon been toying with them the whole time? He'd let them think they had the advantage. He'd feigned all of that? There was no way. No human way.

"I'm sure you're confused," Solomon said, as even more weapons punched into Ryan's Avatar. It was all he could do to encircle his core with as much mana as possible, to keep them from driving any deeper inside. Every ounce of Ryan's power was now focused on keeping his core safe.

"How?" Blake croaked out. His form was flickering with grey mana. It was clear Blake was trying to go ethereal, yet unable to do so. Whatever the Exalted One had done to him held him captive.

"I told you before. Anyone who stood before me today would die." He chuckled, raising a hand to the sky. White light again pulsed from him, rushing out across the battle-field. "This mana, the mana of life, isn't even the secret to my strength." He grinned, puling more mana outwards. "The real secret is in my core."

From the back of the army the diamond core suddenly disappeared, reappearing high above Solomon, floating there as it pulsed with a white light.

"No mortal, no matter how powerful, can harness enough mana to become a god." He said simply. More and more glowing weapons appeared around Ryan and Blake. Solomon was enjoying this.

"That was a universal truth in my time. The strongest you could ever hope to climb, was Diamond 1. God Tier is a myth. An impossible task." He grinned. "At least, for most."

The orb above him began to glow brighter. "The final aspect to reach godhood was to be able to harness the amount of mana needed to ascend and become a god. Luckily for me, with Life mana, and enough time, I could create a vessel capable of holding that type of power." He smiled. "I could create an orb of my own. To harness all the power of Life once again. With my hands, I could become the true God of Life."

He rose a hand towards the glowing orb. A connection of light appeared between the two, the white mana flashing between himself and the orb. "You see? With the power of Life, I was able to craft this orb from the shattered cores of hundreds of dungeons. I started collecting them long ago, when I tempted the Church, and man along with it, to turn against the dungeons, claiming them to be evil. Then, with my core created, I needed to make sure no one else could do as I'd done. To ensure no one could grow in power to rival mine. That was why I ordered my followers to corrupt the remaining dungeons. So the Church and Adventurers Guild would remove them.

Prior to the start of this battle, I linked myself to the orb I'd created. And since then, every time someone touched by my mana has died, a portion of their power has funneled into this orb. Sure, I could have killed everyone back in Libertus, or some other city. But doing so would have tainted my name."

He laughed, spreading his arms wide. "This way, everyone will know I ascended trying to save the world from the last dungeon. I ascended leading the Church on its final crusade. I will be revered. And so, I suppose I should thank you for your help today, in playing the part of the villain, and slaughtering all these poor souls." The mana between Solomon and the orb intensified.

"Now—" More mana pulsed from Solomon, completely coating the remainder of the battlefield. Both Ryan's forces and the Church of Justice's, began to glow white. "Now that I've got both of you on Death's door, I can eliminate the rest of this battlefield and claim my place as a God."

The ground began to rumble, and Solomon's smile widened, showing his fangs. "It is always said, the victor writes the history books. Today will go down in history as the day the Bone Dungeon betrayed those who tried to help him. And that only I, Solomon, God of Life, was able to stop him and return balance to the world."

Ryan was done listening now. He'd taken in everything he needed to, and he knew what had to be done. He couldn't help but berate himself for not doing this sooner. Solomon was right about one thing; Ryan had betrayed those who tried to help him. Had Ryan done as the God of Death asked—if Ryan had given his life to the God of Death at the beginning of this battle, all of this could have been stopped. Everyone who had come to help him, everyone who had died on the battlefield today, could have been spared. How selfish had Ryan been, to think his path was the correct one. To think his life was worth more than all those around him. He'd been a fool.

"I'm sorry," He said mentally to Erin and Hel. He sent a wave of emotion through his bond with them, more emotion and feeling than he'd ever thought he could muster. After all, he was simply a soul trapped within a stone. And yet, he had regret. He felt more sorrow now, as he faced his death head on, than he had when the Church had executed him so long ago. Maybe that was because, unlike then, he now had a purpose. He had a life, he had people dear to him.

In the time he'd been a dungeon core, he'd come to appreciate life and he'd felt more fulfilled than he ever had as a human. Perhaps that had been why he had been so reluctant to give his life to the God of Death. Self-sacrifice was so much harder when you truly had things you loved. Even as their emotions rushed into him, he steeled himself. He couldn't give them a chance to change his mind. Because the thought of leaving them, the mere notion of what they would go through at his sacrifice, almost stopped him. He really was a selfish core.

"Speaking of Gods," Ryan said as he forced his Avatar to smile. It was all he could do to keep his voice steady. "I know of one you've angered." He said these words as he pumped all of the power he had into the Crown of Sorrows atop his head. He'd crafted it, in an artistic way, to appear a part of his skull. In doing so, he'd perhaps hidden the true nature of the item. But as it burst to life, as Ryan's remaining mana went into it, Solomon's eyes widened. This time Ryan was certain that emotion pure, unadulterated horror. This time, he was certain, Solomon wasn't faking it.

"No." Even as Ryan's crown began to glow, as Darkness mana swirled around him, Solomon was moving. The Exalted One's entire body burst with massive amounts of white light, as he summoned hundreds, thousands of weapons all around Ryan. The weapons thrust towards him, and from above, a gleaming blade appeared, descending towards him. "I will not lose. I waited, I calculated everything perfectly. Betraying Chaos to serve Justice simply to trick the Goddess, to climb my way to the seat of power. I suffered agonizing pain. You cannot understand all I've done, all I've thrown away, sacrificed. Everything for this moment. I will not let it be ripped away from me by a—"

Everything froze. Ryan was forced back into his core as Death's full presence overcame him. An omnipotent, overwhelming force unlike anything he'd ever felt before. All of his experiences interacting with Death, he realized, he had barely touched against a fragment of the God's actual presence.

"A wise decision, even if a bit late," Death said in Ryan's mind, even as the God took complete control over all of his powers. *"Self-sacrifice alone is a worthy virtue. But what you've undergone, the ability—the reflection—to understand your faults and realize such truths, and to regret and understand the cost of your actions, is even greater. It is an honorable trait. Now, then, as promised."*

Ryan watched, in a disjointed way, as the world was covered in Dark mana. Every ounce of area he'd spread his influence, the vast two-mile radius of his power, was covered in utter darkness. A split second later, it faded away, leaving obvious changes behind.

First, his Avatar had transformed. No longer was it the hulking visage he'd created. Instead, it was a simple skeletal man, covered in a plain purple robe, his form hunched over. In his skeletal hand he clutched a staff, atop which Ryan's core sat. The old skeleton looked down at Solomon, who appeared frozen in time. In fact, nothing around them moved, save for Death.

"Hubris. The greatest flaw of the living. Alone, that sin would have simply brought you to my doorstep but instead, you combined it with countless others. You wanted to become a God, yet to become one, you must care about others, not yourself. To be divine is not to rule. As a God, I rule over nothing. No...my power, all of my siblings' powers, they were meant solely to care for and protect what was passed onto us. I am no ruler. I am but a simple caretaker." He snapped his fingers, and the Exalted One was unfrozen. The man's eyes glanced at Death, and he stuttered, his rant stopping at his lips.

"How?" Solomon tried to step forward, but his entire body was chained with Dark mana. Behind him, Ryan saw a reaper patiently waiting. "I did everything right. It wasn't supposed to happen like this. This shouldn't be happening." He squirmed and fought, but even as he did, Ryan could see the mana flowing from his body into the reaper's lantern. "Again, you would thwart me." Solomon hissed. He spit towards Death's feet. "I knew why you joined my side during the war. I knew you were there to simply ensure balance. That's why I switched sides. Because I knew, then and there, you would never let me grow otherwise." He laughed, his eyes going wide. White light began to swirl around him.

"You aren't a God. You're a tyrant." He continued to struggle, his muscles flexing. The strands of Darkness mana grew denser, fighting to hold him in place. "You speak of your righteousness. You sound like her." He spit again, he was practically frothing. "If anyone is to blame, it's her. She's not fit to lead. She's not fit to be a God. BUT I AM." With a massive heave he ripped free of the Darkness mana. The core high above him glowed brightly, flashing with pure white light, as power ripped into Solomon. "I WILL BECOME THE NEXT—"

Death let out a sigh and stamped his staff on the ground. A rush of power flowed through Ryan's core, the sheer amount of it greater than anything he'd ever felt. Compared to it, his might at Diamond felt like a drop in a pond. It was overwhelming. "You've avoided death for far too long. Come. Rest, and learn what it means to live." All the light around Solomon instantly vanished. His body went grey as his soul was pulled from his body. It hovered for a moment before it flowed into the lantern of the reaper. All that was left of the Diamond 1 dual affinity user, was a simple soul fragment. A soul fragment exactly like all the others Ryan had seen. In death, all things were perfectly equal.

"Please." Ryan's consciousness was still confined to his orb, just as Death had mentioned. It wasn't until Death left, that he was supposed to die. "Spare Blake." Ryan wasn't certain what Blake had done. All he knew was, whatever it was, Blake's time was limited. The sand in the hourglass the reaper beside him was holding was nearly out. Not to mention all the wounds the man had received...

"Blake..." Death looked down at him. The adventurer was lying there, frozen in time by Death's power. "Blake has broken an ancient taboo," Death stated simply. "He did so willingly, to violate the rules of the Gods. Such items were created as a test. To use them in this way is a grave sin." Death moved slowly towards the adventurer. "However, the world finds itself at a unique moment in time." He held out a skeletal hand, gently touching Blake's face. The amount of tenderness in that touch, from the God of Death no less, took Ryan by surprise.

"In the last two days, the world has seen the loss of more Diamond Tier individuals than ever before. And now, with all the death that has occurred today, there is an imbalance. To leave this power vacuum, to leave things as they are, could undo all I am working to fix." He sent a pulse of power into Blake, and the reaper standing behind him faded away. At the same time, all of Blake's injures closed up.

"For his actions today, and for all he has done for me, I will spare him. Today, his existence, his survival, works in favor of the balance." Death chuckled slightly. "Unlike you, this man seems to have good luck when it comes to escaping the calling of Death." Ryan did not appreciate Death's gallows humor.

"About my fate—" Ryan started. Death silenced him with a thought.

"Patience, my dear core." Death pointed his staff at the massive core Solomon had created. The core shattered instantly, and from it all the souls, all the life Solomon had absorbed, were sent free. Reapers appeared instantly, harvesting all of the souls, doing whatever it was that Death did with the cores.

"Now then." He took a step away from Blake and turned towards an empty portion of the battlefield. He set the staff with Ryan's core in front of him as he rose both his hands. He pointed towards the ground with each hand and sent a massive pulse of mana into the earth. The rock and soil twisted violently, as Dark mana rippled across the ground. Slowly, ever so slowly, two massive structures formed before them.

The first had strange white pillars with sculptures of angels adorning it. A golden, inviting light drifted deep within it. The other one had massive, black chains crossing the front of it, and demonic statues stood guard on either side. Within, Chaos mana crackled back and forth. These were dungeon entrances.

Death stood before the two entrances for a moment, waiting patiently. After a few minutes, two figures appeared.

One, from the dungeon with the white pillars, was a woman in gleaming armor, her face exhausted. The other, stepping toward the chains, a man, his eyes blazing with madness. They looked nearly identical. If Ryan had to guess, they were twins.

"Brother, sister," Death said simply. The two looked at him, the female nodding, the man scowling.

"What do you want, D?" The male asked, his voice irritated. "Come to gloat some more?"

Death looked hard at him and the man flinched, stepping backwards.

"Is it done, then?" The female asked, looking from Death to their surroundings. Her eyes lingered for a long moment on Blake.

"For now," Death responded calmly. He looked at the two. "Finally, the last remnants of what you two released upon the world have been dealt with."

The man, whom Ryan figured was the God of Chaos, scoffed. "We *all*," he stressed, "decided living creatures should have free will. That's not my problem."

"Faust," The female, the Goddess of Justice, said. She looked at the God of Chaos, her eyes pleading. "You know we brought this upon the world."

The God of Chaos shook his head. "All we did was create life. How is that our problem? Our father did the same thing."

"We didn't just create life," The Goddess of Justice said. "We neglected our creations. We gave them power and let them run rampant with it. Our infighting allowed this to occur."

The man pointed at Solomon. "That one is yours. He was one of your devout followers. He turned against me in the last war. He's your problem, not mine."

Death chuckled darkly at that. "We both know, Faust, that you had a hand in this."

Faust opened his mouth to speak but stopped as Death raised a hand. "After all, dear brother, I am certain I drained every ounce of Chaos mana from him. Only the act of a God could give him access to that power back."

Faust paled and looked away, refusing to keep eye contact with the skeletal form of Death.

Death continued. "The sins of the both of you are great. Whether or not you accept that," Death shrugged, "is not my concern."

Before the God of Chaos could speak, the Goddess of Justice looked at Death, bowing her head. "How can we atone for all the trouble we've caused?" Ryan could tell, just by looking at her, that she carried a lot of weight upon her shoulders. He had no doubt she blamed all of this on herself. At that, his distaste for her faded. How could it not—only someone who truly believed in justice was willing to enforce it upon themselves.

Death pointed towards the remnants of Solomon's orb, where the reapers were still harvesting souls. "While that mortal did nearly manage to recreate the Orb of Life, he did it the wrong way."

"What's broken, is broken. What's done, is done," Death continued. "Life mana shall never again be a part of this world." He held out a hand towards the twins. "To atone for the damage to this world the two of you caused, both directly and indirectly, your time as Gods has come to an end. Our father, the World Smith, did not give us these powers to cause such disorder in his world. More importantly, our father would not like what has become of his two youngest children. It is time the two of you simply lived. Being a God was too much a burden for the two of you."

"What—that's preposterous! You don't have the—" Before the God of Chaos could continue his tirade, Death hit his staff on the ground again. Even more power rushed from Ryan, and he watched as two objects appeared from within the dungeon. One, a brilliant shield set with an emblazoned sun, the center of which was a gleaming stone. From behind the God of Chaos, another shield, this one covered with a demonic skull, in the center of which sat another stone. Both gems were only half of a sphere. Two halves of the same stone.

"I do have the power. And I have the duty. I was left to ensure this world was kept balanced. It is my responsibility to do all I can, to do as much. Whether or not it pains me, whether or not it hurts me, is of no matter. I will do what is best for the whole world, even if the two of you are my family."

The God of Chaos thrashed against the chains on his dungeon entrance. His form shifted, his eyes grew crazed, and he began a massive demonic transformation. From behind him, two glowing eyes appeared from deep within his dungeon. "You cannot do this. If you think I will allow you to strip my power from me, you're mad." Before he got any larger, before he could do anything, massive strands of Darkness mana erupted all around him, restraining him. At the same time, a wall of shadows appeared behind him, blocking whatever it was he'd been summoning from within his dungeon.

Death chuckled, though Ryan could feel the sorrow in it. This decision was not easy on the God of Death. Even more so, Ryan got the feeling the skeleton was disappointed in his younger brother. The God of Chaos's actions, his words… Ryan could tell they were exactly why Death was making his decision.

Conversely, the Goddess of Justice looked to be ecstatic. Her eyes were filled with tears, and that exhausted look was fading. At her side, a white tiger appeared. The creature looked up at her with loving eyes, and she glanced down at it, smiling sweetly.

"It's come to an end," she whispered to the tiger. "Finally, this nightmare is over." She looked at Death and bowed her head. From what Ryan could tell, being a Goddess had been hard on her. He got the feeling she was much softer than she appeared. In fact, he had a feeling that Erin's personality, her traits, were a reflection of a different side of the Goddess. He had a feeling she had been suffering at the hands of regret and doubt all this time. To her, this sentence must have seemed like a blessing.

Death smiled at her and love flowed through the God. He cared for his siblings, deeply. He was doing this not just for the world, but for them. "Your sentence will be to walk amongst your creations for all time. You will have no power, other than the power of observation. Live alongside the people you created, and hopefully you can relearn the true importance, the true value, of life. And perhaps you can relearn who you once were and how you used to be."

The two shields floated towards him. As they did, they shrunk, until they were small enough to fit a human.

"From this moment on, this dungeon shall serve as the ambassador for both Celestial and Chaos mana. The Bone Dungeon shall serve as the link between these forces and the world. Because he has proven to the entire world that it is not the type of mana you have but what you do with it."

What? Ryan tried to send a message to the God but found his mental connection with the God blocked.

The God of Death sent the shields towards the frozen forms of Erin and Hel. "And these two shall become the protectors of these orbs."

"As you wish, brother." The Goddess of Justice bowed her head, a relieved smile crossing her face. Centuries worth of aging from worry and stress seemed to fade from her. Ryan could tell she was looking forward to her sentence. The God of Chaos, on the other hand took the news much more violently. He continued to struggle against his bindings, his eyes promising murder the moment he was freed. He was going to be a problem…but without his powers as a God, without any mana, he would be a much smaller problem. At least, Ryan hoped.

"Now then, Ryan." Death looked down at his orb, a smile crossing the God's skeletal face. "How about we renegotiate our deal?

Chapter Eighty-Five

"Are you ready for this?" Erin was excitedly flying around as she spoke. She was covered in her gleaming armor, along with the newest addition to her equipment, the Celestial Shield of Justice. It had been almost a month since that fateful day, the day that had seen a change in the very pantheon of the Gods.

Ryan was still trying to get used to everything going on. So much had changed after that fateful battle. The most important ones, of course, being his change in status with not just the Adventurers' Guild but the world. Now, Boneville was the official Headquarters of the Adventurers' Guild, the town working hand in hand with Ryan to carry out their business. Because of his relationship with the adventurers, he figured it only fitting to keep them close by. It not only ensured extra protection for him, but it also meant he could keep an eye on them. And of course, it let him keep his friends and allies close at hand. Additionally, Death had informed Ryan he was the last dungeon that would ever be created, meaning there was no reason for the Adventurers' Guild to be located, or travel, anywhere else. He was now their one and only stop, save for those who had special relationships with the other deities.

The other big change was that he was no longer just a dungeon. Following that battle, following all that had happened, and his discussion with Death, something else had changed.

Ryan had become a God.

"Give me a minute." Ryan chuckled as searched throughout his dungeon. With the conclusion of the battle he'd been given the powers of a God Tier dungeon. Death had granted him that status and spared his life, in exchange for Ryan's agreement to forever keep the two orbs safe. And while the world had definitely changed after the massive battle and the loss of so many powerful figures, it was imperative that Ryan have the power needed to keep his core room safe.

Which, with the amount of power brimming in him, he could now do. Erin and Hel, on the other hand, had been tasked by Death with ensuring they properly guided those who awoke to either of their mana types. In Death's eyes, their relationship—their growing bond—was reminiscent to how the two siblings should have been. How the twins used to be.

He wanted the world to remember that there was no inherent evil within the world. That it was up to each individual to decide what they did with their power, to become the equalizer. The fairies-turned-Goddesses were expected to carry on those teachings. Ryan could sense that Death secretly hoped someday his younger siblings would return to their former selves. Even more so, he got the feeling Death was hoping to remind those two of what they had once been through Erin and Hel.

Erin was excited about this prospect. Though…Ryan felt sorry for any who sought advice from her. He remembered all too well how terrible she was at teaching. Hel, on the other hand, had been both thrilled and dismayed at her new task. She was more than eager to interact with the living races, but the fact she could no longer manipulate and play with them as she once had, really grated on her. He'd heard her groaning more than a few times that she'd not gotten to have enough fun before godhood had been thrust upon her. Erin was always quick to remind her, life wasn't fair.

Ryan knew that all too well. After all, the only reason he was in this situation, the only reason things had played out like this, was because he'd been unjustly killed, so long ago, by the corrupt followers of the Goddess of Justice. Looking back, Ryan couldn't help but wonder whether it had been happenstance, or something more, that had led to this outcome. Had he always been destined to play a hand in defeating Solomon? Or had things simply worked out that way, based on the combined choices and actions of those involved?

Either way, there was no changing the past. All they could do now was use what they'd been given, to move the future, the world, in the direction it ought to go. A world where everyone could live in harmony. A world where Ryan could enjoy skeletal fight club in peace.

Blake

He slowly put on his armor, fingers tracing across the damaged portions of it. Ryan had offered to give him a new set, but he wanted to keep this one. He wanted to be reminded of just how fragile he was, how fragile everything was. Blake had come close to death too many times to allow himself to forget the gift he'd been given.

According to Ryan, Death had sparred him, even though he'd willingly made the choice to give his life away that day. It seemed unfair, for him to be spared when so many more deserving adventurers than him had died. However, Ryan had told him about what Death had said, about the imbalance in the world, and that Blake's life was meant to keep the balance. After further discussion with Ryan over it, they'd come to a conclusion. Blake would use his life to ensure Ryan's dungeon and his two Goddesses were forever protected. Blake's life, the life Death had spared, was sworn to the Bone Dungeon's safety. For as long as he lived, he and Ryan would forever be connected.

Of course, that didn't mean he had to stay at the dungeon. No, he had a pendant that would allow him to immediately come to Ryan's aid if anything should happen. For now, Ryan and Blake agreed he should go out into the world. Blake's place wasn't within the dungeon, but without. For now, Blake had a mission. To root out any remaining followers of Chaos or corrupt members of the Church and bring them to justice. That was the task of a Judicator.

Additionally, Ryan had asked him to keep an eye out for the former God of Chaos, Faust. They both agreed Faust may try to cause trouble in the world, and so Blake was heading out to ensure any sparks of Chaos he tried to start were stopped before they could cause any more suffering.

And there was an even greater perk to his task. He didn't have to carry it out alone. Following the battle, a lot of things had been put into place, and rapidly. All that had been required, given that the Church of Justice had been all but destroyed and the Adventurers' Guild was a shell of what it had been prior to the battle.

Marcus had taken up the mantle of Guildmaster for the Adventurers' Guild. The Whisperer had proven himself time and time again. Many in the land knew of him and recognized his leadership capability. Unfortunately, Marcus also started his official role as Guildmaster instantly with the ire of one of the other Guilds. Apparently, allowing Emily and Matt to ascend had really angered the Mages' Guild, who were supposed to be in line for the next set of ascensions. Blake was not envious of Marcus for having to deal with those issues.

He had a feeling a part of Marcus's agreement to move the Headquarters of the Adventurers' Guild to Boneville was so he could call on Ryan in case anyone tried to cause the Guild any problems. After all, causing troubles for the Guild was a lot easier in Valta than it was in Boneville.

Even with the political drama already unfurling, Blake was excited for the future of the Guild. Ryan had promised to keep his dungeon open to the masses, ensuring generations of adventurers could continue to grow and flourish. Blake was also excited to see how far Ryan could evolve, and what he would come up with, over time. He was looking forward to trying out Ryan's coliseum. So far, frustratingly, Jack had been the only one to try it and survive. Blake didn't like losing to his friend.

Jack and Karan had a large set of tasks ahead of them as well. Following the battle, it was made clear that Jack's decision to call upon the pack had indebted him to them. After a long conversation and intense negotiations of which Blake was a small part of, an agreement had been worked out.

Jack wouldn't join the pack directly, but he was tasked with ensuring the wolfkin had equal treatment and rights moving forward. This task, Jack was uniquely suited to ensuring, as Karan's new role put the bishop in a huge position of power. Karan had been tasked by Marcus with establishing a new Church, one that was specific to Ryan and his two Goddesses. Jack had wanted to call it the Church of Bones but luckily that had lost in the votes...just barely.

Instead, Karan was to head the Church of Balance. The purpose of this Church was to protect, preserve, and watch over the world. It was to respect life, and keep in perfect harmony the world. And since Jack was to be married to the leader of this new Church—well, he had a good amount of say in what rules and policies the Church set into place.

In response, and as part of the negotiations, Sasha and Rasha promised to pledge themselves and their clan, to the service of the new Church. They would act as a new, elite force for the Church. Their duties were to spread the word of the Church and enforce their teachings. Sasha had even volunteered, rather forcefully, to come with Blake on his quest to root out the remaining opposition forces. She had not given up her chase of him. In fact, now that he was Diamond, she seemed even more intent on claiming him. Her interest in him still left him a little unsettled.

Blake had been saved from those…advances, luckily, by Matt and Emily. The two volunteered to travel with him, much to Sasha's dismay. Blake was looking forward to traveling with them. He considered Matt a brother, and he and Emily had been getting close during all their time together. Blake, with his new view on life, couldn't let this opportunity to travel with such close companions pass him by.

And, while there had already been plenty of interesting things occurring following the battle, one more rose up. For as they were discussing their travel plans, they'd been approached by Blaine. He'd been battered and bloody, looking on the brink of death, and yet still he walked towards them with a purpose. After telling all within earshot of how he'd slain over five-hundred members of the Church, he pulled out a set of rings, looking hard at Matt and Emily. A moment later, he handed them over. They bore the mark of the Dragnov family.

It hadn't been announced, but when Blaine had ascended

to Diamond 3, he'd taken over as the patriarch of the Dragnov family. His father's injuries meant the Duke of Blood was no longer the strongest Dragnov, and by his own laws, unfit to rule.

Blaine, in giving those rings to Emily and Matt, had recognized them as members of the Dragnov family—whether they wanted it or not. Along with that, Blaine had given Emily one last item. Another ring, again bearing the signet of the family, but with a ruby in the middle. Along with it, Blake had heard Blaine tell her she was truly the strongest in the family.

Emily didn't take the ring. Instead, she simply smiled and returned it to him. She'd told him she didn't need a token to show her power. Merely that she knew she was the strongest and would continue to be so. His recognition was all she'd wanted, and it was enough.

Blake couldn't help but feel happy for her. The girl who'd once been so meek, was now likely the most powerful woman in the world. Even as the battle ended, tales had already begun to spread of her and her dragon. They were calling her the Crimson Dragon Queen, and Blake had no doubt no one would ever question Emily's powers again.

"You ready, man?" Jack's voice pulled Blake from his reflections. He smiled as he stepped out of his tent. His party members were all there, waiting for him. His eyes drifted fondly over them all, lingering on Emily for a moment. In response, Cynder leapt happily from her shoulders to land atop Blake's. The baby dragon happily tugged at one of the bones on his armor, and with a thought he released the bone, allowing the dragon to chew happily on it.

"But of course." They'd agreed to do one last dive together before Ryan officially opened, a month after that tragic war. Before they headed out onto a new stage of their lives, they'd come together, once more, to do what had initially started all of this. One last dungeon dive.

They had come so far. He couldn't believe this was where his path had taken him. He'd gone from a young man who'd almost gotten killed on his first dungeon dive, to a man who'd finally found his place in the world. A man who'd found friends and family in the darkest of places. A man who'd reached his goals, and accomplished impossible things, all thanks to the people around him, and a Bone Dungeon named Ryan.

The World Smith

The final words crept across the page as an image in his head lingered. That of the party teleporting just outside of the dungeon's telltale entrance, that of a massive wolf skull. Just as the party stepped within the dungeon, the image faded. His inkwell was dry and as he slid the rolled scroll into the shelf, it fit snuggly, filling it up. He'd told many tales in that particular world and was glad everything had finally worked out. Some of the other scrolls, some of the other tales, hadn't ended as happily.

He wondered at times if he'd done right by leaving the world in the hands of his children. That decision had caused the world, his children, and himself so much pain and suffering. Then again, he hadn't had a choice. He couldn't spend all his time, all his power, on a single world. As a World Smith, he'd been tasked with countless worlds. Spending too much time on one of them, meant the others were neglected. Finding the perfect balance was his burden. Being a World Smith was no simple task.

With that thought, he closed the case on that world, the world of his elemental dungeons and looked around. There were countless other worlds and tales he needed to check up on. After all, if he didn't record the history of the worlds he created, who would? A flicker of light from one of his writing desks caught his attention. The light shimmered more brightly this time and he could tell within his soul what the next tale was. There was a new world ready for him to create. A new world to bring to life and to record.

He grinned as he walked over, picking up the quill, dipping it lightly in the ink. He closed his eyes, connecting himself to the world, and the tale that needed telling. The last time he'd done this, was for the world he'd just finished. When he'd created that world, when he'd brought it to life, it had sprung forth so powerfully. His children, those he'd chosen to guide the world, had been his pride and joy. It had pained him, watching as they struggled, as they worked and learned, as they both succeeded and failed.

Sometimes, creating these worlds and watching them thrive, was the hardest part of being a World Smith. He wanted nothing but happiness for his creations. However, he also knew he had to let them live. And living was full of mistakes and learning. It was always hardest, watching those you loved struggle. Knowing they needed your help while you stood back and observed, was the burden he held.

It was the burden of a World Smith. Yet, even with that burden, even with the pain that came with his power, he wouldn't change anything about it. As he began with this new world, calling forth the magic within, preparing to create it, he couldn't help but smile. It was time for something new to be created. It was time for new life to spring forth.

It was time for a new story to be told.

End

Author's Note

We've done it. We hit the end. This is it. My first ever trilogy, is finally complete. How did I do? Honestly, this story, the stress of trying to make the perfect ending to my trilogy, an ending everyone would love and enjoy, has eaten away at me all this time. That, combined with COVID, and just 2020 in general, really have made it hard on me.

That being said, I want to thank each and every reader from the bottom of my heart, once again, for taking one last trip to the Bone Dungeon with me. Hallowed Bones has by far been the most difficult and time intensive story I've written to date, and I really hope it was able to meet a fraction of everyone's expectations. At the very least, I hope it helped you escape the real world for a moment, to a fun filled world of chaos, shenanigans, and skeletal fight club.

If you've enjoyed this story, please, share it with your friends, leave a review, and give it a rating. Everything helps!

This will not be my final book. The Elemental Dungeon Series, and the support of everyone who has picked up my stories, shared them, and left reviews, has set me on the path of being a full-time author.

Writing is my passion and my dream, and as long as you are all willing to give me a moment of your time, I will gladly continue to write stories for everyone to consume. (I would do so even if it wasn't my job...but obviously being able to pay the bills with it helps me write quicker, bwahahaha.)

If you're interested in following my work, and chatting with me and fellow fans of the Elemental Dungeon series, check out my discord.

https://discord.gg/DkJ9mMc

If you're interested in reading some more of my work, though perhaps in a rougher format, please check out my story, Dungeon Core Online, on Royal Road

www.royalroad.com/fiction/21501/dco--dungeon-core-online

And one last bit of self-promotion ... if you want some behind the scenes looks at my work, some advanced chapters here and there, as well as early access to my ongoing projects (notably, a LitRPG in the DCO world, a slice of life tennis LitRPG, and an upcoming western/magic Gamelit...) your support is greatly appreciated (and extremely helpful on the path to becoming a permanent full-time writer) over at my Patreon.

https://www.patreon.com/Glyax

If you're a fan of Gamelit, LitRPG, or Dungeon Core (I'm going to assume the last of you), don't forget to follow Portal Books Facebook group for updates not only on my works, but the other amazing writers at Portal Books:

www.facebook.com/groups/LitRPGPortal/

Finally, if you'd like to sample FREE content from any of the other incredible writers at Portal Books, you can do so by signing up to Portal Books mailing list. Doing so right now will grant access to a short story by me titled Path of Flames (which gives some more information on Emily), as well as over 70k of LitRPG stories set in other Portal Books worlds.

https://portal-books.com/sign-up

For more general discussions about the genre, these groups may be useful to you:

www.facebook.com/groups/LitRPGsociety
www.facebook.com/groups/LitRPG.books
www.facebook.com/groups/LitRPGGroup

If you want to find more great LitRPG Books check out the Amazon store - www.amazon.com/litrpg

Best wishes,
Jonathan Smidt and the Portal Books Team

Join the Group

To learn more about LitRPG, talk to authors including myself, and just have an awesome time, please join the LitRPG Group.